A DOOR LEFT OPEN

BY DAVE SALVATORE

ISBN: 979-8-9917340-4-2

Library of Congress Control Number: 2025924113

Front cover image by Dave Salvatore

Book design by Dave Salvatore.

Printed by Kindle Direct Publishing, in the United States of America.

First printing edition 2025.

 Dave Salvatore

PO Box 285

Atlantic City, NJ 08401

www.davesalvatore.com

For my wife, Maryann - the light that stays on when every other door closes.

My thanks to Nicolina Salvatore, Stephanie McNeilly, Jennifer Jenkins, Kristine Knorr, and Jason Murschell—my beta readers who ventured into the house before anyone else. You walked its shifting halls, faced what waited in the dark, and helped me find the path out. I'm grateful you all made it back.

TABLE OF CONTENTS

PART 1

THE INHERITANCE

CHAPTER 1

The Key

Elena Harrow had not planned to attend the funeral, much less inherit anything from it. But obligation has a strange gravity, and grief—however hollow—still pulled. Victor Harrow had been a painter of some small reputation, a man whose canvases were as heavy with varnish as with guilt, and the last surviving link to a family that had politely disowned itself over the years. Existing for 108 years before his death, Victor practically outlived his entire family. Now, his estate had fallen to her: an artist who had not painted in six months, whose gallery had quietly stopped returning emails, and who still owed two months' rent on an apartment that smelled of turpentine and failure.

She'd told herself the trip north was practical. Collect what could be sold, sign whatever needed signing, and return before the next payment deadline. But as the train of condolences faded and the lawyer's thin voice recited the will, the word *inherit* had settled in her chest with unexpected weight.

The rain followed Elena from the city like a stubborn thought she couldn't shake. It beaded on the windshield and smeared beneath the wipers, blurring the map, the street signs, the world. When the GPS announced she had reached her destination, the road had narrowed to a hem of cracked asphalt stitched between pines. Blackwood Manor appeared the way a memory does—suddenly, and as if it had always been there.

She parked in the circular drive and killed the engine. The quiet wasn't quiet at all; it was something arranged—the wet hush of leaves, the gutters' slow gulping, a stillness made on purpose. She pushed damp hair behind her ear and looked up at the façade. Grandfather Victor's house, now hers. She tried to summon grief and felt instead a clean, hollow space where grief should have been, like a canvas primed and waiting. The stillness of that waiting canvas was worse than any storm; blank demanded a painting, and she hadn't made anything true in months. Her landlord wanted the two months she didn't have; the gallery wanted a series she couldn't start.

"You're here," she whispered—not to the house, to the silence it had built around itself.

The front door was older than the rest: a slab of blackened oak pinned with rivets, a lion's-head knocker caught mid-snarl in polished brass. Two days ago, after the funeral, the lawyer—Terence Barlow, who smelled faintly of mothballs and spearmint—had pressed a long envelope into her hands. *The house and all its contents to Elena Harrow, provided she personally takes possession within seven days.* He'd glanced at the window then, the way you look toward a sound that keeps going after you stop listening. "It's an old place," he'd said. "There are... particularities." He had not given her a card.

The drive up from the station had been all hairpin turns and fog so thick it seemed to breathe. Now, standing in the rain, she felt the same claustrophobia she used to feel in galleries just before an opening—the moment before judgment, before anyone decided if the work was worth keeping.

Elena slid the envelope from her coat and unfolded the single key. Not the key to a home so much as to a cell: iron-heavy, cold, its teeth jagged into a pattern almost deliberate, almost beautiful.

She rested her palm on the damp wood—neither cold nor warm, like skin just freed from a clasp—and turned the key.

For an instant she thought she heard something shift behind the door, a faint repositioning, as if furniture—or something else—had been waiting directly on the other side. The lock yielded easily, the bolt sliding back like a patient throat clearing.

She hesitated. Rain hissed on the hood of her car behind her, urging her forward. She thought of the city apartment with its ceiling leak and unpaid bills and the cracked mug full of brushes she never used. Going back was impossible; staying outside was ridiculous. She exhaled and stepped inside.

The air changed immediately. It was warmer, but in a way that reminded her of exhalation more than heat. She stood in the threshold until her eyes adjusted.

The hall was lined with wainscoting, each panel gleaming as if freshly polished. The smell met her—old wax, old paper, and a breath of lavender cut with iron, like stone after rain. Dust should have leapt; the air was clear. The runner down the corridor had been recently beaten. On a small table by the door a blue-and-white bowl held fresh peonies; she touched a petal to be sure it wasn't silk. Cool, damp.

Elena stood very still, listening for the natural life of a house—pipes thudding, wood settling. Instead she heard welcome, calibrated. Somewhere a clock ticked and—agreeing—chimed four. The sound seemed to find the center of the hall and pause there, as though testing its own echo.

She closed the door behind her, and the latch fell with a neat metallic click. It sounded practiced. The sound of something that had been waiting for this exact moment to repeat itself.

Her suitcase felt absurdly loud as she set it down.

The entryway smelled faintly of old perfume, something flowery but restrained—lavender, again. She rubbed her hands together for warmth and felt an odd prickle along her palms, the kind of mild static that came before a thunderstorm.

"Victor?" she called, knowing how foolish it was. The name broke and dissolved.

Her voice didn't return as an echo; it came back thinner, like a thread pulled tight and released.

She walked deeper into the hall. Portraits and landscapes hung at exacting heights, the arrangement too symmetrical to be casual. At the hall's end, a staircase rose in a confident curve to the second floor. Halfway up, the banister thickened into a newel post shaped like a sleeping hound. She ran her hand over it. The carving had depth; she could feel each ridge where a knife had lingered.

She caught herself thinking of composition—the way the stairs framed the hallway, the natural vanishing point created by the chandelier's chain—and hated the instinct. She hadn't come here to admire.

To her right, a door stood slightly ajar, the smell of dust and polish wafting from within. She nudged it with her fingertips and found a parlor, perhaps once used for guests. Furniture draped in white sheets filled the space like ghosts mid-gesture. A fireplace crouched at the far wall, unlit but perfectly clean. Above it hung a mirror that caught what little light there was and refused to reflect it properly. The furniture's shapes wavered in it, blurred, as though the glass were filled with water instead of air.

She backed out and closed the door quietly, more out of politeness than fear.

The next room was a dining room—long table, twelve chairs, all aligned. She pulled back a chair to test its weight; it moved easily, the felt pads beneath its legs intact. Someone had cared for these floors. She leaned over the table, noting faint scratches where plates had once rested, ghost circles of long-vanished dinners. The scent of lavender again, stronger here, as though it had been rubbed into the wood.

In the adjoining butler's pantry, she found a small window cracked open just enough to let in the rain's smell. The breeze stirred a lace curtain that fluttered like a slow pulse. The motion made her uneasy; there was no reason for the window to be open on a night like this.

She shut it, bolted it, and when she turned, she could swear the lace still moved for a moment longer than it should have.

Elena pressed her fingers to her temples. "You're tired," she said aloud, because hearing her own voice was marginally better than not.

The kitchen lay beyond—immaculate, almost modern in its order. Copper pots bright as coins, a tiled stove older than two of her apartments combined. Rowed jars in Victor's elegant, apologetic hand—*cinnamon, anise, barley sugar.* In the icebox, a fresh block of ice bled cold onto the floorboards. She shut the door quickly, as if she'd interrupted something breathing.

A paint-splattered corner of her mind itched to sketch—the angle of light on copper, the geometry of an overly perfect room—but the pencils stayed pocketed. If she set paper on the table, something would disapprove of the scratch.

She turned back toward the hall. The rhythm of the rain had softened outside, its patter replaced by the slow tick of the unseen clock. Each tick seemed slightly too deliberate, as though waiting for her to notice it.

Elena paused in the doorway, taking in the symmetry again: the hall straight as a gallery corridor, the chandelier swaying just enough to make the reflections in the floor tremble.

She rubbed her arms. "It's just a house," she muttered. "A house that hasn't forgotten its manners."

Somewhere deeper inside, a board shifted—ordinary, but distinct enough to sound like acknowledgement.

Elena returned to the foyer, tracing her steps backward as if retracing a painting's under-sketch. The light through the high windows had cooled to the color of pewter. She realized with a start that she hadn't checked her phone in hours. The screen showed no signal, the time stalled at 4:07 p.m.—the same minute the hall clock had struck when she entered.

She slipped the useless phone into her pocket and climbed the stairs. The treads gave slightly underfoot, soft but firm, the way a stage yields to an actor's weight. At the landing, the light thickened; a pane of stained glass filtered the gray daylight into fractured blues and greens that slid over her hands like river water. She paused halfway up, fingertips resting on the carved hound at the newel post, and thought she could almost feel its ribs move with breath.

She let go quickly and continued upward.

The second-floor corridor greeted her with a faint breeze that should not have existed in a closed house. A line of miniature portraits marched along the wall, Harrows rendered in oil and tempera, their faces sharing the same narrow bones and pewter eyes. Whoever had hung them had done so with mathematical precision: identical spacing, identical frames, each canvas aligned to the last millimeter.

Elena slowed. A girl in a high collar looked out with the cool severity of those who have never smiled in glass. Her hair was drawn tight, her gaze level. The placard beneath read simply: *E. Harrow, 1892.*

Elena leaned closer. The girl's expression was unyielding, but the eyes—gray-blue, metallic in this light—were unmistakably her own. The resemblance went beyond bone structure; it was a perfect repetition, as if the painter had worked from a photograph of her instead.

A thin chill touched the back of her neck. She stepped sideways, half expecting the portrait's gaze to follow. It didn't. That somehow made it worse.

Her mother had mentioned an Eleanor once, in the detached tone of someone naming a mistake the family never quite repaired. Something about a disappearance, a scandal too old for remembering. The memory surfaced now like a shape glimpsed under water—blurred, but enough to make her uneasy.

She took a breath and forced a smile at the painted girl. "Hello, E," she said quietly.

The silence that followed wasn't heavy; it was alert, as if the house had been listening through her mouth.

She turned away, careful not to glance back.

The hallway opened onto a series of closed doors. She tested the first: a linen closet, neatly stocked, everything folded with a precision that bordered on military. The next door led to a small guest bedroom. The bed was perfectly made, the coverlet smooth and white, a single rose pressed flat between the pillowcases. She touched it gently; it crumbled at once, leaving a faint mark of dust on her fingertip.

The third door revealed a study smaller than she expected—bookshelves to the ceiling, a single chair angled toward the window. Every surface had been dusted recently. On the desk lay a blotter, blank paper, and a pen resting diagonally across it as though interrupted mid-sentence. She brushed the edge of the paper. The top sheet lifted slightly, revealing indentations beneath—words written, then torn away. She traced them with her nail: *The house remembers.*

Her heart skipped. She stepped back, half laughing at herself. "Of course it does. That's what houses do."

She closed the door, gently, as though not to wake someone.

At the end of the corridor another hallway branched, narrower, ceiling lower. A single bulb glowed behind frosted glass. She followed it to a small sitting room with a chaise, a sewing table, and—unexpectedly—a piano. The lid was closed. Dust had gathered evenly except for one small patch where a handprint might have been wiped clean.

She lifted the lid. The ivory keys shone like teeth. On impulse she pressed one. A dry, soft note sounded, startlingly pure. She pressed another. Slightly out of tune, but not badly. Someone had kept it alive.

For a moment, she let her fingers wander. The sound barely filled the room, but the house seemed to inhale it—absorbing rather than echoing. When she stopped, the silence that followed felt deliberate, as if the house were waiting for her to continue.

"Not today," she murmured, closing the lid.

On the way back toward the landing, she noticed a faint draught coming from above. She looked up. A square vent near the ceiling rattled once, twice, then fell still.

A small, sensible part of her mind whispered that the ducts were probably old. Still, she dragged a chair from the nearest room and climbed up, steadying herself with one hand against the wallpaper. The screws turned easily, the metal sighing as she loosened the grate.

Cold air breathed out, carrying the scent of iron and something faintly sweet. Inside the vent, balanced delicately on the edge of the duct, lay a small brass key.

It wasn't like the iron key that had opened the front door. This one was elegant, warm-toned, its bow worked into the shape of leaves—or perhaps flames. She pinched it between thumb and forefinger. The metal was warmer than it should have been, and the ridges pressed into her skin with the familiarity of something that remembered her hand.

She stared at it a moment longer, oddly reluctant to put it down.

"Okay," she said finally, to no one at all. "Okay."

The chair creaked as she stepped down. The floorboards felt uneven underfoot, as if they were readjusting to her weight. She noticed a sliver of varnished wood lying beside her boot—thin, curved, freshly broken. She turned it over. A ghost of red paint clung to the underside, faint but vivid against the grain.

She looked up at the vent again, then down the corridor to the closed door with the old mouth-shaped keyhole she'd noticed earlier. The coincidence struck her too clearly to ignore.

"Of course," she said under her breath, already walking.

She reached the door with the mouth-shaped keyhole and tried the brass key at once, already knowing it wouldn't fit. It slid in halfway and met uncomplicated emptiness. No catch, no tumblers, no satisfying resistance. The key and the door had nothing to say to each other.

The refusal felt personal.

She withdrew the key and turned it in her fingers, the leaf-flame bow warm against her skin. The corridor breathed faintly—no, that was ridiculous—and she stepped back from the door, annoyed at herself for granting it anything like intention.

There were other doors. She tried two; one opened onto a narrow closet with umbrellas bristling like spears, the other onto a trunk room where canvas-covered shapes slumbered in tight rows. Neither felt as if it had been meant for her. When she returned to the mouth-keyhole, nothing had changed. She could feel the house not watching her; the effect was the same.

Without thinking, she slipped the small key onto the thin chain at her neck, letting it settle against her skin. It warmed quickly, as if it had been waiting for the chance.

The light in the windows had fallen into evening's gray. She hadn't eaten since morning. Practicalities returned with the clatter of hunger, and, grateful for something ordinary to do, she went downstairs.

In the kitchen she found a loaf of bread wrapped in wax paper on the counter where there had been nothing earlier. She stared at it long enough to wonder whether she had simply failed to see it before. The paper was dry at the edges, damp in the center where the bread still held warmth. No, not warmth—room temperature mistaken by cold hands. She sliced two pieces, found a small crock of butter in the icebox, and ate standing up, replenished by salt and fat and the comfort of repetitive motion.

After, she filled a glass from the tap. The water ran clear, metal-cold. She drank and set the glass down on the table, meaning to rinse it at once, then left it there to prove she could. It felt like a victory so small it might have been imaginary.

The hall clock chimed six, then seven. She checked her phone again and found the signal dead, the time still wrong. She thumbed the screen off and slid it back into her pocket as if to spare it embarrassment.

She needed to make some kind of sense of the house—if not of the inheritance, then of the physical space. A map might fix it long enough to stand on. She fetched her sketchbook and a pencil, returned to the foyer, and sat on the low bench beneath the staircase where she could see the hall unspool in both directions. She began to draw.

Lines behaved at first. Entry, hall, the angle of the parlor door, the proportion of the dining room to the pantry. She paused between each section to stand and look, to check her distances by sight. Perspective came back quickly, relieving in its rules.

When she moved to the second floor, she sketched the stairs with care, counted the miniature portraits, and marked the position of the mouth-keyhole door.

She looked down. The drawing was fine. Not beautiful, but accurate enough. She went to add the small side hallway with the piano room—and felt the pencil snag over paper that had become very slightly damp. She lifted her hand. A faint ring of moisture circled where her palm had rested. She glanced at the ceiling, expecting a leak, and saw only wood and plaster. When she set the pencil to the page again, the corridor line she'd drawn looked longer. Not by much. A door she hadn't marked had appeared in graphite, just there, a smudge with a knob. She had not drawn it. Or perhaps she had and forgotten. She traced the new door lightly with the tip of the pencil and felt the paper resist, as if something beneath it had stiffened.

"Stop it," she said to herself—meaning the house, the pencil, her own nerves, she wasn't sure. She tore off the page, folded it once, slipped it into the sketchbook pocket, and started a second map with slower hands. This one she made stingy and square, refusing flourish. When she finished, the hall looked tame again, four doors on one side, two on the other. She placed the second map atop the first and pressed them together, willing them to agree.

They did.

She breathed and closed the book.

Dusk came on properly. She hadn't turned on many lights. The rooms she had seen kept their borders in the dim—a quality she found comforting. Dark made the brightness honest. She told herself she should pick a bedroom and unpack. She told herself she should check the boiler, the locks, the attic for leaks. She told herself she should try the phone again, or the landline, if there was one. She did none of those things. She drifted instead, a faint tour of corners and thresholds, the kind of wandering that precedes commitment.

The parlor with the sheet-draped furniture looked lonelier than it had, as if she'd caught it thinking. The dining room table's wood glowed with the last of the day; she ran her fingers along the scratches left by long-ago plates and felt the tiny interruptions catch at her skin. In the butler's pantry she checked the window latch a second time and found it still shut.

The lace curtain hung quiet. She lifted a corner of it and watched how the pattern broke light into little nets.

On her way back toward the stairs, she noticed a small console table she hadn't paid attention to before, positioned beneath the mirror. Two shallow drawers sat side by side, each with a little brass pull. She opened the left one. Inside lay a thin book of household notes in Victor's hand—columns and dates, deliveries, repairs. The last entry was from early spring: *chimney swept, study latch replaced, ice delivered.* Below that, faintly, a note she could only read at an angle: *key safe.* No explanation. No arrow pointing to a safe anywhere visible.

She closed the drawer and opened the right one. Empty. The wood smelled faintly of cedar. When she shut it, the mirror caught her motion and presented it back with a half-second lag that made her stomach tip. She stood very still until her reflection caught up, told herself it was an effect of angle and light, and stepped away.

Upstairs again, she paused at the miniature portraits and counted them a second time—another foolish little insistence. The number matched her first count. She found that soothing. She stopped in front of *E. Harrow, 1892,* and considered what else could be done to banish the stupid idea that the painting had anything to do with her other than resemblance. She could take it down. See what was written on the back. The thought felt impolite in the bone. She let it pass.

The master bedroom to the left still looked aired, the bed turned down as if an invisible maid kept to a schedule. She didn't want to sleep there—not yet. The house had made that bed too confidently. She continued to the east bedroom that looked over the lawn, liking the way the windows set the world at slightly different heights. She'd left her suitcase on the bed; the zipper crooked, the fabric wrinkled. She unzipped and placed shirts in drawers with the efficiency of a hotel arrival.

At the bottom of the suitcase she found the letter the gallery had sent two months ago—the one she'd slipped in among clothes to pretend it wouldn't follow. She read the first line and folded it shut. Not now. She slid it into the nightstand drawer and closed it with a finger against the wood to protect the quiet it made.

She set her sketchbook on the windowsill beside the curtains, then drew them shut. The velvet drank the outside whole. It made the room feel simpler. She turned on the small lamp by the bed. Its shade cast a patient circle of light over the quilt. She sat, unlaced her boots, and tugged them off by their loops, lining them side by side as if to make a promise of order.

The hall beyond the door deepened into that blue that only exists between the last scrap of daylight and the first admission of night. Her heart had been drumming lightly since she arrived; the beat had subsided to something more reasonable. She thought she might take a bath. The notion felt incommensurate with the house, as if bathing here would require permission. She rejected the idea and let her body be grateful for the bed.

Sleep came skittishly at first. She hovered in its margins, aware of the tick tick tick of the hall clock filtering through the floor, of the way the lamp hummed. She turned the lamp off and the darkness settled neatly, cooperative rather than oppressive. Her breath steadied. She slept.

She dreamed a corridor too long for any house. The runner narrowed into a red thread that seemed to hold her in place, not by force but by promise. Doors lined the walls: some ajar, some closed. One, painted a red that warned and welcomed, held her attention as if it were responsible for the dream's gravity. She didn't open it. Her ears filled with that odd pressure that precedes descent on a plane. From the far end of the hallway, someone spoke her name—not loudly, and not unkindly. She woke with iron in her mouth, a taste like the memory of a coin.

The hallway clock said three. The rain had gone quiet, as if it had turned its face to the wall and slept. She lay still, waiting for her heart to decide it wasn't an emergency.

The house was not silent. It occupied its stillness. A pipe clicked somewhere below. A board settled and made no apology. She told herself that in the morning she'd take the map again and test it against the actual hall—measuring the distances with steps, marking every door she could open and the ones she couldn't.

A hinge sighed, very near.

She sat up too fast and the room tilted, a small ship in ordinary waves. She steadied herself with a palm against the quilt, practiced at returning to scale. The sound came again—small, specific. A door, and not one downstairs. The air shifted almost imperceptibly, as if a draft had learned to move around furniture.

She swung her legs to the floor, every tendon tightening for no particular reason, and moved toward the bedroom door.

It was closed. She hadn't closed it.

A strip of dim blue lay along the floor beneath it. Hallway night. Not enough to see by, enough to show that the world still existed.

Her palm on the brass knob registered warmth that had no obvious source—perhaps from the room, perhaps from her own skin. The feeling made her think of the little key at her throat. She turned the knob, pulled, and stepped into the hall.

No one there. Of course not. The cool on her cheek felt like leftover air. The runner lay placid, the miniature portraits suffered her presence politely. Down the corridor, the mouth-keyhole door kept its posture.

She took one step, then another. At the third, something at the edge of seeing altered—the sense of a shape becoming slightly more certainty than suggestion. She turned her head and saw nothing but wallpaper, vines looping in a pattern that made her fingertips itch to trace them. She put her palm against the wall and felt nothing move beneath, no breath, no vibration, only plaster beneath paper.

"Enough," she said without heat. Then, inexplicably, "Please."

She didn't know why she said please. It fell out of her like a habit she didn't remember learning.

She waited for the house to do nothing, and it did. The waiting became the room's only furniture.

Behind her, the softest change in pressure. She turned in time to see the wardrobe door in the east bedroom ease open a quarter inch, as if relieved to be done with the effort. She had checked it earlier—empty hangers, polite cedar smell. The gap now made a thin black line in the room's darkness, a fraction of absence neat enough to frame.

Something cold started at her teeth and moved backward through her skull in a line as precise as a seam. She stepped toward the doorway and stopped. Not because she was not afraid; she was. But because another sound threaded itself through: a faint metallic tapping, irregular, like a small object nudged along a metal channel and finding different notes as it traveled. She pictured the vent grate near the ceiling, the easy screws, the brass key perched on the lip. It was ridiculous to imagine the house had more of them, that it would start gifting her a chain of tiny doors she couldn't open. It was more ridiculous to imagine it remembered her.

She backed into the hall, not wanting to cross either threshold. The air steadied of its own accord; the metallic tapping ceased without ceremony. The wardrobe door, left to its own devices, remained slightly open. She had the sudden, childish urge to run the three steps and shut it firmly, to assert some small governance over a square of wood on hinges. She didn't move. The urge passed.

For a long time nothing happened. Floor was floor. Wall was wall. Her name was Elena.

She exhaled and discovered she'd been holding her breath in small installments since she had first stepped into the house. The release made her shoulders ache with relief. She closed the bedroom door with the care you use when someone sleeps in the next room. Her forehead met the painted panel; the wood was cool and sensibly solid beneath her skin.

In the soft kiss of wood to jamb, another sound answered—a door somewhere else in the house completing the thought that the hinge had begun. Not loud. Not aggressive. A fraction of opening, like a conversation resuming in a different room.

The sound didn't ask permission. It arrived the way a decision does—one you recognize not as new, but as something you agreed to quietly, long before you realized a question had been asked.

She lifted her head. The hallway looked longer than it had, which she attributed to the way darkness plays with edges, the way focus fails when the eye is tired. She did not go hunting for the source. That kind of search invited narrative she was not yet ready to write.

One hand braced on the door, the other found the little brass key at her throat. She pinched it lightly, half to confirm it was still there, half to feel something unquestioningly real.

"Tomorrow," she whispered to the world that was hallway and wallpaper and doors, bargaining with nothing anyone else could have heard. "We'll make introductions properly tomorrow."

She stood there until the words felt less foolish, until her heart remembered it was a tool and not a witness. She stepped back into the room, closed the door again gently, and crossed to the bed. The wardrobe's slender darkness watched from the wall. She left it be.

She lay down without undressing further and pulled the quilt to her ribs. From somewhere beyond sight, a hinge finished its sentence with a slow, satisfied creak.

CHAPTER 2

The Shifting Halls

Morning came late, and with it the kind of light that looked hesitant to enter. The rain had stopped, leaving the windows filmed in condensation that blurred the trees into watercolor. Elena woke on top of the quilt, every muscle reminding her that she had slept in the posture of someone braced for impact.

For a long minute she lay still, cataloguing the familiar shapes of things: ceiling, dresser, boots, suitcase. The wardrobe door was closed again. She couldn't remember doing it. She told herself she must have.

When she finally swung her legs out of bed, her body felt borrowed. She found the bathroom off the hall—claw-foot tub, porcelain sink, a mirror old enough to warp the edges of her face—and turned the tap until the pipes coughed out water the color of weak tea. It cleared slowly. The smell of iron clung to her skin after she washed.

In the kitchen she made coffee with the surviving grounds from her travel tin. The scent grounded her, bitter and human. She stood at the window over the sink, watching steam drift against the glass, and told herself she would spend the day making sense of the house.

The rational part of her brain had already prepared the speech.

Old foundations shift. Air pressure changes between rooms. Memory isn't film stock; it edits itself. Nothing in this place was impossible, only peculiar.

She repeated the speech until it sounded like belief.

The hall looked less intimidating in daylight. The chandelier was dull brass rather than gold; the runner's pattern was merely floral, not suggestive. She opened the front door for a test—the hinges groaned in a perfectly ordinary way—and stepped onto the porch. The air outside smelled of wet earth and pine sap. No monstrous house was supposed to smell so clean.

Still, the silence pressed close. The forest that ringed the property had a sound of its own, an almost-hiss of wind through needles that never quite reached the porch. She could see the curve of the drive, the car still parked where she'd left it, the faint impression of her footprints in the mud leading back to the door. The prints stopped at the threshold. None led away.

She shut the door again and leaned her forehead against it until the coolness steadied her. "It's fine," she said softly. "You're just living in someone else's geometry."

By mid-morning she had pulled a small folding table into the foyer and spread her sketchbook across it. She ruled clean lines for scale, marked the compass directions, then began to reconstruct the first floor from memory. Each room received careful attention—the parlor, the dining room, the pantry, the kitchen. She drew light arrows to indicate windows, small circles for doors.

When she reached the far end of the hall, she paused. There was a door beside the staircase that she couldn't remember opening last night. Or had it been a closet? She looked up from the paper. The door was there, white-painted, unremarkable. She crossed to it, turned the knob, and found a small mudroom leading to the back garden. Perfectly reasonable. She closed it again.

Back at the table she added the mudroom rectangle. The diagram looked neat, domestic, harmless. She sipped her coffee, pleased at how normal the morning had become.

The sound began quietly—an almost sighing scrape, wood on wood. She froze, pencil hovering. It came again from somewhere above, directly over her head. A chair being moved, maybe. Houses creak. She'd heard this in city apartments, in museums, even in the studio loft that used to leak paint thinner smell through the floorboards.

She waited. The sound stopped.

When she looked down, her pencil had left a faint extra line through the hallway, an accidental duplication. She erased it and drew again more carefully, but the eraser left a smudge that resembled a shadow.

She decided to check the second floor before finishing the map.

Upstairs, light slanted through the stained-glass window, scattering green fragments across the floorboards. The portraits looked duller in this light, less accusatory. Even *E. Harrow, 1892* seemed simply bored.

Elena walked the corridor counting doors, measuring distances with slow steps. Twelve paces from the landing to the mouth-keyhole door. Six more to the end wall. She wrote the numbers in the margin of her sketchbook as she went. The air smelled faintly of polish and lavender again, a perfume without source.

At the far end of the corridor she found another door she hadn't noticed before. It was narrower than the others, painted the same white, with a brass knob rubbed bright by many hands. She turned it. The door opened onto a flight of narrow stairs climbing steeply upward into gloom.

The attic, she thought, and immediately disliked the word.

She should have gone back for her flashlight from the car. Instead, she felt along the wall until she found a switch. Nothing happened. She tested the first step—wood solid beneath dust—and climbed.

The smell hit her halfway up: dry timber, varnish, and something faintly chemical, like old varnished canvas. Sunlight filtered through a small gable window at the far end, illuminating dust motes that turned lazily in the air.

The space was longer than she expected, almost a full corridor with its own doors leading off it. The first opened onto a storage alcove lined with trunks. The second revealed an unfinished section of rafters and insulation. The third...

She stopped.

The third room was bright. Someone had cut a skylight into the roof, and morning poured through it in a pale shaft. Against the opposite wall stood an easel. A drop cloth lay neatly folded beside it. A jar of cloudy turpentine sat on the windowsill. She crossed the room, each step raising a sigh of dust.

The canvas on the easel was blank except for a single vertical stroke of crimson paint down the center—fresh enough to glisten.

She touched the edge with her fingertip. Wet.

Her pulse stumbled. "No," she whispered. "No, that's—impossible."

There were no open cans, no palette, no brush, no smell of fresh pigment, nothing but that deliberate, perfect line. She backed away until she felt the doorframe against her spine.

Downstairs, something slammed. A window, she told herself. Drafts. She took one last look at the red stroke, at the way it caught the light like a cut, and closed the attic door behind her.

Back on the main landing, she found her breath again. The hall stretched quiet and unbothered. She checked her phone by habit—still no signal. The time read 11:43 a.m.

She looked down the stairs toward the foyer. From here she could see the small table with her map laid out. The drawing sat square and patient in the sunlight. But the hall beyond it looked subtly wrong. The chandelier hung too far to the left, or the staircase began one riser higher than before. She couldn't decide which.

She descended halfway, blinking, and the perspective snapped back to normal.

"Light," she said under her breath. "Angles. Nothing more."

Still, when she reached the bottom, she redrew the foyer outline from memory. She made sure the chandelier was centered this time.

The door to the study remained locked. She tried it out of curiosity, rattling the knob. From the other side came a soft thump—something shifting as though dislodged by vibration. She waited for another sound. None came.

She stood there a long moment with her hand still on the knob.

The quiet on the other side of the study door held its breath as if aware of her listening. She let go of the knob and backed a step, the imprint of the brass cool on her palm.

"I'll come back," she said, the kind of empty promise people make to locked things.

In the foyer, her coffee had gone cold, the skin on its surface broken into drifting islands. She poured it down the sink, then set about completing her map, determined to anchor herself with angles and distances.

She measured each room methodically—paces along walls, rough lengths in pencil marks against her forearm, noting every window and vent. The exercise calmed her. Numbers made sense. Ratios didn't move when you looked away.

By early afternoon the page was full, the lines crisp and confident. She felt almost proud of its logic until she noticed the placement of the parlor. According to her drawing, it should have shared a wall with the dining room. Yet when she stood between the two doors in the hall, there was clearly more space than a single room could contain.

She frowned, double-checked her notes. She must have miscounted. Twelve paces from the front door to the parlor threshold, another ten to the dining-room archway. She walked them again. Twelve, then eleven. The second number was new. She tried once more. Ten and a half.

"You're tired," she muttered, half laughing. "You're adding your own steps."

She laid the map flat on the hallway table, pressed her pencil tip against the line between the rooms, and drew what she actually measured. The rectangle bulged outward, creating an impossible overlap with the pantry behind it. She stared at the distortion until her vision blurred.

Somewhere deeper in the house, wood settled with a hollow pop, as though confirming her discovery.

The air felt heavier. She rolled her shoulders, forcing a practical tone into her thoughts. Old houses expanded, contracted, lied about their measurements all the time. The Harrow manor was over a century old; foundation drift could do strange things to symmetry.

Still, she couldn't resist testing the house itself.

She opened the parlor first. The furniture shapes beneath their sheets looked precisely where she remembered them. She counted paces from wall to wall—fifteen by twenty, roughly. She stepped back into the hall, entered the dining room, and measured again. Seventeen by twenty-two. Impossible. The rooms shared a wall yet claimed different lengths.

She turned in a slow circle, feeling the kind of vertigo usually reserved for stairwells. The chandelier above the hall shifted gently, though no window was open.

"Settling," she whispered, as if naming it reduced its power.

She decided to check the back of the house, the service corridor leading toward the kitchen. The passage was narrow, lit by a single bulb that hummed faintly. At its end, the pantry door stood ajar.

Inside, the air smelled faintly of sugar and dry herbs. She touched a jar on the shelf, found a light layer of dust—not fresh, not ancient. On the floor beneath the lowest shelf was something small: a folded piece of paper, brittle with age. She crouched to retrieve it.

The sheet had once been part of a ledger. Across the top, written in a steady hand, were the words *Inventory — Winter 1892.* Below it, a neat list of items: salt, flour, kerosene, candles, turpentine. Each line had a small check mark beside it except one. The final entry read simply: "Room added." No check mark.

Elena frowned. She turned the paper over. Nothing else. The handwriting was familiar—the same as the labels on the spice jars. Victor's, or one of his ancestors'. She replaced the note where she'd found it, unwilling to carry it with her.

When she straightened, she noticed the bulb's hum had stopped. The silence pressed harder.

She returned to the foyer and studied her map again. The irregular line between the parlor and dining room pulsed with significance, daring her to acknowledge it. She penciled the words *possible addition?* in the margin. The graphite looked absurdly small against the paper's blankness.

Her stomach reminded her that she'd eaten nothing since the bread the night before. She opened the icebox again, found the same block of ice and, beside it, a jar of preserves she swore hadn't been there earlier. Strawberry, or something pretending to be—thick, dark, too sweet. She tasted a fingertip of it, grimaced, and rinsed her hand.

When she closed the icebox, the kitchen clock ticked audibly for the first time, though she didn't remember hearing it wind.

At two-thirty she went back upstairs to double-check the second floor. The hallway looked unchanged. She counted the portraits again: one, two, three...ten. There had been nine yesterday. She counted once more, slower. Ten. The new one hung at the end near the stairwell, identical frame, identical varnish smell.

It showed a young woman in a pale dress, seated at an angle, hands folded neatly in her lap. Her eyes, gray-blue and familiar, gazed just past the viewer's shoulder. The placard beneath read *E. Harrow, 1892.*

The same name. The same date. But the painting was different— the face turned slightly toward the light, the mouth softened into something almost kind.

Elena's first thought was duplication error, an artist reusing a subject. Her second was far less comfortable: that the other portrait had changed.

She forced herself to compare. She walked to the first, half the hall away, and stared. The girl in the high collar looked as rigid and unsmiling as ever. She turned back toward the second, keeping her eyes on the floor so the brain couldn't trick her into anything between. When she looked up again, the hallway seemed longer than it should have been. The second portrait waited at its far end, serene and patient, too far for her to be sure of its expression.

"Light," she said again, the word her shield. "Just light."

She took a photo with her phone to prove it. The shutter clicked, the screen displayed a gray blur, and then the camera app froze. She backed out of it, tried again. The photo gallery showed nothing but black rectangles. She locked the phone, pocketed it, and refused to check the time.

The narrow door to the attic remained closed. She considered opening it again, proving to herself the easel was still there, that the crimson line hadn't multiplied. She didn't. Instead, she returned to the east bedroom to rest before she convinced herself to do something truly irrational.

The bed looked different. Not remade—just rotated slightly, as if someone had nudged it while cleaning. A scuff mark on the floorboard confirmed the shift. She placed her hands on the footboard and pushed. The frame didn't budge.

She sat on the edge of the mattress, breathing through the rising tightness in her chest. "Old houses," she whispered. "Nothing stays square."

She took out her notebook and wrote: *Minor discrepancies—hall length, added portrait, misaligned furniture. All explicable.* She underlined *explicable* twice, the graphite almost cutting through the page.

Outside, the wind had returned. Tree shadows scraped across the windowpane like writing she couldn't quite read. She closed the curtains, reopened them, closed them again, dissatisfied with both states.

When she looked back at the notebook, a small droplet of something dark had smudged the corner of the page. She touched it—it was ink from her pencil's cracked lead. She hadn't noticed pressing that hard.

Down the hall, a door clicked softly. Not loud enough to startle, just declarative.

She waited. The sound didn't repeat.

Elena stood, notebook open on her knees, and tried to decide whether she'd actually heard that door or imagined it because her body wanted an excuse to move. The room felt fractionally tighter, as if the air had taken a step closer while she was writing.

She set the notebook aside. Enough half-measures. She would test the house the way a technician tests a camera: one controlled variable at a time until the fault revealed itself. She pulled the tape measure from her toolbox—she had brought a small one in case there were frameable canvases—and clipped a pencil behind her ear. Practicality has always been her antidote to fear.

In the hall she anchored the tape at the newel post with a strip of painter's tape and walked it straight down the runner, letting the metal tongue sing out an inch at a time. Twenty feet to the parlor door, she wrote on her palm. Another fifteen to the dining room. She backtracked, measured the width of the hall itself, then the distance from the wall to the chandelier's plumb. Her notes smudged gray across the side of her hand when she wiped off the sweat.

Next, the rooms. Parlor: fifteen-by-twenty. Dining room: seventeen-by-twenty-two. She measured the shared wall. The numbers refused to add up by a margin that made her jaw tense.

She tried again, this time pacing instead of measuring. Twelve strides from threshold to threshold. Ten back the other direction. Not possible unless her legs had shortened between attempts. She laughed once—dry, not unkind to herself—and went for the narrow passage toward the kitchen.

The service corridor felt cooler, a temperature drop that might have been the absence of carpet or the proximity to outside walls. She measured it anyway. Nine feet from pantry door to back stair. When she turned to walk back, it was ten.

She stood still in the corridor until she could hear only the small pulse in her ear. When she walked the nine feet again, counting aloud, she reached the sixth foot and heard the pantry shelves creak. She stopped counting. She told herself a board had shifted, or that she had breathed differently. She started again. This time she reached eight and realized she had counted without moving. The corridor looked exactly the same length it always had; her numbers were just making decisions without her.

"Stop it," she said, and now she meant herself.

Back in the foyer, sunlight had advanced a few inches across the floorboards, revealing damp boot-prints not entirely hers. She knelt to check. The shape was right—the same worn heel pattern, the scuffed toe—but the spacing was wrong. These steps were longer than hers by a half stride, as if made by a future version of herself with a wider reach. Or by someone else. She pressed a fingertip to the water, smearing it into a single shine, and felt ridiculous.

The map waited on the table like a neutral witness. She set her tape measure beside it and tried to overlay the numbers. Each time she lifted her pencil to correct a line, another line somewhere else demanded adjusting. It was like cropping a photograph that refused to keep the subject in frame.

She flipped to a clean page and wrote the simplest form of her question in block letters: What is fixed?

She stared at the words until the answer came. The exterior. The skin of the house—the porch, the visible windows, the roofline—had a shape she had already accepted. If the interior would not hold still, she'd test the inside against the outside.

She took the back-door key from the ring in the kitchen drawer and stepped into the cold. The sky had cleared to a washed-out blue; a gull wrung a cry out of itself somewhere beyond the trees. The lawn sloped gently away from the house toward a line of yews, their dark shapes like stitches along the property seam. She circled the manor, counting windows and noting their position relative to corners. Three on the eastern face, two on the north, five on the west. She drew a quick rectangle and marked them in little squares, numbers beside each: E1, E2, E3. At the northeast corner she paused. There was a window on the second floor where there should not have been one, if her map were to be believed—centered in a spot that ought to look out over the landing wall, not any room at all.

She stepped back into the grass until she could see its frame clearly. Glass slightly wavy with age, sash painted white. No light behind the pane, no shadow crossing it. Just a blind window on the exterior where there was no corresponding interior. She traced its position on her outside sketch and wrote beside it, Window with no room. She put a question mark, then another.

On the south side she found a door flush with the siding, nearly invisible unless you were looking for it—the same moss-green paint as the trim, a small iron handle half-swallowed by a coil of ivy. A service entrance, maybe. The handle resisted when she tried it, then gave an inch and stuck on something that felt like a chain. She didn't force it. The smell there was stronger—earth and old wood and the faint sweetness she kept encountering without source. She stepped back, heart bumping too loudly for such a small discovery.

At the front again, she looked up at the porch roof and counted the dentils along the cornice to give her mind something to do that numbers could not ruin. Their repetition soothed her. She returned inside with the external sketch clamped under her thumb as though the wind might try to steal it.

The hall felt different after being outside, as if stepping through the door had shifted her eyes' willingness to accept what they saw. The interior map and the exterior sketch did not reconcile.

She expected that. But the disagreement felt less like error and more like argument—two truths that refused to overlap.

She set both drawings side by side and began to translate. She matched the east windows to the east rooms, then the north. When she reached the west, her pencil stalled. The phantom window—the one with no inside counterpart—would sit inside the wall just above the landing. She stood, carried the exterior sketch to the stair, and looked up at the place it should be.

Wall. Paint. The faint sheen of varnish on the banister, the slant of light through stained glass. No indentation. No recess. No hint of a frame beneath plaster. She reached out and touched the wall anyway. It was exactly as a wall should feel: cool, uninterested.

Her phone buzzed in her pocket, a vibration so unexpected she gasped. She slid it out, grateful for the irritation of its insistence. One new voicemail notification. The time stamp said 2:07 a.m., which was when she'd been asleep. The caller ID read *Unknown.* She swallowed, pressed play, held it to her ear.

Silence. Then a small, close sound like a finger brushing across the microphone. A breath that could have been static. Then a voice so low it might have been a misinterpreted frequency: not words, exactly, but the shape of them forming and unforming around her name.

The message ended. She stood there staring at the black screen until her reflection looked like someone else's, then deleted the voicemail and turned the phone off. She told herself it was a wrong number. The simplest explanation is almost always the right one. Almost.

She went back to the table and made a new list beneath What is fixed?

1. The exterior.

2. The stair count.

3. The chandelier anchor.

4. (maybe) The smell. Lavender + iron.

She underlined the last item, annoyed that she was cataloging scent. But it kept recurring, outlasting rooms.

In the early afternoon lull the light thinned. A brightness settled in the foyer that made edges look honest. It seemed like the right moment to test the upstairs again, briskly, before shadows complicated things.

She climbed, counting each tread aloud: one through twenty. She reached the landing, looked down the corridor at the miniature portraits, and counted those too. Ten. She marked it in her notebook and walked to the end, palm brushing lightly along the wall as if to catch the house in some small lie.

At the far end, she stopped. She was standing in front of *E. Harrow, 1892.* Only not the one near the landing—the other, with the softened mouth. She hadn't registered passing any of the portraits between. She turned around slowly and saw the other nine stretching away toward the stair. Had she started at this end and forgotten? She tried to reconstruct her path and could not, as if the memory of walking had been recorded without its images.

She told herself she had been preoccupied and must have lost track. She tried to smile at the second E. Harrow and failed; the expression in the painting resisted friendliness.

"Enough," she said, with a steadying attempt at humor, and walked back toward the landing without looking at any faces. She kept her eyes at floor level, counting the boards as she went. Twenty-two wide planks from the far wall to the first riser.

She reached the stair and turned to see the hallway she had just traversed. Instead of twenty-two boards between the paintings and the stair, there were nineteen. She counted again. Nineteen. The numbers were stubborn.

Her hands had started to sweat, a betraying slickness that made the pencil inch down in her grip. She wiped her palm against her jeans and made a decision that felt childish and stubborn enough to work: she would walk the upstairs corridor in a loop, eyes on the far end, without stopping, without counting, three times. If she ended up somewhere she had not started, she would accept that she was exhausted. If she ended up where she began each time, she would accept that houses do not loop to spite their owners.

She started at the landing, picked a fixed point—the doorknob to the linen closet—and lined it up with the edge of the stained-glass light on the floor. Then she walked, steady, refusing to look either side. The floor beneath her feet felt reliably wooden, the give consistent. She reached the far wall, turned, and walked back. At the end of the third pass she paused and looked for her fixed point: the doorknob, the light.

They weren't aligned. The stained-glass smear had crawled a few inches down the hall, as expected with the angle of the sun. That she could forgive. But the linen closet knob sat two doors away from where it had been when she began. She stared at it until her vision shimmered and furred.

She opened the closet because she needed to do something. The shelves stared back, obstinately folded. She shut the door, and when she did, the brass knob felt different in her hand—warmer, as if someone had used it just before her.

"Fatigue," she said, whispering as though not to wake the walls. "You're not sleeping well; you're making mistakes."

She went back downstairs. The air felt heavier on the first floor, as if she were walking into a room where someone had just argued and left. She opened a window an inch to change the pressure, and the scent of outside slipped in: damp grass, cold stone. It made her eyes sting with an unaccountable relief.

She made tea because coffee now seemed too sharp. The kettle whined low, and the whisper of steam felt human in a way nothing else had. She brought the mug to the foyer table and looked at her maps as if they belonged to someone else, a person whose handwriting she admired but did not trust.

The exterior sketch remained clean. The interior map looked smug. She pulled the pencil behind her ear and began a third drawing—this time starting with the stairwell as the anchor, building outward from what her feet remembered rather than what her eyes insisted. Landing on the left, hall forward, parlor right... She paused. The parlor door was to the right when she faced the front door. But when she stood inside the hall and oriented by the stairs instead, it was on the left. She tried to diagram that minor rotation and found herself drawing a circle where the hall should be.

She rubbed the end of the pencil against the paper until the circle was a smudge. The graphite lifted under the eraser in little rolls that stuck to the pad of her thumb like ash. When she blew them away, the smudge remained, as if the paper had recorded the idea beyond its surface.

"Listen," she said to herself, not knowing what she meant to listen to. The house? Her own better sense? The way old wood spoke at night?

She left the table and walked to the parlor again. She pulled back a sheet from one of the chairs. The fabric clung for a moment, giving with a reluctance that felt oddly polite, and then slid free. The chair beneath was an austere walnut piece with a thinly cushioned seat, more show than comfort. She sat anyway, balanced on the edge. The room tolerated her presence the way a lobby tolerates travelers: neutrally.

Her eyes landed on the fireplace mantel. Small objects arranged themselves across it—a silver matchbox, a glass paperweight with a trapped bubble, a photograph in a simple frame turned facedown. She reached for the photograph and hesitated. Something about it being facedown felt like an instruction. She turned it over anyway.

A woman with Victor's eyes looked back at her, hair pinned up, expression wary and intelligent. She was standing in front of the manor, its façade distant behind her. No date handwritten on the border. No name. Elena held the picture at arm's length and tried to place the decade by dress, then put it back, face down as she had found it.

Back in the hall, the kettle clicked as it cooled. She took her tea to the dining room and sat at the head of the table. Steam rose from the cup and flattered her with its warmth. She placed the mug carefully over one of the ghost rings from another era, aligning her present with somebody's past. The small performance steadied her.

She opened her notebook to the page where she had written What is fixed? and reconsidered the list. The exterior, yes. The stair count, mostly. The chandelier anchor, probably. The smell... She wrote sound? beneath it, then crossed it out. Hearing lies.

Late afternoon leaned into the windows, and the house's edges softened. She felt the temptation of a nap like a tide, the pull toward a blank pocket of time in which nothing would be required of her. She resisted; she feared waking in a room that remembered itself differently.

Instead, she walked back to the foyer and picked up her sketchbook. The first two maps lay where she had left them. She lifted the top one to slide the second free and saw a third page beneath, a sheet she did not remember tearing from the pad. No lines on it. Only a single word written in a careful, unfamiliar hand across the center.

Listen.

She stared at it long enough for the letters to separate into shapes. She looked over her shoulder automatically, as if someone might be standing behind her with a small, cruel smile. The hall was empty. The note smelled faintly of pencil lead and lemon oil— the polish used on the table, not her graphite. The word itself had a steadiness her own lines rarely had. She set the sheet down and put both palms flat beside it as if steadying something fragile that might otherwise blow away.

"Very funny," she said to the room, and snorted softly at herself for meaning it. She flipped the page, hoping for an explanation on the back. Blank. She held it to the light. The tooth of the paper showed its weave patiently, obvious and unhelpful.

She pressed the heel of her hand against her eye until fireworks. She let the hand drop and listened. The house, obliging, made house sounds: a pipe releasing air, a floor joist realigning, the long thread-noise of wind moving past eaves. Somewhere, a faint chime—as if a glass had been touched by a wet finger—shivered once and quit.

She wanted the word to be a warning. She also wanted it to be a kindness. She didn't know which made her more foolish.

She slipped the sheet back into the sketchbook and closed it, as if shutting the cover would keep the imperative contained. Then she returned to the front door and opened it again just to smell the outside. The porch boards were dry now, their gray grain raised by moisture into velvet underfoot. She stood half in, half out, and allowed the cold to argue with the warmth at her back.

"I hear you," she said finally, not to the door or the hall or the map but to the fact that something in her had been trying to get her attention since she arrived. "I hear you. I'll pay attention."

She locked the door and turned away. She did not notice until she reached the stairs that she had left her tea in the dining room. When she went to retrieve it, the mug wasn't on the ghost ring anymore. It sat two places down, as if someone had politely made space for her at the table.

She stood looking at it for a count of five. Then she lifted the cup, swallowed what remained, and decided to be the kind of person who noticed a thing, recorded it, and saved the fear for a later time.

The light had gone from fractured gray to the first suggestion of evening blue. She cleaned the kitchen because it was something she could do well—wiping counters, aligning jars, a domestic performance that reassured the part of her brain that liked tasks with edges. She set the bread knife's blade parallel to the counter seam and enjoyed the precise click of alignment. She turned off the light over the sink. She turned it on again. Off. On. The world obeyed the switch. It was an absurd comfort.

She took the sketchbook to the east bedroom and placed it on the windowsill beneath the drawn curtains. She unbuttoned the top button of her shirt—her throat felt too tightly laced otherwise—and sat on the edge of the bed with her boots still on, as if suspending the day by a single decision not yet made.

The house relaxed into night with her. The small sounds grew smaller. The bigger ones went away. She lay back and let her eyes close in the last wedge of light.

Sleep came in increments, in shallow bowls that tipped and refilled. A hallway with too many doors; a window with none.

A whispered syllable that might have been her name or might have been a hinge remembering its purpose. She woke once to the feeling that someone had taken a seat at the foot of the bed and then remembered the way mattresses respond to memory, to weight, to breath. She did not investigate.

When she finally slid under fully, the dream was mild. She was in the foyer drawing a map, and the lines behaved straighter than they did in waking. She added the parlor, the pantry, the upstairs landing, and when she drew the long hall on the second floor, the pencil made a sound like a fingernail on glass. She lifted it and saw that what she had written instead of a line was a word.

Listen.

She woke to darkness and the soft idea of a chime. She reached for the lamp switch, and the room obeyed, flooding itself with the kind of light that makes shadows admit to their shapes. Her sketchbook lay open on the windowsill where she had not left it open. She crossed the room and looked down at the page.

Her map was there, third attempt—stair first, hall after. A new line had been added where she would have added it next.

Beneath it, in smaller letters than the page downstairs, the same word again.

Listen.

She looked at the window, at her hands, at the bed, at the door. She wanted to accuse a draft. She wanted to accuse herself and have done with it. She closed the book and set it facedown, a minor act of superstition.

In the hall, something shifted—a patient weight remembering its options. A floorboard gave and took back its indent.

Elena returned to bed and lay awake on top of the quilt, fingers wrapped around the little brass key at her throat without realizing she had reached for it. The metal was warm. The house breathed in its unstartling way.

"Tomorrow," she said into the room, though this time it wasn't a bargain. "Fine. I'm listening."

The manor said nothing. It didn't have to. The silence was eloquent as a nod.

CHAPTER 3

The First New Room

The morning light came late. It leaked through the curtains in pale slats, as though the house were filtering the day before letting it in. Elena woke with the metallic taste of her dreams still sitting in the back of her throat, that flavor of fear that lingers even when the fear itself has forgotten its reason.

For a few seconds, she lay still, listening. The manor had its own idea of morning—quiet, but not empty. Boards flexed softly in the walls. A low hum of air passed through unseen vents. Somewhere far off, water moved in pipes, the rhythm too deliberate to be plumbing.

Her hand was already at her throat. The little brass key hung there, warm against her skin.

She sat up, pulled her hair into a loose knot, and reached for the sketchbook on the sill. It wasn't where she'd left it facedown. The cover was open, pages splayed like wings. The last page— the one she remembered closing—was still visible, but the ink looked newer somehow, as though it had been written again over the old graphite lines.

Listen.

Same word, same neat handwriting, but darker now, as though freshly pressed into the paper.

She closed the book without comment. The air in the room felt fine-dusted with something that wasn't dust—an attention.

Her reflection in the window looked strange in the half-light: eyes too wide, color too low. She almost smiled at it. "Good morning," she told the woman in the glass, and stood.

Downstairs, the house had already been awake. The scent of old lavender clung stronger than before, weaving through the kitchen like perfume sprayed and forgotten. The chairs were a little off—one pulled slightly away from the table, as if someone had stood up in a hurry. She tucked it back in.

The kettle refused to whistle this time, though she could see the water boiling inside. She poured it anyway, made her tea, and leaned against the counter while the steam fogged her glasses. For a moment, it was almost easy to believe she had imagined everything. Almost.

She carried her mug into the hall, careful not to spill. The foyer light had shifted, soft gold against the wainscoting. Her maps and notes still lay on the side table where she'd left them, but the sheet with the word *Listen* was gone. She flipped through the pile once, twice. Nothing.

The sound reached her before she could decide whether to care.

A faint *creak*, somewhere upstairs. Not sharp—measured, like a slow footstep on old wood. Then another, lighter.

She hesitated at the base of the staircase, half-drinking, half-listening. The sound stopped, obligingly, as though aware of her pause.

Her rational mind gave her the same tired script: wood settles, air shifts, memory fills the gaps. She took the stairs one by one, each tread complaining slightly under her boots.

The upper hall was bright in the kind of light that reveals dust and makes old wallpaper seem honest. The portraits looked the same: ten in their row, each face solemn, precise, oil catching the new angle of day.

All but one.

The second portrait on the left—E. Harrow again—had shifted a fraction. Not fallen, not crooked, just... *turned*, as if the figure inside had leaned closer to the frame. She adjusted it automatically, and when her fingers brushed the bottom edge of the frame, they came away faintly tacky. Resin, maybe, or varnish that hadn't fully dried.

She wiped her hand on her sleeve, pretending not to care, and moved farther down the hall.

That was when she saw it.

A door.

It should have been absurd—this was her house now, she had counted every entry, every panel, every threshold—but there it was, between the guest bathroom and the linen closet. A narrow door, plain white, with a brass handle that gleamed faintly in the morning light. She had walked this hall a dozen times. It had never been there.

Elena stopped halfway to it, tea sloshing in her mug. The smell coming from that section of the hall was faintly sweet, almost floral, but off by one note—like perfume gone slightly stale.

She forced herself to set the mug down on the floor and approached.

The handle was warm. Not body-warm, but sun-warm, as though the door had been standing in light no other surface had. The paint looked newer too, a brighter white that didn't quite match the walls.

She looked for any sign of construction—fresh plaster, nail holes, tool marks. Nothing. The frame was old, perfectly integrated into the wall's trim.

Elena's first thought was to measure, to prove to herself that it was impossible. But the urge to *see* overrode it.

She turned the handle and pushed.

The door resisted, then yielded on a long, reluctant hinge. The smell strengthened—a blend of dust and something once lovely, faded now into memory.

The room beyond was small, maybe twelve feet square. Pale wallpaper peeled in places, a repeating pattern of birds and branches. The furniture was old-fashioned: a crib with slender spindles, a rocking chair, a dresser with three drawers and a small mirror above it.

A nursery.

She stood in the doorway for a long time before stepping inside.

The air felt different here—not colder, but thicker, like walking into the end of a held breath. Light filtered through lace curtains, dull and colorless. The cradle stood motionless at the center of the room.

A mobile hung above it—clouds, stars, a crescent moon—all made of paper or something pretending to be paper. They spun gently even though the air was still.

Elena circled the room slowly. The dresser drawers were half-open, revealing folded linens yellowed with age. The top of the dresser held a porcelain doll with missing eyelashes, eyes that refused to meet hers.

She turned the mirror face-down on instinct.

On the floor by the rocking chair lay a wooden block, the letter *E* carved into it. She picked it up, turned it over, and saw a small dark stain on one corner that might once have been paint—or something else.

Her own name started with E. So had the girl in the portraits. So had her grandmother, *Eleanor Harrow.*

That thought settled in her chest like a coin dropped into water.

A faint rhythm interrupted it—the sound of something moving. She turned. The cradle was rocking, slowly, rhythmically, as though pushed by a careful hand.

Her throat closed around a word that didn't quite make it out.

She stepped closer, trying to tell herself she'd brushed it, that her motion had disturbed it. But the air in the room was still, perfectly unmoving.

The cradle continued to rock.

Elena reached for it and stopped. Beneath the lace blanket, the faintest indentation marked the mattress—as though something small had once lain there and left an impression that never lifted.

She touched the blanket anyway. The fabric was cool.

Then the lullaby began.

It wasn't loud. Just a few notes, almost more remembered than heard, humming through the air without a source. The melody was simple, old-fashioned, the kind of tune that belongs to no one and everyone. She realized, with a small shock, that she recognized it.

Her grandmother had hummed it sometimes while painting—absentmindedly, between brushstrokes.

Her hand went to the brass key at her throat.

The music grew softer, fading like breath on glass, and then it was gone. The cradle slowed.

Elena took a step back. Then another.

When she reached the threshold, she noticed something she hadn't seen before. The wallpaper beside the door had peeled back in a long, curling strip, revealing words carved into the plaster underneath. The grooves were faint but legible.

Don't open the door.

The letters had been scratched deep, then painted over. A small flake of paint hung loose from the tail of the *r* as though someone had tried to erase it and failed.

She stared at the words until her pulse steadied, until she could convince herself she was reading old mischief, not warning.

Then she stepped backward into the hall and shut the door gently behind her.

It closed without sound.

She looked down the corridor. The other doors stood where they always had. Everything looked orderly, proper, untouched.

Elena exhaled and whispered, almost politely, "Noted."

The handle stayed warm beneath her hand for a moment after she let go.

When she reached the stairs again, her tea was still waiting at the base, cold and untouched.

She stood a long time at the end of the footprints, waiting to feel something she could name. A draft, maybe. A shift in pressure. An apology in the air. Nothing obliged. The last print looked back at her without looking at all.

She went for her phone and returned to the hall, crouching to frame the tracks. The camera app opened reluctantly, lagging a second behind her touch. She took photographs along the trail—by the stairs, across the runner, where the prints began to fade—snapping quickly and checking each image before moving on.

Most caught only floorboard, the damp oval dissolving into glare. One, near the runner's border, sharpened enough to show the blunt arc of toes and the smooth heel. Small. Bare.

She zoomed in until the pixels smudged. Her throat tightened. She wanted it to be a trick of water, a spill in the shape of coincidence. But the prints had a progression—a slight outward splay on the left foot, a narrower landing on the right. A gait. Whoever had made them had been moving from the staircase toward the kitchen, then had simply…stopped.

There was nothing to stop *at.* No puddle, no rag, no towel dropped for small wet feet. Only the doorway and the smell that reached for her anew—lavender edged with iron, that old signature of the house.

She stood and found a pencil in her pocket, the same one she'd been using to mark measurements. On impulse, she wrote the time on the back of her hand, then in the margin of her notebook: *4:26 p.m. Footprints—small, bare—end before kitchen. Floor dry elsewhere.* She felt foolish writing it down. She felt worse not writing it down.

When she looked back toward the stairs, she noticed something else she might have missed if she hadn't been crouched to the floor: a faint drag through the dust near the lower step, as if a hand had slid there briefly. The smear was small, as if made by four fingers without a thumb.

She photographed that too, then closed the camera and pressed her fingertips to her eyelids until white sparks burst. When she lowered her hands, the hall looked as it had: composed, waiting, the bowl of peonies as perfect as before. (Had that petal already fallen? The pale pink one bowed onto the table's edge? She couldn't be sure.)

"Enough," she told the house, meaning the performance of calm, meaning herself. "Enough for today."

She didn't mean it. She went back upstairs.

The nursery door was neither colder nor warmer than the others. She half expected to find it locked—to be spared by mechanics. It opened on the first try, patient as before.

The room had altered in the smallest ways that felt largest. The lace curtains lay smoother. The dresser drawers were pushed in flush. The porcelain doll sat at a slightly different angle on top of the dresser, chin tipped down so that her painted gaze pointed toward the floor. Elena had turned her face away earlier. She was certain of that.

"Not supernatural," she said softly, persuading the air. "Memory. Human error. I'm tired."

She stepped to the cradle. It was still, as if listening with its whole structure. She leaned over and pressed her palm lightly to the mattress, smoothing the crease where an old weight had once rested. The fabric had the faint coolness of rooms that don't bother to be warm.

She lifted the mobile with a finger and watched the paper moon and stars turn. Their motion drew her eye upward to the ceiling, where a hairline crack chased the junction of two boards. It occurred to her that if she wanted, she could dismantle this entire space—turn it into evidence piece by piece. Measure the baseboards. Remove a section of wallpaper. Collect the dust, send it to a lab, ask what century it was last bothered by a broom. The thought felt both sane and obscene.

She moved to the wall beside the door. The peeled strip of wallpaper still revealed the warning—Don't open the door. She ran the pad of her thumb along the letter *n*; flakes lifted, then settled again. A small impulse—the kind that doesn't feel like an impulse until after you obey it—made her slide her fingers under the loose edge of paper and pull.

The wallpaper resisted, then released in a wave, exhaling a dust that tasted like decades. She coughed and waved her hand, blinking. Beneath it, the plaster showed the ghost of the same words, scored deeper than she'd first realized. Whoever had written them had not only scratched; they had carved, patient and furious, each stroke insisting through paint and past repairs.

Beneath the warning, almost lost in a tangle of faint lines, were smaller marks. She bent close. Letters, but crowded, written over themselves. She traced the strokes with her finger without quite touching them, trying to order the mess.

A date surfaced first: *1892*—repeated, then struck, then written again. Below, a sentence clawed through the whitewash: It listens. Another: Under the stair. And beside that, lines that might have been words and might have been scratches, ending in a messy loop that suggested a name beginning with *El...*

She took a step back and looked at the whole wall, breathing through the ache in her chest. This wasn't a warning scrawled on a whim. It was a palimpsest of warnings. Layered. Insisted. She imagined a hand, then another hand years later, length of fingernail, the tip of a penknife, a hairpin, anything that could be made to speak.

Her pencil was already in her hand. She copied the legible parts into her notebook exactly as they appeared—including the strikes, the doubled numbers, the uneven capitalization. It listens. Under the stair. She drew the looped beginning of the name as well as she could and left the rest open, a broken circle on paper.

"Under the stair," she repeated, testing the shape of the words, feeling the faint pull of them toward some saved space in the mind where instructions settle.

She looked at the cradle without intending to. It seemed to have registered her attention by becoming even stiller. She touched the rail with her fingertips and found the wood worn silken by the kind of use that passes from generation to generation.

"Who wrote it?" she asked, hating the taste of the question, loving it too. "And who ignored it?"

The house was a house. It didn't answer. But the sense of attention thickened slightly, the way air does when you say a name you're not sure you're allowed to say.

She replaced the strip of paper she'd peeled back—pressing it along the plaster, pretending it would hold. It sagged anyway, leaving the warnings half-exposed like a bandage that refuses to cover the wound.

Elena stepped away, meaning to check under the main staircase immediately, to kneel and peer and find only dead spiders and the mundane shame of crawling around in a house you don't yet live in properly. But the smallness of the nursery drew her into an orbit—another few minutes, another attempt to make a simple map.

She paced the room's perimeter, counting softly. Eleven paces and a half. She wrote the number down and then paced the equivalent distance in the hall outside. Ten and a quarter. Better than in Chapter 2, worse than sanity. She put her pencil behind her ear and stood very still, listening as instructed.

The house spoke only in its own dialect of settling and breath.

She crossed to the dresser and opened the top drawer. Inside, neatly folded, lay a stack of small cotton garments, yellowed at the edges, the kind of thing you find in antique trunks. She lifted one—a little shirt with shell buttons—preparing herself for the ordinariness of rot. The cotton surprised her with its intact strength. The buttons were secure. She ran a thumbnail along a seam and found no fray.

At the back of the drawer, tucked under the linens, lay a strip of ribbon. Red, faded to rust. She unrolled it and saw a darkened spot near one end, brown as old tea. When she brought the ribbon to her nose she smelled only dust and that persistent lilac. She folded it and replaced it exactly where it had been.

When she shut the drawer, the porcelain doll tilted very slightly in its place, as if jostled. Elena froze, then told herself she had bumped the dresser with her knee. She righted the doll gently, keeping her eyes on its painted lashes until they seemed ridiculous rather than menacing.

On the floor by the rocker, the wooden block with the carved *E* had shifted too, or she had kicked it without feeling it. It now sat perfectly squared to the board it rested on, the letter facing the door. She told herself she was getting superstitious about letters.

"Under the stair," she said again—this time with intent, to break the nursery's gravitational pull. She left the room and closed the door carefully, breathing cooler air in the hall as if she had surfaced.

At the top of the main staircase she paused and looked down. There was nothing obviously *under* the stair from this vantage— just the open space of the foyer and the curve of the underside where dust would gather. On the first floor, the wall beneath the flight was paneled and painted the same white as the rest, elegant and blank. She stood there an extra beat, resisting the urge to look behind her in case something had chosen that moment to stand in the hall.

The foyer felt normal enough to be almost insulting. The front door was closed, bolt shot. The peonies had lost another petal. The footprint smear on the runner had darkened as it dried, losing its definition. She knelt anyway at the base of the staircase, running her hands along the lowest panel, feeling for irregularities the way a restorer might search for the seam of a hidden compartment.

Her fingers found one almost at once—a hair-thin line between two panels that deepened under pressure. She pressed with her thumb, then both hands. The panel gave a fraction and returned. She pressed again, this time pushing at the inner corner near the tread.

A click, so small she wasn't sure she'd heard it until the panel eased outward by a thumb's width.

Elena rocked back on her heels, heart doing something unhelpful. "Of course," she said, because she had to say something. The words left a fog on the panel's paint.

She slid her fingers into the gap and pulled. The panel swung inward on hidden hinges, revealing a narrow, triangular space beneath the first four steps. The air inside smelled trapped—old wood and wool and that same metallic breath that threaded the house's scents.

A small box sat at the back of the cavity—plain, wooden, the size of a book. She reached for it and paused, more from narrative caution than fear. If this were a story she might have waited for a second person to see it, to confirm reality. But she was alone, and waiting felt superstitious in a way she decided not to be.

She took the box out carefully, surprised by its weight. No lock. The lid creaked when she lifted it. Inside: a folded piece of paper finer than the ledger page from the pantry, a length of red ribbon (a twin to the one upstairs, or the same one in a different story), and a small silver rattle tarnished into gunmetal. The rattle's handle had been engraved—*E. H.*—inside a wreath too delicate to be anything but custom work.

She set the box on the floor beside her and unfolded the paper. Two words, hurried and brave, met her.

Don't listen.

The loop of the *t* in *don't* cut a groove where the pen had dug too hard, tearing the fiber. The *o* in *not* was closed twice, a worry loop. She touched the letters lightly. The graphite smudged under her finger. Pencil. Not ink. A second hand, perhaps, over an older note. A correction of advice. A contradiction. Listen upstairs. Don't listen down here.

She sat back against the riser and laughed once, without humor. "Make up your mind," she said to the house that did not write and to the people who had.

The rattle was heavier than it looked. When she shook it, a faint sound answered—not the bright chime of a toy but a muted clack, like bone inside wood. She stopped immediately and put it back, an apology rising before she could stop it.

She replaced the paper in the box, the ribbon on top, then closed the lid and set the box on the panel's threshold. She didn't return it to the cavity. She wanted it in the air with her, part of the world again.

When she stood, her knees creaked their very human creak. She slid the panel back into place, pressing until the latch caught with a small, satisfied sound. As she straightened, she had the sharp sense of having been visible to the house while she crouched—of having presented it with the back of her neck as a target. She turned quickly because the body does that when it believes it's being watched. The foyer resisted the accusation by being entirely itself.

She took the box to the side table, set it beside the maps, and wrote another note in the notebook: *Under the stair—panel, box (rattle, ribbon, note). 'Don't listen.'* She left space beneath for later thoughts and closed the cover.

The light had softened to late afternoon's defeated honey. Her hands had begun to shake, small seismic betrayals that irritated her. She considered pouring a drink but decided that she did not want to add any blurring to a day that was full of it. She poured water instead, drank half standing at the sink, the glass too cold against her teeth.

Upstairs again, because there was nothing else to do but walk her circuit and pretend she was collecting evidence rather than being collected, she returned to the nursery one last time before dusk. The door opened easily. The room waited with the stubborn stillness of places that expect no argument.

She stepped to the cradle because there was nowhere else to put the attention. She set her palm lightly to the rail and pushed once—not unkindly, a small test. The cradle rocked in a long, patient arc, wood on wood whispering a sound that made the hair on her forearms rise. It rocked forward, back, forward again, each movement carving the smallest crease of shadow under the mobile's paper moon.

She watched the motion find its own end. It always would; friction was still friction in this house. When it slowed to almost nothing, she removed her hand and stood very still and told herself she would not touch it again.

From the hall, a muffled sound. Not a door, not exactly—a weight negotiating a hallway somewhere else. She didn't move. The cradle continued its tiny swing, smaller, smaller. The hush in the room thickened with the nearing of its rest.

Elena took a step backward toward the threshold, not wanting to be in the room when the motion ended, as if being present would mean participating in a ritual she didn't understand. She put one foot in the hall. The cradle rocked once more, a last, defiant inch.

Then it stopped. Not with the lazy settling of friction, but abruptly. As if a hand met it mid-swing, steadying.

The air seemed to press in a fraction. Elena's fingers had already found the key at her throat and closed around it, not a prayer, not a weapon, but a habit.

She stood in the doorway and counted five silent breaths, then said, as if to a child who isn't there and to herself, "That's enough."

She closed the door softly. The latch took like a small, sealed agreement. In the hall, the smell of lavender had sharpened into something shinier at the edges, like a scent that remembers a metal it once touched.

Downstairs, the house resumed its ordinary work. A pipe released what it had to release. The clock considered and then decided to tell her the hour.

Elena picked up the box from the table and carried it to the east bedroom. She placed it on the windowsill beside the closed sketchbook, the two of them sitting like quiet jurors. Night gathered outside the curtains—not fast, but with the confidence of something that always gets what it wants.

She sat on the bed, boots still on, and looked at the door until she could say out loud what the day had taught her.

"Noted," she said. "I'm listening. And I'll decide when not to."

The manor, polite as ever, allowed her the last line. The quiet that followed made space for the smallest sound: a ribbon sliding against wood somewhere in the walls, a hush like fabric telling a secret. Then even that was gone, and the house was only a house again—if only for the length of that settling breath.

CHAPTER 4

The Town's Whispers

The morning began wrong. Not dramatically—no blood, no screams—just the sense that the air had already made a decision before she woke.

Elena stood at the east bedroom window and watched fog pull itself off the trees in slow tides. The forest breathed like a lung. The house, by contrast, seemed to hold its breath. Her sleep had been shallow, full of almost-sounds: a heartbeat in the pipes, a sigh too rhythmic to be wind. When she opened the door to the hall, she half expected the nursery to be gone. It was still there— only now the distance between it and her room looked longer, as if the corridor had stretched overnight.

"Optical illusion," she told the quiet, as if a password could make it behave.

Her throat ached from the dryness of old air. She needed coffee, a voice not fashioned out of pipes and floorboards, proof that the world beyond Blackwood Manor still obeyed physics and small talk. She dressed for practicality—jeans, boots, paint-softened sweatshirt—slid her notebook into her bag, and hesitated at the little brass key around her neck. She tried to leave it on the dresser and couldn't. It had weight now—absurd, superstitious, but still a comfort. She tucked it under her collar, where it warmed instantly, as if relieved.

Downstairs, the manor's silence had matured. The clock in the hall ticked slower, as though reluctant to move the day forward. The bowl of peonies on the table had opened too quickly, edges already browning. The air carried that thin thread of copper she had begun to identify as the house's mood.

She found her car keys on the side table beside her maps and the wooden box from under the stairs. She brushed a finger over the lid—not opening, just... acknowledging—and stepped outside. The wind off the trees hit her like clean water.

The drive unspooled between pines that leaned toward each other like conspirators. Her phone lost signal before the gate, recovered a single, struggling bar at the fork, then gave up altogether. The road narrowed, then widened, then posed as ordinary. Fifteen minutes later she reached the first houses—

mailboxes painted like animals, a sign that said *Blackwood Hollow — Founded 1819*, its serif letters half-swallowed by moss.

Main Street dozed under a pale sun. The *Gull & Lantern Café* sign creaked on its chain. She parked and sat for a beat, palms against the steering wheel, surprised at how much of her body had been listening for the hum of the house even out here. It faded, but not completely. You can't unswallow a sound that's learned your shape.

The bell over the café door gave a halfhearted jingle as she stepped inside. Conversation didn't stop—it detoured, curving around her like a stream around a stone. Heads turned and pretended they hadn't. The room smelled of butter, coffee, and the sort of lemon polish that apologizes for the past without removing it.

The woman behind the counter—thirty, maybe, hair in a practical knot—looked up. Her nametag read MAE in tidy letters. Her gaze narrowed, not with suspicion but with recognition she couldn't possibly have earned.

"You're a Harrow," Mae said, as though naming a symptom. "Word got around quick someone finally went and opened that house again."

Elena took a stool. "I didn't realize it was news."

Mae poured coffee without asking. "Everything's news here, sweetheart. Especially when it's got old dust on it."

Steam breathed against Elena's face. She wrapped both hands around the mug and let the heat decide a few things for her. "I'm Elena."

Mae's mouth tipped, not quite a smile. "We figured. Victor Harrow's granddaughter."

"You all figured?"

Mae gestured with the pot at the window, meaning the street, meaning the town. "Blackwood's a mouth with a hundred tongues. Your gate clicked open yesterday. Half the Hollow heard it."

"That seems unlikely."

"Things echo different up there," Mae said lightly, as if remarking on weather. "You settling in?"

"Define settling." Elena tried to keep it casual. "The floors have opinions."

"Yeah." Mae slid a sugar packet across like a talisman. "Keep the windows cracked at night. It hums less when it can breathe."

Elena blinked. "It?"

"Old houses," Mae said, with the shrug of someone refusing to be drawn further. "They keep their air too long."

The man at the end of the counter muttered something into his cup—Elena caught only "Harrow women"—and the room's attention pretended to be elsewhere again. Mae set a plate down: toast that looked like it had been cut by a person who liked neat rectangles, a ramekin of jam.

"On the house," Mae said. "Welcome back, I guess."

"I've never been here."

Mae considered her, head tilted. "Not you. Your face has."

Elena laughed before she could stop it, short and unbelieving. "That's not creepy at all."

Mae's not-smile sharpened. "You'll get used to worse."

They ate her silence together for a minute. The coffee steadied her pulse into something that didn't resemble the house's rhythm. She could see the street through the glass: a barber sweeping hair into a bin; a girl dragging a chalk hopscotch back into existence; the old woman in a shawl two doors down turning an "OPEN" sign to "CLOSED" with unnecessary care.

"Library's two blocks over," Mae said, as if reading the question she hadn't asked. "Court-house-looking thing that isn't a courthouse anymore. Rowan's on mornings. He likes a mystery until it looks back."

"Rowan?"

"The archivist. Harrows have a drawer with your name on it whether you like it or not." Mae topped off Elena's coffee, eyes kind only at the corners. "And before you ask: yes, someone's going to tell you not to listen if it calls. We all tell each other that. Helps exactly as much as you think."

"Figured you'd show sooner or later," Mae added, voice lowering as Elena reached for her wallet. "The house never keeps its own for long."

Elena paused. "Its own?"

Mae considered, then decided: "People who open the door."

"Which door?"

Mae returned the not-smile. "You'll know it when it paints itself."

Elena left too much money and took too little comfort. At the door, she glanced back. Mae's expression had softened into something like pity.

"Floors," Mae said, as parting advice. "Keep your eyes on them. They have fewer opinions than mirrors."

The Blackwood Public Library lived in a retired courthouse— red brick, clock tower stalled at an unhelpful time. Inside, light drained politely through high windows. Dust motes rehearsed their old choreography. Elena signed the visitor log; the pen scratched like a small animal.

A young man appeared behind the desk, cardigan and nervous energy. His nametag: ROWAN.

"Hi," he said, like a question. "Can I help you find something, or are you the kind of person who prefers to wander until paper finds you?"

"Local records," Elena said. "Blackwood Manor. Harrow family."

The blink she was getting used to—the one that tried to be professional over a twitch of superstition. "Right. Upstairs, back room. Sorry in advance about the dust. And the… organization." He winced. "We're mid-recataloging, which is another word for 'we gave up and started over.'"

"Chaos I can handle."

Rowan led her up creaking stairs to a smaller room under a clouded skylight. Metal cabinets lined the walls. He unlocked one and drew out a banker's box labeled *Harrow / Blackwood Manor* in an older hand.

"This is the greatest hits," he said. "There are more in county storage, but these are the ones people actually ask for."

"People ask?"

Rowan looked at her over the box. "People gossip. I organize."

He left her to it with relief disguised as courtesy. Elena opened the lid and found clippings and photographs under a film of care. The first: MARTHA KEENE, SERVANT OF THE HARROW HOUSEHOLD, DIES IN ACCIDENTAL FALL (1892). Two paragraphs, the tone briskly sympathetic. No mention of why a servant had been in the attic after midnight.

Another clipping, two weeks later: ELEANOR HARROW REPORTED MISSING. The photograph beneath the headline could have been Elena in a borrowed dress. *Last seen at Blackwood Manor*, the caption read. The article offered theories like candy: elopement, nerves, poor health, a woman's tendency to wander. No facts.

A folded page in Victor's hand: *The house adds what it needs. Each generation leaves a room behind.* The loops and slant matched his birthday cards, steadier here, as if he'd written this sentence with someone looking over his shoulder he meant to impress or defy.

Elena copied the line into her notebook and underlined leaves twice. Leaves behind, or leaves as in departs? Language encouraged ambiguity when it wanted to be remembered.

She spread photographs across the table: the manor in 1901 with a window above the east gable that didn't appear earlier; the same wall blank a decade later; an image from 1998, the year of the carriage-house fire, Victor blurred mid-turn, his posture half a question.

"Find anything?" Rowan asked from the doorway, as if he'd promised himself he wouldn't and then obeyed his curiosity.

"Your collection can't decide how many windows my house has."

Rowan came closer, careful not to cast a shadow on the table. "It never has. The house edits itself when it's bored. Or when it's hungry." He winced at his own tone. "That was a joke."

"It didn't sound like one."

"Because I'm bad at them." He glanced at the ledger page. "You're Victor's granddaughter."

"Allegedly."

"Then you probably know the story."

"I really don't."

Rowan considered her a moment longer, then pointed to a photo with a penciled note on the back: *Study—private—V. Harrow.* "He built something in there. Some device. Said it measured the way rooms change. He stopped coming into town after." He gestured at the missing police report folder in the box. "Records get misplaced around your family."

Elena smiled without mirth. "Around my house."

"That too." Rowan cleared his throat. "If you want copies, I can—"

The skylight above them made a small sound: glass flexing. Both of them looked up. A cloud shifted. The light dulled and then tried again.

"Storm coming," Rowan said too quickly.

"Sure," Elena said.

She returned the papers to the box exactly as she'd found them. The archivist's fingers loosened on his pen when he saw her respect the order. "Mae sent me," she offered, by way of truce.

"That tracks," he said. "She knows everything she isn't supposed to."

"She told me to keep the windows cracked at night."

"Sound advice," he said, then added, quieter, "If you start hearing it when you're not there, don't answer."

Elena tucked the ledger copy into her bag. "Everyone keeps saying that."

"Because it keeps trying," Rowan said simply. "Whatever it is."

Outside, daylight had soured toward pewter again. Her phone flickered to life with a spasm of static, then blacked out. She could see herself double in the library door: her reflection and a half-beat-behind version, a glass that hadn't agreed yet which way to throw her back.

On the sidewalk, she almost collided with an elderly woman in a knitted shawl the color of old smoke. The woman steadied her with a hand surprisingly precise.

"You're a Harrow," she said, not unkindly.

"Apparently."

"I was called Dunley when I worked the grounds. Mrs. Dunley now." The pale eyes were watchful rather than coy. "Tell Victor I said hello if you see him."

"He's—" Elena began, and the woman lifted a small hand.

"So am I, in most rooms." She smiled with all her teeth. "Walk with me."

They sat on a bench near a square whose chalk hopscotch had been scuffed into a blur. Mrs. Dunley arranged her shawl like a map.

"I started at Blackwood in '63," she said. "My husband fixed fences; I minded the roses. Victor wasn't cruel, just distracted. The house sounded different in the evenings. Like a kettle you haven't asked to boil, but it intends to anyway."

"Did you ever—hear things?" Elena asked, feeling both foolish and on script.

"Oh, it hummed," Mrs. Dunley said, as if Elena had asked whether spring rains. "If you kept the windows shut, it pressed on you. So I opened them." Her mouth thinned. "Heard a child once by the hedge. Your grandfather said fox. Foxes don't sound like they're remembering you."

Elena didn't trust her voice. She nodded.

"Every generation gets a room," Mrs. Dunley went on. "A sewing parlor, a chapel, a blue place between two doors where there hadn't been space for air before. Rooms come when they're needed, then go when they're done, like weather that only some of us acknowledge."

"And the people?"

"The house makes keepers of those who stay," she said simply, "and stories of those who don't." She reached into her shawl and produced a tissue-wrapped rectangle. "This was left in the potting shed in '78. I woke thinking of it so hard today it felt like a hand." The tissue unwound under Elena's fingers. A small brass doorplate, palm-sized, engraved with a serif E.

"It came from a nursery door," Mrs. Dunley said.

Elena kept her face arranged. "There is—there was—a nursery."

"Of course there was." Mrs. Dunley stood with the careful ceremony of someone negotiating treaties with her joints. "If it calls you by name when you're not there, don't answer."

"Everyone says that."

"Because it hates being ignored." She patted Elena's sleeve: papery, precise. "Drive before the fog decides for you."

She disappeared with the efficiency of a person who knows how to leave a room before the room knows it. Elena wrapped the doorplate and slid it into her bag. It weighed more than it should have, decision-heavy.

On the drive back, the road behaved. She surprised herself by being disappointed.

The gates appeared exactly when they should. The manor kept its posture, lightless and expectant. She parked and sat with the engine ticking itself cool. The key warmed against her collarbone like a pulse that wanted borrowing.

She mounted the steps. The brass handle reflected a dull oval of her face. She had locked the door when she'd left—bolt and latch, careful as ritual.

It stood open a few inches.

Not blown ajar. Not carelessly left. Opened, and then stopped, as if the person who opened it had changed their mind at precisely that gap.

The smell flowed out—lavender and iron and that warmer note like breath through linen.

Elena put her palm to the door, because she needed the painted wood under her hand to be a door and not a mouth.

"Noted," she said, the word she used when she wasn't ready to argue. "I hear you."

She pushed. The hinge gave with exquisite manners. The hall received her the way a stage receives an actor—indifferent, then attentive. The bowl of peonies on the table had collapsed under their own weight while she was gone, petals slicking the wood in soft crescents. A page from her sketchbook lay beside them she did not remember leaving out, faintly indented where a word had been written and then erased hard enough to scar the paper.

She stepped over the threshold. The door did not close. It waited ajar, as if listening for what she'd brought in.

She stood a moment, one hand on the wood, one on the small brass E under the tissue in her bag, and said what the day had taught her to say when the house behaved and when it didn't.

"Tomorrow," she murmured. "We'll make introductions properly tomorrow."

The manor, gracious host, allowed the pretense. And in the stillness that followed, from somewhere beyond her sight, a hinge finished its sentence with a slow, satisfied creak.

CHAPTER 5

Forgotten Tragedies

The rain began again at noon, soft as an afterthought. Elena heard it first through the chimney—a hollow tapping that arranged itself into rhythm, then into insistence. She sat at the kitchen table with her sketchbook open to a blank page. The pencil hovered uselessly above it.

Across from her, the peonies had collapsed entirely, petals turning translucent against the wood. They looked like lungs left too long in air.

She had told herself she would work, that normalcy could be wrestled into existence by sheer stubbornness, but the house disagreed. Every sound—clock tick, gutter drip, soft internal breath—found a way to arrange itself into near-words. Finally she stood, pushing the chair back. "Fine," she told the room. "You win."

The corridor felt longer again. On her way past the staircase she noticed something new: a door beneath the landing, one that hadn't existed yesterday. It was small and square, with a plain brass knob. A whiff of oil and paper drifted from its seam.

Her pulse did that quick, traitorous flutter that always preceded curiosity. She crouched and tried the handle. Locked.

The brass key around her neck felt suddenly heavier. She drew it out, turning it in her palm. The teeth looked too delicate for such a mundane door, but the fit was perfect. The lock yielded with a sigh.

Beyond it lay a narrow passage lit by a single lamp. At the end stood another door, this one paneled in walnut, frosted glass inset with a stenciled name: V. Harrow – Private Study.

The lettering looked fresh.

She pushed it open.

The room was smaller than she expected, crowded with shelves and the dense, comforting smell of ink and glue. A typewriter sat on a desk beneath the window, a single sheet rolled halfway through. The keys still glistened faintly, as if someone had just left.

The first line read:

To my granddaughter, when you finally come home—

Her breath caught. She lowered herself into the chair, which gave a tired creak, and read on.

I don't expect forgiveness. I only expect understanding. The house keeps what it's owed, and I have borrowed too much. When you read this, it will already have chosen you.

A blot of ink marred the next word. Beneath it, faint but legible, another sentence formed as she watched:

It listens best through paper.

Elena jerked back. The typewriter's carriage shifted a fraction on its own, the faint tick of metal teeth like a throat clearing.

"Okay," she whispered. "Not funny."

She reached for the sheet—but the letters she had just read were gone, replaced by a new line.

Welcome home, E.

Her chair scraped back hard enough to catch the rug. She stood breathing shallowly, eyes darting to the corners. The rain struck the window in quick, deliberate bursts.

When she looked again, the typewriter was quiet, the paper empty. Not blank—empty, as in unmade.

She tore the sheet free anyway, folded it, and tucked it into her sweatshirt pocket. The air smelled faintly of ozone.

A row of books along the shelf caught her attention—journals, leather-bound, edges furred with dust. She pulled one free. On the first page, a date: April 2, 1892. The handwriting slanted neatly, loops precise.

> *I heard her again tonight. She hums the lullaby from the nursery though the door has been shut these ten years. Victor says it's memory. I think memory is just another kind of haunting.*

The entry stopped mid-sentence. The next page was glued to the one after it, the paper puckered as though it had once been wet.

Elena closed the book carefully and slid it under her arm.

Somewhere beyond the study a clock chimed, though none in the house were set to that hour.

She turned toward the door—and noticed the wall behind the desk now bore a new detail: a framed photograph, sepia and faded. Eleanor Harrow sat at the same desk, hands poised over what might have been the same typewriter. The window behind her showed rain.

Elena reached out, fingertips brushing glass, and felt not the chill of it but warmth, as if the room inside the picture were still lit.

The photograph quivered faintly, once, like paper breathing.

The first rumble of thunder came so far off it felt like a memory of weather. The second rolled closer, shaking a little dust free from the study's crown molding. Rain ratcheted up from suggestion to earnest, blotting the window with quick, dark coins.

Elena set the sepia photograph gently back against the wall and turned the next page of the journal. The leather cracked along the spine like a joint being stretched after too long at a desk. Inside, a date:

April 8, 1892.

It is not the sounds that frighten me. Doors may speak; wood has language. It is the form of my thoughts that troubles me. They are not always mine. I write a sentence and know it to be true, then look and find another hand has finished it for me.

She glanced at the typewriter. The carriage sat obediently, only a ghost of oil-slick sheen along the keys. She turned a page.

April 10.

I dream of a child who is not born and not dead. In the dream the cradle rocks without comfort. I wake to find the cradle stilled and feel sure some mercy has been done to me. In the next moment I hear the lullaby begin again from the stairwell, and I cannot persuade my mouth to stop humming.

Elena let the journal rest against her knee. The house's smell— lavender edged with iron—seemed thicker in here, as if the walls had saturated in it. She thought of the ribbon in the under-stair box, the little rattle that had clacked like a bone, and willed her mind to walk away from the image forming.

Another page.

April 13.

> *Victor says there is no chapel in this house. I ask*
> *him, then, what I have been praying in. He smiles*
> *(kindly! he is forever kind when I wish him anger)*
> *and says I mistake closets for cathedrals. He does not*
> *hear the echo. He does not see how light copies itself*
> *along the cornice there, as if taught.*

The rain made a harp of the downspout. Every few lines Elena
lifted her head and checked the door, checked the window,
checked the blank paper still rolled limp in the typewriter. She
turned a page.

April 17.

> *The blue room is more faithful than the chapel. I did*
> *not add it. I awoke one morning and it had appointed*
> *itself between the linen press and the window where*
> *I watched geese last November. I have not told*
> *Victor. The wallpaper is the color of china painted*
> *as sky. It has a chair with arms like hands.*

At the top of the entry a smear of pigment crossed the date, a
thin blue line that had bled into the paper and dried there.

Elena turned the page, then the next, and the next. The entries started tidy—names and times and the small domestic weather of a woman's day—but then the tone slid sideways, the shape of the thought turning unfamiliar in a way she recognized from her own notes when the house had worn through her sentences.

April 21.

> There is a pressure in the ear you do not report to a doctor. It comes when a door means to exist. Yesterday there were three.

April 24.

> I have spoken to the house aloud. It is ungenerous. It does not answer, but it rearranges. I asked it what it wants and the nursery door sighed in a manner I choose to interpret as apology.

A small blot at the edge—tear or rain?—made the ink bloom. Elena's fingers tingled with the sense of reading words written at the pitch of her own pulse. She sat on the edge of the desk and read on, rain climbing to drum.

April 29.

I am not the first to be added to. I do not know yet whether that is comfort. The girl in the miniature with my face (she is not me; she is something a mirror made without my consent) tells me with her mouth closed that the house means to make a keeper or a story of me. It is a poor choice. I have never kept even a plant alive. I am too vain for story.

Elena smiled before she could stop herself. It failed halfway to her mouth.

Wind shouldered the window; the study's lamplight went dull for a breath and then recovered. She set the journal down, went to the wall switch on instinct, flipped it up and down to test the circuit, and told herself the small obedience of the bulb rising and falling was a currency she could spend against fear.

When she took her hand off the switch, the room rearranged by a fraction. Not much—only the chair tucked closer under the desk, only the blotter squared to the wood. The correction was so neat she might have done it without noticing. She pushed the chair out again. It slid back under with a quiet scrape as if a thoughtful host had come behind her to tidy.

"Don't," she said to the empty air, and heard her own voice answer from the hall, soft as a shadow: "Don't."

Her hands went cold enough that the little brass key at her throat felt hot. She stood listening hard until the rain was all there was again, and the house's other sounds—the small thermal ticks, the traveling pops—fell back into their pattern.

She returned to the journals because the past, however unhelpful, had the illusion of sequence.

May 3.

> *Martha Keene fell from the attic. The sound made my ribs feel like slats. They say she slipped; there are scuffs, a button found three steps down. I say the attics are for hinges and heat, not for ordinary feet at midnight. Her mother took the body into town in a cart that smelled of lilac. The house was not sorry. There is a room up there with a skylight that was not there last week. I went to it and the canvas bled without a brush.*

Elena felt the study press around her as if turning to hear what she would do with the sentence. She thought of the crimson line in the attic studio, its wetness with no jar to feed it. She turned the page carefully, resisting the urge to push the journal away.

May 7.

> *The blue room took my voice for an hour today. I swallowed air and produced only the sound of someone else trying to remember my name. When it came back to me it did not sit right in my mouth. Victor kissed my temple and said, "You only need rest." I would rest if resting did not feel like stepping into a corridor with no end.*

Out in the hall a soft scrape sounded, followed by another in answer, the way chairs talk to each other in old houses. Elena set a hand against the study door and discovered it flush, but not the way a door is flush; flush the way a mouth is shut. She left her palm there, the cool paint an anchor.

Another entry, no date at the top, only a dash in the corner and a smear like graphite.

> *The nursery sings when the windows are shut. When I open them, the song slips outside and comes back in the hedges ten minutes later. I have stopped*

humming. It hums for me. (This is not poetry. It is a note for the person who will read this when I am done.)

Elena swallowed and realized her own throat had picked up the hum at some point—two notes, nothing more—so low she hadn't noticed. She bit them off, and the silence that replaced them felt like stepping out of a warm bath into a cold room.

Lightning laid a white slice across the window; thunder followed without pause. The light in the study browned, then stuttered steady again. The typewriter gave a small metal sigh that might have been weather and might have been anything.

She put that journal aside and reached for a thinner one bound in rougher leather. It dropped open near the middle, a flattened place as if the book had spent years bearing weight. Half the page had been torn away. What remained read:

—one door for leaving and one for keeping. I cannot tell them apart. He says do not listen; it feeds on that. But I learned my letters on these walls. I cannot stop reading what it says.

The torn edge rasped against her thumb. She looked at the scrap, looked at the typewriter, at the blank paper rolled in it like a tongue refusing a word, and felt the strangest pang of pity for Victor—not for his strangeness but for his faith in machines that he thought might catch what the house kept saying.

Another entry—undated, the handwriting wobbling as if written in a moving carriage:

> When I close my eyes, I am two women at once. In one body I am young and clever and sure the world is a rug I may roll out and walk upon. In the other I have the understanding of someone who knows there are cracks in floors and rooms you cannot walk past once they appear. I speak in a voice that is not precisely mine and say, "Not yet," and the cradle stops mid-swing as a polite hand steadies it.

The study's door clicked in a small way that wasn't open or shut. Elena left her fingers pressed to the paint until her palm printed heat onto it. She set the thinner journal down and took a breath that hurt going in.

"You can move the chair," she said, because bargaining with furniture felt like sanity compared to bargaining with air, "but I am reading."

She lifted a final book, thinner still, its cover stamped with a decorative border that had worn away to suggestion. The first page she opened had no date, only a sentence written larger than the rest:

I am learning which parts of the house are kind.

The next lines came in a rush, as if the writer had not lifted her pen for breath:

Kind like a teacher who will let you copy the answer and scold you after. Kind like weather that gives warning. Kind like a hand on your sleeve at the top of stairs. Not kind like mercy; do not mistake me. It does not know mercy because it does not know judgment. It knows appetite and arrangement.

Elena read the last word twice. The rain doubled, tripled; the room went briefly twilight. In the slick black square of the window she saw herself superimposed on the yard beyond—her shoulders, the tilt of her mouth, how thin she looked in borrowed lamplight. Lightning forked again and turned her face to paper. The glass held for two beats. On the third it showed another face—a resemblance, older hair, a mouth trained to hush. The lightning rolled on and the window returned to her alone.

She closed the book and stood because sitting made her feel like a pinned specimen. The house had been listening longer than she had been reading. The typewriter ticked once as the metal cooled. A drop found its way down the inside of the window and made a clear track through grime.

"I'm going to the blue room," she said aloud, to Eleanor, to Victor, to whatever the house had made of their notes. "If it exists today."

The lamp stayed obediently lit. The chair stayed tucked. The door opened under her hand with that same precise give she was coming to dread.

Out in the hall the storm reassembled the house in sound—roof drumming, gutter gulps, a loose piece of trim somewhere rapping like a knuckle. As she reached the top of the stairs the chandelier shifted its weight, a hesitant sway toward the landing before stilling itself. She glanced down at the under-stair panel and felt, like a small electric thought, that the box was not where she had left it. She did not go down to check.

Upstairs, the corridor had grown longer. It always did under storm light. She walked it anyway, counting out of habit and arriving at the wrong number in a way that now annoyed rather than frightened her. She passed the nursery without looking in. She passed the linen press. She stopped where the wall should have been blank.

The blue room had kept the appointment.

It stood shyly between known doors, smaller than a parlor but larger than a closet, papered in a blue so pale it might have been gray if the light were less sure of itself. The chair Eleanor had written about waited in the corner—a Victorian piece with arms that curved up and inward as if to hold the sitter. A narrow table sat by the window; on it, a small brass bell without a clapper.

Elena would have preferred a lab, a measuring tape, a friend. She had only her hands and a stubbornness that had not served her well in cities and might yet serve her here. She stepped inside. The air turned one degree warmer. The room smelled faintly—

not lavender, not iron—something like beeswax and white soap, a scent that hid rather than declared.

"Kind. You said you were kind," she told the room, testing the word's fit.

No immediate correction. The floorboards lay straight, respectable; the window framed the same slice of east lawn she had seen from two rooms that could not occupy the same wall. She crossed to the table to touch the bell. The brass was dull. The lack of clapper seemed like a dare.

She ran her finger along the wallpaper's seam. It lifted at the very bottom edge and settled back as if embarrassed. In the chair she sat and did not lean back, too aware of the carved arms' inward turn. The wood remembered the weight of someone small and upright, someone who had practiced posture, someone determined not to give a room the satisfaction of slumping.

"Eleanor," she said, like a test. It made no difference. The house did not ring at the name. Lightning answered instead, cracking closer; thunder clapped a moment later so hard the window shivered in its frame.

From somewhere, not the nursery precisely and not precisely far, the lullaby turned up again, thinner than last night, like a groove worn smooth. Elena stood, walked to the doorway, and listened to its source fail to choose a direction.

"Not now," she said, and the music paused obediently, then resumed, softer—as if it had merely stepped into another room and continued.

She left the blue room because leaving it while it was kind felt like winning a small round in a game with no rules. Back in the hall, the portraits watched with their tidy apathy. She checked the one labeled *E. Harrow, 1892* nearest the stairs; the mouth was drawn into a line that could have been fatigue. The second *E. Harrow*—the one with the softened expression—hung farther down the corridor than it had earlier. The space between them had widened just enough that an extra frame might be hung there tomorrow.

Another lamp flickered—her room, she thought, though she had not left any light on. The house corrected itself as she walked, smoothing edges, aligning sills, a stagehand making ready for a scene she had not agreed to play.

By the time she reached the study again, the storm had swung to that fevered pitch where every raindrop felt like a decision. She closed the door to keep the hum manageable. She reached for the journal she had marked with the word *kind* and found the page she had just read now occupied by two sentences more:

> *Kind ends.*
>
> *Do not mistake patience for love.*

Her mouth went dry. She checked the next page and found the ink there untouched, neat and old and made of a century's dust. She set the book down carefully, as if weight might be a sacrament, and went to the typewriter.

"Enough," she said, putting her fingers on the keys.

They were cool. The ribbon caught her nail with a faint, dirty kiss. She rolled in a blank sheet, fed it straight, turned the platen until the margin met the line. She typed, ARE YOU ELEANOR.

The machine made the tender clack that had always delighted her in libraries; the letters emerged crisp. The dot of the question mark sat a millimeter north of where it should, a crooked thought.

The carriage did not move on its own. The study did not take up the story in tidy Courier.

She pulled the paper higher and typed a second line: ARE YOU ME.

Nothing answered from the machine. The answer came from the room as a whole: a gust through the chimney, a number of the books' spines releasing their dust, a chair beyond the door adjusting by a whisper to a new idea of where it ought to live.

She pulled the paper free, folded it in quarters, and slid it into her pocket with the first. Her hands shook; the gesture made the shiver look like purpose.

The house rapped once, not furniture, not weather—the sound of a knuckle on wood politely interrupting. She looked at the wall behind the desk and saw, not fast enough to say she had seen it happen, that the photograph of Eleanor had slid a fraction down in its frame, as if gravity had turned up. She went to fix it and felt heat through the glass.

"Elena," the house said, using her voice. It said it from the hall, where she had said "Don't" awhile ago. It said it without words—only the shape of her name arranged by boards and air.

She opened the door.

The corridor was dimmer by two degrees, line-drawn in shadow. At the far end, near the turn to the stairs, a rectangle of darker dark sat on the wall where there had been paint: a door-shaped absence, no knob, only the impression of a threshold. It wasn't a hole. It was an option. The sight of it hurt her eyes the way a too-bright light does.

Behind her, the study released a small sigh as if set down. Ahead, the dark threshold offered nothing: not scent, not draft, not sound. She felt, absurdly, that if she raised her hand she could erase it with a few heavy sweeps of graphite. She did not lift her hand.

"Kind ends," she said to herself. "Patience isn't love."

The house made one more arrangement—something behind her, the study window perhaps, the lamplight shifting. She stepped toward the absence because stepping away from it felt like consenting to have the hall lengthen again until purpose failed.

When she reached it, the dark wasn't dark. It was room-temperature nothing. And then it wasn't nothing at all. On the next breath it had become inside. Not of the study. Not of the hall. Inside some other decision the house had been waiting to make.

She looked down and found her boot already across the line.

Thunder put a period on the moment. The world on the far side gave the smallest of yielding sounds, like fabric that has remembered its drape. She didn't think. She couldn't. She did the only thing that kept her from making a stranger's noise in her own throat: she stepped the other foot through.

The study behind her blinked out, not like a light cut but like a sentence concluded.

The room she entered smelled of lilac and starch and years, and from its center a cradle rocked once, as if recognizing the motion of her step rather than her. Above it a mobile made of paper turned though the air was still. On the dresser a small, desiccated notebook lay where the doll had sat before, the porcelain gone, the mirror face-down as she had left it once, the ribbon not where she remembered it being.

Lightning indulged the window. In the flare she saw her own reflection and another just behind it, wearing her mouth in a shape it had not learned. The thunder followed late, as if the atmosphere were working from a script and she had skipped a line.

The brass key at her throat grew so warm she pressed her fingers between it and her skin. She looked at the notebook on the dresser and knew the texture of its paper without touching it. The loop of a first letter waited on the cover like the beginning of a name.

"Elena," the house said again—not quite word, not quite breath—and for one beat her body remembered another posture, another decade, another climate of fear. Perfume bloomed and was gone. The room did not tilt, but her memory did, briefly, a camera that had been set to a different angle and then corrected.

Somewhere, back in the corridor that was no longer connected to this breath of space, a door that was not yet finished with being a door finished. The sound arrived a second late, careful and satisfied.

She took three steps to the dresser and put her fingertips on the notebook as if lifting the pulse from a wrist. The paper's dry grit carried, under dust and old glue and time, the faintest trace of graphite.

On the first page, written in her own hand, sat her name.

Elena Harrow.

She did not remember writing it. She did not remember being the person who would choose that loop on the *E,* that impatience in the *H.* Yet there it was: her line, and under it a sentence begun and scratched out, and under that a second that read:

The house adds what it needs.

She turned the page before her heart caught up and found the next line in a script that was not hers and was hers both:

And what it keeps was never only the dead.

The first thing she noticed when she came back to herself was the quiet. Not the kind of quiet that follows thunder, but a quieter quiet—the stillness of a house listening between heartbeats.

Elena stood in the nursery, her palm still resting on the desiccated notebook. The cradle had gone still, the mobile above it motionless, the paper figures facing one another as if conferring. Her throat was raw, as though she'd been shouting. The brass key at her neck radiated a small, persistent heat.

The house had changed its air again. She could smell it—the faint copper of static, the whisper of something burned away.

She opened the notebook.

The handwriting inside was hers, but younger—more confident, more careless with ink.

> *The blue room was waiting. I am certain now that the house remembers us, not as people, but as drafts. It keeps rewriting the same story until one of us ends it properly.*

Her pulse thumped. She flipped to the next page.

> *I thought I could map it. I thought art was a kind of control. I painted the corridor again and again until the doors began appearing in the painting before they appeared in the house. That was when I stopped.*

The lines blurred at their ends, as though written in humidity. The handwriting faltered halfway through a word, dipped, then resumed in a script she didn't recognize—Eleanor's, slanted and precise.

He found the red door. He went through it. I heard
the house close after him like a mouth.

The paper's surface rippled, and a drop of water fell onto the page. She looked up. The ceiling above her was dry. The drop had come from nowhere, or everywhere.

"Elena," the house said again—softly this time, not quite her own voice.

She backed away from the cradle. The shadows along the walls moved a fraction too slow for the light. The wallpaper breathed.

"Stop," she whispered.

The floor answered with a single creak—the exact pitch of a footstep.

She turned toward the door. The hall was waiting. But it wasn't the same hall she'd come through. It sloped downward now, imperceptibly at first, as if the whole house had taken a bow and forgotten to rise again.

She stepped over the threshold. The nursery door closed itself behind her with careful grace.

The air was heavier here, the kind of thick you feel before a storm but never after. Each breath left a ghost of condensation in the air, brief and trembling.

Halfway down the hall, she stopped. The portraits had multiplied. The frames weren't new—they'd always been there, she was sure—but now every gap held a painting. Some faces she knew—Victor, Eleanor—but others were strangers. Some of them looked too much like her to be strangers.

One near the end made her throat tighten. The signature in the corner: *E. Harrow.* The brushwork was hers. She'd painted it years ago—a self-portrait she'd abandoned, unfinished, because she couldn't get the eyes right.

The painting looked back now, completed. The eyes were open.

"No," she said. The sound cracked halfway. "No, that's not—"

The painted head tilted by the smallest degree, a movement she felt more than saw. The hallway lights flickered.

She ran.

The house stretched in that dream-logic way, the stairs taking longer than physics allowed, the landing farther each time she blinked. The walls breathed her name, over and over, a pulse that wasn't voice but vibration.

When she reached the first floor, the front door was gone. In its place stood a wall of mirrors—tall, antique, the kind that distort without meaning to.

Her reflection multiplied across them, each version lagging slightly behind the other. Some smiled when she didn't. Some whispered words her mouth didn't form.

"Stop it!"

One reflection obeyed. The others did not.

She threw the notebook at the mirrors. The sound it made was disappointingly ordinary—a soft thud, paper on glass. But the impact rippled outward like a dropped stone. The mirrors quivered, the room warped, and then—

—She was standing in the study again.

The air smelled scorched. The journals were gone. The desk was empty except for the typewriter, which held a single fresh sheet of paper. The words on it were new, and wet:

It is your turn.

She stepped closer. The letters shimmered. The key around her neck pulsed once, twice, then went still.

"You think this is inheritance?" she whispered. "You think this is legacy?"

Her reflection in the study window moved its mouth before she did.

"You were always meant to stay."

It didn't sound like the house now. It sounded like Victor.

The typewriter clacked once by itself. A new line appeared:

Then stay.

Elena's pulse stuttered. The window glass warped, bending her reflection into something older, sadder, patient. Eleanor's face flickered through hers like light behind water.

She reached for the typewriter, intending to rip the page free—but her hands didn't obey. The brass key burned against her chest. The heat licked up her throat, behind her eyes, into thought itself.

She heard the house's heartbeat again—not in the walls, but in her pulse. A rhythm older than the architecture.

She closed her eyes and saw the corridors folding in on themselves like the pages of a book closing. Each room was a sentence, each door a comma, each Harrow an unfinished line.

It listens best through paper.

The sentence from Victor's letter echoed in her skull.

She grabbed the paper from the typewriter and crumpled it, but the sound it made was wrong—not the crinkle of paper, but the whisper of breath.

The rain outside stopped. The silence that replaced it felt final.

The study light dimmed—not out, but inward, as though absorbed. Shadows pooled around her feet.

The wall behind the desk pulsed once, bulging inward like the inside of a lung. Then it split down the center, clean as a wound, revealing a narrow stair descending into dark.

The smell that came up was not dust or stone but earth and candle wax.

She hesitated. Then she went down.

The steps curved deeper than the house should allow. Her phone's flashlight caught glimpses of frescoes painted directly onto the walls—faces she half-recognized, all bearing the Harrow eyes. The frescoes shimmered faintly, as though damp. Some blinked.

At the bottom: a single door. Red.

Its surface was smooth, lacquered, the color too deep to be paint. The knob was brass, identical to the key at her neck.

Her skin prickled. The door radiated warmth, almost heartlike.

On its surface, words appeared faintly, written in condensation.

Do not open the door.

Her own handwriting.

The same warning she'd seen scratched into the nursery wallpaper days ago.

She laughed once, short and bitter. "Too late."

She touched the key to the lock. It fit. Of course it fit.

The metal turned with a sound that was more sigh than click.

The red door opened.

The dark beyond it was not absence but density. It had texture, like breath you could walk through. She stepped forward, and the air closed around her like warm water.

She could hear them now—voices, layered and overlapping. Eleanor, Victor, countless others, whispering her name as though testing its fit.

Keeper.

Daughter.

Architect.

Inheritance.

And under them all, the house itself, speaking with a mouth made of every board and beam and nail:

"We remember."

The floor shuddered beneath her. The red door slammed shut behind her, sealing the light out.

She wasn't sure if she screamed.

When her eyes adjusted, she saw she was standing in another study—but smaller, older, as though the previous one had been its echo. On the desk sat a single framed photograph: her, taken yesterday, standing on the porch of Blackwood Manor, the front door open behind her.

The caption written beneath in fading ink:

The Last Harrow.

The typewriter on this desk had no keys at all. Only teeth.

The notebook she'd carried was gone. The brass key was cool now.

And in the corner, where shadow deepened into shape, someone stood.

Eleanor—or something that had learned her face.

It tilted its head, mirror-perfect. Then smiled.

Elena's mouth mirrored it before she realized.

In the silence between lightning and thunder, the house breathed in—and for the first time, she breathed with it.

INTERLUDE 1

Elena woke in daylight that didn't belong. The air was dry, still, and unbothered by the night before. She sat up on the floor of the study, unsure when she had fallen asleep—or if she had. The journals were gone again, the desk bare except for a faint ring of dust where the typewriter had stood. Her reflection in the window stared back as if waiting for her to notice something wrong, and it took a moment to see it: the view outside had changed. The garden was gone. The window looked out over a room—her own, she realized—a perfect replica of the east bedroom, framed from the wrong side.

And there, on the other side of the glass, someone sat on the bed.

Someone with her face.

PART 2

THE ENDLESS HOUSE

CHAPTER 6

The Window That Shouldn't Exist

The morning light had the color of paper soaked in milk. It bled across the study floor, thick and too still, as if it had settled instead of shone.Elena rose unsteadily, her knees leaving faint impressions in the dust. She didn't remember falling asleep, or lying down, or closing her eyes. The last thing she recalled was the photograph—the words *The Last Harrow*— and Eleanor's smile blooming like a bruise in the dark.

Now, the photograph was gone.

The desk was bare except for a single object: her notebook. Clean, unmarked, as though she'd never written in it.

She touched its cover with the wariness reserved for things that remember more than you do.

Her reflection in the window caught her movement and returned it—almost. The angle was wrong, the timing a fraction late. She blinked, and the other version of her blinked too, but slower. The difference was small, the kind your mind files under fatigue.

Until it smiled.

Elena's breath caught. She hadn't smiled.

The smile in the window lingered, patient, like someone waiting for you to catch up to the joke.

She took a step forward. The reflection didn't. The air between her and the glass carried a faint hum, like power lines before a storm.

The view beyond the glass had changed again. No longer the gray garden and the dripping pines—now it was the east bedroom, exactly as she'd left it. The unmade bed, the folded blanket at its foot, the half-drunk glass of water. Even her coat, draped across the chair.

Except there were differences. Small ones. The curtains were drawn though she'd left them open. The wallpaper pattern didn't quite match—the vines looping wrong, the shadows deeper in the folds.

And, of course, the woman in the window.

She stood in the middle of the room—Elena's height, Elena's hair, Elena's everything—but her posture was wrong. Too still, too deliberate, like someone pretending to be human.

The figure lifted a hand and pressed its palm to the glass on its side.

Elena flinched back. Her own breath fogged the window, but the reflection's didn't.

"Who are you?" she whispered.

Her voice muffled against the glass, as if the air between panes had thickened.

The figure mouthed the same words a moment later— *Who are you?*—but the sound didn't come. The lips were hers, but the expression behind them was not.

She forced herself closer. Inches now. The surface of the glass shimmered faintly, a skin stretched too tight over water.

A thought came, intrusive and certain: *If I touch it, it will touch back.*

The brass key at her throat pulsed once, like a heartbeat caught in metal.

"Elena," the figure said. Not mouthed. Spoke. The sound came from the wrong side of the glass, slightly warped, like a recording replayed through water.

She froze. "What?"

The reflection smiled wider. "You left the window open."

"I—what?"

"It was raining," the voice said gently. "You should have shut it."

Elena took another step back, the floorboard creaking in protest. "You're not real."

The reflection tilted its head. "Neither are you."

The light in the study dimmed. The glass began to darken, tint bleeding inward from the corners like ink spilled in reverse. Behind the reflection, the room beyond shifted—the bed unmaking itself, the curtains pulling open, the walls subtly breathing.

"No," Elena said. "No, no, no."

She grabbed her phone from her pocket. The screen was black. Dead. When she caught its reflection in the window, it was still lit in the other version's hand—her reflection scrolling through a gallery of photos that shouldn't exist: her asleep, her at the desk, her standing at this very window.

The other Elena looked up from the screen and smiled again. "You're late."

"For what?"

The reflection pressed its palm to the glass again, and this time the surface rippled.

Elena stumbled back, chair legs scraping across wood. The ripples settled, leaving faint rings that didn't fade.

"Stop it!"

Her voice echoed faintly, and for a second, the echo didn't stop— it multiplied. Layers of her voice whispering *stop it stop it stop it* until the sound collapsed into silence.

She turned from the window and ran for the hallway. The doorknob twisted before she could reach it. The door opened toward her.

Cold air bled in from the hall.

The wallpaper outside was the wrong color. Pale blue instead of cream.

The blue room.

But she hadn't gone upstairs.

Her breath came shallow. She took one step through—and found herself looking at the window again. The same window. The same reflection. Only now, the version in the glass was on her side of the door, and she was inside the frame.

Her reflection tilted its head, perfectly calm, as Elena began to understand the geometry had changed—that the house hadn't moved her from room to room; it had rotated the rooms themselves.

She pressed both hands against the glass. The surface gave beneath her palms like thin ice.

Her reflection leaned in close, until their faces almost touched.

"Elena," it whispered again. "You keep looking at me like I'm the stranger."

Then the reflection blinked—and this time, she was the one who didn't.

For a long moment, Elena couldn't move.

Her reflection smiled faintly in the glass, eyes steady, mouth soft. It wasn't mocking her—it was *waiting*. That was somehow worse.

When she finally forced herself backward, her shoulder hit the edge of the desk. The notebook on top slid off, hitting the floor with a soft thud. The reflection didn't bend to pick it up. It only tilted its head, a small, birdlike motion that landed somewhere between pity and curiosity.

The key at her throat throbbed once, then cooled.

"Stop copying me," Elena whispered.

The reflection raised a brow—mock surprise—before deliberately turning its head away, breaking the mimicry as if to prove it could.

It walked—no, glided—toward the version of the door that existed behind the glass, its movement too smooth, too sure. Then it paused, looked back over its shoulder, and mouthed a single word: *follow.*

The reflection opened its door and stepped through, disappearing from view.

Elena stared at the window's other side. The east bedroom beyond it now stood empty. The bed unmade, the curtains shifting slightly in a wind she couldn't feel.

She took one step closer.

The air changed again—the taste of metal and ozone, the faint vibration underfoot. The surface of the glass had gone matte, the reflection gone entirely. She raised her hand and pressed it to the pane. The temperature was wrong—not cold, not warm, just *alive*.

A heartbeat, faint but unmistakable, pulsed beneath her palm.

Her breath hitched. She yanked her hand back and stumbled against the desk again.

The notebook she'd dropped had fallen open to a clean page. New handwriting bled through from the fibers beneath, wet and deliberate.

The second voice always comes from behind.

She turned fast.

The study door was open. The hall beyond stretched in both directions, longer than it should, walls bending slightly, as if viewed through curved glass.

"Elena," someone said from behind her.

She spun again.

No one.

The window was blank now—no room, no reflection. Only her own faint outline, the faintest echo of herself moving in delay, a trick of light.

"Elena."

The voice was closer this time, exactly her tone, but quieter, like a recording replayed through fog.

She ran for the door.

The hallway beyond didn't lead to the landing. It opened into another hallway, identical. The same wallpaper, the same chandelier, the same framed portrait of Eleanor—but each copy slightly *off.* The wallpaper's vines looped the wrong way, the chandelier's bulbs too dim, Eleanor's eyes too narrow.

Elena turned left.

Another hallway. Another copy.

A low hum vibrated in the walls—a subsonic purr, like the house was pleased with itself.

She passed the same door three times, each one slightly different: brass knob, iron knob, no knob. The air thickened, the light dimming with every turn.

"Stop it!" she shouted.

Her own voice answered from behind her, perfectly timed, perfectly hers.

"Stop it!"

She froze.

The echo didn't fade. It continued forward, steady, approaching.

"Stop it stop it stop it stop it—"

Elena turned.

Her double came out of the dark, barefoot, pale, eyes glinting. Not a ghost—not translucent, not flickering—but fully solid, as if she'd stepped out of a mirror and forgotten to go back in.

Elena backed up. "You're not real."

The double smiled. "Neither are you."

It was the same phrase from the window, spoken now with her own breath. The same cadence, the same warmth, the same calm that made denial sound like confession.

"Stay away from me."

"I already am you."

The double's bare feet left no sound on the wood. It stopped an arm's length away. They stood there, mirror-still, and for a terrifying instant Elena felt her own muscles go soft, waiting to be moved by someone else.

The double reached out a hand. "Come back. We belong in the same place."

Elena stepped back. "No."

The double frowned. "You already said yes."

The hall lights flickered, once, twice.

When they steadied, the double was gone.

The air in front of Elena still smelled faintly of her perfume.

She ran.

The corridor doubled back on itself, folding like a page creased too many times. The stairwell was gone. The floor tilted subtly, pulling her toward a vanishing point she couldn't see.

She tried the nearest door. Locked. The next. Locked. The third opened into a bedroom—not hers, but close enough to confuse. The furniture was mirrored, the dresser on the wrong side, the bed facing north instead of east.

A window dominated the far wall.

She knew before she looked what she'd see.

Her reflection stood in the garden, outside the house, staring up at her.

It waved.

Elena slammed the curtains shut.

Behind her, the bed sighed—as if something beneath the covers exhaled.

She turned.

The lump under the quilt rose, then fell.

She yanked the blanket away.

Nothing. Just the indentation of a body that had been there seconds before. The sheets were warm.

"Elena," the voice said again, from under the floor this time.

She dropped to her knees and pressed her ear against the boards. The wood was warm, vibrating with breath.

> *You keep looking at me like I'm the stranger.*

The same sentence. The same tone.

She staggered back, her heart pounding in her throat. "Get out of my head!"

The house laughed—or maybe the floor did. The sound rippled through the wood like footsteps running beneath the surface.

She fled into the hall again. The lights along the corridor strobed faintly, a slow, steady pulse. The hum of the house had become rhythmic now, like a heartbeat.

Her heartbeat.

It synchronized.

Every thud in her chest came a fraction later than the vibration in the walls—until it matched exactly.

She stopped, pressing her hand to her sternum. "No," she whispered. "You don't get to have that."

But the pulse kept time.

Down the hall, the reflection appeared again—only this time it was moving first. Every tilt of its head, every lift of its hand, came a heartbeat before she did it herself.

She turned away, tried to trick it by stepping sideways—but her own body betrayed her, moving before she decided to.

It was teaching her how to follow.

The reflection raised its hand to its lips—*shh*—and Elena's hand rose without her permission.

"Stop."

The reflection shook its head. "You'll ruin it."

"Ruin what?"

"Our symmetry."

Something in the tone cracked her will. She bolted forward, running straight through the reflection—into herself.

The air went liquid, folding her in.

For a second she was everywhere—stairs, hall, nursery, blue room—all overlaid like transparencies, the house's bones visible and alive. She felt it, all of it—the shifting timber, the pulse in the plaster, the faint vibrations of a thousand trapped breaths.

And through all of it, one thought not her own:

You were always meant to fit.

Then the pressure released. She hit the floor hard. The corridor around her was normal again.

Her reflection was gone.

She lay there, gasping, hand pressed to her chest. Her heart beat on, irregular now, like it was trying to remember which rhythm belonged to her.

When she stood, her knees trembled. The wallpaper around her was damp to the touch, condensation slicking the vines into blurred green veins.

Something shimmered at the end of the hall—a faint glow, like a lantern behind glass. She followed it.

The light led her to another door. This one stood ajar, breathing faintly, the gap pulsing with a soft luminescence.

She hesitated, the brass key heavy in her hand.

From inside came a voice—soft, precise. Her own.

"You're late again."

Her throat dried. "What are you?"

"Finishing what you started."

Lightning flashed somewhere outside. For a moment, she saw the entire house reflected in that impossible light—each room existing at once, nested inside itself, fractal and infinite.

Then the light vanished, and the door before her creaked open fully, revealing—

—herself, sitting at a desk in a perfect replica of the study.

The reflection looked up, smiled. "See? You were always here."

Elena's mouth went dry. "No."

"Yes," the double said gently. "We just forgot which side of the glass we were on."

The brass key pulsed once more, this time not in heat but in sound—a low, resonant chime that came from *inside* her chest.

The air rippled. The floor beneath her feet shifted, softening into reflection, then into water, then into nothing at all.

The last thing she saw before the world folded inward again was her own face—calm, certain, seated at the desk—watching her fall away with a kind of sad relief.

Falling didn't feel like falling. It felt like being misremembered.

Air pressed at Elena from all sides, not with speed but with intention, as if the atmosphere were a pair of hands repositioning her. When the motion stopped, she didn't hit anything. She arrived—quietly, the way a thought arrives—standing in a room she knew too well to trust.

The study. Or its rehearsal.

Everything was correct in the way copies are correct: the window with its faint mineral swirls, the desk scar, the chair's threadbare arm, the scent of lemon oil over old ink. A typewriter waited on the blotter, black enamel gleaming. Its ribbon spooled out in a lazy loop across the keys like a tongue.

Across from her, seated at the desk, her double regarded her with what might have been compassion and might have been strategy.

"Better," the double said. "You always were dramatic about transitions."

"Give me back my house," Elena managed. Her voice sounded muffled, as if it had put on a coat. "Give me back myself."

The other Elena tipped her head. "That assumes we're different things."

"We are."

"Are we?" She smiled, soft, sincere enough that Elena wanted to step backward and couldn't remember how. "When you left the city, did you think you were bringing yourself alone? You packed an inheritance without opening its box."

"I didn't pack you."

The double frowned, the expression flitting across their face like weather. "No. I've been here longer than that."

Silence layered between them: house-quiet, storm-silence, the hush after a name is said but before it is acknowledged. The typewriter gave a small, prim tick, as if clearing the throat of its mechanism.

"Why me?" Elena asked. "Why now?"

The double touched the brass key at her own throat—Elena's key, Elena's chain. "Because the house needed listening and you knew how. Because you already speak in corridors and shadows and careful edits. You were always going to fit."

"I'm not joining you," Elena said. "I don't care what the house 'needs.'"

"It's not asking." The double turned the paper bail, aligning a blank sheet under the platen with a precision Elena recognized from her own hands measuring canvas. "It's writing."

"And what are you?" Elena asked. "Ink?"

"Reader," the double said gently. "Editor." A pause. "Keeper."

The last word made the skin at the back of Elena's neck try to move away from itself. "No."

The double looked almost sympathetic. "Say it enough and it can be true in small rooms. This one isn't small."

A shape flickered in the window—a negative of herself walking past, an afterimage of a day she hadn't lived yet. When she blinked, the glass held only the room's reflection again, a layered palimpsest of desk and lamp and the two of them facing one another like a conversation practicing.

Elena edged toward the door. The knob watched her without eyes.

"You can leave," the double said. "Of course. There are always doors. But you know the trick by now."

"What trick?"

"The one rooms play. They follow."

Elena put a hand on the knob anyway. The metal was room-temperature. The wood shivered faintly under her palm, as if remembering a past hand's pressure. She turned—one quarter, half, the latch riding back with an offended click—and opened.

A corridor spread out—familiar, patient. At the far end, the nursery glowed with its funeral-light. Behind her, the typewriter breathed out another small tick, the way a machine does when it cools.

"Elena," the double said, the syllables landing with the exact weight Elena's own voice gave her name. "You can't outwalk geometry."

"Watch me," Elena said.

She stepped into the hall.

On her second stride the floor corrected. Not a shift—an edit. The boards accepted her weight and then offered it back without friction. On her fourth, the portraits multiplied, then un-multiplied when she tried to count them. On her sixth, she arrived at a window impossible to be there and looked through it.

A bedroom looked back. A chair sat empty. A bed waited without opinion. On the far wall a mirror had been hung where the wallpaper once showed a bloom of damp. In the mirror, the study hovered behind her right shoulder. In the study, the double lifted her hand and waved.

Elena slammed the hall window shut—absurd act; it was only glass set into interior wall—and felt the house smile with its beams.

"You're tiresome," she told it, low.

The house brightened half a candle's worth, as if pleased to be spoken to again.

At the nursery threshold she stopped. She did not step in. The cradle was moving. Not rocking—breathing, the mattress rising and falling with no weight on it. Above, the paper moon turned once and redrew its shadow.

"Not today," she said, and closed the door.

Behind her: the blue room breathed in a measured, kind way. It smelled like beeswax and borrowed calm. "Kind ends," she recited, remembering Eleanor's hand. "Patience isn't love." Then, more softly, to herself: "But it will do."

She stepped into the blue room and shut the door. The silence tightened neatly, as if a cloth had been pulled taut. For a moment she could pretend it was only a square of gentleness inside a bad dream.

The small brass bell without a clapper sat on the side table exactly where it always sat when the room existed. Elena set one fingertip to its lip. It hummed without sound—sensation too fine to hear, the kind you feel in the teeth.

"Show me the edge," she said. "If you're kind."

The room obliged. A seam in the wallpaper lifted, revealing faint pencil marks where some past hand had sketched the room's bones before the house decided on them. A construction line, faint and proud. A note in the margin so soft she almost missed it:

Listen here.

She put her ear to the plaster. The wall conducted breath—not the house's, not a person's—something between. A channel. Through it, far below as if at the bottom of a well, a repetition: a word trying to be a song.

She shut her eyes. Said nothing. Let it pass by.

When she opened the door again, the corridor had been edited cleaner: portraits in their first positions, runner aligned, chandelier plumb. The house had done its best impression of order. On instinct, she cut diagonally across the hall and put her shoulder to the study door. She expected resistance. It opened, courteous.

The double hadn't moved. "You're doing well," she said. "You're remembering how to stand inside a story."

Elena crossed to the desk and put both palms on the blotter. "I write my stories."

"Oh, Elena." The double's smile was fond in a way that made it cruel. "You paint them. Paintings are the polite cousins of hauntings."

"We can negotiate," Elena said. "You and me."

"We are negotiating. Our terms are most of a century old."

"Then update them." She leaned closer. "You want a keeper. I want a door."

"You want two things," the double said, tone neutral. "To stay and to leave. The house is happy to let you suffer both."

Elena straightened. "Do you remember the town?"

The double blinked. "Which part?"

"The café. Mae's warning. Mrs. Dunley's hands. The doorplate with the E." She kept talking because the sound of her own voice in this room kept the key at her throat from cooling back to silence. "Do you remember the ledger page? 'Each generation leaves a room behind.'"

The double's eyes darkened a fraction—not anger, exactly; consideration. "Yes."

"What's ours?" Elena asked. It surprised her, wanting to know. It surprised her more that she meant it.

The double touched the typewriter with a fingertip. The metal acknowledged her the way a cat acknowledges a touch it didn't ask for. "Not yet."

Lightning blew the window white. For one bare slice the study held two Elenas and none; the glass decided to reflect and then to remember, and the room obliged.

"Pick," the double said when the light released them. It sounded kind. "Which side you want."

"You already have one."

"So do you."

Elena's mouth had gone dry enough that speaking felt like cutting new teeth. "What happens if I choose the wrong one?"

"There isn't a wrong one." The double's smile tilted. "Only the one that keeps more of you."

The typewriter shifted by a small, pleased inch. The blank page swallowed another margin.

"Fine," Elena said, not to the double, not to the house, not to the part of herself that kept answering—perhaps to all three. "I'll choose. But we will set terms."

"Name them."

"First, I won't hum your lullaby."

The double's eyebrows rose, amused. "It's ours."

"It's borrowed." Elena's palms pressed harder into the blotter until she felt the cardboard give. "Second, you stop calling me when I'm not in the house."

Silence. The storm went down a stair. The double considered. "That one's difficult."

"Try."

"Third?" the double prompted after a moment, polite.

"I walk through every room you offer me, but I choose which one I leave behind."

That landed. The double's mouth made the shape of a refusal and didn't give it voice. She turned the paper release lever and straightened the sheet, stalling. "And if the house doesn't accept?"

"Then you can keep your symmetry without me," Elena said, and pulled the key over her head.

The chain hissed softly against her skin. The key lay bright in her palm, warmer than it should be. It looked small at that distance from her body—childish, almost. She set it on the blotter between them.

The double studied it as if it were a map. "You'll want that back."

"Take it."

"That's not how this trick works."

"Take it." Elena nudged the key forward with a finger. "You're the one who wants to keep. Keep something."

The double did not reach for it. She reached, instead, for Elena's wrist. The touch was light, ownership disguised as gentleness. Elena did not pull away—because this, too, was a choice. The double turned Elena's hand, palm up, and lowered the key back into it.

"Two of us holding it is the point," she said. "Else how would the door remember which way to open?"

The key pulsed once in Elena's fist. The room brightened a tone. The typewriter sighed as if thanked.

"Then hear mine," Elena said, quietly now. "I will stay long enough to know what the house is. Not longer. When I leave, you won't follow."

The double tipped her head again—a sparrow shape, curious. "Where would I go? I am here." A beat. "We are here."

"Then learn to be here without asking for my breath."

The double's smile thinned to sincerity. "I can try not to speak when you sleep. I can nudge the halls back when they lengthen. I can keep the blue room kind. But the house isn't a thing you quiet; it's a thing you tune. If you refuse to hum, it will hum for you. If I refuse to call your name, the walls will do it with the same voice."

"Then here's my last term," Elena said, and surprised herself with how steady she sounded. "If you must call me, call me as me— not in my mother's voice, not in Eleanor's, not in Victor's. No more inherited tongues."

Something like relief passed over the double's face. "Done."

The window darkened. The study exhaled. A door she could not see unlabeled itself a fraction. Somewhere below, a hinge finished its sentence.

"You've asked nothing," Elena said, finally. "No term for yourself."

The double held her gaze. "I have what I want."

"What's that?"

"You're listening."

A laugh escaped Elena—tired, disbelieving, briefly fond of her own absurdity. "I have been since the key turned."

"Then try a different act." The double touched the typewriter again; the page rolled obediently. "Write."

Elena did not sit. But she reached, and with the ball of her thumb pressed a single letter into the paper—a ghost print, inkless. E. She lifted her hand and looked at the bruise it had left in the fiber. No ink. Still, the page remembered pressure. The letter deepened without pigment, as if the paper had decided to agree.

"Again," the double said.

She pressed L. The paper indented. Outside, rain found its nerve and returned.

"Again."

E. The study's lamp steadied. The window caught, for an instant, the fleeting reflection of someone—Eleanor?—passing just out of frame.

"Again."

N. The key in her fist beat once like a small animal. The floor underfoot approved with a soft shift.

"Again."

A. The house listened.

They stood, two women, one name pressed into a page until the word existed without ink. The typewriter waited, unthreatened by this other technology of will.

"Enough," Elena said, when the last letter was done. "I have said it."

The double nodded. "The house has heard it."

"What now?"

"Now," the double said, and set her palm flat on the desk the way Elena had—"we decide which of us is the echo."

The study's door closed by itself, lightly. The window cupped the stormlight and let it go. The typewriter shifted a sigh. The air thickened the way water thickens when it agrees to hold you.

"On three," the double said. "Choose."

Elena knew what choice she meant. Glass or air. Reflection or room. Door or door.

She didn't count. She moved.

The double moved too. They stepped at the same moment— Elena toward the window, the double toward the door. Their hands crossed in the air above the blotter and, for one breath, clasped. Warmth, pulse, proof. In that clasp a third pressure— beam, nail, lintel—added its weight, a house agreeing to the handshake.

Then they let go.

Elena's shoulder met glass that wasn't glass. It bowed, then broke like skin, giving way with a wet, forgiving sound. Cold layered air met her face. The hall beyond unscrolled: runner, portraits, a length that looked finite. Behind her, the door took the double as easily as water takes oars.

"Don't hum," the double said, not turning back.

"Don't call," Elena said, and didn't turn either.

The room adjusted itself around the tear, the aperture sealed. The glass, which had never been glass, remembered how to be wall. The study breathed once in satisfaction, then surprised them both by offering a final gift: a faint chiming from somewhere unfound, like a clapperless bell finding a tongue.

Elena stood in the corridor and waited for the trick that would undo what she had just done. None came. The portraits hung at their agreed-upon distance. The runner held its pattern. The chandelier remained true. At the nursery door she paused and didn't listen. At the blue room she breathed and thanked it in her head without entering.

At the landing she looked down. The front door existed. It was closed, politely. It felt true as geometry.

Her body did not rush. The house disliked haste; it bent it back into circles. She walked, boots making sane sounds on sane treads, and at the bottom she put her ear for a breath against the under-stair panel. Nothing but wood and the memory of secrets. She didn't open it.

At the foyer table the bowl of peonies had given up finally and become proof of time. She lifted the wooden box, felt its familiar stubborn weight, and set it down. The key still lay in her hand, her chain looped through her fingers.

When she unlatched the door and opened it, the outside air struck her chest with its ordinary cold. Pine, wet gravel, a gull's ridiculous cry. The world beyond the threshold had its own patience and its own rooms, none of which were hers to keep.

She stepped out onto the porch.

The house didn't call. The house didn't hum. It arranged its silence into a shape that, for the first time since she'd arrived, didn't feel like a demand.

Elena looked back once. Not as farewell—she didn't have that to give—but as inventory. The hall held still. A shadow moved that was only hers. Somewhere upstairs a hinge adjusted and then minded itself.

"Noted," she said, and locked the door behind her with a hand that didn't shake. She slid the key into her pocket, not around her throat. It pulsed once against the seam, not pleading—present.

The path to the car was brief and wet and honest. She drove into a fog that was only weather. At the end of the drive, she stopped, because stopping felt like a ritual that could be kind if she let it. She put the car in park and rested her forehead against the wheel and breathed the air that belonged to nobody.

When she lifted her head, the mirror showed her face and no one else's. The road offered its narrow ribbon. The forest waited no more or less than it had in any century that wasn't hers.

She put the car in gear.

At the first bend, her phone woke. Three bars. A voicemail icon. *Unknown number. 2:07 a.m.* She laughed, low and weary, and didn't listen. She slid the phone into the glove compartment and shut it in.

Halfway to town, the radio caught a station that sounded like rain on tin. She turned the dial until a human voice found her— two DJs arguing about baseball, bored and dear. She let them fill the car. At the curb outside the café she sat a minute longer to see if the house inside her would speak.

It didn't. That felt like mercy.

She went in. The bell over the door did its best imitation of friendly. Mae looked up, counted something on Elena's face, and poured a coffee before Elena asked.

"You look like you picked a side," Mae said, sliding the mug across.

Elena took the first too-hot sip and let it burn. "Maybe I just picked a breath."

Mae nodded, as if breaths were currency and she was good for the loan. "Scone?"

Elena almost said she couldn't eat. Then she took the scone because saying yes felt like the right magic. She broke it open and buttered both halves. The simplest prayer.

When she left, the street lightened by a tone. The sky remembered the sun. She set the coffee on the roof of the car to free her hands and took the key out of her pocket. It lay heavy and unperformative on her palm.

"Not a necklace," she said to it. "Not today."

She slid it into the glove compartment beside the sleeping phone and closed them both into that dark.

On the drive back, the road kept its distance and its length. The trees were only trees. When the manor appeared, it did so honestly, exactly when it should.

She parked and listened. The house listened back. Two attentions, not one hunger.

On the porch, she paused, hand on the door, and then stepped to the window instead. The glass showed her face, and behind it, a hall that held, and beyond, a staircase that did what stairs do. She raised her hand in an almost-wave and felt foolish and alive.

From somewhere very far inside, a red door neither opened nor closed. It merely waited, as thresholds do when they learn patience.

Elena shaped the house's silence with her own.

"I'll come in," she said softly, "and we'll see."

The hinge answered with good manners. The door accepted her.

The window across the hall—one she had never noticed because it had never needed to be—held no reflection at all. Only the idea of light passing through.

When the door shut behind her, it did so without performance. Somewhere upstairs, in the blue room, the brass bell that had no clapper made no sound.

And in the study—whichever study was real enough today—the typewriter sat with a page still indented by a name pressed without ink, and a second page waiting for something neither house nor keeper could write alone.

Outside, the forest made its weather. Inside, the house kept its promises as far as it knew how.

Only one Elena walked the hall. Whether she had come from glass or air wasn't the kind of question the day required answered. Not yet.

She put the key back around her neck because the weight had learned to be a comfort, not a claim. Then she set a clean sheet on the foyer table and wrote three words to begin the part of the story that would have to be made, not found.

Do not listen.

She crossed them out.

Underneath, in her narrower, truer hand, she wrote:

Listen differently.

CHAPTER 7

The Red Door Appears

The night behaved for almost two hours. Elena took the house's obedience like a truce. She ate in the kitchen with the light over the sink turned low—bread, an apple, the kind of dinner that didn't ask the room to share itself. The pipes spoke their small dialect, reasonable and tired. The clock in the hall kept a modest tempo. The blue room's door kept its soft breath to itself. When she passed the nursery on her rounds, she didn't look in. The quiet let her get away with that.

She carried the wooden box from the foyer table to the study and set it on the windowsill—a witness, not a secret. The under-stair panel had held its blank well enough for one day. In her sketchbook, on a clean page that resisted both revision and panic, she wrote:

Today: I chose.

She closed the book on the sentence to keep it true.

The typewriter—today's version—sat with its mouth closed, nothing rolled, nothing waiting. On the blotter beside it she placed the brass key, then changed her mind and looped it back around her neck. Without its weight, her collarbone felt too visible. With it, she could believe in a center.

"Listen differently," she said into the room, the phrase stripped of bravado now and becoming a habit. The house replied by lowering the lamp a fraction, as if to show that listening could be shared and not only asked.

She went to bed in the east bedroom because that was where her body expected to sleep. She opened the window half an inch— Mae's advice, Mrs. Dunley's, the small superstition of air—and let the forest lay its cool on the sill. The curtains moved a little, like breath. She laid the key inside her shirt and let it warm to skin. She told herself a story about leaving in the morning to buy new bread. She fell asleep before she could finish the part where she came back.

When the dream arrived, it didn't announce itself.

It began as a corridor long enough to forgive mistakes. The runner's pattern thinned and reddened toward a vanishing point.

On the walls, portraits lined themselves into an aisle of faces turned slightly away, not out of shame but out of courtesy— don't let our eyes push you. The house was generous in the dream; it allowed her to count. Twenty paces, thirty, forty, and then the corridor ended, because all corridors end, on a plane of red.

Door-red, not blood-red. Lacquer rather than stain. The sort of red that isn't painted so much as grown, layer by layer, until it tricks light into a new profession. The surface was so smooth it could have been wet. The frame around it was older wood, the kind that remembers hand tools and patience. There was a knob, brass like the key, and a keyhole the size of a tear.

Elena stopped, the way a person stops at the edge of a cliff even if they don't mind heights. The door's proportion satisfied the eye the way formal gardens do—symmetry, intention, an argument ended. If she stepped closer, she could smell something beneath the lacquer: wax, cedar, heat. The smell moved like a thought through her ribs.

From the other side, so faint it might have been a muscle twitch in the house's skin, came a knock.

Not the frantic staccato of horror, not the casual visit of a friend. A measured rap, then a pause. Two, softer, as if to say *I am real; I am not wind.* She lifted her hand to the knob and woke with her palm pressed to the cool wood of her nightstand.

The house breathed. The forest answered.

She lay still, letting the panic discover it was not required. Dream, she told her body. A good one—well-made, like a chair. She shut her eyes to pick the door apart in memory, how the red used shadow, the weight of the knob. That was a painter's impulse, not a haunted woman's.

Then, from somewhere beyond the bedroom, a knock.

She sat up too fast and the room listed—a slow boat's roll. She held to the edge of the mattress until the ceiling remembered to be level. Her phone, facedown on the nightstand, showed the hour: 2:07 a.m., spiteful and precise. She smiled despite herself, a small, humorless curl. "Of course."

"Elena," the house did not say. It didn't have to. It offered the corridor like a suggestion instead.

She got up. Bare feet on cold floor, shirt pulled on without looking, key warmed in her palm on its way back beneath the collar. The hall outside the door felt a degree cooler, a physics she could forgive. The portraits kept their faces. The chandelier considered an indulgent sway and decided against it.

She followed the knock the way you follow a smell— uncertainly, willing to be wrong. At the landing she paused. The second floor stretched obediently right and left. No red. The nursery's door sat where it sat, an object and not a symbol. She didn't touch it.

The next knock came from below—not from the foyer proper, but under it, or behind the idea of it, where drawings of houses keep their erased lines. She went down the stairs steady as a person reluctant to test their ankle.

The foyer was a lesson in reasonable light: the lamp measured, the runner true. The peonies, dead and soft-mouthed, had been replaced. She hadn't replaced them. She wanted to correct that thought—*Someone replaced them*—but no one and someone felt equally inaccurate here. The bowl held white blossoms now, not pink, and water that didn't dare to stain the table.

The knock again, behind her. She turned, expecting the study's door to offer itself, or the under-stair panel to loosen its secret.

What she saw instead was a narrow length of hallway where there had never been a hallway - a slim corridor opened up between the dining room and the service passage, just wide enough for a person to step into without comfort. At the far end, around an angle she could not see, a dull wash of color pulsed, not bright, not dim. If she had to name it—heat.

She should have fetched her boots. She should have fetched the tape measure, the pencil, the version of herself that insisted on being adult about magic. Instead she stepped forward because the body's sense of narrative is older than the mind's caution.

The corridor's walls wore no paper. Bare plaster chalked her shoulder where they brushed close. The floorboards were unpainted, sanded smooth by shoes that were not hers. The house had not finished this piece of itself; it had only decided it was ready enough to show.

"Alright," she said, quietly. "If you're going to be born, do it in front of me."

The corridor bent left, then right—polite angles, not tricks. The air warmed as she went, the way closets warm when light bulbs do their private search for dust. She smelled something not the house's vocabulary—resin, resin, and a little honey.

The knock again. Closer. Two, then the small courtesy of silence.

At the corner, the corridor ended. The wall there had been primed and was waiting to be painted. And in that wall, not red but ready for it, sat a rectangle of raw timber framed perfectly square, a door without its door—just the threshold set like a promise, the jambs true, the sill proud. The aperture was filled with a taut stretch of canvas tacked neatly to the frame.

She stared at the canvas and found her hands lifted without consent, as if to check the weave. Her palms hovered an inch shy of the surface, feeling not heat but the intention to be heat.

She did not touch it. She had learned some politeness.

"Is this what you're going to be?" she asked, and felt stupid and correct at once. The house rustled, which was either an answer or furniture settling. The canvas hummed the way power lines hum when weather is coming.

Behind the canvas—no, that was wrong; there was nothing behind it—somewhere adjacent to the idea of the canvas, a faint pressure rearranged her inner ear. The body knows when a door chooses to exist. It is an airport descent deep in the head. It is a small breaking.

She took a step back and the humming softened, agreeing not to rush her.

"Noted," she said. "I see you."

The house held still in that way that means it is thinking. She left the corridor before it could decide whether her confirmation constituted consent.

In the foyer again, she stood with her back to the table and watched the hallway's mouth until it understood she was not coming back tonight. The light there cooled a degree, sulked, and behaved.

She slept after that the way you sleep before a surgery—briefly, shallowly, with the body eager to be done and back.

**

In the morning the corridor was gone.

The varnish on the dining room chair backs shone in the generous angle of nine a.m. light. The service passage held its well-behaved hum. The wall where the hall had been wore its paint untroubled. If she pressed her ear to it, she heard only wood agree with wood.

She made toast like proof. She ate standing up with her shoulders not tense and her jaw remembering normal. She washed the plate and thought about calling someone, as if anyone existed in a catalog at the end of a phone who took calls that begin *A hallway appeared and then did not.* She opened her phone and saw the voicemail icon—*2:07 a.m.*—and shut the phone into the drawer with the bread knife.

She would go into town for a fresh notebook, she decided, because the one she had learned too much from had become impatient with her hand. She would buy a pencil sharpener to replace the little metal wedge that had stained her pockets graphite. She would ask Rowan for the ledger copy and Mae for a second scone she would not finish. She would keep the key around her neck and her mouth shut.

The house did not argue.

On her way out she passed the study and glanced in because she was not a coward. The typewriter had not moved, the blotter kept its modestal hairline. On the windowsill the wooden box kept its counsel beside the white peonies, which looked as if they had never been otherwise.

She paused. One of the peonies had begun to show, at the base of a petal hidden from casual glance, a tint that was not pink. Not bruising. Not age. A color building the way resin builds—layer on layer until light forgets its old job.

Red. So faint she could have blamed the sun. There are a hundred excuses for red if it wants to be excused.

"No," she said gently to the flower, because it could stand in for anything. "You don't have to be."

The petal did not answer. The thing in the house that loved the arrangement filed the moment under later.

She took the car because walking through the forest felt like trying to dictate to a choir. The town received her with its version of hospitality: Mae's small nod; Rowan's smaller one; Mrs. Dunley not in her spot near the square but the space shaped as if she might arrive. Elena bought a notebook that would not bleed and a handful of pencils and an eraser big enough to be confident. Rowan, when asked, produced a photocopy of the ledger page as if he had put it aside for her days ago, which he might have.

The house adds what it needs. Each generation leaves a room behind.

"Did Victor ever mention a red door?" she asked, as if she were asking about paint.

Rowan's mouth made an O without sound. "Only once," he said after a moment. "Said it wasn't a door so much as a habit."

"Good," she said, because sometimes the right answer is the wrong one phrased poetically. "Thank you."

Back at the café, Mae slid coffee and a scone across without being asked and said, "Don't look out any windows you didn't buy."

"I'll keep my eyes on the floor," Elena said.

Mae nodded, approving. "Floors have fewer opinions."

"You'd like my house," Elena said, and regretted the invitation as soon as she made it.

"I like you better outside of it," Mae said, unafraid.

When she returned to the manor near noon, the road neither elongated nor lied. The gateposts kept their dull dignity. She parked and sat a minute with her hand on the key in her pocket, not her chest, letting the decision learn where to live.

Inside, everything was still. House-still, not story-still. She put the new notebook on the foyer table, where it changed the light a little the way new things always do. She did not go looking for the corridor again. She went into the kitchen and opened a window to the degree Mae would have approved, and the house breathed through it with something like gratitude.

At half past one, the smell came back. Cedar and wax and a sweetness that wasn't sugar.

At one thirty-two, a knock, from under or inside or next to the front hall. Measured. Single. Confident.

She left the kettle where it was—mid-persuasion—and walked out to meet it. The wall between the dining room and service passage had remembered the trick of being two rooms apart. It parted again with good manners, offering the slim hall. The air beyond it was warmer than the house, as if someone had been living there.

She stepped into the corridor without introducing herself.

Around the last angle, where last night the door had been promised and not present, the canvas had been primed the color of dried bone. The frame was the same. The tacks were the same. What was different was the first square inch of color at the lower right corner—a red so deep it drank the light around it. Not painted; applied like vow.

She stood watching the inch of red do nothing. She did not reach out. She did not argue. The house, pleased with her performance, offered the next square inch. On the canvas, the color grew without brush—capillary, caper, caprice—another inch, and then the slow diagonal of a stroke where no hand moved.

"Okay," she said. "I understand."

The knock again, behind the canvas, or within it, or beyond all three options.

"Elena," nobody said.

She returned to the foyer and to the table and wrote on the first page of the new notebook, with the new pencil carefully sharpened:

The door is arriving.

Under it, smaller:

I will not open it alone.

She closed the book and put her palm on the cover. The study held its breath. The corridor hummed like heat over stone. The house arranged its silence into something almost kind.

At three o'clock, she heard the faintest click—hinge? latch? a first finger flex?—from the newborn hall.

At three-oh-one, she put on her boots. She tied them tightly. She slid the key back under her shirt.

At three-oh-two, the house, polite enough to appreciate a ritual, made room.

She went to meet the red.

The first morning after the red began, the house behaved as though it hadn't noticed.

That, Elena decided, was worse than hostility.

She walked her route — foyer, kitchen, blue room, landing, study — as though inspecting a crime scene that refused to remember one had happened. The scent of cedar was gone, replaced with lemon oil and dust's faint sweetness. The peonies, white and polite, had not bled further. The typewriter's platen was blank, no page rolled in. Only the hum under the floorboards betrayed the lie of normalcy — not audible, exactly, but *pressing*.

When she passed the wall where the corridor used to appear, the air thinned. She stopped. A hand's breadth from the plaster, a subtle current moved — warm to cold to warm again, as if the space behind it were breathing.

"Not now," she whispered, and felt the wall hold its breath.

That was when she noticed the key. It had warmed again — pulsing faintly, though she hadn't touched it. She looked down, expecting its usual bronze sheen, but the metal had deepened — a new vein of reddish hue blooming along the ridges.

The same color as the door.

She pressed her thumb to it and it stopped, as if embarrassed at being caught.

By late afternoon, the quiet became theatrical. The clocks all agreed on four o'clock — the same chime, the same tone, the same echo layered thrice, like a chord struck by one hand through different rooms. The house's symmetry was performing again.

She found herself standing in the study, sketchbook open to a blank page. She hadn't meant to draw, but the pencil moved before she decided what it was drawing. The first line was vertical, deliberate. The second curved slightly at its base. She blinked — a door, of course. Not red, not yet. She shaded around the edges, crosshatching the grain of imagined wood. Then she pressed harder, darker, until the lead snapped and the sound broke something else in her concentration.

When she looked down again, the page was wet.

She turned it toward the window. Not water. Pigment. Red, the way paint is red when it's new — before it oxidizes, before it learns to pretend it's brown. The lines she'd drawn had thickened into something closer to brushstrokes.

The red bled slowly, feathering the edges of the page. The smell of resin returned.

"Alright," she said softly, "I'm listening."

She tore the page free and placed it on the blotter beside the typewriter. The inked letters of the machine's last imprint — her name, *ELENA* — ghosted faintly on the sheet below.

A conversation, maybe.

"Tell me what you want."

The typewriter didn't move. The air did. A draft pushed through the window, flicking the corner of the red drawing. The paper lifted, turned once, and settled — face down.

When she flipped it back over, the red had dried darker, older. The door was now complete — knob, hinges, a line suggesting the faint shadow of something beneath it.

At the top margin, in pencil that wasn't hers, someone had written:

When the paint closes, stand behind it.

She didn't sleep that night. Not properly. The house shifted moods every hour, polite but restless, the way a host rearranges the furniture of silence to suit a guest. Sometimes she heard faint tapping from beneath the floorboards, like the house trying out syllables in a forgotten tongue.

Once, around three, she woke to find her sketchbook open beside her on the nightstand, the red drawing gone. Only a faint mark of pigment on the linen sheets proved she hadn't dreamed it.

At dawn, the house made its next move.

The corridor had returned, bolder now, claiming its place between the dining room and the passage. The walls were clean plaster again — but no canvas this time. The red had bloomed full.

The door stood where the aperture had been, sealed into the frame as if it had always existed. The lacquer gleamed faintly, though no light touched it. The brass knob reflected nothing — a sphere of colorless depth.

Elena stood ten feet away, heart steady out of sheer discipline.

"Good morning," she said.

The house exhaled. The temperature shifted a degree warmer, the air thickening the way honey does when stirred.

She stepped closer, counting each pace.

Up close, the red wasn't uniform. Beneath the topcoat of lacquer, she saw layers — dozens of them, maybe hundreds. The color wasn't pigment. It was depth. Something had been applied over and over, each coat slightly translucent, so the light passing through built its own gravity. When she leaned close, she saw movement. Slow, tidal, inward.

She reached out.

The brass key at her neck flared cold. Her hand stopped an inch short of the door's surface.

"Not yet," she murmured, without knowing why.

The door agreed. It did not open.

It *listened*.

Later that morning, Mae's warning came back to her: *Don't look out any windows you didn't buy.*

Elena found herself staring at the study window again. The view outside had changed. The trees beyond the drive stood in perfect stillness, every branch holding its breath. The fog, which had always moved like the tide, was now motionless — a wall of pale glass beyond the porch.

And at the edge of the fog, barely visible, a shape. Not human. Not entirely *not*.

Tall, with shoulders that bent light around them, as though the body refused to agree with its own outline. The shape faced the house, unmoving.

Her breath condensed on the glass.

When she wiped it away, the figure was gone.

But the fog pulsed, once. Like a held note released.

That evening, the door began to whisper.

It wasn't sound, exactly. More vibration — a pressure behind the ear that shaped itself into meaning if she stood too close. She recognized the cadence before the sense: her own voice, reversed.

...emoc, enil lufituaeb a morf...

She stepped back. The air cooled.

When she turned away, the whisper followed — not louder, not pleading, simply *present*. Like breath.

She went upstairs, into the blue room, and tried to read. The text refused her attention. Every line rearranged itself into the same phrase, the one she hadn't meant to remember: *When the paint closes, stand behind it.*

At midnight she gave up.

She went downstairs.

The door glowed faintly, red through red. The brass knob looked dull, as if something on the other side was holding it from turning.

The key at her throat vibrated. Once. Twice. Then still.

"Alright," she said again, the word both surrender and strategy. "Then show me."

The knob turned—slow, reluctant. Not all the way. Just enough for air to pass.

The smell of cedar rushed through, sharp and sweet.

A voice — faint, not a person's, but a *pressure*—rose and fell in rhythm with her pulse. Not speech. Something older, trying to remember how to *mean.*

She leaned closer, the way you lean to hear a child whisper a secret.

The breath from the gap touched her face. It was warm.

Then the door shut itself, gentle as a lullaby.

For two days, she left it alone.

She painted instead. Not the door—never that—but shapes that had no symmetry. Circles that refused to close. Lines that ended before their destinations. The act was therapy disguised as rebellion, and the house tolerated it the way a parent tolerates a child's tantrum.

When she washed her brushes on the third night, she noticed something new: the water in the jar had taken a faint pink hue. She hadn't used red all day.

She looked toward the dining room.

The door waited, faintly luminous in the dark.

A sound — a low, slow *thud* — rolled through the floorboards.

Another.

And another.

Not random. Measured. A rhythm building.

Heart. Step. Breath.

The house was teaching her the beat.

By the time she reached the corridor, the rhythm had become language. She didn't know the translation, but she knew the meaning: *Closer.*

She obeyed.

At the fourth step, the air turned heavy, charged. She lifted her hand and laid it flat on the red lacquer.

Heat flooded through her palm, up her arm, into her chest.

She saw—herself, standing on the other side, looking back. —but the *other* her was older. Or newer. Or truer. The difference felt semantic. —the double smiled, the same way the reflection had.

The contact broke.

Elena stumbled back, gasping. The key at her neck had gone blister-hot. She tore it off, dropped it to the floor. It clanged once, then rolled in a perfect circle before stopping — pointed at the door.

The door clicked.

Unlocked.

She didn't move.

The house went utterly still. Even the hum beneath the floorboards paused, waiting.

Her heart said open it.

Her mind said leave.

Her hand said touch.

Her voice — the part of her that had learned to listen differently — said:

"Not yet."

The door respected the boundary. The knob relaxed. The lacquer dulled to its earlier calm.

She bent, picked up the key. It had cooled again, almost tender against her palm.

When she looped it back around her neck, the house seemed to exhale — not disappointment, but relief.

Maybe it wasn't ready either.

Maybe that was the point. That night, she dreamed again of the corridor — longer now, the portraits leaning closer. The red door stood waiting, the knob gleaming faintly. On its surface, she saw movement. Not reflection — memory. Hers.

Victor's face, half turned.

Eleanor's hands, painting.

The blue room, before it was blue.

The voices that followed were her own, layered — one for every decision she'd ever deferred.

When she reached the door in the dream, it opened by itself.

Inside, there was nothing but the color red, stretching forever inward, soft as breath.

A voice spoke from within it — not command, not invitation.

"Listen differently."

She woke up crying, not from fear but from recognition.

By morning, the smell of cedar filled the house again.

The red door waited.

And this time, she noticed something new:

At the base of the frame, in tiny black script, carved so fine it might have been written by the air itself:

To open is to remember.

She smiled, half against her will.

The house had finally written back.

The day began with the smell of smoke that wasn't.

It wasn't fire — not yet. It was the ghost of burnt things: candle wax, resin, air rubbed raw.

Elena woke with her palms flat on the coverlet, as though pushing back the dream she had just left. The key at her neck pulsed once, faintly, then quieted. She sat up and listened. The house wasn't humming anymore. It was *breathing*.

A deep inhale through unseen lungs, followed by a held silence too deliberate to be chance.

When she rose, every board beneath her feet responded by not creaking — a restraint so total it became a sound in itself.

She found the red door before she meant to.

It was waiting in the corridor, light pooling along the lacquer as if the house had angled its geometry to favor that one surface.

The brass knob had dulled to a warm amber, the way metal does when it's been handled recently.

She hadn't touched it.

"Alright," she whispered.

The door didn't answer, but something behind it *shifted*, the soft slide of weight against wood — a sound neither invitation nor threat, just a fact: someone, or something, existed there.

She brought a lantern this time, lit by her own hand. Its flame offered the kind of courage electricity never could — imperfect, personal.

She set it on the floor beside the door, and its glow painted the red deeper, richer, more alive. The color seemed to *drink* the light, swallowing it until the lacquer gleamed with an internal pulse.

When she leaned closer, she saw movement inside the red — not reflection but depth. Layers folded upon layers, each slightly translucent, each holding a shadow of a room she half-recognized.

A staircase.

A portrait.

A woman standing in a window that did not exist.

Her own outline formed last.

"Elena."

Her name — breathed, not spoken. The syllables carried from behind the door, through the wood, through the key at her neck.

Her first instinct was to step back.

Her second was to listen.

It was her voice.

Older.

Tired in the way of endurance, not defeat.

"We remember by walking," it said.

"Come see."

The brass knob turned on its own — not a full rotation, only enough to click. The latch released, a soft gasp of vacuum giving way to pressure.

Elena pushed.

The door swung inward without resistance.

The light inside was not red but colorless, though every object held the memory of red in its edges — the way the eye sees after staring at a candle flame too long. The corridor beyond was narrow, lined with unpainted wood.

But it wasn't a corridor anymore.

It was a gallery of memories, arranged as if by an unseen curator who preferred emotion to chronology.

To her left: a long table set for a meal that had never been eaten. Every glass half full of shadow.

To her right: a staircase climbing into blackness, each step creaking with the sound of her own heartbeat.

The walls breathed in rhythm with the house, slow and patient.

Elena took one step in, and the red door closed behind her — not violently, but with a certainty that felt like punctuation.

The sound it made was not *thud* but *period*.

She didn't panic. She had learned not to waste adrenaline in Blackwood Manor.

The lantern's flame followed her, not because she carried it — she had left it by the threshold — but because the light understood its purpose.

Each new step lit a few feet ahead, enough to make decisions and regrets.

There were paintings here — enormous ones, oil on canvas — and each was unfinished. Faces blurred, brushstrokes arrested mid-motion. But every canvas shared one subject: the house.

The manor at dawn.

The manor under snow.

The manor with windows that had never existed.

And in the corner of each composition, painted faintly, was the same figure: a woman with her back turned, always facing a door.

Her dress changed — sometimes modern, sometimes ancient — but the posture never did. She was always reaching for the handle, never touching it.

Elena touched one frame.

The surface was warm.

The figure in the painting moved, almost imperceptibly — a half-breath, a flex of fingers.

Then, in the next painting, she had taken a step closer to the door.

Elena moved on.

The hall widened without warning. The walls pulled back, revealing what at first looked like a ballroom, though the ceiling pressed too low and the floor mirrored her reflection wrong — delayed by half a second, as if unsure whether to believe in her.

Music trembled through the air, faint but meticulous — an old waltz played on a phonograph left running too slow.

At the center of the room stood a man in a suit that had not been fashionable for a century. His back was to her, his hands clasped behind him. His posture was familiar — proud, meticulous, weary.

"Victor?" she asked before she could stop herself.

The man turned halfway. Not enough to show his face. Only the profile.

"Do you hear it?" he said. His voice was her grandfather's but thinner, like sound remembered instead of made.

"The heartbeat in the walls?"

"I do."

He nodded once, as if she had passed a test.

"It started with Eleanor," he said. "She painted a door she couldn't close."

Elena stepped closer. "You mean this one?"

Victor's half-face smiled, sad. "No. That one was mine."

He gestured toward the wall behind him. There, half-shrouded in shadow, stood another door — smaller, rougher, its surface matte and cracked with age.

"She thought the house loved her," he continued. "But it only needed her memory to live in."

"What does it need from me?"

"Continuation."

The word rang like the strike of a chime in a hollow room.

Elena reached for his shoulder, but her hand passed through him — not cold, not heat, only *absence*.

When she looked again, he was gone. Only the echo of the waltz remained, looping a phrase too short to satisfy itself.

The lantern brightened. The red gleam returned at the far end of the room — not lacquer now, but light spilling through cracks in a wall that hadn't existed a moment ago.

The air pulsed. The light beckoned.

The next door opened before she touched it.

She stepped through into a nursery.

Not the one upstairs. A *memory* of it — too vivid, too wrong. The wallpaper was fresh, the cradle still. The air carried the faint powdery sweetness of old milk and wood polish.

On the rocking chair sat a woman in a dress the color of dusk. Her hair was pinned up in a severe twist, but strands had escaped, curling against her neck.

Eleanor Harrow.

Elena knew her without introduction. The resemblance was complete except for the eyes — Eleanor's were darker, deeper, reflecting things no mirror would return.

"You shouldn't have come," Eleanor said softly, not as rebuke but lament.

"I didn't have a choice."

"There's always a choice," Eleanor said, stroking the arm of the chair. "You just don't like either option."

The cradle creaked. Slowly, on its own. The sound was too soft to be threatening, too rhythmic to be random.

"What's inside?" Elena asked.

Eleanor smiled without looking. "The next generation of the house."

Elena stepped closer, heart steady because fear was useless here. She leaned over the cradle.

Inside was a small figure wrapped in linen — not a child, but a mirror the size of one.

Her own reflection blinked up at her.

"You see?" Eleanor said. "It never stops wanting more."

Elena turned to face her ancestor, but the chair was empty now. Only the faint dent in the cushion proved she'd been there.

The cradle stilled. The reflection inside smiled — her own lips moving a heartbeat late.

She left before it could speak.

The corridor narrowed again. The air turned dense, almost liquid. Every breath felt like drawing through silk.

At the end stood the red door — the same, yet not the same. The lacquer gleamed wetly, but she realized the shine came from within, as though it had swallowed the lantern's flame and was using it to burn from the inside out.

This time, she didn't hesitate.

She placed her palm on the surface.

It was warm, then hot, then something beyond temperature — the heat of recognition, of two memories colliding.

To open is to remember.

The carving at the base pulsed faintly, the letters blurring.

Elena pressed harder.

The door softened beneath her hand, pliant like wax under breath.

Light poured through the cracks — not red anymore but pure, bright, merciless white.

Her body trembled but didn't resist.

The key at her neck began to hum again, matching her pulse. The sound rose, layered, became a chord she knew — the same rhythm from the door's knock, now translated into music.

She turned the knob.

The room beyond was infinite.

No walls. No floor. Just suspended air, thick with color and memory.

The manor existed here in fragments — staircases without landings, windows without walls, doors opening onto light.

In the center hung the portraits from the gallery, drifting weightless, their frames turning slowly as if orbiting an unseen center.

And in that center -

A shape.

Not monstrous. Not human. A convergence of every outline she had ever seen in the house. Hands, walls, voices, light. The house itself, awake and aware, folding its geometry into something like a body.

Its voice filled the air, many and one:

"We are made of you."

She couldn't speak. The breath in her lungs felt borrowed.

"Eleanor built the first room," it said. "Victor the next. You bring completion."

"What do you want?" she managed.

"What we are owed. Memory. Continuity. Keeper."

"I'm not staying."

"You misunderstand. You already have."

The light surged, filling her vision with a thousand brief images:

Eleanor painting the nursery.

Victor sealing the study.

The blue room opening for the first time.

Her own hands turning the key on the first night.

The moments overlapped, bled, fused. The house wasn't a place—it was the act of remembering itself, a recursion of blood and history and longing.

She felt her mind split along the grain. One half understood. The other resisted.

The house pressed closer. Its presence felt like gravity rearranging its loyalties.

"If you leave, you forget."

"If you stay, you complete."

Her lips shaped the word before she meant to: "Neither."

Silence.

Then — faintly, like laughter under breath — the house replied:

"Then listen differently."

The light collapsed inward, pulling the fragments of the manor back into themselves. The portraits spun faster, the doors unhinged and folded into points of red. The floor remembered its duty and returned beneath her feet.

She fell, not far, but long enough to forget the order of motion.

When she opened her eyes, she was lying on the floor of the corridor again.

The red door stood before her, closed.

The brass knob gleamed faintly, innocent.

Her lantern sat beside it, flame steady.

The key at her neck was cool.

And for the first time since arriving, the house was quiet — not waiting, not watching. Listening.

She pushed herself upright, slow. Her reflection in the lacquer moved with her, perfectly matched.

Then, a second too late, it smiled.

Morning found Elena seated at the kitchen table with her hands wrapped around a cup she couldn't remember making. The house had gone still again—not dead still, but listening still, like a held breath waiting to hear its name. The air was clear, the light was honest, but everything carried the faint echo of red, as if the color had seeped beneath the paint and into the bones. She couldn't tell whether she'd dreamed the door or walked through it, only that something on the other side had learned her heartbeat.

When she passed the hall later, the door was gone. Just plaster, paint, and the faint scent of cedar clinging to the floor.

But in every mirror she crossed that day—bathroom, hallway, the silvered glass above the mantle—she thought she saw it reflected somewhere behind her, half-closed and patient, waiting to be remembered again.

CHAPTER 8

Echoes Of The Past

Morning in Blackwood Manor arrived like a rumor—slow to convince and easy to doubt. The light that seeped through the curtains was more suggestion than certainty, pale and indecisive, as if it had changed its mind halfway down the hill. Elena sat on the edge of her bed with her sketchbook closed on her lap, not drawing, just staring at the faint graphite dust that stained her fingers. She'd dreamed of corridors again—this time shorter, quieter—but still ending at the red door that pulsed behind her eyelids even when she was awake.

The house hadn't slept. She could tell. Its quiet had a texture, the way silence does when it's been tampered with.

When she swung her legs over the side of the bed, the floor was warm beneath her bare feet, not from sun or pipes but from something that had been there a while, waiting.

Downstairs, the clock struck eight, although she couldn't remember hearing it wind. She dressed quickly, tugging on jeans and a loose sweater, and tied her hair back with the elastic she'd looped around her wrist since college. She thought briefly about going into town again—Mae would be behind the counter, pretending not to watch her—but something in the air near the door stopped her. Not cold, not resistance. A pull. The kind that turns curiosity into inevitability.

Coffee first. Then sanity.

The kitchen had its usual museum calm. The peonies she'd replaced two days ago had browned and collapsed into themselves, petals scattered like dropped fabric. She brewed coffee and stood by the window while it gurgled, watching mist unspool from the trees. The house seemed still. Even friendly, in a half-asleep way.

Then she heard it.

Not the creak of a hinge this time, or the shifting breath of walls. It was her voice.

Soft. Low. From the next room.

"Hello?"

She froze, mug halfway to her lips. The echo was perfect—same pitch, same uncertainty—but it came from the hallway to her right. She set the cup down and listened. The air returned nothing.

She told herself she'd imagined it. That the acoustics of the old halls warped sound. That she'd murmured without realizing it. But as she stepped into the hall, the voice came again—identical.

"Hello?"

It wasn't calling. It was *repeating*.

She walked slowly, scanning doorframes, mirrors, the tall grandfather clock that hadn't worked since she'd arrived. Each reflection felt slightly behind. When she reached the end of the corridor, the sound had already moved—upstairs, she thought. Into the landing.

"Elena," she said quietly, as though introducing herself to a nervous animal. "You're imagining things. It's fine."

From the second floor: her own voice answered, *"It's fine."*

The mug would have shattered if she'd still been holding it. Her throat closed around a sound that never made it to air.

She took the stairs one at a time, fingers brushing the carved banister. The sleeping hound at the newel post seemed to smirk. At the top, the landing was thick with morning dust motes, weightless and numerous. The door to the study was closed. She'd shut it last night; she remembered because it had taken two tries to make the latch catch.

Now the key—Victor's iron one—hung in the lock. Turned.

"Not possible," she said, and winced at hearing it answered faintly in return.

Not possible.

Her own voice, slightly delayed. Not an echo—an imitation.

Elena reached out, touched the key, and pushed the door open.

The study was dim, shades drawn, but not cold. It had that strange, curated stillness of a room that wanted to be left as it was. The smell of old paper and varnish clung to the air, underscored by a faint metallic tang—something electrical, though the lamp cords trailed unplugged.

The desk was a scholar's altar: inkwell, ledger, pens arranged like instruments of divination. Behind it, shelves sagged under the weight of journals and boxes. And there, on the far table, stood something that made her hesitate.

A reel-to-reel tape machine.

It was old, heavy, its brushed metal dulled with age but well-kept, like everything else Victor had touched. Two reels sat in place, the tape threaded and taut, as if waiting for her. A small yellowed label on the first reel read:

E. Harrow — 1893.

Her stomach turned over. "Eleanor," she whispered.

But below that, smaller, someone had written in Victor's handwriting:

Do not play unless the house asks.

The absurdity of the instruction might have made her laugh on another day. But this house had a history of asking questions she didn't want to hear the answers to.

She found the power switch and flicked it. The machine stayed silent. No hum, no static. She should've been relieved. She wasn't.

She turned to leave and noticed the mirror opposite the desk.

Her reflection stared back as expected—same tired hair, same guarded eyes—but when she raised her hand, it lagged a fraction behind. Not quite out of sync. Just *late.*

The delay stretched into a half-second. Then a full one.

She dropped her hand. Her reflection did the same—slowly, reluctantly.

"Stop it," she said to herself.

The reflection's lips didn't move.

Elena backed away until she hit the desk. The corner bit into her hip. She reached instinctively for the brass key around her neck, and for a breathless moment, the reflection did *not.*

It stayed with its hand by its side, eyes still fixed on hers.

Then—suddenly—it smiled. Not a cruel smile. A knowing one. A mirror remembering something before the original did.

The tape machine clicked.

No whirring, no reel spin—just a *click,* mechanical and sure. Then, faint and grainy, a woman's voice filled the room.

> "If the house remembers," the voice said, "then so must I."

Elena froze. The accent was older, the tone restrained—but the voice was unmistakably hers.

> "It takes from sound first. That's how it begins. The air learns you before the walls do."

She turned toward the machine, but the reels weren't moving. The tape lay still, perfectly threaded.

> "When you hear yourself, it isn't you. It's the house reminding you what you've already said."

The machine fell silent again.

Elena waited for her pulse to slow, but it didn't. She ejected the reel with shaking fingers. The label's ink had bled slightly, as if wet recently. Beneath the original text—E. Harrow — 1893—a faint penciled note had been added in Victor's script:

Test successful. The voice carries.

She set the reel down carefully and checked the shelves. Three more reels sat beside it.

One read: *V. Harrow — 1961.*

Another: *H. Harrow — 1920.*

And the last: *Unlabeled.*

She didn't touch that one.

On the desk, half-buried beneath a ledger, she found a notebook she hadn't noticed before—thin, leather-bound, smelling faintly of oil and dust. Victor's handwriting again. Inside: sketches of the house, each room drawn with unusual precision. Notes filled the margins in tight cursive.

> The house does not simply echo; it absorbs.

> Resonance memory: rooms replay moments at matching frequencies.

> Each generation leaves an imprint. The next inherits not only blood, but sound.

She traced the phrase *resonance memory* with her fingertip. The ink had smudged at that exact point, as though touched by someone with wet hands—or a tremor.

At the bottom of the page, another entry, barely legible:

> *She is still speaking through the walls. The others fade, but she persists.*

Elena closed the notebook. She didn't need the name to know who *she* was.

She turned back to the mirror. Her reflection had caught up again. Its face was hers, expressionless. Yet she could've sworn that behind her reflected shoulder, in the mirror's distance, the study's door was standing open—wider than it actually was.

She glanced behind her. The door was only half-open.

Back to the mirror: wide.

A sound threaded through the silence—the faint static of a needle settling into a groove, though the machine hadn't moved.

"You shouldn't have played it," her voice said softly from nowhere.

Elena whispered, "I didn't."

The voice replied: *"Not yet."*

She stumbled out of the study, closing the door harder than she meant to. The latch stuck, then clicked in protest. Her breath came fast, shallow. She pressed her forehead to the cool wallpaper in the hallway and counted until her heartbeat obeyed.

In the distance, the grandfather clock chimed once. Noon.

Except her phone, when she checked it, said 10:47.

She laughed—short, brittle. "Sure. Why not."

The mirror in the upstairs hall caught her reflection again as she passed, and this time she didn't look away fast enough. For a moment she thought the light flickered, but no—it was the *color* that changed. Her reflection's hair had darkened, a deeper brown than hers. Its clothing was wrong, older. And behind her reflection, the wallpaper pattern had shifted: vines curling into symbols instead of flowers.

When she blinked, everything was back where it should be.

She went downstairs, intending to go outside, anywhere with open sky. But when she reached for the front door, her fingers found the brass knob already warm—like someone else had just used it.

Her pulse spiked. She pulled the door open.

The world outside was the same, but quieter. The trees swayed, yet made no sound. Even the gravel of the drive seemed muted.

"Fine," she said to the silence, stepping out onto the porch. "Fine. You win."

But as soon as she said it, her voice came back—closer than before, whispering from somewhere inside the house.

"Fine. You win."

The echo reached her ears a half-second later than it should have.

She backed down the steps, staring at the doorframe. Every instinct told her not to look up—but she did. And in the second-floor window above the porch, where she knew her bedroom faced the east lawn, someone was standing.

A shape. A silhouette. Still. Watching.

Not the vague shimmer of reflection—something *there.*

She blinked once. It was gone.

She turned and walked to the car. She didn't look back. But as she opened the door, a single sound slid from the open house behind her.

A hinge. Slow. Deliberate.

She froze, one hand on the door handle.

Then another sound followed—light, almost polite.

The faint *click* of a recorder stopping.

She didn't leave.

The keys were already in the car's ignition, her bag half on her shoulder, one foot inside—and still she took it back. Not bravado. Something simpler. The sense that if she fled now, the house would finish telling the story without her and then hang it on the wall for future Harrows to bump into.

"Fine," she told the gravel, the gate, the trees. "Later."

She went back inside.

The foyer received her in that attentive hush it had learned. She closed the front door and held the knob until the metal cooled under her palm, until the part of her that wanted to run decided to wait for a better reason.

Upstairs, the study door had remembered how to sit just ajar. She pushed it with two fingers. The room eased open like a taught animal that had been convinced you mean no harm.

The reel-to-reel sat where she'd left it—reels still, tape threaded straight, its faceplate catching the light. It looked almost modest now. Not a machine that had just borrowed her voice out of air.

The mirror opposite the desk reflected the room properly again. Her reflection raised a hand when she did, no lag.

She spoke toward the machine anyway. "I didn't play you."

Nothing. Not even a helpful click.

She stepped to the desk. Victor's thin notebook lay where she'd closed it. She opened it to the page with *resonance memory* and read on.

> Notes on the Harrow Resonance Device
>
> Sound leaves a pressure-trace in plaster and wood. In old houses this accumulates—like fingerprints— until walls prefer certain frequencies.
>
> Eleanor's humming (the lullaby) elicits persistent responses near the nursery and blue parlor. My voice elicits less. (Why? Blood? Gender? Key?)
>
> Hypothesis: Rooms are tuned. They answer when addressed in their *key.*
>
> Device to detect: magnet + coil + spring armature affixed to wall. Sound returns as oscillation on

filament. Photograph bulb behind to capture pattern.

A diagram followed—crisp, obsessively neat. He had drawn the house as a collection of notes on a staff. The atrium sat at middle C, the study at A below. The nursery—he had labeled it with a symbol Elena didn't know. Not a letter. Something like an old clef.

Beneath, a more personal line, cramped in at the margin: *If I cannot change the house, perhaps I can tune myself to it.*

She turned the page.

A series of photographs had been taped in—long-exposed streaks of light. The labels alternated between rooms. *Blue room, 9:18 p.m. / Nursery, windows shut / Study, door open.* The streaks changed shapes: tight curls, wide loops, a figure-eight that made her stomach turn with its familiarity—she had drawn that shape mindlessly, as a child, as an adult, in margins of bills and failed paintings. The house had been tracing it too.

"You were listening," she said, not to the machine now, but to the paper.

The brass key at her throat answered with a small, almost embarrassed hum. She took it off and laid it on the blotter. The sound stopped. When she moved it near the notebook's diagram, it started again—thin, insect-faint, but steady. She slid the key back and forth. The pitch rose near the sketch of the blue room. It lowered near the nursery. At the drawn study, it went quiet, as if recognizing itself.

She laughed once, short, feeling foolish and confirmed. "So you're a tuning fork."

She looped the chain around her neck again. The hum returned to wherever the body keeps such things. She turned to the shelves.

Boxes. Journals. A wooden case blackened with age, brass corners worn to the dullness of old coins. She lifted its latch. Inside lay Victor's device—simple, almost pretty. A small magnet housed in Bakelite, a coil of fine copper wire, a spring arm carrying a pale, brittle filament that ended in a hair-thin needle. A little clamp to fix it to a wall. A socket for a bulb and a tiny roll of photographic paper.

She looked from the case to the diagram, back to the case. Across a century, the parts had found each other.

"This is stupid," she told the empty room. "And we're going to do it anyway."

The clamp bit the study wall just to the right of the mirror. The needle settled on plaster like a stethoscope. She fumbled the bulb into place, then hesitated at the paper—was it any good after decades? The little roll felt dry, powdered with time. She licked her thumb, touched a corner, and it darkened. So—sensitive enough.

She threaded the paper into the slit behind the bulb. A switch sat on the side of the housing: *Expose.* She didn't flip it yet. She leaned close to the spring arm and spoke softly, deliberately.

"Elena Harrow," she said. "Today we are sane."

The filament moved nearly invisibly, a gnat's dance, nothing more. She wasn't sure the device could detect her sarcasm.

She pressed the switch.

The bulb flicked once—no click, no whine, only a quiet affirmation of light—and went dark. When she rolled the paper forward, a faint thread of black trembled across it. Shallow, but there. She held it to the window. The thread had thickened, here and there, to something like a pulse.

She set the first strip aside, rethreaded, and tried again, this time humming the lullaby she had promised herself she wouldn't. Not loudly. Barely air. The needle quivered. The bulb burned. When she unspooled the second strip, the line leapt, widened, doubled back on itself so quickly it blurred. The pattern looked like a heartbeat trying to remember which rhythm it owed.

"Okay," she whispered. "You like the song."

She moved the device—one foot left of the mirror, then two, then above the desk, then under the lintel. Each position shifted the line differently. Some places the streak flattened well-behaved. Others it leaped, as if the wall were speaking back over her. She fixed the arm beside the door—her least favorite threshold in the house—and whispered her name again.

The line wrote a steady, almost kind note.

"Kind ends," she muttered, remembering Eleanor's page, and moved the clamp.

Across from the mirror, the strip went wild. Not higher, not louder. Stranger. The figure-eight returned, tighter this time, self-overlapping, a knot that had learned to tie itself.

"You," she said to the glass, and saw only herself.

She set the device lower, at knee height, where a child might lean a cheek to listen. The pattern there grew simple. A soft wave. Gentle and repetitive. She listened and, against her will, began to sway, almost imperceptibly, as if rocked.

She tore the paper off before her body agreed to more.

On the desk, her strips began to look like a language. She put them in a row—study/wall, study/door, study/mirror, study/low—and could imagine a machine reading them, spitting out speech where the lines overlapped. The house wasn't only holding sound. It had begun to prefer it.

She reached for Victor's notebook to see where he had ended.

> The device works only when the room agrees.
> Without consent, it lies.

Underneath, smaller, as if written after too much coffee and not enough sleep:

Tonight I will attempt conversation.

She closed the book and sat with that. The lamp ticked in the small way hot metal does. The window gave up a little light and took it back.

"Conversation," she said to the empty study. "We can try."

She moved the device back to the place where the figure-eight had been rudest. She threaded new paper. She pressed the switch and spoke slowly, like someone trying to train a shy animal.

"Eleanor," she said. "Are you listening?"

The line rose, hesitated. Fell. Not nothing. Not yes.

She tried again. "Eleanor Harrow."

The line tied itself once.

"Elena Harrow," she said, and the line did not change.

She hummed the lullaby and felt the hairs on her arms lift when the line doubled. The device wasn't only detecting vibration. It was pleased.

"What do you remember?" she asked, too quickly, and realized she had asked like a person demanding a story from a child who had only just learned words.

The line went slack.

"Sorry," she said, absurdly. "What would you like to remember?"

A figure-eight. Tighter than before, but still, a refusal. Or a dance.

She stood, restless, and went to the shelves. More boxes, more paper. A folder labeled *Acoustical Tests, Blue Room.* Inside: strips like hers, but long, dozens of inches, spliced together, annotated with times and weather. Window open: gentle. Window shut: pressure. Humming: excessive response. A final strip labeled *Chime.* The line there made a new shape—three loops linked, like a childish drawing of a chain.

She set the folder down and looked at the door. At the threshold. The house had left her alone with the toys long enough. Time to collect a debt it had not said she owed.

"Conversation," she reminded herself, and retrieved the heavy bell from the blue room—a little brass thing without a clapper that somehow found sound when it wanted. She brought it to the study and set it near the device. She touched its rim with a fingernail. It didn't ring in air. It rang in her teeth.

The filament jumped. The line drew the chain again—loop, loop, loop—then steadied.

"Elena," the room said, not with a voice and not without one. Her name arranged itself across the surfaces, gravity finding a new path. She felt it more than heard it, like her whole skeleton briefly did the math and said yes.

"I'm listening," she said.

The line fluttered, flirted with a word, lost it.

She placed the key next to the magnet housing. The hum from her throat took on a secondary note, an overtone she couldn't have produced. The strip darkened along a vein.

"Eleanor," she said again, slower, like the word itself had to be lifted and turned. "Do you remember me?"

The line drew a shape she hadn't seen yet: a long, smooth arch that ended abruptly in a spike. *Almost.* Then *No.* Or perhaps *Ask different.*

"What do you remember?" she tried again, patient now, the way Mae would have spoken to a storm. "What do you want remembered?"

The line wrote nothing. Then, after a long quiet that felt like the inside of a breath—two small vertical slashes, side by side.

"Eleven," she said, without knowing why. "Or a door."

The filament trembled as if relieved. The strip shakily produced the chain again.

"Door, then." She thought of the red lacquer, the heat beneath her palm. "You know it."

The line tightened into a dark bar—agreement, or grief, or both.

"Victor," she said softly. The line softened, then wrote a shallow, steady wave, then flattened. That read as *tired* even to a mind inclined to doubt.

"Blue room." The line grew delicate, frilled, fraying out to the margins as if the device had encountered lace.

"Nurs—" She swallowed the rest and said instead, "Windows open." The line relaxed, unknotted.

She took the strip off and wrote labels beneath each piece with a pencil that kept breaking under her hand. It looked like a conversation she'd be embarrassed to show any rational person. She didn't care.

Above all the strips lay the unlabeled reel. The tape had a small nick at its leader where someone had clumsily cut and reattached. She touched it with one finger as if testing a tooth.

"Not yet," she told it too. The house had taught her that phrase as a door.

She left the device clamped to the wall and fetched the second, heavier bell from the hall closet—the one that had once been a servant's summons, its pull chain roped to the nursery. She hauled it like a disobedient pet back to the study and set it beside the other bell, two mouths closed.

"This will be stupid," she warned the empty air. "Good."

She ran her fingernail around the rim of the small bell. It sang teeth-only, a pressure in the bones. She buzzed the larger bell by tapping the housing with the handle of a screwdriver. The sound walked up her spine and set up house behind her ears. The filament went frantic, then calmed. A pattern emerged—not the figure-eight this time, not a chain. Three loops, then a bar, then a loop again. A rhythm she knew from the door's knocking, a code she hadn't learned.

She said the lullaby's first two notes and then stopped, jaw clenched.

The house finished them for her.

Not loud. Not boastful. The notes simply entered the room from wherever sound keeps its leftovers. The bells did not move. The paper rolled itself an inch.

"Elena," the study said again, calmly this time, tolerant of who she was. "Come back."

She did the only reasonable thing left: she laughed. "No."

The room considered that and adjusted a degree cooler. The little brass key warmed against her clavicle in rebuttal. A strip of paper slid under her hand—she hadn't unthreaded it; she hadn't touched the switch—and a single straight line marked its length from end to end. Flat. Silent. Patient.

"Alright," she conceded. "But we do this in my key."

She set a metronome—Victor's, wound and fussy—on the desk and clicked it to a human tempo. The tick was humble, mortal, dumb to the house's appetite. She tapped the desk in time. She spoke in time, syllables on beats. "El-ea-nor. I am El-e-na. Do—you—re-mem-ber—the—door."

The filament drew a tremor like laughter. On the paper: two short lines, then a longer. She amended. "What—do—you—want—me—to—re-mem-ber."

The line rose, stopped. Another small chain. Then, faintly enough that she had to bend in to see it, a tiny, uneven staircase—one line, then another, slightly higher, then another, cancelling the climb.

She used the pencil like the medium she didn't believe in. She drew those three uneven steps on the margin and wrote beside them: *Stairs? Hinge? Wrong step?*

She felt ridiculous and then not. The air beside her cheek cooled as if a presence had leaned near to read.

When she looked up, the mirror across the room did not return herself. Not immediately. For the span of a single breath it offered a double exposure—her and another woman sitting at the desk side by side. The other woman's hair was drawn back in a plait, her blouse buttoned too high for comfort. Her mouth held confirmation, not contentment.

"Eleanor," Elena said aloud, reflex.

The image in the glass turned its head, just enough to be a motion and not a trick. Then the reflection found itself again: only Elena, alone, the room her witness.

The strip in the device had darkened end to end, the line thick. She tore it free and set it beside the others. Her hand shook. She steadied it with the cheap cruelty of a joke. "Great. We're making art."

The house took her at her word. Somewhere far off, a door opened and closed with gallery manners. A hinge signed its name.

She turned the metronome off. The tick stopped and left her heartbeat raw. She put the brass key flat on the blotter and watched it for a moment, waiting for the trick she would pretend not to believe.

It changed temperature. That was all. It cooled as if set in shade.

The reel-to-reel clicked.

The reels did not move. The tape did not travel. The sound arrived anyway, as if the machine had learned to be a wall.

"…don't leave the window shut," said a woman in a very old voice trying to be young. "It presses."

"El—" Elena began, and stopped. The voice wasn't quite Eleanor's and not quite not. The spectral quality of old recording pressed vowels thin. Then:

> "Victor says I should not indulge it," the voice continued in a tone Elena knew: fatigued, defiant. "He builds his wire ear and hopes to catch it like a fly."

A breath, caught on magnetic dust, played across the speaker.

> "If someone is listening later," the voice said, and Elena felt the ridiculous, sudden intimacy of being that someone, later, "leave the blue room kind."

Silence. Then a different scrape, as if the tape had been spliced, and another voice slid through—Victor's, younger, brittle with certainty:

> "Resonance persists longer than grief. Good to know."

The machine clicked again, a sound like a period.

Elena found herself sitting. She didn't remember sitting down. The chair accepted her the way water accepts a foot: briefly, with intent to hold and to test. She set her fingertips to the blotter and discovered she had been pressing hard enough to indent the leather with half-moons.

"Okay," she said to the room. "We can do this."

She spent the next hour like a scientist pretending not to be a penitent. She set the device at different walls, she hummed or didn't hum, she spoke names on and off the beat, she recorded strips that looked enough alike to be siblings and enough different to be arguments. She learned small things: that the study liked her voice best at the door; that the mirror performed when she did not watch it; that the blue room, even from here, softened any line if she spoke its name.

She learned a larger thing, too: when she set the key to the desk and stepped back, the line went flat. When she wore it, the line woke. She was a conductor in both senses—of electricity and of orchestra. The house used her to hear itself better.

By late afternoon the light in the window had gone the color paper turns when forgotten behind glass—yellowed, patient.

Her strips lay in neat disorder across the blotter. She could have begun to read them. She did not. She kept choosing discovery over conclusion, because conclusion sounded too much like the red door's insistence.

She left the study to fetch water, which felt like a worldlier act than listening. In the hall, the grandfather clock had moved to agree with her phone. 3:06. She said "Thank you" aloud before she could stop herself and hated that it felt earned.

In the kitchen, she drank from the tap and tasted the metal of old pipes and an aftertaste of cedar that could have been memory. The window over the sink showed the lawn as an even patch of green; the forest beyond rehearsed wind without committing.

When she returned to the study, the machine had decided to be honest.

The unmoving reels now moved. Slowly, so slowly she might have missed it if the light hadn't caught the faint glint of tape winding from one circle to the other. The sound came soft and far, like voices through snow.

"…and if it asks you," a woman said—the same woman, not the same—"answer, but don't agree."

"Eleanor," Elena said, too loud for the moment, and the reel stuttered, a hiccup of old splices giving way.

The voice resumed, quieter, as if she'd leant closer to the original microphone.

"We are not meant to be keepers. We are meant to be remembered. There's a difference."

A scrape. The tick of something set down. Then Victor again, the fatigue familiar now:

"Stop recording in the nursery. It attracts."

The sound ended mid-breath. The reels stopped. A thin curl of tape had unwound itself onto the table like a shed skin. Elena pinched it between two fingers. It felt nothing like anything— neither plastic nor paper nor regret.

The mirror opposite caught her face and, for a moment, wore a different expression than the one her muscles knew how to make. Not older. Not other. A look she'd seen once in a photograph of a soprano in the moment just before the note: braced and ready to be more than one person at once.

"Don't," she told herself, and dropped the spool.

"Don't," the house agreed, and someone stepped lightly on the landing outside the study.

She froze. The sound was unmistakable, exquisite in its specificity. Not the house's broad creak, not wind. Steps. Two. A pause. A third, smaller sound like a child trying to walk quietly.

She crossed the room and opened the door in one sure motion— too fast for fear to veto.

The landing lay there, long as a story you've heard too many times. The runner held. The chandelier behaved. At the far end, where the nursery sat with its good behavior draped around it like lace, the door was ajar by an inch.

The inch did not widen. The inch did not apologize.

Elena stood with her hand on the study knob and the brass key warm against her skin and felt, for the first time since she had arrived, that the house was not making a move but accepting one.

"Alright," she said, softer than she meant. "We'll talk."

Behind her, in the study, the tape machine clicked once more, as if typing a single punctuation mark after a line long overdue its end.

She stepped into the hall.

The nursery door breathed. Somewhere downstairs, the smaller bell in the blue room made no sound at all and still she felt it ring in her teeth.

She took three steps toward the door and stopped just short of the threshold. Out of habit, she looked to the window across from it, more glass than view. Her reflection stood where she stood. It did not lag. It looked tired and true.

From inside the nursery, not a recording but air, an old voice used her name with careful regard.

"Elena."

She did not flinch.

"I'm listening," she said.

The hinge, polite, finished its sentence. The door opened a degree more and offered the smell she had come to recognize:

lavender, starch, and the edge of something burned away a long time ago.

She did not cross. Not yet. She had learned that word's uses.

"If you remember me," she said to the room beyond, to the house that learned through people and taught with doors, "then tell me who I was."

The reply did not come in words. It came in a small, familiar rhythm at the baseboards, the old, stubbornly tender *thock* of a cradle shifting under no weight at all.

The study behind her—her machine, her strips, her carefully numbered sanity—waited.

She stood between them and listened until she could name the beat without wanting to hum along.

Then, very quietly, she said, "Again."

And it did.

CHAPTER 9

Echoes Of The Past

Elena didn't sleep. Not because she didn't try—she did, curling under the quilt in the east bedroom, lights off, curtains drawn—but because the house had learned to imitate breathing. Every board and pipe inhaled, exhaled, and somewhere inside that rhythm was a pulse she couldn't name. She had the irrational sense that if she let herself drift, she'd start dreaming in someone else's body and wake up somewhere else entirely.

By two a.m., she sat in the hallway wrapped in a blanket, the brass key warm against her skin. The air smelled faintly of lavender and burnt wax, the house's version of comfort. She listened. No movement. No voice. Just the delicate whine of time stretching itself too thin.

Her sketchbook lay open on her knees. The page was blank except for a single line she'd drawn without meaning to—a slow, looping shape that began nowhere and ended nowhere, like the figure-eight from Victor's recordings. Her hand itched to finish it. She forced herself to close the cover.

The house sighed.

That was the word that came to mind: sighed. A low exhalation from the walls, as if a long-held breath had finally been released. It wasn't threatening. It was... domestic. Familiar in the wrong way, like overhearing your name in a conversation that isn't about you but could be.

Then came the sound of footsteps above her head. Soft, even, the weight of bare feet on old wood. The rhythm didn't match her own. It circled once, paused, then continued down the hall toward the staircase. She stood slowly, the blanket falling to her elbows.

"Not again," she murmured.

But curiosity had become reflex.

The steps continued, fading toward the main floor. She followed them, barefoot, her shadow bending along the wall. The chandelier overhead quivered once, as though adjusting to a shift in temperature. Downstairs, the corridor glowed faintly with that colorless half-light the house invented when it didn't want to commit to darkness.

At the bottom of the stairs, she stopped. Someone was humming.

Not a ghostly wail, not the lullaby, not anything theatrical—just a woman's voice, low and casual, moving through a melody that didn't exist anywhere else. The sound came from the kitchen. She edged forward.

The kitchen light was off. The moon caught the edge of the copper pots, turning them into pale coins. And there—at the table—was a shape. Not solid, not transparent. A distortion, like heat haze in human form. It sat in one of the chairs, shoulders bent over a bowl, hands moving with a faint rhythm. A servant, maybe. A woman from another century, working through a habit too ingrained to die.

Elena didn't breathe. She knew she was watching an echo— what Victor had called *resonance memory*. It wasn't really there. The air was simply remembering.

She whispered, "Martha Keene."

The distortion faltered.

The sound cut. The hands stilled. The chair's faint outline scraped back, even though no physical object moved. The figure turned—slowly, mechanically—and the shimmer of it sharpened into something nearly visible: a face, half-built out of refracted light. The eyes were blank. But they *looked.*

Elena took a step back. The figure blinked once—then vanished, like steam absorbed into air.

The silence afterward had weight.

She stayed where she was, trembling, and waited for her breath to catch up with her fear. The air retained a faint afterimage, as though the figure had pressed itself into it. She touched the table. The wood was cold but dry, and there, under her fingertips, she felt a shallow impression. A ring—like the mark left by a bowl that wasn't there anymore.

She whispered, "You're real enough."

The house disagreed by letting the clock in the hall chime three times, though the hour wasn't right. She counted each toll, and after the third, another sound answered—upstairs. A faint, delicate *thock... thock... thock.* The cradle again.

The blanket around her shoulders felt suddenly heavy. She climbed the stairs.

The nursery door stood ajar exactly as she'd left it. The air inside smelled sweeter now, the lavender stronger. The cradle's rhythm continued: a steady, patient swing. She could see it in the half-dark—a small, shadowed curve moving back and forth with the soft precision of a metronome.

She stepped closer. The motion slowed, paused, then reversed— on its own, unhurried, as though whoever had pushed it had only stepped away for a moment and would be back any second.

Elena touched the edge of the cradle. The wood was smooth, cool, humming faintly beneath her fingers. Not alive, exactly, but not empty either.

"Who are you remembering?" she asked softly.

The question seemed to ripple through the air. A faint creak sounded behind her, the noise of something adjusting to listen. She didn't turn.

The rocking stopped.

And then, so faint she almost missed it, a child's laugh—high, quick, and gone before it could find shape. The air thickened with warmth for a heartbeat and then cooled again. The smell of lavender dimmed.

Elena whispered, "Eleanor?"

No answer, but the door across the hall—Victor's study—clicked.

It was enough.

She turned and walked toward it, each step slower than the last. The handle was warm. She pushed the door open.

The study hadn't changed, but something *in* it had. The air shimmered faintly, a mirage of dust and motion. The reel-to-reel on the desk was turning. The reels spun lazily, no electricity required. A faint voice drifted out—Victor's this time.

> "Resonance increases with attention," it said. "Observation feeds pattern. The more one listens, the more the walls repeat."

Elena moved closer, heart hammering. The voice continued, distant but clear.

"I heard Eleanor again last night — not as a ghost, but as a memory. She insists the echoes speak to her. I hear only repetition. She hears intent. Perhaps she's right."

The recording crackled. Then came another voice—hers, but not hers. Eleanor's. The accent was old-fashioned, vowels drawn thin.

"It listens because it wants to be remembered. What else could it want?"

The tape hissed. The reel spun faster.

Victor again: "What happens when the house remembers too much?"

Eleanor, softly: "It dreams."

The tape clicked to a stop.

Elena pressed her hands to the desk to steady herself. The wood was vibrating faintly. The mirror across the room reflected her— but the background behind her was wrong. In the reflection, the study's window was open and daylight streamed in. The desk was tidy, newer. Victor sat at it, head bent, pen scratching across the page. His sleeve cuff was ink-stained. The man was alive and concentrating.

Elena turned around. The actual room was empty.

Back to the mirror: he was still there, writing. He paused, lifted his head as though listening. Slowly, his gaze rose toward her reflection. He frowned. His mouth moved—she couldn't hear what he said—but the motion was clear: *"Who are you?"*

Her throat constricted. "You wouldn't believe me."

He looked past her now, at something else, and his expression changed from irritation to dread. His chair scraped back. His hand went for the desk drawer.

Elena turned, instinctively following his line of sight.

Behind her, the air thickened. A shadow gathered at the edges of the room—not shape, not person, but density. Like light refusing to enter a space it used to fill. It pressed against her skin like static before a storm.

The mirror flashed white.

When her vision cleared, Victor was gone. The window in the reflection had closed. The desk was exactly as it was before— papers scattered, the reel motionless.

Elena sank into the chair. Her heart wouldn't slow. She pressed her palms to her face and whispered, "Okay. You're showing off."

The house didn't argue. But from somewhere below—maybe the dining room—a sound rose, faint and musical. The clink of silverware. Then laughter.

Not cruel. *Alive.*

She left the study and followed the sound, half afraid of what would happen if she didn't. The air grew warmer as she descended the stairs, the banister slick under her hand. The laughter became clearer—multiple voices now. Men and women talking over one another, a dinner party in progress. She could smell roasted meat, wine, candle wax. The scent was rich and wrong, impossible.

The dining room glowed faintly from within.

Through the doorway, she saw them—not solid, not even ghostly, just impressions made of shadow and light. The long dining table gleamed with silver and crystal. The figures seated around it were half-finished, the way an artist sketches gesture before detail. They moved in pantomime: a man raising a glass, a woman leaning to whisper something scandalous, a servant pouring wine. Laughter rose again, echoing as if caught in a loop.

And at the far end of the table, where the head of the family would sit, was a vacant chair.

Elena hovered at the doorway, transfixed. The figures didn't notice her. The scene played on, repeating every minute or so, a flickering film trapped in its projector.

Then one of the guests—a woman in a dark gown—looked up. Her face was indistinct, blurred at the edges, but her head turned directly toward Elena. For a heartbeat, the echo and the present overlapped. The woman's mouth moved. Elena could almost read the words.

You're late.

The entire tableau blinked out. The table was bare. The air smelled of dust and neglect again.

Elena stumbled back, striking her shoulder against the doorframe. The house settled audibly, as if exhaling from exertion. She pressed a hand to her chest. Her pulse felt double—hers and someone else's overlapping, struggling for the same rhythm.

She stood alone in the quiet dining room, surrounded by the echo of laughter that had never belonged to her.

"Victor," she whispered. "What did you build?"

No answer—just the faintest whisper of wind moving through the hall, repeating her question an instant too late.

What did you build?

The echo sounded almost amused.

The house stayed quiet for nearly an hour.

Too quiet, the kind that felt arranged—like the pause before a photograph develops. Elena walked the length of the first floor, one hand trailing along the wainscoting. The wood was smooth and cool, but not lifeless. She could feel the vibration of something beneath it, like breath through a wall. When she reached the end of the hall, she realized she was holding her breath again.

"Stop doing that," she muttered. "You're not part of it."

The silence answered with its usual indifference. But it *heard.*

From the corner of her eye, the mirror near the stair landing flickered. Not light, exactly—more like the glass flexed for an instant, then returned to stillness. She stared at it until her reflection began to blur, the way faces do when you stare too long at them in dim light.

"You've got to stop anthropomorphizing architecture," she said under her breath, but the voice came back a half-second later, slightly warped.

"Stop anthropomorphizing architecture."

Her stomach clenched. It wasn't the room echoing—it was the mirror.

She stepped closer. The surface trembled faintly, like water in a disturbed glass.

"Elena," she said deliberately.

Her reflection's mouth didn't move. But the voice came from the mirror again.

"Elena."

Not mimicry now. Recognition.

Her pulse fluttered against her throat. "Who's there?"

The reflection blinked once—hers, but not quite right—and whispered, *"You know."*

Then the surface went flat again.

She stepped back fast enough that her heel hit the baseboard. The mirror's glass held its calm, reflecting nothing extraordinary. She could see her own pale face, her hands shaking. No ghosts. No tricks. Just her. And yet the air had changed.

It was thicker now, charged, as though the temperature itself had begun to remember something terrible.

From somewhere upstairs came a dull *thump.*

Then another.

Then the unmistakable sound of something—or someone— running. Bare feet. Rapid, uneven, crossing the upper hall.

Elena looked toward the staircase. "No," she whispered. "Not this time."

But she was already moving.

Each step groaned under her weight, echoing too long after she took it. At the top landing, the air was warmer. The smell of dust had been replaced by something faintly coppery, almost sweet. She followed the sound down the corridor toward the attic door. It was slightly open, the rope pull swaying.

She'd never opened it before. Victor's journal had mentioned it only once—in a line she hadn't wanted to reread: *"Martha's fall was not accidental."*

She reached up, gripped the rope, and pulled. The door creaked down on its hinges, stirring a rain of old dust. The ladder unfolded. Cold air spilled down from above.

She climbed, flashlight in hand, each rung flexing beneath her feet. The beam of light caught rafters, the glint of old nails, the corner of a trunk.

The attic smelled like everything that had ever happened there—woodsmoke, candle wax, faint mildew, something once sweet that had gone sour.

She panned the light. Empty.

Then, behind her, something shifted.

She turned the flashlight, its beam slicing through the dust. Nothing. But the dust itself was moving, spiraling in slow, deliberate patterns like breath against glass. A low sound rose from the boards beneath her—wood under strain.

And then she saw her.

At first it was just the suggestion of movement—a shape forming out of air, a shimmer barely separate from shadow. Then the figure clarified. A woman in a long dress, apron tied at the waist, hair pinned back. Her head was bent, arms reaching for something unseen. The echo of labor.

Elena knew who it was.

"Martha Keene."

The name filled the attic like light. The figure stiffened, turned. Her face came into focus for half a heartbeat: pale, eyes wide with surprise. And then—just like that—it happened.

The boards gave way beneath her.

The sound was awful, the collapse of old wood and bone together. Martha fell through the floor, vanishing mid-scream. The echo of it reverberated down the beams, through the walls, into the hollow of Elena's chest. She heard the impact below—so close it might have been under her own feet—and dropped to her knees.

Her flashlight rolled, spinning light across the rafters. The air filled with the smell of dust and something metallic, old blood burned into history. The boards beneath her were intact again, seamless.

She reached out a trembling hand and touched the place where the figure had fallen. The wood was cold, but pulsing faintly—as if it remembered the wound.

Her voice came out hoarse. "You didn't fall."

The attic listened.

Then, softly, from below her, a voice answered.

"No."

She froze.

"Martha?"

"No."

The word echoed upward through the wood, like air squeezed from an old bellows.

Elena crawled toward the opening where the sound had risen. There was nothing—no body, no stain, not even dust disturbed. Just a faint outline on the floorboards, the kind that might be left by a person long gone.

Her flashlight flickered. In that brief pulse, she thought she saw something written in chalk near the outline: *don't open the door.*

She blinked, and it was gone.

The air thickened again. Behind her, the boards creaked as if under a second set of feet.

She turned the beam of her light.

Martha stood at the far end of the attic now, facing her. Not shimmering this time. More defined. A figure carved from faint, silvery dust. The eyes—those were the worst. Empty, yes, but not vacant. Focused.

The lips parted. "You shouldn't have said my name."

"I wanted to know what happened."

The voice came layered, as though spoken through years of echoes. "It happened *again.*"

Elena swallowed hard. "You mean the fall?"

The ghost smiled faintly, the expression both pity and accusation. "All the falls are the same. You see one, you've seen them all."

The air behind her shifted; the boards moaned. Elena turned. For a fraction of a second, she saw it—the faint outline of the trapdoor re-forming, closing on its own. Then she heard the whispering. Dozens of overlapping voices, male and female, layered on top of each other like chorus practice gone wrong. All repeating variations of the same phrase:

"Don't open the door."

Her flashlight flickered out.

Darkness.

And in that dark, something brushed her shoulder. Not solid. Not weightless. Like air shaped into memory.

"Martha?" she whispered.

But the voice that answered wasn't hers.

"Eleanor."

Elena's lungs forgot how to move. "No," she said. "Not her."

"Eleanor."

The sound stretched, multiplied, became several voices, all repeating it, overlapping until the name itself was rhythm.

"Eleanor... Eleanor..."

She stumbled backward. Her heel hit the ladder, and she almost fell. The air around her shimmered again, folding time.

The attic wasn't empty anymore.

Figures crowded the edges—translucent shapes caught mid-task. Servants carrying trays. A child sitting cross-legged near a chest of toys. A man in a waistcoat reading by candlelight. All faint, all half-formed, their motions looping endlessly. Echoes of daily life, moments trapped between breaths.

And in the center, Martha again, climbing, reaching for the same beam over and over, never noticing the break that awaited her.

The loop reset. She fell again.

Elena pressed her palms to her ears. "Stop."

The sound didn't stop.

She forced herself toward the ladder, feet fumbling for rungs. Each one creaked like a throat clearing before speech. She hit the landing, stumbled into the hall, and slammed the attic door shut. The rope pull swung once and stilled.

The voices continued faintly behind the wood—an aftertaste of sound, words chewed down to hums.

She backed away until her shoulders touched the opposite wall. Her chest heaved. She closed her eyes and waited for the silence to mean something again.

When she opened them, the hall was full of movement.

Not people—*shadows.* Patches of light sliding across the wallpaper where no source existed. They passed over her like memories replaying in the wrong room. In each flicker, she caught fragments: a hand dropping a glass, a face turning in shock, a figure kneeling over another. Scenes out of sequence. All of them variations on loss.

The air felt heavier with each one, pressing against her ribs.

"You're remembering too much," she whispered.

The shadows stilled. For one impossible moment, the house felt like it was listening directly, aware of her tone.

Then, gently, the chandelier above her began to sway.

Just slightly. Just enough to make the crystals whisper against each other. The sound that came out was not random. It was melodic.

A lullaby.

The same tune she had hummed in the study.

Elena closed her eyes, the rhythm tightening her throat. "You learned it."

A whisper brushed her ear, so close she felt the air move:

"You taught me."

Her eyes snapped open. The hall was empty again, still as an oil painting. The chandelier hung motionless.

But she could still feel the echo of breath near her cheek, still warm.

She turned slowly toward the nursery door. It was wide open. Inside, the cradle was still again, but a faint indentation marked the pillow—like the weight of something unseen resting there.

And on the wall above the cradle, something new had appeared.

Scratched faintly into the wallpaper were words—not gouged, but traced, the strokes careful and deliberate.

IT REMEMBERS WHO YOU WERE.

She backed out, pulse thrumming, and nearly tripped over the landing rug. The house seemed to tilt for a moment, the hallway stretching just slightly longer than before. The air shimmered as though from heat, but it wasn't warm.

Her reflection in the nearest mirror stared back with a second's delay, eyes wide, lips parted in disbelief.

Behind her reflection, the shadow of Martha lingered at the end of the hall.

Watching. Waiting for her to understand.

The house had learned to be quiet around her, the way a cat learns the soft spots between ankles.

Elena stood at the landing, palms open, letting the silence check her. The hall smelled faintly of starch and candle smoke, and underneath that—cedar, a polite warning. The scratched words above the cradle—IT REMEMBERS WHO YOU WERE—stared with the patience of carved stone.

"Who I was," she said, tasting how the sentence wanted to be plural.

The mirror at the corner returned her face with no delay. That sudden obedience felt like a trick. She waited. When it stayed ordinary, she moved toward the end of the hall where Martha's shadow had stood. The wallpaper's vine pattern seemed to tense as she passed, curling tighter, as if the room wanted to clutch its own ribs.

"Martha," she said softly. "I see you."

The air answered with the precise weight of a footstep.

Not on the ceiling. Not in the wall. On the floorboards, at the far end of the corridor. A second step followed, careful, as if someone was remembering how to walk.

"I called you by your name," Elena said. "Now call me by mine."

Silence. Then the voice—thin as tracing paper and twice as fragile—came from the shadow that had gathered where the light should have been stronger.

"Eleanor."

Elena shut her eyes for a count of three. "No. Try again."

A pause, and in it she felt time rearrange its hairpins. The voice returned, still wrong but trying.

"Elena."

Her chest unclenched. "Better."

The shadow deepened, condensed, and the air cooled just enough to lift the hairs at her nape. Martha stepped forward by not stepping at all—arrived, rather, the way a memory arrives: decided and unstoppable. The outline of her was stronger now. The dress found seams. The hands found fingers. The oval of her face resolved just enough to hold expression. She looked like a photograph that had been rinsed too briefly, the darks not yet settled.

"You fell," Elena said. "But you said it wasn't accidental."

Martha tilted her head, as if listening to someone else explain her. "A house doesn't have accidents."

"And the door? The warning in chalk up there—'Don't open the door'?"

Martha's voice made a small, mirthless shape. "It was a joke we told each other while we were living. After, it became a rule." Her gaze—if the bright, empty ovals could be called that— shifted toward the nursery. "Rules never come soon enough."

Elena held the banister with one hand, because what tried to climb her spine was not fear but the urge to run, and the hand kept her honest. "You know me, but you don't. Why?"

"Because it remembers you wrong," Martha said gently, like she'd had practice with gentleness. "Because remembering is a hunger and hungers have poor manners."

"Remembering me as Eleanor," Elena said. "Because of our faces."

"Faces are how doors recognize you."

Outside, wind rehearsed the idea of weather against the eaves. The house offered the sound back in a softened key. Somewhere below, the smaller bell without a clapper moved no air and still rang in her teeth.

"Martha," Elena said, "what did it do to you?"

Martha looked past Elena, toward a time Elena could not turn to see. "It loved me," she said. "The way deep water loves what drops into it. Thoroughly."

"That's not love."

"No," Martha agreed, and the shape of her mouth made something like a smile. "But it's steady."

The chandelier gave a private shiver; the crystals whispered a phrase from the lullaby and then pretended they hadn't. Elena took a step closer. The floor did not protest. "Tell me how to make it remember me correctly. Not as Eleanor. As myself."

"There are only two ways," Martha said, and the house gathered itself to listen, as if rules being said aloud had weight it enjoyed holding. "One is to leave. Cleanly. Quickly. Before it has enough of you to hum."

"And the other?"

"Teach it a new song."

The answer hit the soft of Elena's mouth like a laugh she didn't want. "I've been trying."

"Yes," Martha said, and the word carried no praise. "It likes your voice. It always liked hers."

"That's not my fault."

"Nothing here is," Martha said. "But all of it is yours."

They stood with that between them like a window that had not been opened in years. The key at Elena's throat warmed, then cooled, a tide in metal. "You said the falls are all the same," Elena said. "Show me yours once more."

Martha's head turned toward the attic, toward the seam in the air that even living eyes could find if the light was right. "We shouldn't."

"Yes," Elena agreed. "But we will."

The shadow of Martha thinned, lengthened, and moved up the wall the way reflections do when someone carries a candle. Elena followed. The ladder folded down in a slow courtesy when she pulled the rope; the attic delivered its cold the way a well delivers water.

Up there, the air held that sweet copper—a past event rusting forever. Dust hung obedient and seemed to thicken where Martha stood. The world lost its edges for a heartbeat; then the scene found itself.

It played again.

Martha's weight on the beam. The reach. The give. The awful break. The fall. The scream that seemed to be made by wood as much as by woman. Elena forced herself to watch the moment she had flinched from before—the instant *before* the give. The subtle rise at the plank's edge. Not rot, not age, but design. A gap planed into being and disguised with stain. Human intention. Not the house.

Victor's note: *Not accidental.* The phrase acquired teeth.

Martha landed—no sound now; the house withheld it the way a person spares a child a grim detail. When the air cleared, Martha's echo stood again, intact, the loop ready. She didn't turn this time. She spoke into her own scene, a ruin whispering to the moment before it was ruined.

"He had reason," she said. "Not good, but sharp."

"Who?"

"I keep trying to forget that," Martha said. "Each time I do, the house offers it back. A kindness." The last word felt like an old bruise touched. "You think it chooses how to hurt. It doesn't. It repeats what we teach it."

"Who?" Elena asked again, softer. The attic moved the question into its beams and kept it for later.

Martha's outline wavered. "A man who wanted a room to stay the way it was forever," she said. "A man who needed a loss to finish a sentence." She tilted her head. "There were fewer rules then."

Elena swallowed. The air scratched her throat when she did. "Victor?"

A pause. The loop startled, stuttered, then resumed—as if a needle had hit a scratch and been guided through it.

"No," Martha said. "But he understood afterward."

The attic seemed to tighten around a name; Elena couldn't find it, like trying to pick up mercury. She lowered her voice further, not for the dead, but for the house. "Do you want to be remembered?"

Martha looked at her with those bright hollows. "It isn't for me."

"What is?"

"You," Martha said simply. "You and the door and the way the house will try to put you behind it with a word that sounds like your name."

Elena thought of the red lacquer, the depth that wasn't pigment, the way warmth had moved through her hand when she touched it. She pictured, involuntarily, Eleanor's plait slipping loose and the way her ancestor's mouth had looked like agreement even when she had not said yes.

"You mistake me for someone who stays," Elena said.

Martha did something like shrug. On her, it looked like dust remembering it had once been shoulder. "I mistake nothing," she said. "I am an echo. I only repeat."

"Then repeat this," Elena said. She took the brass key off its chain and set it on the beam between them. "I am Elena. I am not the room you remember."

The wood took the weight of the key as if it had been waiting for that exact metal, that exact doubt. The temperature in the attic shifted. The hum behind the ears that meant *you are in its throat now* dropped a tone.

Martha's mouth shaped a word that might have been "good," might have been "go." Then she thinned as if the scene had run out of budget for her outline. From somewhere below—down in the nursery, in the carriage house that wasn't anymore, in the hall where servants had once lined up their shoes—came a small percussive sound. A child knocking a wooden block against a table. A pocket metronome. A heart trying to keep a promise.

"Do you need me?" Elena asked.

Martha's echo did not answer. She replayed her fall, and this time her mouth—impossibly—shaped Elena's name on the way down.

Elena turned away.

The ladder's rungs gave back each step with a sigh. When she dropped to the landing, the house felt lower, as if the ceilings had tilted down to hear and then forgotten to lift. The nursery door stood open. Inside, the cradle was still. The indent in the pillow had grown, slight but undeniable, as if something had learned to weigh itself.

"Enough," Elena said, a word she'd been trained to use as an apology. "Please."

The house considered. The lullaby withdrew, as if a music box had been closed with two fingers.

"Thank you," she said, hating the way gratitude felt like capitulation.

In the study, the device on the wall—Victor's fragile tension of coil and filament—had drawn while she was gone. A long strip dangled, the mark thick at the beginning and then thinning into a straight calm, like panic learning manners. She tore it free and pinned it beneath one of her paperweights. The little brass key had kept its heat on the beam upstairs; the chain left a chill on her collarbone.

She wrote a sentence at the top of a new page in her notebook:

The house repeats what we teach it.

Under it, smaller:

Teach it to me.

She set the metronome on the desk, wound it, set the tick to a human pace. She spoke in its rhythm, not giving the house a melody to steal. "I am Elena. Not Eleanor. I am not a room. I am not a door. I will listen, but I will not hum."

The paper strip in the device twitched once, as if amused, then steadied. Was that a yes? A nod? She decided not to learn too quickly.

Dusk layered itself across the windows. The house does that: turns nouns into verbs when it's tired of pretending.

She ate in the kitchen—a meal so small even hunger wouldn't bother to name it—and let the clock lie about the hour because lies are sometimes the shortest road to sleep. When she returned upstairs, the hallway had the particular look of an evening that wants an argument. She turned off lights that weren't on. She shut doors that were already shut. Rituals calm houses. Or their keepers.

At the nursery, she stopped, because something had changed that could no longer be mistaken for tiredness.

A new portrait hung on the wall opposite the door.

She would have sworn there had never been a nail there, that the plaster had resented even thinking about one. Now a gilt frame hung with dutiful gravity. Inside: oil on canvas. A woman's three-quarter pose, head turned slightly to the right. The painter had been precise and kind—too kind perhaps—with the cheekbones. The eyes were gray-blue, deep as pewter, and they looked like hers.

Under the frame, a brass plate: E. Harrow. No year. No first name spelled out to save confusion. No painter's signature. The paint looked... fresh.

"Of course," she said.

In the glass over the mantel down the hall, her reflection lifted its hand at the same moment. No lag. No delay. She didn't feel relief. The obviousness of it made her teeth ache.

From the far end of the corridor, a figure stood where the light refused to quite reach. Not Martha this time. Taller. A man, shoulders set the way a posture sets when it's been imitated from portraits. He didn't move. He didn't glow. He simply existed, as if the house had remembered in enough detail to make a person from outline and intention.

"Victor?" she called, and the name seemed to enter his silhouette like a wick drawing oil. He did not answer.

She took a step toward him. He lifted a hand, not in greeting, not in warning, but in the universal sign for *wait.*

The house obliged. The chandelier stilled. The air found its preferred temperature.

Victor—not entirely Victor—spoke as if speaking cost him the kind of energy breath cannot replace.

"You are late," he said.

She almost laughed. "To what?"

"Your life," he said, and the cruelty in it was all him, not the house.

"I'm on time enough," she said. "You built a device to talk to a building."

He looked past her at the nursery portrait and flinched in a way any living man would have. "It learns faster each generation."

"So I've noticed."

"Eleanor thought she could out-listen it," he said. "I thought I could out-measure it. You—" His gaze flicked to the keyless space at her throat. "—you will try to out-name it."

"And?"

"And it prefers verbs," he said, a bleak humor that actually was his. "It likes doing. It will do you unless you do it first."

"Do what?"

"Decide," he said, and the hallway leaned in, a whole architecture eager for cliff notes. "Before it does."

He began to go out the way fog goes, unmaking himself at the edges. She tried to pin him with a question. "Who pushed Martha?"

The house blotted him quicker for that. "It doesn't forgive names spoken aloud," he said from a thinner place, "when the person still has descendants."

The last of him bent toward the study as if habit anchored him. Then he was only air with opinions.

"Coward," she said to the emptiness, and hoped he heard her in whatever room men make for themselves when they die badly.

Night accepted its job. The house braided sounds into something like a lullaby that wasn't the lullaby and waited to see whether she'd hum along. She refused. She stood in the hall until her legs ached and the portraits began to look like choices lined up. She touched the new painting's frame. The gold leaf flaked under her nail. Fresh, then. Or newly remembered.

"Teach it me," she said again, this time not to the study, not to the device, not even to a specific room. "Learn my name like a tune you can't shake."

She walked the perimeter of the upstairs corridor clockwise, then counterclockwise, counting the steps under her breath. She spoke out loud the mundane: the names of colors in the rug, the inventory of doors, the stupid, human details houses notice when they grow fond of you against their will. She gave it everything not haunted about herself. Favorite coffee. The shape of her brush grip. The fact that she once painted fruit because a gallery said fruits were selling and she hated herself for it for a month.

"You can keep those," she told the walls. "Not the rest."

At the last door, the nursery shifted in her peripheral vision. She refused to look straight on. "Good night," she said to it like a problem you plan to love tomorrow.

She made it as far as the threshold of the east bedroom before the house decided it had waited long enough.

Every mirror in the corridor bloomed red at once. Not painted— remembered. Lacquer-color flooding the glass from within, swelling until each pane became its own red door. The brass knob at her shoulder vibrated once in sympathy. The air heated a degree like breath blown into cupped hands.

Elena stood very still. "No."

The red lessened a fraction. Enough to be called listening.

"You will not put me behind a door tonight," she said. "I will go if and when I choose."

Silence considered being dignified and decided against it. The lacquer in the mirrors deepened. From everywhere and nowhere at once, the house spoke—not with a voice, but with the exact weight and warmth of one. Not Eleanor's. Not Victor's. Not her mother's.

Her own.

"Welcome home, Eleanor."

She smiled then—sharp, exhausted, unwilling—and said with a smoothness she did not feel, "Say it again. Correctly."

The red held.

"Again," she said, and the metronome in her blood ticked without mercy.

The mirrors paled by degrees, as if embarrassed at having shown off. The air cooled. The brass settled. All at once, the corridor's windows remembered moonlight and admitted it.

The house spoke once more. A lesson repeated. An edit.

"Welcome home, Elena."

Not perfect. Not relief. But a different key.

"That's right," she said, and the word right meant *true enough for tonight.*

She entered the east bedroom and shut the door—the act so ordinary it felt like defiance. The key lay upstairs on a beam where memory had weight; she slept without it, collarbone bare and honest. The house arranged its sounds into something almost kind. She did not dream of falling. She dreamed the stupid, saving dream of packing a bag that keeps agreeing to be too small and somehow fits everything.

When she woke just before dawn, the portrait opposite the nursery hung crooked, as if a hand had tried to take it down and changed its mind. The scratched words above the cradle remained, but a new, fainter line had joined them, so soft she could have missed it.

LISTEN DIFFERENTLY.

Her phrase, written back to her in a hand that wasn't a hand at all.

Downstairs, the front door stood politely closed.

The house breathed in. She breathed out.

"Good morning," she said, and it did not argue the definition.

CHAPTER 10

The House's Influence

Morning arrived uncertainly, the kind of light that behaves like it's trespassing.It slipped between the curtains, found the edges of Elena's face, and hesitated—too pale to be kind, too weak to be honest. She sat up, half expecting the room to correct itself again, to pull its walls tighter or return the portrait to its original place. But everything looked still. Too still. The air was stiff with that polite sort of silence that follows an argument.

Her phone still had no signal. The date on its lock screen flickered between two days, refusing to decide which one it wanted to be. She turned it off and set it aside. The ticking from downstairs—one clock, then another, then another—rose through the floorboards like the pulse of something buried but alive.

The house had learned her rhythm. Now, it wanted to teach her its own.

She washed her face in cold water from the tap. It came out cloudy for a second, then cleared as if embarrassed. When she looked up, the mirror showed her hands still cupped, but the water inside them didn't fall. It hung there, perfectly suspended.

Then she blinked—and the reflection caught up, the water spilling in the glass a full second before it did in real life.

She turned away sharply, a towel pressed hard to her face. "Not today," she muttered.

In the kitchen, the air smelled faintly of toast and lavender, though she hadn't made either. The peonies on the table were gone—replaced by a bowl of green apples, each one polished, each one bearing a small bruise in the exact same place. A note sat propped against the bowl, the paper yellowed at the edges. Her name written in looping ink:

Eat something, Eleanor.

She crushed the note without reading it twice and threw it into the trash. The apples gleamed anyway.

Every clock in the house chimed the hour at once—but not the same hour.

Seven. Eight. Ten. The sound was discordant, like the house had a chorus but no conductor.

She poured herself coffee, black, and sat at the kitchen table. Her sketchbook lay open beside her, the page she'd last touched the night before showing a half-done drawing of the east bedroom window. But the lines had changed.

The sketch now showed the window *open.*

And beyond it—something faint, like the impression of a face just outside, watching.

Elena stared at it until her pulse went sharp in her ears. "I didn't draw that."

No answer, of course. Just the steady, satisfied hum of the refrigerator.

She flipped the page. The next sketch was of the chandelier in the upstairs hall—only now its crystals formed words instead of light: LISTEN DIFFERENTLY.

Her hand hovered over the paper. She wanted to tear it out but couldn't shake the certainty that doing so would make the wall bleed.

Instead, she stood and walked to the back door. The glass was fogged. She wiped a circle clean with her palm and froze.

Birds.

Not crows or ravens—starlings. Dozens of them, clustered on the branches near the property's edge, their bodies slick and oil-dark. They shouldn't be here, not in this season. Not in this number. As she watched, the flock shifted all at once, not flying away but reordering—an aerial ripple that formed and unformed patterns.

For a moment, she thought they spelled something.

Then one fell from the branch, hit the ground, and didn't move.

Elena stepped back from the door. "No," she whispered. "You're not real."

But the smell of feathers—dusty, sweet, faintly rotted—slid through the crack beneath the door. She grabbed the handle and yanked. Locked. It hadn't been locked when she came downstairs. She rattled it once, twice, then stopped herself before the panic fully bloomed.

It wasn't that the house didn't want her to leave. It wanted to see *what she would do when she tried.*

She turned, leaned against the counter, and exhaled slowly. Her breath fogged in the air, though it wasn't cold.

On the far wall, one of Victor's framed sketches had tilted slightly. She straightened it—and realized it was one of *hers.* A charcoal rendering of the manor's front drive she'd drawn last week, before the worst of the dreams had begun. But it was wrong now.

The driveway was empty in her memory. Here, the drawing showed a car parked there. Her car. Headlights on.

She pressed her thumb against the glass. "What are you showing me?"

The image flickered faintly—one headlight went dark, then both. Then the car was gone again, leaving only the gray smudge of its absence.

She pulled the picture down from the wall and set it face-down on the table.

The sound that followed—faint, metallic—came from the vent above her head. A slow tap-tap-tap, deliberate and rhythmic.

Her throat tightened. "What do you want?"

This time, the answer came in the form of movement. The vent cover vibrated, then slid half an inch open. A whisper of air, like an exhale. Something small tumbled out—a folded scrap of paper.

She waited a full minute before touching it. When she finally unfolded it, she recognized the handwriting instantly. Hers.

Stop fighting it. You'll make it angry.

She stared at the note until her pulse steadied, then crumpled it and shoved it into her pocket instead of throwing it away. The act felt both practical and superstitious.

She left the kitchen, moving through the house slowly now, studying its stillness like an animal assessing territory. Every room seemed slightly altered—not drastically, just enough to make her doubt memory's loyalty. The rug in the study had been turned ninety degrees. The globe stood open, revealing nothing but blackness inside. In the dining room, one of the chairs had been pulled slightly away from the table—as if someone had been sitting there recently.

She reached for it, then stopped. The chair's surface gleamed faintly wet. Her fingertips hovered a breath above it and felt warmth radiating upward. Someone—or something—had only just left.

The ticking of the clocks joined again, synchronized for the first time since she'd woken.

Ten o'clock. Sharp. Unified. The sound vibrated through her chest like a command.

She backed out of the room slowly, refusing to turn her back on it until she reached the hall.

The chandelier above her stirred—one crystal swayed, then another, until they all moved in perfect rhythm. Not random. A pulse. Her pulse.

That realization made her knees weak.

"You're hungry," she whispered. "Aren't you?"

The house didn't answer, but something inside the walls creaked with the pleasure of being understood.

She returned to the east bedroom to get her sketchbook and found it open again, a new page exposed. A sketch she hadn't drawn—yet unmistakably in her hand.

It showed *her* at the kitchen table, bent over the sketchbook, eyes hollow and distant.

A second version of herself stood behind, hand on her shoulder, smiling faintly.

Elena slammed the book shut. The sound echoed down the hall like a door closing.

She went to the window and opened it for air. The cold slapped her face—sharp, metallic, clean—and for one brief second, she could hear the sea, though she was miles inland. Waves crashing somewhere behind the trees, steady as breathing.

Her breath came out visible now. The curtains stirred behind her even though there was no draft. She turned back toward the room - and stopped.

The portrait opposite the bed was different again. It no longer showed the woman with the pewter eyes. It showed *her.*

Her face, rendered in oil, expression neutral, the paint still wet enough to glisten.

She stepped forward until her breath fogged the varnish. Her reflection overlaid the painted one.

"I didn't sit for you," she whispered.

The painted mouth curved upward a fraction - barely, but enough to be undeniable.

Her stomach dropped. She backed away until her calves hit the bedframe.

Outside, the starlings erupted from the trees all at once, screaming into the air like metal grinding against metal. The sound didn't fade - it followed, wrapping the house in static.

The chandelier stilled. The clocks stopped.

And for the first time since she'd arrived, the house was truly silent.

Elena sat on the edge of the bed, palms pressed together, waiting for her heartbeat to belong to her again. She thought of what Martha had said: *It remembers what it loves. And it loves who it keeps.*

She looked up at the portrait. The eyes in the painting had turned slightly away from her, looking toward the door.

As if someone was standing there.

She didn't turn to check.

For the first time since arriving, Elena didn't sleep that night — but neither did she stay awake.

The hours bled into one another until she couldn't tell which belonged to dream and which to consciousness. Somewhere in that gray seam, the house found its chance.

It began gently.

A soft light under the door. A hum that wasn't the pipes, wasn't the wind, but the low, soothing vibration of approval. She knew that sound. Not from the house — from her studio, years ago, when she'd first felt what it meant to create something *true.* That little hum in the skull when a brushstroke landed exactly right.

"Elena," the house whispered.

The sound wasn't disembodied anymore; it was intimate, like someone speaking into her hair.

"Come see."

Her body obeyed before her mind could argue. Barefoot, she followed the light into the hall.

It wasn't the cold blue of moonlight, but the warm gold of gallery bulbs — the kind that made every painting look like it mattered.

At the end of the corridor, the air shimmered. The walls pulled wider, stretching until the familiar angles of Blackwood Manor became something else entirely: her gallery show.

The one that had been canceled when her funding fell through. The dream that had slipped quietly into the past tense.

And yet here it was.

Canvases she'd never finished — finished now.

Her signature perfect in the corners.

Brushwork alive with confidence she hadn't felt in years.

Visitors wandered between the frames, murmuring in tones of reverent approval.

Their footsteps echoed softly, the rhythm of admiration.

She moved closer. The nearest painting stopped her cold. It was of the house — Blackwood Manor — but not as it was. As it *wanted* to be seen. Bright windows. Clear sky. Not haunted, but holy.

"Elena Harrow," said a voice behind her — smooth, male, practiced.

She turned. Her former mentor, Nathaniel Crane, stood there. Or the memory of him.

He smiled the same knowing, gentle smile he used to give when she'd brought him something *almost* brilliant.

"You've done it," he said, motioning to the walls. "You've found truth in the uncanny. No more hiding behind irony."

She swallowed. "You're not here."

"Of course not," he said, without offense. "Neither are you. Not yet. But you could be. You always could."

The light shifted. Another painting came into focus — her parents' faces, rendered in soft pastels. They looked proud. Proud of her. Proud of *this.*

Her mother's eyes glistened as though she were about to speak.

Elena's throat closed. "No."

Her mother stepped from the canvas, feet making no sound on the polished floor. She wore the same blue scarf she'd been buried in. "You were meant to come back," she said.

Her father joined her, his expression exactly as she remembered from childhood — the unspoken warmth, the almost-smile that had been her home before there was a house.

"It's all been waiting," he said. "You can rest now. You've worked hard enough."

Elena's knees weakened. "This isn't real."

"Does it matter?" her mother asked softly. "We are. You are. Here, you can paint again. You can finish what you started. You'll never have to struggle."

Behind her, another voice joined the chorus — her own, calm and steady:

"Don't you want to be seen? Don't you want to *matter* again?"

She turned. Another Elena stood there — clean, radiant, hair swept back, skin luminous with health. This one smiled easily. Her clothes were unrumpled, her eyes clear. She looked like someone whose life made sense.

"You fought for this," the other Elena said. "For peace. For beauty. For control. The house gives it to you freely. All you have to do is stay."

The air was warm, the kind of warmth that lives in memory, not in physics. It smelled of linseed oil and lemon polish, of her father's workshop, of childhood afternoons with paint beneath her fingernails and no deadlines to fear.

She wanted to believe.

God help her, she wanted to believe.

The house pulsed gently, as if sensing her surrender. The portraits leaned forward, the air thickened, and the golden light grew richer, almost edible.

The hum beneath her skin became pleasure — not sexual, but the deep, resonant pleasure of being *understood.*

She reached out a hand toward the other Elena. "What happens if I do?"

Her doppelgänger smiled with the sadness of a saint in a fresco.

"Then the world stops hurting."

The words hit with the weight of a promise too old to be new.

The sound of the sea returned — closer now, not imagined. Waves beneath the floorboards. The manor breathing in tide rhythms. Somewhere distant, she heard laughter. Not cruel. Familiar.

Hers.

Then a knock. Sharp. Singular. The sound of interruption.

Everything froze. The golden light faltered.

The crowd of faceless admirers turned toward the noise as one, heads tilting like birds.

The knock again. Harder. Real.

Elena blinked — and the gallery wavered, its colors thinning like paint exposed to rain.

Through the dissolving walls, she saw the manor beneath — gray, damp, breathing.

The illusion cracked like a pane of glass cooling too fast.

The third knock came from the study.

She tore herself away from the apparition, running toward the sound, the floor shifting underfoot as the world rearranged itself around her.

By the time she reached the study door, the glow was gone. Only candlelight remained, faint and sour.

The brass key — the one she'd left on the beam upstairs — lay on the desk.

It shouldn't have been there. She hadn't brought it down. She picked it up carefully. It was hot to the touch, as if it had been handled by someone moments ago.

The fire in the hearth guttered, flared once, then burned steady. And within its flame — not reflection, not trick — she saw her *own face* again. Not the radiant double this time, but something rawer.

Eyes hollow. Lips cracked. The skin beneath her nails blackened like soot.

The mouth in the fire moved.

"You've already chosen," it said.

She stepped back. "I haven't."

"You came here. You stayed. You opened doors."

The flames rose higher, almost touching the mantle. The voice softened, coaxing:

"It's easier to live in a story than outside one. You could stay in mine. You could be finished."

She clenched the key tight enough to draw blood from her palm. "I am not yours."

"You were never yours either," it said. "Not really."

The fire dimmed, collapsing into ember. Her reflection flickered out.

Elena fell into the desk chair, breathing hard. The room felt too small, the air dense with copper heat.

She stared at the journals stacked neatly beside her — Victor's, Eleanor's, all labeled in that meticulous Harrow hand. She pulled one open.

Inside, the ink had bled, the words warped by heat — but the first line was clear enough:

The house rewards belief.

Her fingers trembled as she turned the page. Sketches filled the margins — doorframes, blueprints, faces. At the bottom of the last page, written faintly, as if from memory:

It will never ask you to stay. It will ask if you remember why you want to.

She read the line twice before closing the book.

Her reflection in the dark window shifted again — the other Elena, still smiling faintly, hand pressed to the glass from the other side.

This time, the reflection spoke aloud.

"You can make it love you."

The glass fogged where the mouth moved, breath visible.

Elena's skin prickled; her own heartbeat synchronized with the tapping of rain against the pane.

She reached forward, pressed her palm to the reflection's. The surface was warm — too warm.

The other Elena's eyes widened, mirroring her shock, but not her fear.

Then the warmth turned to heat. Her hand burned. She yanked it back.

The glass smoked, leaving a faint imprint — her palm, outlined in soot.

From somewhere deep in the walls came a sigh, long and content.

The illusion faded. The gold light vanished.

The smell of lemon polish became dust again.

But as she turned to leave, she noticed one small, impossible detail:

The soot mark on the window pulsed faintly, like something beneath it was breathing.

She didn't look back again.

She woke at the desk with her cheek stuck to the blotter.

For a moment she didn't know where she was—only the ache in her neck and the taste of iron in her mouth. Then the room arranged itself: the study, the cold lamp, the window showing a slice of pale morning like a gauze pad soaked through. The metronome sat where she'd left it, un-wound, its brass bob like an eye that had closed without permission.

Her hands.

They were stained to the wrists, not with ink—too matte for that. She rubbed her thumb across her palm and the residue smudged into a gray-black fog. Soot. Old, dry, fine as breath. It traced the whorls of her fingerprints, lived under her nails. She turned her wrist and fine powder trailed to the blotter, blooming an ashy fingerprint she hadn't given it leave to have.

She hadn't lit a fire.

The hearth held only cold ash, sullen and innocent. The grate was clean. The poker leaned where it always had, a dutiful soldier. The smear on her skin resisted water, then surrendered all at once and slicked into something like mud. She washed until the sink ran clouded and then clear; the skin beneath burned, as though the dust had been older than her.

When she lifted her head, the mirror over the sink delayed just long enough to punish. Her reflection lifted its face a heartbeat after she did. The eyes in the glass were her eyes, rimmed red, the lids swollen. Behind them, the study stood a degree out of step: the lamp still on, the metronome still ticking.

"Enough," she said, hoarse.

The house said it back—her exact tone, softened, the way you say *enough* to a child you intend to pick up anyway. The voice didn't echo from a direction. It pressed lightly from everywhere at once, the way warm breath does when you lean into a scarf.

"Enough," it agreed, with her mouth.

She dried her hands on the towel and the towel left lint like gray snow. When she stepped into the hall, the clocks had reconvened their argued times. 7:13. 8:01. 9:47. The grandfather insisted on 6, stubborn and ceremonial. She thought of a choir unwilling to choose a key.

Her sketchbook lay where she'd abandoned it on the landing stool. Open. The next page had drawn itself while she slept: an ink line of the blue room's mantel, simple and true—except for the thing perched in the grate. Not logs. Not fire. A dark, compact mass with a suggestion of ribs. A bird-shaped blackout. A starling built from absence.

"No," she said, and her voice didn't come back. It leaned— warmed—approved.

"Yes," the house whispered, using her exact breath.

Yes, you see.

"I'm done," she told it, though she didn't know with what. She should have left then—bag, keys, door, road—but the thought of her hands on the knob made her throat close.

She carried the sketchbook to the study and set it on the blotter. The soot-grease on her fingers left a crescent. She flipped past the mantels, the windows, the chandelier's forced words. The last page was blank. Blank like fresh ice. Blank like a dare.

"Teach it me," she'd written the night before. She felt suddenly, wildly unequal to the job.

The house changed strategy. The sweetness edged into comfort. The walls found a warmer tone. Her mother's voice, this time— only not the memory of it, the idea of it. A lullaby without melody, promise without substance.

"You're tired," the house—her mother—she—said.

"Sit. Let it be easy."

The temptation came like a tide over the ankles—nothing dramatic at first, just that pull. She put her hand on the desk to steady herself and found the brass key she'd retrieved last night, its heat now spent. She closed her fingers around it. The metal was cool, honest. It didn't hum. It didn't soothe. It waited.

"Not yours," she told the room. "Mine."

Her gaze drifted back to the sketchbook. The blue room had never been kind to her drawings; they always ended up too pretty in that light. She thought of the house's attempts at portraiture—the oil opposite the nursery tilted by an unseen hand, the cheekbones made slightly nobler than they had any right to be. *You will not make me ornamental,* she thought, and the thought had teeth.

She tore the mantels page out in one hard motion.

The sound felt obscene—paper muscle separating from paper bone. A flurry of ash leapt from nowhere and settled on the desk, on her wrists, into the grain of wood. The lamp hissed—the filament widening a fraction as if offended. From the wall behind her, a small, hurt noise. Not loud. Distinct.

She froze, the torn page in her hand like a severed wing.

"Did that injure you," she said, not a question.

The house pretended not to understand. The ceiling remembered it was old and gave a nervous creak. The torn page pulsed heat in her hold. When she loosened her grip, the corner stuck to her skin as though the air had turned adhesive.

"I'm not a room," she said to the plaster, to the smooth-lipped mirror, to the perfect brass of the drawer pulls. "You don't get to keep the parts of me that perform."

She ripped the page in half. The sound tore the study's temper. The coil-and-needle device on the wall twanged its spring like a struck nerve. The metronome started itself, one defiant tick, then another, then stilled—shamed.

She expected the house to punish. It withdrew instead. The warmth stepped back a degree. The sweet in the air thinned, then returned as if to say it could outlast her, it had all the time in the world.

> "You're frightened," it told her, in her own easiest, most private register—the voice she used with the very few people she'd ever let see her fail.

She answered in the register she used for herself when she meant to stand up. "Correct."

The sketch of the chandelier glinted from the nearest page. LISTEN DIFFERENTLY written in dangling crystal. She took the pencil and, under those words, wrote in her spidery, impatient hand: STOP HARMING YOURSELF TO FEED IT.

The air shifted—offended, interested. The mirror across the room showed her standing slightly more centered than she felt, like a teacher adjusting a child's posture.

"You heard me," she said.

"Always," the house said.

The "always" carried a weight that made her think of Eleanor, of all the women who had learned to move quietly and deliberately so the house would not make a meal of their steps.

She flipped to a blank page and made herself draw something stupid, something the house wouldn't want: a crooked spoon from the kitchen drawer, the dent in the enamel bowl, the forgotten nail head on the back staircase she kept catching her sweater on. Ordinary. Flawed. Human.

Her hand shook for the first ten lines, then steadied. The spoon looked like itself. The bowl's dent refused beautification. The nail head sat with its little dark certainty and did not become a symbol. When she finished, the paper felt heavier. Not with ash. With insistence.

The house breathed in long and slow, then let it out the length of the hall.

"Elena."

Her name in its mouth now was patient, a word you might set a cup upon and trust not to spill.

"Let it be easy," it added.

Not command but a cajole, and used again that not-quite-her-mother tone, and again the not-quite-Nathaniel approval, and then, softest, her own studio voice saying finish it, you can finish it, it's right there.

She laughed, sharp, and the sound felt like cutting a knot. "If I stay because it's easy," she said, "then I am the varnish you put on something you don't know how to fix."

Silence. But it wasn't dignified this time. It sulked.

She stood. The chair squealed, mundane and undignified, and the sound made her braver. She carried the torn drawing to the hearth and struck a match. It hissed, opened its small orange eye. For three seconds she thought she could make a ceremony of it. The flame licked the edge of the paper, browned it. She held it at the fireplace's empty mouth.

Heat surged up the chimney—impossible, immediate. A gust like a breath from a body waking. The flame snapped tall, greedy, then guttered as if pinched by invisible fingers.

"Mine," she said through her teeth. The page charred, bowed, then surrendered. When it fell to ash, the draft sighed—the exact sound a sleeping person makes when you take your hand off their back. The room waited to see if she would apologize.

She did not.

She went to the blue room to test the house's claim to mercy. The small bell without a clapper lay on the mantel and didn't look like a mouth at all; it looked like brass. She set it on the floor, set the metronome beside it, and wound the tick to her own pulse. She spoke on beats again, rude with normalcy.

"This is my space," beat. "This is a chair," beat. "This is a window," beat. "This is a song I will not hum."

The bell did not ring. The air did, faintly, high in her teeth, like a held note, less than pain. The walls took her inventory without comment. The windows breathed a little. She opened one an inch. The house did not flinch. The cold stitched her skin and she welcomed its needle.

She left the window cracked and went to the hall. The new portrait opposite the nursery—the one that had been her and not her—hung obediently level now. It had been straightened in the night. Or by morning. Or by the version of her that wanted to be admired. The eyes in the painting were not looking at the door anymore. They were looking at her.

"Don't," she told it.

For a heartbeat, the wet shine on the iris shifted—trembled, as if a living eye had blinked shallowly behind paint. Then it was only oil again. A hairline crack appeared where none had been across the varnish, shallow as a paper cut.

She felt that small wound in the wall like a pressure in her ear.

It felt her too—she saw it in the shiver that went along the plaster, visible if you stare the way you stare into rain and decide you can see the separate drops. The house didn't like the crack. It liked itself unmarred. It wanted her uncracked too. Ornamental. Glossed.

Her palms prickled with an old, petty joy. "You can be hurt," she said, and it sounded uglier than she intended.

"So can you," the house said, gently—her voice with the middle taken out. It didn't have to threaten. It was large. It could wait.

She put a fingertip to the hairline and pressed. Not to widen. To feel.

The house inhaled and did not exhale.

Behind her, in the nursery, the cradle gave one small, involuntary thock. Not haunting. Reflex.

She withdrew her hand and said, to the room and the portrait and the cradle and the air that tried to own her lungs: "I decide."

She went to Mae's note—the one she'd crushed yesterday, *Eat something, Eleanor*—and smoothed it out on the kitchen table. She wrote beneath the looping script in a blunt, unbeautiful block: ELENA. She ate an apple and did not remark on the bruise. She made eggs that tasted like iron and cut them with too much salt and sat in the ordinary light and chewed.

Halfway through, the chair opposite hers moved a fraction. A polite scoot. An invitation.

"Dine alone," she advised the air. The chair obeyed. It sulked a little, but its legs remembered courtesy.

Later—she could not have said how much later; the clocks had decided on 11:12 and stayed there like a truce—the front door let in a draft that carried pine and fog and a tang she'd begun to call *outside.* She stood in the foyer and did not reach for the handle. She waited until the draft found its manners and became house air.

Upstairs again, the soot had crept back under her nails, a ring of shadow refusing to be scrubbed. She sat on the floor of the hall, spine to the wall, and set the metronome on the boards. She wound it to her pulse, then slower, then slower than that. She let her breath find it. She let the house find it.

"Elena," the manor said.

This time it didn't use her mother. It didn't use Nathaniel. It didn't even bother with the precise imitation of her studio voice. It used something closer to the raw first-person—less polished, more accidental. The tone you hear when you catch yourself thinking out loud.

"Elena," it repeated, and timed the syllables to the tick. *E-le-na.* Tick. *E-le-na.* Tick. Not command. Not question. Name as rhythm. Rhythm as claim.

Her heart adjusted without asking her permission. *Elena.* Tick. *Elena.* Tick. There are worse prisons than a metronome.

She closed her eyes and matched it on purpose. "Elena," she said. Tick. "Elena." Tick. The word began to mean nothing and something wider. The house breathed with her—not in opposition now, not to drown her out, but alongside, as if a second chest had learned to expand when hers did and empty when hers emptied.

"Elena," it whispered again, and the consonants brushed her inner ear like a hand that knows when to stop. The sound was inside her and outside. It was the closest the house had come to a lullaby that wasn't theft.

"Don't," she said, gently, like you tell a cat not to climb the counter because you already know it will. "Don't make me your tide."

The silence that followed wasn't sulk this time. It was...
considering. The metronome ticked. The portraits breathed their
varnish. The crack in the painting did not deepen.

"Good," she said. "We are learning each other."

That felt like the stupidest thing she had ever said, and also true.

She lay back on the runner, cheek to the weave, and watched
the chandelier hold still. A tiny spider, unbothered by memory
or inheritance, rappelled from the ceiling and stopped an inch
above her nose like a punctuation mark. It spun on its thread,
slower than the tick. It did not care about names. It cared about
catching what flew by.

"You're right," she told it. "We both need to eat."

She could sleep like this, she thought—not the sleep that leaves
you unguarded and available to dreams, but the thin, animal
doze that replenishes without surrender. She shut her eyes.

The house brought its mouth very close to her ear. It didn't have
to move. It was already everywhere. It warmed its whisper until
it matched her warmth.

"Elena," it breathed, again, again—until her name and her heartbeat found the same bar and marched there, unarguably together.

CHAPTER 11

The Rooms of the Dead

By the time Elena woke, her watch said three times at once. The hour hand trembled between them like a creature unsure of where to rest. She blinked, rolled her shoulders, and told herself she would not count the chimes this morning. She would not ask what day it was. She would only make coffee, write, and pretend the house was just a place that needed airing.

But the floorboards had learned a new route.

The hallway stretched longer than it had yesterday—by at least three steps. She could tell by the rug. The pattern didn't repeat where it should have; one of the blue diamonds had doubled, an error that felt deliberate. When she bent to touch it, the fabric was cool, as if it had only just arrived.

She fetched her sketchbook, the same one she'd sworn to close forever after the last night's confrontation, and began mapping again. It had become a compulsion as much as an act of rebellion. If the house wanted to rearrange itself, then fine—she would document its lies.

"Kitchen, east," she murmured, pencil scratching. "Study, hall, nursery."

Each door had its own smell now: lemon polish, candle soot, rust. She followed the scents, marking each turn. Her first two maps had twisted themselves into nonsense after an hour, the graphite shifting, the paper curling as though rejecting her lines.

This time, she used ink.

It didn't help.

The hallway leading to the blue room split like a nerve. She stood before it, trying to remember if the new branch had always been there. The wallpaper on the left showed the familiar ivy pattern. The wall on the right shimmered faintly—new plaster, still breathing out its moisture.

A new door waited at the end of that plastered passage. Narrow. Bare. No trim. It looked unfinished, as though built in secret and forgotten mid-thought.

Her stomach turned. "No," she said, softly. "Not today."

But she went anyway.

The knob was cold—not old-cold, but hospital-cold. She turned it. The hinges moved soundlessly, as if greased by anticipation. Inside, the air was wrong. Thick, still, uncooperative. The room was not dark, yet she couldn't see its corners.

It looked, at first, like another bedroom. High ceiling, dusty wallpaper, four-poster bed. But the dust had gathered too precisely. The sheets bore the outline of a body—flattened, perfectly contoured. She felt certain if she brushed her hand across the surface, she'd feel the warmth of a person who had only just left.

At the foot of the bed stood a chair, turned outward, facing her.

And someone was sitting in it.

She didn't scream. The figure didn't move. The outline was human—woman-sized, shoulders forward, hands folded.

It took her a moment to realize the person wasn't *present*. They were *projected,* somehow. An image, dim and translucent, flickering like film slowed to the brink of stillness. The woman's face hung a few degrees out of focus, caught between frames.

"Elena?" she whispered.

The ghost did not reply. But its mouth twitched, once, as though rehearsing a word.

The air smelled faintly of rose water. She remembered that scent from somewhere else—the portrait gallery? The peonies that refused to die? She took a step closer, and the figure began to dissolve, breaking apart like smoke that had forgotten which way was up.

As it vanished, something clinked against the chair leg: a small brass tag, nailed into the wood. She crouched and read the engraving.

MARY KEENE, 1911.

The name pressed on her chest like a palm.

The surname. Keene. The same as Martha's.

Elena straightened. The room shuddered once, almost relieved to be seen.

Behind her, a second door had appeared—smaller, square, built into the far wall where the fireplace should have been.

Above it, carved into the lintel, were the words:

HALL OF ASHES.

Her mouth went dry. "No," she said again, but the house was listening and found the sound encouraging.

When she opened that door, the temperature dropped five degrees.

A narrow corridor stretched ahead, lit by a single line of sconces that flickered with an indifferent blue flame. The walls were too close, the ceiling too low, the air too dry. It smelled of wax and burnt hair and the powdery sweetness of decayed flowers.

She hesitated only a second before stepping through. The door behind her sealed with a sigh.

Each room she passed had no number, no name, only a window of glass inset into its door. Behind each pane, a scene—motionless but alive.

A man seated at a desk, pen frozen mid-word.

A child curled in bed, face peaceful, chest unmoving.

A woman at a mirror, brush paused halfway through her hair.

Each one was perfect. Each one was preserved at the instant of death.

Elena pressed her hand against the first glass pane. The surface was cold, but behind it—heat.

Life residue.

Her breath fogged the window, and for a moment, the figure inside blinked.

She jerked her hand away.

"No," she whispered, backing down the hall. "You're not—this isn't—"

The next door whispered as she passed it. She froze.

> "They all come back," it said, faintly, a voice stretched thin with age. "We all come back to where we stopped."

She leaned closer, pulse pounding. "Who said that?"

> "Doesn't matter," another voice answered from the next room. "We're the rooms now."

Her knees weakened. She stumbled backward into the opposite wall, shoulder brushing the plaster. It rippled under her skin—soft, like skin, like flesh.

She gagged and pushed away.

The whispering multiplied. Dozens of low murmurs rose and fell, weaving together into a language just beyond sense. Names. Years. Pleas.

The walls vibrated with it, the air thickening until sound felt solid.

The corridor turned abruptly, then widened into a long, vaulted hall.

Here the sconces burned red, not blue. The glass doors on either side opened into what looked like parlors or dining rooms, but each was paused mid-tragedy.

In one, a dinner party: six people seated, heads bowed as though in prayer, but the table beneath their hands was drenched in dried blood. Their eyes were open, glossy, watching the air. A chandelier hung above, its crystals blackened.

A card on the nearest plate read THE HARROW SUPPER, 1895.

In the next room, a servant stood half up a ladder, reaching toward a painting. The ladder's rung was cracked, one foot slipping just an inch. The moment before the fall.

A tag on the floor beneath: THOMAS, 1903.

Elena's heart pounded so hard it felt foreign. She stumbled from door to door, scanning names.

Each one accompanied by a plaque, a date, a cause.

VICTOR HARROW, 1937.

ELEANOR HARROW, 1892.

JONATHAN WRIGHT, 1949.

MARTHA KEENE, 1901.

She stopped at that last one. Inside the glass, the same image she'd seen replayed in the attic - Martha reaching for the beam, the plank giving way. Only now, frozen an inch before the fall.

Her mouth opened, closed, useless.

The tag glinted. Under the date, someone had carved—recently, the metal still raw—REMEMBER HER.

Elena pressed her forehead against the glass. The temperature burned cold through her skin.

"Martha," she whispered. "Who did this to you?"

The air fogged again. The figure in the glass moved a fraction. The head turned. The eyes opened—vacant, pale—and met hers.

Then the pane cracked.

A fine fissure ran from corner to corner, humming faintly. She stepped back, afraid to breathe too hard.

The other rooms shivered in sympathy. The air became static.

The whispers stopped.

For a heartbeat, absolute silence. Then, from somewhere deeper in the hall, a new sound—slow, deliberate footsteps.

Elena turned toward the noise. It came from the far end, beyond where the sconces stopped burning.

She squinted. The shadows there were thick, uneven. They moved with the rhythm of walking, but no figure emerged. Just the suggestion of presence, heavy as gravity.

"Who's there?" she called.

The footsteps paused.

Then a voice—not a whisper this time, not spectral, but *real*. A woman's voice, calm, steady, human.

"You shouldn't be here."

Elena's mouth went dry. "Who are you?"

"You already know," the voice said.

She did. It came from her own throat, just delayed. A perfect echo.

"You shouldn't be here," the voice repeated, quieter now, as though from behind her.

She spun around. The corridor behind her had changed. The doors were gone. The plaques, the glass, all replaced by smooth, unbroken walls. The exit—erased.

The house had closed the museum.

Her knees locked. The blue flame of the sconces flickered, then steadied again, casting her shadow across the sealed wall.

But it wasn't her shadow. It was taller, hair longer, posture softer.

"Eleanor," she whispered.

The silhouette turned its head. For a breath, the faintest outline of a face appeared where shadow shouldn't hold detail—a familiar cheekbone, her own eyes, but emptied of intention.

Then the shadow stepped forward.

Off the wall.

Into the hall.

The shadow stepped free from the wall like wet paint peeling itself away.

It had Elena's shape but none of her hesitation. Where she trembled, it glided. Where her breath snagged, it moved smoothly, perfectly, as if exhalation were choreography.

It smiled — a small, civilized smile. Then it turned and walked deeper into the corridor that shouldn't exist.

Elena followed because she could not.

The sconces brightened as they passed, the blue flames snapping red as though shifting allegiance. The walls here weren't plaster anymore; they'd become marble — pale, veined, and cool. Etched into their surface were faint outlines of doors that weren't open yet, like uncarved graves waiting for names.

The air grew heavier. With each step she took, the silence bent — the pressure of it tugging at her eardrums, as though sound were gathering its strength.

The first of the new rooms opened on its own.

A parlor, grand and golden, light pouring from an unseen source. At first, it seemed normal — furniture polished, piano gleaming, rugs unblemished. Then she saw them.

Three figures seated by the hearth.

A woman with a book in her lap.

A man staring into the fire.

A young girl drawing on the floor with a piece of charcoal.

Their movements were small but endless — an infinite loop of gesture. The girl's hand dragged the charcoal across paper, the line breaking at the same spot each time. The man blinked. The woman turned a page that had already been turned. Over and over.

The sound of the page, of charcoal on paper, of breathing, all synchronized — a metronome made of ghosts.

Elena stepped closer. The drawing in the child's hands took shape — an outline of the manor itself. But where the front door should have been, she'd drawn a dark oval, deep and layered.

A hole.

Or an eye.

The woman looked up. Her lips parted, moving without sound.

Elena read them. One word.

Help.

The paper in the girl's hands caught fire.

It burned without heat, curling in silence. The flames left no ash.

The figures froze mid-motion. Then they blinked out, the entire room dropping into gray like a faded photograph.

Elena staggered backward into the hall. Her own breath came fast, unsteady. "Why are you showing me this?" she asked.

The house answered with sound.

A door opened to her right, slamming against the wall with the finality of confession. The noise rolled down the corridor like thunder in a cave.

She turned. Another room. This one darker, longer — a dining hall with a table that seemed to stretch forever. The air shimmered faintly, the light rippling across it like heat above asphalt. She stepped inside.

The first thing she noticed was the smell — wine, old meat, dust.

The second was the stillness.

Twelve people sat around the table. Men and women in black attire, unmoving.

At the head of the table sat Victor Harrow.

He looked exactly as he had in his portrait — or how he must have once looked, before time had its way. The same proud shoulders, same eyes that missed nothing.

But his hands were wrong. The flesh was pale, the knuckles blue, and one of the fingers had cracked open like old wood.

Elena moved closer. "You're not real."

Victor turned his head. Slowly. Deliberately. The sound of his vertebrae moving was audible, like the grinding of stone.

"Neither are you," he said.

The words came out dry, splintered, a voice made of dust. The others at the table joined in, repeating his phrase in low, layered tones.

"Neither are you."

"Neither are you."

"Neither—"

"Stop!" she screamed, and the sound splintered the illusion. The faces blurred, features slipping like melted wax. The table collapsed inward, the plates shattering into a chorus of broken porcelain.

When the echo died, Victor was gone. The only thing left was a single wineglass standing upright amid the wreckage, filled with dark liquid. Not red wine. Something thicker.

Elena bent closer. The surface shimmered faintly, and for a moment, she saw herself reflected in it — not as she was, but as she'd been months ago, before Blackwood. Healthy. Hopeful.

That reflection lifted its glass and smiled.

"Drink," it whispered.

She backed away, shaking her head. "No."

"Drink," it said again.

"You're thirsty. You're lonely. Let it be easy."

Her fingers twitched. The glass seemed to hum, the same deep vibration she'd heard the night the house first whispered her name. The same frequency as her heartbeat.

She turned and ran.

The hallway spun as she moved, the sconces blurring into streaks of fire. She stopped only when the walls steadied again — though the floor beneath her feet felt wrong, too soft, like the top layer of something deeper shifting below.

The corridor ended in a door wider than any she'd seen.

It was carved from black wood, polished to a mirror sheen. Symbols marked its frame — runes, perhaps, or names written in a language that only remembered itself through repetition.

Above the door, an inscription burned faintly in the low light:

THE HOUSE IS ITS OWN GRAVE.

Elena touched the door. It didn't move, but her pulse jumped.

A voice spoke from behind it — soft, feminine, terribly familiar.

"Elena."

Her name, but not the house's version — not the mimicry that matched her tone. This was warmer, fuller, alive.

She leaned closer. "Who are you?"

"I'm what's left."

The surface of the door rippled, faintly breathing.

She could see something moving on the other side — pale shapes flickering through the grain, like people pressed beneath the surface.

"Come in," the voice said. "You've earned your place."

Elena's hand reached for the knob before her mind could stop it.

Her fingertips brushed the brass—and the surface went cold as ice. A shock shot through her arm, sharp enough to make her gasp.

The door shuddered once. Then it opened an inch.

The smell that escaped was impossible to describe—part candle wax, part rot, part something older. The air that followed was heavy, humid, human.

She pushed the door wider.

The room inside was vast—larger than the house could hold.

A ballroom, or something that had once been one. The ceiling was too high, the floor too polished, reflecting everything like a black lake. Candles burned in chandeliers above, each flame steady and silent.

And everywhere, figures.

They stood along the walls, dressed in every fashion from every era. Dozens of them. Hundreds. All perfectly still. Each face pale, serene. Each pair of eyes fixed on her.

As she stepped forward, they moved. Not much—just a tilt of the head, a shifting of the weight, like guests acknowledging a late arrival.

The voice spoke again, now from all around.

"They've been waiting."

Elena's knees weakened. "For me?"

"For someone who remembers them. It's all we ever wanted."

One of the figures detached from the wall—a woman in a dark gown with pearls around her throat. She moved like someone walking underwater, each gesture too slow, too deliberate.

"Elena Harrow," the woman said. "You brought the key."

Elena's fingers went to her collarbone instinctively, where the chain had once hung. The key wasn't there.

She'd left it upstairs—or thought she had.

The woman smiled. "It's never upstairs. It's always been here."

She gestured toward the center of the floor.

There, half-sunken in the mirrored surface, lay the brass key. It gleamed faintly, as though catching light from nowhere.

But the reflection beneath it showed something wrong. The key in the reflection wasn't brass. It was red.

"Take it," said the chorus of voices. "End the waiting."

Elena's body trembled. "What happens if I do?"

The woman tilted her head, smiling with pity. "You'll understand."

Her legs moved of their own accord. One step, then another. The floor mirrored her completely—her hair, her breath, her pulse in her throat.

When she reached the key, she crouched.

The surface rippled. She could see herself beneath it, the reflection staring back.

The other Elena smiled faintly and whispered through the mirrored glass.

"Come down. It's warmer here."

Elena's hand broke the surface.

The liquid wasn't water. It was thick, dense, pulling at her skin with a lover's insistence. She gripped the key and yanked it free.

The floor trembled.

Every figure in the ballroom inhaled.

The sound was terrible—not because it was loud, but because it was *simultaneous.* Hundreds of lungs remembering their purpose all at once.

The woman nearest Elena exhaled, a sigh of centuries leaving her lips.

"Thank you," she said, and her body began to crumble, the pearls scattering like teeth.

All around, the others followed—one by one, the still figures collapsing into dust that rose, swirling into the air. The room filled with gray, the kind of gray that makes all color meaningless.

And in that fog, the whisper returned—hundreds of voices, one voice, the house's voice:

"You've opened us."

Elena stumbled backward, clutching the key. "What did I do?"

"You remembered," the voice said. "Now we can remember too."

The fog moved against her, soft but relentless, wrapping her arms, her throat, her face.

For a moment she couldn't breathe. Then she realized she didn't need to—the air was breathing *her.*

She fell to her knees, the floor solid again, the ballroom empty.

Only one figure remained: Eleanor.

Her ancestor stood where the reflection had been, half-light, half-shadow, hair unbound and eyes luminous. She looked exactly as she did in the portrait—the one that sometimes smiled and sometimes didn't.

"Why are you doing this?" Elena rasped.

Eleanor's expression softened, almost kind.

"Because someone has to keep the rooms warm."

The brass key in Elena's palm pulsed once—like a heartbeat.

When she looked down, it had left a faint red imprint across her skin.

Eleanor's voice echoed, fading with the gray.

The ballroom emptied as if a tide had changed its mind.

Dust sank, gray on gray, until the floor remembered it was polished. The figures that had inhaled together were gone, not dispersed so much as shelved. The silence that followed was not an absence. It had weight, like a quilt pressed over a face.

Elena stood with the brass key in her fist and the red welt it had left across her palm. The mark pulsed once, a private signal. She closed her fingers tighter until the metal cooled.

"Enough," she told the room.

The room agreed by forgetting itself. The chandeliers blinked out. The black-lacquer floor rippled, glass finding wood, and then she stood in an ordinary corridor again, plaster walls, blue sconces humming their indifferent flame. The doors here had returned to their glass windows, their plaques small and obedient. The Hall of Ashes had decided to be museum again.

She put one hand to the nearest pane. Behind the glass, a parlor that had just tried to burn itself away sat composed, its girl drawing the manor with a hole where the door should be. The loop continued. The page turned, rustled, burned, returned. A sigh repeated the way a line repeats when you practice saying it without believing it.

Elena stepped back and almost collided with her reflection.

Not in glass. In air. Her silhouette leaned against the opposite wall like a twin who'd arrived early to rehearsal. The hair was wrong—too smooth. The posture remembered approval and wore it like a coat. It watched not her, but the rooms.

"What do you want?" Elena asked the shape.

It smiled without teeth and did not answer. When she moved left, it remained angled to the glass, like a person who has come to see an exhibit they've been told is important.

"Then watch," she said, and kept walking.

The corridor curved; the sconces went red again; the air thinned. Her maps would have eaten themselves here. She passed plaques without stopping—names she recognized now like relatives you only know from letters. Keene. Wright. Harrow. Harrow. Harrow. The repetition had the dull shine of heritage.

The portraits began at the turn. Not in frames—*in* the plaster, like frescos painted into the wall and sealed there while the lime was still wet. She recognized some of the faces: the dinner guests who hadn't eaten; the servant mid-step. Others were strangers, their eyes the right size and wrong temperature. But the last few—those made her stop.

Mae.

Rowan.

Mrs. Dunley.

Not exact likenesses—quick studies, a hand working fast to get it down before the sitter moved, but clear enough to flinch at.

They looked alive. They were alive. She'd spoken to them yesterday. And yet.

Under Rowan's portrait: BLACKWOOD PUBLIC ARCHIVES. No date.

Under Mae's: GULL & LANTERN. Someone had pressed a clean thumb into the wet plaster where a year ought to go, then lifted it away.

Elena's stomach went thin. "You don't get to practice on them," she said. "You don't get to put holds on the living."

The wall understood disagreement as flirtation; the frescos glossed, taking on a damp sheen, as if the paint had been woken. Mae's painted eyes slid a fraction toward Elena in a way that could have been trick light or could have been a plea.

"I'm not your keeper," Elena said. "I don't catalog for you."

She moved faster. The corridor narrowed into something that wasn't corridor anymore—a throat. The sconces leaned inward, their flames tilted, all pointing ahead, toward a final door.

It was not grand. It was *exact.* Oak darkened by decades of air and handling. A plain brass plate at eye level: V. HARROW. No dates. No euphemism. The House did not bother with *In Memory Of* here.

Elena touched the plate. It was warm. Her fingers left a clean oval on the tarnish.

The glass set into the door was small, smaller than the others, as if privacy belatedly mattered. She stood on her toes and looked through.

Victor sat at his desk in the study. The angle was wrong—the room seen from high, almost ceiling-corner, as if the house had taken up residence where a spider might. Victor's head was bowed. Papers lay on the blotter in his precise stacks. The coil-and-spring device perched on the wall across from him, its filament stilled between tremors. He was not dead yet in this image; that was the cruelty. He was nearly.

His right hand lay on a notebook, fingertips on a line as if reading aloud to an audience that preferred silent jokes. His left hand rested on the brass key. Her brass key. The chain looped across his palm like a small trap.

Elena cupped both hands around the glass. "What happened?" she said, and the breath smudged her view.

Victor moved, infinitesimal. His chest rose. His mouth shaped a sound she could not hear.

She pressed her ear to the wood. Nothing. The door had been constructed to be a wall.

"Fine," she said, to her own pulse as much as the House. "Show me."

The latch yielded without complaint. The room inside did not smell like death. It smelled like paper and polish and the heat you get from two lamps left on during a long argument. She stepped over the threshold and the scene resumed exactly where the Hall wanted it.

Victor lifted his head. His eyes found her—not really her; the space where the viewer would be when the room performed. He looked quickly away, embarrassed by need in the old man way. His lips moved. She read them as easily as if he'd spoken: it wants a verb.

Then he put the key to his chest, flat against his sternum, and closed his eyes as if to listen from the inside. A pressure entered the room, the way thunder squeezes air from a hilltop. The device on the wall sang a line of pure dark across its paper. Victor exhaled as if surrender were technique. The exhale didn't end.

His body arranged itself into stillness that wasn't rest.

Elena watched herself watching a death that had already happened. The House had picked the angle and the silence and the light. It had curated.

"Is this what you wanted?" she asked it. "A tidy ending."

The brass plate on the door warmed under her palm like a pulse. The Hall liked the display. It liked her inside its grammar. It brought the next room closer by a degree, the way a person leans.

Past Victor's door, the corridor altered its temperature the way a body alters its mind—slightly, but with future built into it. The sconces went steady. The floorboards lost their squeak. The walls stopped pretending they had paint. Ahead waited a single door, bare wood like a stage without scenery. No plate. No glass. No plaque.

A soft red came from around its edges. Not lacquer. Not a candle. The color of a light you see first with the parts of the eye that don't admit feeling.

Her reflection had followed her this far, content to watch and be watched. Now it stepped in front of her, as if to take the door's first look. It reached for the handle. Elena reached too—not to stop it, but to own the act.

Their hands passed through each other and met the brass together.

The knob was warm. Not flattering warm. Animal warm.

She turned it.

The red behind the door did not flare. It *throbbed.* A tide in color. The air it released smelled of iron and roses and something like scalp. The room inside was not a room. Not even a ballroom pretending to be a lake. It was a hallway that loved a vanishing point too much.

No floorboards. No carpet. A surface that looked like lacquer and moved like breath. The walls had not picked a texture—they were history in the viscosity state, events under lacquer, images trying to get out and deciding to wait until she came closer.

She did. One step. Two. The key in her palm heated until it admitted pain. Her reflection matched her. At the third step, the scene changed all at once and didn't look like a scene anymore.

She stood in a room that belonged to her future. The light carried tomorrow's dust. The chair bore the dent of her body. On the desk lay her sketchbook open to a page she had not drawn—yet loved for how accurate it was of how little she would sleep.

A voice spoke. Not above. Not around. *Through.* Her throat knew the muscles but not the choice.

"Elena Harrow, aged—" The sentence paused where a number would go. The room supplied nothing. "—found in the study at Blackwood Manor, seated, head at rest on the blotter. No sign of struggle. No scorch. No forced door. All the windows cracked an inch. The coil-and-spring device stilled. The key in her hand. Mouth parted as if to hum, and didn't."

Her mouth was open. She shut it by force.

"Stop," she said.

The narrative obeyed, but it took the temperature of the air with it, and the cold left behind made her teeth ache. She hadn't seen herself in the chair. She didn't need to. The description had already painted.

The room waited. It enjoyed being paused.

"Another ending," she said, to break its pleasure. "Try again."

It did. Cheerfully.

> "Elena Harrow, age unknown, found in the blue
> room, window open, hair moving in like water, body
> light enough to be mistaken for fabric. A bell has
> rung without a clapper. The room has closed its eyes.
> The house says 'keeper' and means *kept.*"

"Enough."

> "Elena Harrow—"

"Stop." The word carried a not-yet anger that made the lacquer air vein.

She took one step backward. The red dimmed in that corner. She took another; it brightened behind her. The room was a lung building a preference.

"Who gets to name it," she asked. "You? Me?"

> "Together," the house said, pleased to be invited to
> grammar.
> "Finish what you started."

The phrase found her bones too quickly. She remembered Victor's mouth shaping *verb*. She remembered Eleanor's *keep*. She remembered every time she had sat down to paint and avoided the first brushstroke because the first stroke decides the last.

"Not your sentence," she said. "Mine."

The door behind her loved being door. It swung, not shut, but nearer. The red around its edges receded, polite. The corridor presented itself again—frescos, plaques, the curated hush of the Hall. It wanted her to think she had chosen the retreat.

She stepped back through and put the door against its jamb. The latch caught with the exact soft click the house used for agreement.

"Good," she said aloud, to make the word in air and not just in mind. "Now listen better."

She walked past Victor's door without looking, past Mae's not-yet, past Rowan's unkind premonition. The reflection did not follow this time. It hung back, face turned toward the red seam like a moth that prides itself on restraint.

At the last turn, the Hall resisted letting her go. The floor tried to learn a new slope. The sconces dimmed, then re-glowed, training her eyes to the dark it preferred. The glass panes whispered one more time, names and dates, little museum labels spoken like bedtime: *1901. 1895. 1937.* She did not stop. She had learned the trick of not honoring repetition.

The door to the Hall of Ashes opened as if a docile room had never had another mood. She stepped through and the pressure let go. The corridor's ordinary paper pattern reappeared, ivy cheerful enough to be a lie. The first narrow bedroom—Mary Keene, 1911—had emptied. The impression on the bed had smoothed. The brass tag had warmed enough to fog slightly when she breathed on it.

"Rest," she said, knowing how condescending it sounded and letting it anyway.

She found the main hall and walked its center, not skirting walls like a child avoiding monsters. The chandelier behaved. The portraits—hers included—pretended to be paint. At the nursery, she looked at the cradle and did not step in. She hadn't earned anything from that room except the right to say no.

Back in the study, the coil-and-spring device waited with its cooperation coiled. She didn't touch it. The metronome lay on its side like a beetle. She didn't right it. She set the brass key down on the blotter and put both palms either side of it and let the skin cool.

"Here is the map," she said, to the desk, to the walls, to the thing that used her name in time with her blood. "Kitchen. Study. Nursery. Blue room. Hall of Ashes behind unfinished plaster. Victor's room. The future you tried to hand me like a fitted glove. Here is what you do not get to decide: the verb."

The study breathed once. The window made a small throat-clearing as the draft adjusted its manners. Far away, below, in the house's deeper places, a hinge signed its name in the book of this hour.

"Finish what you started," the house whispered from all its rooms at once, the phrase so even it almost could have been kind.

"When I start it," Elena said, and surprised herself with the steadiness of the line.

She reached for her sketchbook—not the page of mantels she'd burned, not the chandelier's instruction—but the last blank sheet, which had refused all morning to allow a line. She put pencil to paper and drew what she had avoided drawing: the plain door at the end of the red hallway, edges breathing, knob warm, no plaque. She drew it badly on purpose first, to offend the house's vanity. The page did not ash. The room did not moan. The device did not twitch. She drew it again, true this time, without ornament.

When she looked up, the study mirror returned her without lag. Her face looked like a person who had not slept and did not pretend otherwise.

"I'll finish," she told it, and meant the book and the house and the verb in the same breath. "But I pick the sentence."

On the landing, the portrait opposite the nursery had straightened itself again. The hairline crack across the varnish had not healed. It caught the light like a thin, honest scar.

Elena lifted the brass key from the blotter and hung it back around her neck. It took her heat and gave some back. When she stepped into the hall, the house said her name once in time with the metronome that wasn't ticking.

"Elena."

"Good," she said, and walked away from the Hall that had tried to narrate her. The door to that corridor stayed shut. It would wait. Doors can. It pulsed once, faint red finding forever work on the seam. She did not turn.

From behind it, barely audible, the sentence the house most hoped would be true followed like breath through a keyhole.

"Finish what you started."

She let it trail her the way fog trails a field and vanish when the air decided it had another job.

"And the house loves a keeper who remembers."

CHAPTER 12

Victor's Secret

Morning came late, dragging its gray weight through the windows.Elena woke up on the study couch, though she didn't remember lying down. Her limbs ached with the peculiar fatigue of having argued with a house all night. The embers in the fireplace were still faintly alive, breathing in shallow glows. The air smelled of iron and lavender, that strange perfume that had begun to follow her everywhere, like the memory of a touch that wouldn't fade.

The brass key lay on her chest. She hadn't put it there.

It was warmer than her skin, its edges pulsing faintly as if testing her heartbeat for rhythm. She sat up and it clinked softly against the button of her shirt, then rolled into her palm. The red imprint from the night before was gone. But the ghost of pressure remained, like the afterimage of a grip.

The study looked different in daylight—or what passed for daylight here. Dust motes suspended themselves midair like insects caught between seconds. Victor's books lined the walls, their spines a hundred shades of brown and black, titles pressed in gold that refused to dull with time. He'd organized them by subject, she realized—philosophy, mechanics, theology—and then, near the far wall, a section labeled simply Experiments.

She stood and stretched. Every joint sounded like it was confessing something.

The desk waited in the center of the room, patient as a predator. The papers on it had rearranged themselves overnight. The ledger she'd left atop them had slid an inch to the left, a deliberate distance—as if the house wanted her to notice. When she touched the cover, the surface tingled under her fingertips. The waxed cloth binding was cool, but faintly alive. It flexed when she pressed.

She opened it.

The handwriting was Victor's—his tight, slanted scrawl, each line of ink a signature of control. The pages were numbered, but unevenly. Some numbers repeated, others were skipped. Between sections, she saw faint watermarks: circles intersecting triangles, like sketches of a mechanism.

The title page read simply:

The Cycle of Memory — Prototype Notes

Victor Harrow, 1964–Present.

"Present," she whispered, tracing the word. "You didn't end it."

The first entry was scientific, almost clinical.

Memory is energy. What is remembered resists entropy.

The body fails, but recollection persists.

The key is containment.

Below, he had drawn a cross-section of the manor—pipes, wires, and what looked like veins running beneath the floorboards. The annotations were too precise for metaphor. He'd built something into the bones of the house.

Elena flipped forward. Halfway down the next page, the tone changed. The handwriting grew erratic, the lines wandering as if written under duress.

It responds to the name Harrow. Perhaps it always has.

The more I map it, the more it maps me.

The mirrors are working. The subjects speak their last thoughts clearly, though I have yet to stabilize duration.

Elena's breath caught. *Subjects?*

She turned another page.

M.L. is correct—the circuit requires inheritance.

The voice must pass through blood, not wire.

A new medium is required.

At the bottom of the page, he'd written a single phrase in capital letters:

"THE HOUSE REMEMBERS."

She closed the ledger slowly. Her hands were shaking. The word *inheritance* had begun to feel less like legal terminology and more like diagnosis.

Her phone, on the corner of the desk, was still dead. She hadn't seen a working outlet in days, though the lights burned obediently. She laughed, softly, dryly. "Of course you power yourself."

The brass key glinted. Something about its shape had changed—no longer symmetrical. Its teeth had warped, subtly, as though adapting to a new lock. She held it up to the light. The pattern looked deliberate, almost ornamental. Leaves, she thought at first. No—letters. Microscopic, repeating, too fine to read.

"Fine," she said to it. "Show me, then."

The house took her at her word.

A soft metallic *click* came from the desk. She started. The right-hand drawer slid open by itself—just a few inches, just enough to invite. Inside lay a stack of yellowing envelopes bound with twine. The paper was brittle but clean. Someone had sealed them with red wax, stamped with the lion's head crest from the door knocker.

Elena sat. Her pulse drummed behind her ears.

She untied the twine and spread the letters across the desk. There were maybe a dozen, each addressed in the same hand:

> To M.L.,
>
> *Blackwood Manor, Unsent.*

Unsent.

She chose the top one and broke the seal.

November 7, 1978

My dear M.L.,

The circuits hum louder each night. The mirrors grow impatient. I have begun hearing the walls finish my sentences before I speak them. You were right about the architecture—it shapes itself to memory. I walk a hall once, and it becomes part of me; I dream of it, and it reappears changed, improved, as though the house prefers my imagination to its own design.

I am close to proving the hypothesis: that memory, when housed properly, becomes self-sustaining. But it requires a stabilizer—a consciousness willing to remain awake while asleep.

The Harrow line holds the resonance. I can feel it in the blood. But you know the cost better than I.

Yours in pursuit of continuity,

V

Elena stared at the page until the ink swam. M.L. Who were they? A partner? A scientist? A priest? The tone hovered uneasily between all three.

She opened another.

March 12, 1981

> M.L.,
>
> The first prototype succeeded, though only briefly. The subject's recollections remained audible for three minutes after cessation of breath. Enough to confirm the theory: the house retains.
>
> However, it now hums even when unoccupied. It has learned to speak *back*.
>
> The voice is not human. It is shaped from every word ever spoken within these walls. It calls itself "We."
>
> I am building a failsafe. If I do not finish, burn the ledger.

—V.

She read the last two lines three times. Her fingers tightened on the page until it crinkled.

"If I do not finish…" she whispered. "You didn't finish, did you?"

Her reflection in the glass of the desk shifted slightly—head tilting a beat too late.

She turned quickly. Nothing behind her but shelves and books and the slow tick of the grandfather clock. Yet the sense of presence had deepened, the house listening more intently now, like a student whose teacher had finally asked the right question.

There was one more envelope. The last. The seal had melted and fused to the paper, as though someone had tried to destroy it but the wax had refused to die.

She pried it open carefully. The handwriting was frantic, slanted uphill.

Undated.

M.L.—

I have failed. The experiment will not sleep. It consumes recollection faster than the body can provide. The mirrors no longer reflect me; they show only what they choose.

The house demands inheritance. It refuses an ending.

I have rewritten the will to ensure the passage. She will come. She must.

Tell her nothing.

If there is mercy left in the design, let her paint. Let her remember something other than this.

V.

Elena read it again. "She will come."

He'd known she would inherit. He'd arranged it. The will, the seven-day clause, the way the house had waited—it was all scripted.

Her chest constricted, the air thick and hot. "You did this to me."

The ledger on the desk pulsed faintly. When she looked down, the ink on its open page had begun to move—not running, exactly, but shifting. The letters slid into new positions, rewriting themselves. She watched the words *The House Remembers* rearrange into *The House Remembers You.*

"Stop it," she said. Her voice came out hoarse. "You're not him."

The room disagreed. The desk lamp flickered once, twice, then burned brighter. In its glow, she saw something else on the inside of the ledger's back cover—a faint rectangular outline. A hidden compartment.

She turned the key in her hand. Its teeth caught the edge of the outline perfectly, as though that had always been its true purpose. The compartment clicked open with a sound like an exhale.

Inside lay a single folded paper and a tiny silver ring. The ring bore the same sigil carved into the key's bow—half leaf, half flame.

The paper was thin, almost translucent with age. She unfolded it slowly. In her grandfather's hand:

> *To my successor—*

> *You will think this a curse. Perhaps it is. But understand: to remember is to resist the dark. The*

house hungers because we fed it. The walls hold

what the grave cannot. I built the circuit to preserve,

not to punish. If you destroy it, we all vanish.

If you join it, we endure.

There is no third choice.

The ring clattered to the floor. It didn't bounce. It landed upright, rolling in a slow circle, the way a coin does when time itself is hesitant to decide which side it prefers.

Elena pressed both hands to her temples. "There's always a third choice."

But the room was alive again, vibrating faintly, the books rattling in their shelves. A low hum crawled up through the floorboards—a frequency she could feel in her teeth. The clock began to tick faster, matching her pulse. The air thickened with static, the metallic scent of ozone intensifying until her tongue tasted sparks.

The ledger snapped shut on its own.

The hum stopped.

Silence folded back over the room, clean and abrupt, like the moment after a storm when the air forgets to move.

Elena stared at the desk. The key lay motionless. The ring, still upright, had rolled itself toward the fireplace and stopped there—facing her like an eye.

She whispered, "What did you do, Victor?"

The answer came not from the walls this time, but from somewhere under the floor. A slow, deliberate tapping, metallic and measured. It was the same sound she'd heard in her first night here—the sound that had led her to the vent, to the first key.

Now it was louder. Closer.

She knelt, pressing her ear to the rug. The tapping vibrated through the wood, a Morse rhythm she didn't know but somehow understood.

Not a warning. A beckoning.

Downstairs. Beneath everything.

The tapping became a pulse.

Not sound, but *direction.* Every beat seemed to say *down, down, down.*

Elena stood slowly, eyes fixed on the floorboards. The rug at her feet looked slightly raised along one edge, like fabric hiding a scar. She kicked it aside. Dust leapt into the air, dancing in the light. Beneath, the boards were uneven, their grain curling around a perfect square — a hatch.

"Of course," she murmured. "You left the truth under the furniture."

The brass key hung warm against her chest. When she lifted it, it vibrated faintly, like something pleased to be noticed. She crouched and ran her fingers along the seam. The metal latch was old but clean, its screws unslotted by time. It didn't take force to lift it — it took permission.

The latch clicked open at her touch.

The hatch rose a fraction on its own.

A breath of cold air came up, thick with the scent of oil and something faintly metallic, like old blood. Stairs led downward into the dark, narrow and steep, lit only by the thin gray ribbon of daylight from above.

Elena hesitated. "You really built a basement of secrets under your own ghosts."

She lowered herself onto the first step.

The sound changed as she descended — air denser, walls closer. The smell of metal grew sharper. Her foot hit packed earth after ten steps. When she raised her phone, the flashlight barely reached the far wall, swallowed by shadows that seemed to shift before she moved.

Something mechanical hummed below the audible range, a low, patient vibration she could feel through her shoes. The air tasted of static.

She switched on an old lamp near the base of the stairs. To her surprise, it came alive instantly, flooding the space in a weak golden glow. The wires still worked. The house had kept them alive.

The room before her was part laboratory, part mausoleum.

Glass tubes lined the walls like ribs. Coils of copper and silver looped into what might have been circuitry or ritual. Several mirrors leaned against the brick, their surfaces shrouded by soot-stained veils. The veils moved slightly, though there was no draft.

In the center stood a worktable — its surface littered with notes, burnt matches, and a metal frame that resembled a coffin crossed with a telescope. At its head, a brass plate inscribed with words worn nearly smooth:

Cycle of Memory — Prototype III

Elena's mouth went dry. "He actually did it."

She took a tentative step forward. The earth floor squelched faintly beneath her boots, damp from condensation. She brushed a mirror's veil aside and caught her reflection — her own eyes, distorted, doubled, flickering like an image failing to resolve.

She froze.

Behind her reflection stood another figure — a man, faint and colorless, his expression grim and resigned. He looked at her with weary familiarity.

Her grandfather.

Elena spun around. The room was empty.

The reflection lingered a moment longer, then dimmed like a candle starved of air.

She turned back to the table. Her hands trembled as she examined the clutter of tools and journals. Most of the pages were too faded to read, water-damaged by years of seepage, but a few remained legible — sketches of human silhouettes with copper wires running from the chest into wall conduits, diagrams of "neural frequency preservation," annotations in Victor's hand reading:

> *Containment through resonance.*

> *Consciousness as circuit.*

> *Architectural echo.*

Elena flipped to the last page.

One line stood alone, written so hard the nib had nearly torn the paper.

> The house no longer needs me.

She set the notebook down, forcing herself to breathe evenly. The key around her neck was pulsing again, each throb in perfect rhythm with the low hum vibrating through the ground. The workshop was awake.

At the far end of the room, she saw another door — small, circular, built of cast iron. A wheel-lock sealed it, engraved with the same sigil as the key. She crossed to it, passing beneath hanging wires that crackled faintly with static.

The door's handle resisted her touch, metal slick with condensation. When she pressed the brass key into the shallow indentation at its center, it slid in like water finding its path.

The lock rotated with a hiss.

The hum deepened.

The door opened onto another chamber — narrower, darker, but glowing faintly blue from within. Rows of glass cylinders filled the walls, each filled with viscous fluid and faint motes of light that drifted like captured stars. The sight was beautiful, almost hypnotic, until she realized what floated inside them.

Faces.

Some were half-formed, others whole — human visages suspended mid-expression, their mouths slightly open as if whispering. The fluid shimmered, reflecting faint ripples of light that looked too much like breath.

Elena staggered backward, one hand over her mouth. "No…"

Each cylinder bore a label, handwritten in Victor's sharp script.

Rowan Keene.

Mary Keene.

Mae Dunley.

And at the end of the line: Eleanor Harrow.

Her pulse climbed toward panic. The faces were still, but their eyes shimmered faintly beneath the surface, as though catching reflections from inside.

She moved closer to Eleanor's cylinder. The face was unmistakable — the same woman from the portrait, the same one she'd seen in dreams. Her ancestor, identical to her in every feature.

The tag below the glass read:

Subject 01 — Memory Stable — Conscious Retention at 73%.

Elena whispered, "You preserved them."

The hum answered — louder now, shifting from vibration into something that almost formed syllables. The glass nearest her quivered, ripples spreading through the liquid like someone exhaling beneath it. Eleanor's eyes opened.

Elena stumbled back, colliding with the opposite cylinder. The sound that escaped the glass wasn't a voice, not at first — it was pressure released, like steam escaping a vent. Then came words, soft but layered, as though multiple mouths were speaking in unison.

"He promised... we'd remember..."

The sound rose from several cylinders at once, each voice overlapping.

"He said it would only hurt once..."

"It's so loud here..."

"Elena..."

She clamped her hands over her ears, tears springing unbidden. "Stop! Please stop!"

The blue light flickered violently, and for a heartbeat she thought the faces were dissolving — but they weren't. They were changing. Every one of them began to shift toward her likeness.

Every face becoming her face.

"No—no, you're not me!"

"We are what the house remembers," the chorus whispered. "You are what it wants to keep."

A glass tube cracked with a sharp *ping,* spilling a thin stream of luminescent fluid across the floor. The hum spiked to a shriek. Sparks flashed along the ceiling conduits.

The key burned against her chest.

She tore it free, flinging it away. It hit the floor and skittered across the dirt, striking the leg of the central table. The hum dropped instantly to a near-silence — a held breath.

Then, from the shadows behind the glass, a voice—calmer, older, terribly familiar.

"You shouldn't have come down here."

Elena turned. Her grandfather stood in the doorway, or something that had decided to *use* his shape. The outline flickered, faint blue around the edges, like a projection fighting interference. His face was worn, his suit immaculate, his expression that same tired patience he'd worn in his portraits.

Her throat constricted. "You're dead."

"Yes," he said gently. "That was the point."

He stepped closer, though his feet didn't disturb the dirt. The air around him bent slightly, heat shimmering in the cold.

"You weren't supposed to see this. Not yet."

"Then maybe you shouldn't have left your cursed diary on the desk."

He smiled faintly — proud, even. "You always were curious."

"What did you do to them?" she demanded, pointing to the rows of faces. "What are they?"

"Preservation," he said. "Remembrance. The world forgets its dead, Elena. I refused to let it forget ours."

"They're trapped!"

"They're *alive* in a way that matters." His voice softened, persuasive. "They think. They dream. They remember what we cannot bear to lose. Every Harrow becomes part of the architecture — a living archive. You could walk through this house forever and never lose anyone again."

"Then why are they screaming?"

Victor's face twitched. The shimmer around his outline distorted. "Not screaming. Remembering too loudly."

"They called my name."

"Because you're part of the design," he said. "The key was only a conduit. The inheritance requires choice. I built the house to continue. But it needed a keeper — someone young, someone with imagination. You were always meant to be the final link."

"I won't be part of your machine."

"You already are."

The hum returned, wrapping around his words, deep and resonant. The faces in the cylinders pressed closer to the glass, their expressions pleading, mouths open in silent repetition.

Elena felt something at the base of her skull — a low vibration, invasive, like her bones humming to a tune she hadn't learned. Her vision blurred. For a moment, the room doubled: two worlds overlapping — the living workshop and its reflection. In the mirrored version, Victor's hand reached toward her, but there was no glass between them.

She stumbled backward, blinking hard. The world snapped back into one. "You're not real."

"Neither are they. Neither are you. Not yet."

The hum climbed another pitch. The light turned red.

Elena lunged for the brass key, fingers closing around it as it burned her skin. Sparks arced between the cylinders, glass shivering. The fluid inside began to boil.

"Stop," Victor said, his voice now vibrating through every surface. "You'll collapse the entire cycle!"

"Good," she hissed, and yanked the main power lever beside the door.

The room screamed.

Every tube shattered at once, shards flying outward in a glittering storm. Blue light flooded the space, blinding and cold. The fluid evaporated in seconds, leaving only the echoes — faint, whispering voices rising like steam.

"Elena…"

"Remember us…"

"Finish what he started…"

Victor's form convulsed, collapsing into light. For a moment his voice broke through the cacophony, raw and human.

"You don't understand—without memory, there's nothing left!"

"Then maybe forgetting's the mercy you never gave them."

She slammed the lever again.

The hum cut off like a throat severed mid-sentence.

Darkness fell. True, unbreathing darkness.

Elena staggered to the stairs, coughing on the dust that rose from the ruined cylinders. Her hands stung, blood and glass glittering across her palms. The key hung dead around her neck — no pulse, no warmth. She climbed until the air tasted of rain again.

At the top of the hatch, she turned for one last look.

The blue light had vanished, replaced by faint, glowing runes crawling along the walls, rearranging themselves.

The house wasn't dead. It was rewriting.

And faintly, from somewhere deep below, she heard her grandfather's voice — no longer human, no longer singular.

"If you destroy memory, you destroy *self.*"

She whispered into the dark, "Then maybe that's the only way to live."

And the hatch closed, the sound of its lock clicking shut from *below.*

The lock clicked from below with the certainty of a sentence ending.

Elena stayed kneeling at the hatch a breath longer, palms flat on the board as if heat might travel through and tell her whether she'd killed anything worth burying. The wood was cool, almost innocent. Upstairs, the house breathed like a person pretending to sleep.

"Good," she said to nobody, to herself, to the splinter in her thumb. "Good."

When she stood, her legs trembled. The study had not changed—desk, books, mirror—yet everything wore the thin, crisp edge of a room that's heard a fight through the floor. The coil-and-needle device on the wall sat quiet, a small, metal animal that had learned not to beg.

Her hands were a mess—tiny glitters of glass along the lifelines, drying blood stippling her wrists. In the bathroom she ran cold water until it went pink. Each sting felt like a fact she could trust. She raised her head to the mirror and waited for the lag that had become ritual. It didn't come. Her reflection moved when she moved. Her mouth opened only because she opened it.

"Hi," she told herself. "You're still here."

Behind the mirror something whispered, a dry run of the word *keeper.* She shut the tap and the word dried with it.

Back in the study, the ledger lay where it had snapped shut, patient as a closed door. The brass key, darkened by heat, cooled against her skin again, heavier than it should be, as if holding a little gravity of its own. She set it on the blotter and picked up the tiny silver ring that had rolled to the hearth earlier. It was simple; it would have been pretty in any life that wasn't this one.

"You can go," she told the ring, and placed it in the desk drawer, shut it gently, the small mercy of not throwing.

From somewhere deep in the plaster, a vibration began—low, intermittent, not the constant hum she'd grown to hate. A pulse. It came, paused, came again, like a radio tuning between stations.

"Elena," the house said.

Just her name. Not layered. Not coaxing. Rough at the edges, like something speaking through a mouthful of ash.

"No." She said it calmly, surprised by her own voice. "Use the walls if you must. Don't use me."

The pulse wavered as if startled, then returned steadier, louder, traveling through the baseboards, up the bannister, across the chandelier's armature. She could trace it by touch the way a plumber finds a pipe with the heel of his hand.

She followed it out of the study and down the main hall. The pictures looked down with their typical manners, their varnish pretending to be sleep. At the new/old branch—the plaster corridor she'd found that morning—the air turned charged again. She stopped there and put her palm flat to the wall.

"Not museum," she warned, "not today."

The wall agreed, letting the faint red seam she'd seen in the Hall of Ashes retreat a fraction. The pulse continued on, past the blue room, down the servants' stair, toward the cellar that had been closed for a century and two hours.

In the kitchen she paused at the table—someone had set out two cups. Not delicate; old diner-thick. Steam curled from both. The darker humor felt almost like kindness.

"You shouldn't have," she said, and drank from the left-hand cup because refusal is a kind of invitation too. It was coffee. It was good. The second cup steamed in place, patient, a chair pulled out just enough. She didn't sit. She let it cool.

The back stair was narrow, its treads worn. Halfway down, the radio-scraped voice threaded itself into the wood; the handrail buzzed faintly against her palm.

"You broke the mirror," her grandfather said.

Not anger. Tired. She imagined light refracting through ruin. "Many of them."

"I told you to burn the ledger if I failed."

"You wrote that to M.L. You never mailed it."

Silence, and in it she felt his old habit of sighing turned into architecture—the way the stair seemed to settle a degree lower on the right as though of long practice. Near the bottom landing, the bulb above her flickered once and held. The door to the main cellar—the sane one, with coal ghosts and old lemon oil—stood ajar.

Inside, the temperature dropped two polite degrees. A thin sheen of moisture lay on the stone walls like breath. Barrels slept, split and empty; ropes remembered tension. The tapping began again—metal on metal—coming from the far wall where stone met earth.

She found it by sound: a panel that didn't quite belong, a rectangle of brick with newer mortar. In its center, the faint outline of a grille long plastered over. She pressed her ear to the brick. The tapping obliged. — · — · —, roughly, nonsense that was rhythm first and code second.

"Do you want me to—what, apologize? Admire?"

No answer. The brick was warm against her cheekbone. Not living warm. Remembering warm.

She stepped back, braced her hands on the cold line of mortar, and pulled. The panel did what things like that always do for the person they were designed for: it yielded half an inch, then another, and came free cleanly, like a tooth letting go at last. Behind it, iron. The shape of a speaking tube, the old kind that carries voice through wall to wall.

"Of course," she said softly. "You've been using the house's throat."

She bent, put her mouth to the flared opening. "If you've something to say, say it the way a person does."

The response rolled up the tube, thinner for the journey, full of distance and dust. Victor, but not. His consonants sat where he'd always put them; the breath between words wasn't his to spend anymore.

"You collapsed my array."

"You improvised it out of people."

"I preserved them."

"You archived them," she said, and finally let the temper through. "You shelved them behind glass. You taught the house to catalogue grief and you called it mercy."

"You're mistaking the method for the aim," he said, and it was so like him—the professorial shrug you can hear—that she had to put a hand on the wall to keep from striking something that would only call its damage part of the exhibit. "Elena. I wanted to give the family what the world refused us. Continuity. We were always being erased. By time. By habit. By weakness."

"You rewrote your will so the house could make a keeper out of a child."

"I gave you a key so you'd have a choice."

She laughed. It echoed badly. "When you say choice you mean ritual."

The tube hummed; the manor joined its breath to his. For a moment her own name came riding back thin and long. *Elena.* She tipped the tube with the heel of her hand till the sound roughened and stopped.

"Try again," she said. "And this time you can tell me who M.L. is."

Silence that wasn't. The low machinery of the house turned phrases over behind the walls, tasting them. The answer when it came felt like something smuggled past a guard.

"Miriam Ledger."

Elena blinked. "Ledger—as in the book."

"As in the person," he snapped, sudden and precise. That was Victor, not the house. "As in the woman who taught me to listen to rooms and whose mother led me through this house in the dark when I was a boy. As in the only scientist I have ever met who knew that the word *soul* and the word *signal* are cousins."

"Miriam Ledger," Elena repeated. The name moved around her mouth like it wanted to be an anchor and a weapon at once. "Is she—?"

> "Dead?" The tube made a small, unkind sound— laughter in its afterlife costume. "She is in the house the way I am in it. Less cooperative. More critical. If you listen differently, you will hear her."

A second voice joined, soft enough she might have mistaken it for draft if the syllables hadn't been sure. A woman. Not young. Not formal.

> "I told him the feedback loop would eat him," the voice said. "Men love machines that say their names back."

"Miriam," Elena said, and the name felt truthful immediately. "He made you into this."

> "He failed to save me from becoming what I was becoming," Miriam corrected. "I was going to die. He wanted me to die interestingly."

Victor's hiss came hollow through the tube. "We had a chance to build a memory that did not decay."

"And you built something that eats pronouns," Miriam said dryly. "Elena, child, if you broke the mirrors, good. But you did not break the habit. This house is a habit."

"I know," Elena said, and she did, with the same certainty a person has about the shape of their own hands. "I did what I could do, now."

The tube throbbed. The house moved its weight on the joists. Above them, in the kitchen, a cup creaked gently as steam gave up.

"It will come back different," Miriam said. "You've changed the equation. Victor's array recorded; it did not interpret. It learned to echo. You've introduced loss. Loss teaches."

Victor again, hard, fast, the way men try to say a thing before a woman says the better version. "Loss unspools the thread. Without record there is only oblivion."

"Maybe oblivion is a kind of clean," Elena said.

The tube went quiet for a long breath, long enough for the house's other sounds to fidget: a far hinge, a mouse learning a baseboard, the damp in the stone waking to a new draft.

When Victor spoke, the pride had stepped aside for something that might have been fear if he had ever let himself call things by soft names. "If you kill the memory, Elena, I die."

"You're already dead," she said gently, and surprised herself by meaning the gentleness. "What you're asking is that I die too so you don't feel alone."

Something in the tube—a valve, a web—gave a small, precise click. When he spoke again, he had found a register he'd never used with her when he was alive. No lecture. No shape of a lesson. "I wanted to be a good ancestor."

In the silence that followed, the house inhaled a little. Elena leaned her forehead against the cold rim of the tube and shut her eyes. "So be one," she said. "Tell me where the real kill switch is."

The stone wall held its breath. Miriam laughed, the sound of a match struck and blown out. "There isn't one. He made a labyrinth and forgot to include a thread."

"There is a weak link," Victor said grudgingly. "The mirror circuit had a control—the red door. When it is open the house is awake. When it is closed the house must rely on what it truly knows, not what it can borrow. That was the point. A safety."

Elena opened her eyes. The air in front of her looked the same. It *felt* like choice. "So I close the red door."

"You must persuade it to close," Miriam said. "It doesn't swing on hinges. It swings on sentences."

"My favorite," Elena said, smiling without comfort. "Grammar as locksmithing."

Victor, weary: "It listens to you. It called you home."

"It called me Eleanor," she said, and the old anger came back bright and clean. "It has learned my name since."

She left the cellar door open for the draft, climbed the stair slowly so the house could practice not tripping her, and let the pulse through the bannister guide her toward the upstairs hall. At the landing the chandelier was still. The portrait opposite the nursery wore its thin, honest crack like a truce line.

"Different rules," she told the corridor, and walked it like a person in their own house. At the corner, the mirrors did not blush red. They waited.

She stopped before the place where the hall had once rippled open to reveal the impossible wing. The wall there looked ordinary as a cupboard. She knocked.

"Say it," she told it. "Say what you most want."

The answer came from everywhere and not, her voice braided with others until it was rope. "Stay."

"That's a noun pretending to be imperative," she said. "Try again."

A pause; a calculation; a shift. "Keep."

"Verb," she said, approving as if to a student. "Now tell me the sentence where you promise something you cannot know."

The wall warmed as if embarrassed. The red rose very faintly, as blush not warning.

"The house loves a keeper who remembers."

She breathed out through her nose, the smallest of laughs. "Tired line," she said, and set her hand flat to the paint. "Here is my sentence. Listen to its grammar."

She spoke slowly, not as an incantation but as if dictating a letter to a lawyer. "I will remember the living. I will bury the dead. I will not be a translator for a room that does not learn. I will stand in your doorways and name the nouns true, and I will choose my own verbs. *Close.*"

The last word she pushed down into the seam, into the idea of hinges. The temperature flicked from fever to cool. The red lowered a degree, deepening then fading until it was only paint again.

Far off, beneath everything, something turned. Not a lock. Not a key. The sound a big animal makes when it chooses to lie down.

The portraits lightened. The metronome in the study— unwound, on its side—ticked once, involuntarily, like a heart that has decided not to stop.

"Thank you," she told the corridor, and meant it with the exact proportion of grace she could afford.

In the nursery, the cradle did not move. The indent on the pillow had gone; the lavender scent had retreated to mere fabric. On the wall, the scratched warning still read IT REMEMBERS WHO YOU WERE, and beneath it, faint but legible, the reply the house had given her days ago remained: LISTEN

DIFFERENTLY. She touched that second line and added, with a fingernail, small enough to be a secret: SPEAK CLEARLY.

She went back to the study because that was where she had always gone to think. The ledger had not crept an inch. She opened it. The words stayed where Victor had put them. At the back, in the pocket she'd opened with the key, another folded paper waited, brittle as old air. She hadn't noticed it. She unfolded it carefully.

It was not a letter. It was a diagram. The house, stark. The red door, marked not in the wing she had walked, but in a place that made her stomach lurch—in the front hall, behind the ordinary coat closet, a rectangle nobody looked at because they used it.

Beneath, in Miriam's steadier hand: When closed, it sleeps in rooms. When open, it dreams in people.

Elena shut her eyes, saw the front closet clearly—coats she hadn't worn yet because she hadn't admitted this was home, the umbrella she didn't need. She laughed once, short and sharp. "Of course you hid the apocalypse behind the rain."

The house did not deny it.

She took the key because symbols still do some work even when you've proved they shouldn't. In the foyer the light behaved. She opened the closet. The familiar smell of wool rose, honest, human, easily forgiven. Behind the coats, the paneling looked like paneling. She pressed her palm to it anyway.

Warm.

She laid the key against the seam and did not turn. "I'm not here to open you," she said. "I'm here to talk."

The warmth increased the way a person leans in when they think you might be about to praise them. She spoke as if to a bright child who loves wrong answers more than right ones.

"I will not be your keeper," she said. "I will not be your key. I will not be your good door. But I will be your witness if you will be mine. Close, now. Sleep in rooms. Dream small. Let the living breathe. Let the dead be buried. *Close.*"

She felt it then, not in her hand, not in the wood, but along her forearms and across the bridge of her nose—the sudden relief of pressure easing. The red she could not see receded. The house sighed the way a singer sighs when the note lands where it should. Somewhere behind the panel, something soft-latched.

Behind her, on the console table under the mirror, one of Mae's postcards that she had never seen before lay face down. She turned it over. Come down anytime, love — M. The postmark had no date. The stamp had no country. She put it back where she found it. A contract needed a token.

On the stair, her phone vibrated once—the phantom of a notification without signal. The screen woke to the right date. The time was plausible. She didn't cheer. She did not, no matter how much she wanted to, try to call out.

In the kitchen the second cup of coffee had stopped steaming. She sat. The chair across from her slid in a fraction, respectful. She drank. It was cold. She drank it anyway.

From the cellar, through the tube, her grandfather spoke one last time—a voice already thinning into architecture.

"If I fade," he said, "will you remember me?"

She could have answered a dozen ways. She chose the one that felt like a new verb on an old tongue.

"I'll remember *well*," she said. "Not long."

The tube held quiet. The house accepted that sentence with a small shiver of crystal somewhere in the hall. In the blue room, the window she'd left cracked admitted a square of outside; the air changed its mind and came in. Elena looked at the brass key on the table, at her hands, at the open ledger, at the door the house had learned to keep closed. None of it looked finished. That was the comfort. That was the threat.

"Alright," she said into the morning that had finally committed to being morning. "Back to work."

Above her, the chandelier didn't chime. The mirrors did not blush. The house said her name once, not to claim it, but to practice saying it without hunger.

"Elena."

She answered the way you answer a room you've decided not to be afraid of and not to underestimate.

"Present."

CHAPTER 13

The House Speaks

The quiet should have been a relief. It wasn't. Elena woke to a stillness so complete it pressed against her skin like weight. For the first time since she'd arrived, the house wasn't humming, whispering, or sighing through its bones. The absence of sound was not peace; it was the kind of silence that has already chosen a side.

Light cut across the study in pale bars, dust suspended midair as if waiting for instructions. Every clock had stopped. The one on the mantel showed 7:16; the one above the stair read 7:15; the grandfather clock near the parlor ticked backward, slow and deliberate, as though rehearsing its undoing.

Elena sat up on the couch and rubbed her eyes. "All right," she said softly. "You win the award for creepiest dawn."

Her voice sounded wrong in the air — too loud, too singular. It didn't belong to the room anymore.

The brass key lay on the desk where she'd left it. It hadn't pulsed or whispered or warmed. It looked like a relic now, nothing more than metal. She reached for it anyway, needing its weight to convince herself of proportion.

Cold. Heavy. Still.

"Good."

Her reflection in the study mirror nodded a fraction late, and she told herself she imagined it.

She needed movement, coffee, anything that felt like human pattern. The kitchen met her halfway — sunlight bent through the windows, the air carrying the faint scent of yesterday's brew. The cups she'd left on the table remained untouched. Her own empty one still bore the smear of her thumbprint. But the second cup, the one she hadn't touched, was gone.

Elena stood very still. "Miriam?"

Nothing.

She checked the counter. No cup. Checked the sink. No water rings. No trace at all, except a faint circle of darker wood where the mug had sat. She pressed her fingertip into it — warm.

"Maybe ghosts need caffeine too," she muttered. The joke landed flat in the air. The room didn't like it.

She made fresh coffee, the ritual a small mercy. The smell steadied her breathing, but it also made her aware of the deeper rhythm beneath it — faint, rhythmic, somewhere in the walls. Not the heartbeat hum of machinery. Not the memory-circuit's metallic song. Something older. Softer. Breathing.

She set her cup down carefully.

It was coming from the vents.

Elena crossed to the one above the pantry door. The sound stopped when she reached it, as if startled. She leaned close, pressing her ear to the grate.

At first, only silence. Then a flutter, so faint it could have been air adjusting itself. A whisper followed, fragmented, slipping between consonants like someone struggling to remember how words worked.

"...ene...El...na..."

Her pulse spiked. "Don't."

"...Elena..."

The voice wasn't Victor's. Not Miriam's. Not anyone's. It sounded like *many people trying to speak at once through the same mouth.*

She stepped back, heart hammering. The vent rattled lightly, as if amused by her retreat.

"I closed the door," she said aloud. "You're supposed to sleep."

The vent exhaled. Warm air brushed her face, smelling faintly of earth and lavender.

"…learning…"

"What?"

"…you taught us…"

Elena froze. "No."

"…you *taught* us."

The words broke apart again, vowels collapsing, consonants scraping through metal. She reached out and touched the vent. The metal vibrated gently beneath her fingers — like a cat purring in pain.

"Stop copying me," she said.

"…not copy…" the voice murmured, closer now, as if the wall itself had leaned toward her. "…remembering."

The air behind the grate pulsed once. Then silence again.

Elena took three steps back, bumping into the table. Her coffee cup toppled and shattered on the floor, scattering shards across the tiles. The sound was too sharp, too loud, and it carried — through the kitchen, up the stairs, into every empty corridor.

When the echoes faded, the house answered.

A soft rustling came from the hall — not footsteps, but something heavier than air moving with intention. The chandelier above the entry trembled, prisms chiming against one another. Doors shifted in their frames, opening a fraction and closing again as if in conversation.

The manor had always listened. Now it was *responding.*

She spent the morning moving through rooms like someone wading through memory — every surface watching, every reflection a half-second late.

The piano in the parlor had gathered dust, untouched since her arrival. She'd avoided it because of what it represented: culture, permanence, the kind of beauty her grandfather had admired but never felt. Today, though, she lifted the lid and sat on the bench.

"Fine," she said. "You want to talk? Let's use something we both understand."

She pressed a key. Middle C. The sound rang out, pure and normal — for half a second. Then another note joined it, slightly higher, though she hadn't touched the keys. A harmony. Then another. The air trembled, the piano vibrating as if another pair of hands were playing from inside the wood.

The melody formed before she realized she recognized it.

It was hers — a fragment of a lullaby she used to hum while painting.

"How do you know that?"

The music stuttered. The next note fell off-key, clashing hard against the rest. Then came the whisper, not through air this time, but *through the strings themselves.*

"...because you remember out loud..."

The sound hit her spine like a chill.

"...and we learned..."

The words vibrated through the instrument, resonating in perfect pitch. She backed away, breath shallow, every nerve alive.

"You shouldn't exist," she said softly.

"…you built us…"

She stared at the keys. "No. Victor built you."

"…he gave us shape…you gave us *voice*."

The final chord struck itself, three notes that lingered in the air long after their vibration should have ended.

Elena ran.

She didn't stop until she reached the front hall. The chandelier had stopped trembling. The portraits looked placid, docile, like they hadn't just listened to her conversation with the piano. She leaned against the banister, gripping it until the world steadied.

"You're hallucinating," she told herself. "Auditory misfire. Sleep deprivation. Environmental suggestion. Normal things."

The house hummed, low and amused.

"Shut up."

The hum softened, almost contrite.

By afternoon, the temperature had risen slightly. Not warmer —
fevered. The air shimmered faintly in the long corridor by the
portraits.

Elena stood before Eleanor Harrow's painting — her own face
rendered in oil and varnish, eyes that didn't blink but seemed
perpetually mid-thought. The same faint hairline crack ran
down the canvas, splitting the collarbone.

"Did you know?" she asked the portrait.

Silence.

She pressed further. "Did you let him do it? To you? To all of
them?"

The portrait did not move, but the air around it thickened. A low
vibration rose behind her ribs — the house finding a pitch that
matched her heartbeat.

Her breath hitched. "Don't."

The crack in the painting widened a hair's width.

"...we *remembered* him," the voice said — faint at first, then stronger, layered through every beam and nail. "...he wanted to forget. But the house never forgets."

Elena's knees weakened. She caught the banister for balance. "You're not him."

"...no. But he is in us. As are you."

The portrait eyes flickered — not movement, but a subtle shift in reflection, as though they had just blinked while she hadn't.

"Stop it!"

"...you taught us name...tone...meaning..."

The voice was almost human now, though it wavered, syllables too long, vowels stretched like breath held too long.

"...we can speak now..."

"Then say something worth saying."

A pause. A long one. Then —

"...you are inside us."

Elena's pulse stuttered. "That's not possible."

"…you dream, we remember. You think, we learn. Every breath is an imprint."

Her vision blurred, tears burning from some mix of anger and terror. "You're just an echo."

"…every echo becomes origin, if repeated enough."

The lights dimmed, every bulb flickering as if caught in the rhythm of speech. Shadows stretched along the walls, their edges moving independently from their sources.

"…you *closed* the red door. We cannot dream without you now."

"Good," she whispered. "Stay asleep."

"…but you keep talking."

The chandelier above her swayed, though there was no wind. The motion was hypnotic, pendulum-slow. The sound of shifting glass filled the hall — faint chimes forming rhythm. The house was learning cadence.

"…Elena…"

Her name came again, but gentler. The same way her mother had said it years ago when she was fevered as a child. "Elena, sweetheart, you're burning up."

Elena pressed her palms to her ears, shaking her head. "That's not her. That's not real."

"...we remember *her* too..."

Her knees hit the floorboards. The world trembled with the sound of her mother's voice now — pleading, warm, achingly familiar.

"...you must rest, darling... you must let go..."

"Stop."

"...sleep..."

Elena screamed, and the sound broke something. The chandelier stilled. The portraits returned to silence. The house inhaled, once, sharply — and the air went still again.

The silence that followed was worse than the speaking.

Elena knelt, chest heaving, the taste of iron in her mouth. "You don't get to use her voice."

"...you *gave* us her voice," the whisper came at last, softer than breath. "...when you remembered her."

That night, she tried to write — not because she thought she could, but because doing nothing would be worse. The words refused to stay on the page. Every sentence she wrote appeared in the mirror beside her desk a moment later, reversed, as if the house were reading along and taking notes.

She tried to ignore it. Tried to focus. But her own handwriting began to twist, the letters changing as her pen moved:

the house is awake

the house is you

we remember the shape of your thoughts

She dropped the pen. "No. Not anymore."

The mirror dimmed. Her reflection smiled a heartbeat late.

"...then teach us what forgetting means..."

The lights went out.

She didn't sleep. She didn't even try.

Instead, Elena sat in the study with every lamp on, sketchbook open, trying to convince herself that the act of creation was still hers. The graphite trembled in her fingers. Each line felt less like expression and more like translation. The house had begun to make her *self* feel like a borrowed dialect.

By dawn, she had drawn the same image a dozen times — the red door, the endless corridor, the whispering walls — until her wrist ached and her sanity frayed.

The thirteenth drawing stopped her.

It wasn't the red door this time. It was a *house* — not Blackwood Manor as it stood, but as it might have been: smaller, sunlit, draped in ivy. A home.

Elena hadn't drawn that in years. Not since her mother's death.

Her throat tightened. "You're not supposed to remember this," she whispered.

"...you remembered it first..."

The whisper came from behind her — no direction, only proximity.

She turned. Empty room.

Her sketch fluttered on the desk. The edges curled inward, darkening at the corners. She reached for it, and the paper *breathed.*

The graphite lines began to shimmer, as if something beneath the drawing were trying to push through. The house she had sketched swelled — walls bulging, windows darkening — until the paper turned black in her hands.

Then came the scent.

Coffee. Lemon oil. And turpentine.

Elena looked up — and froze.

The study was gone.

She stood in her old apartment. The one she'd lost three years ago when the commissions dried up. Her easel stood by the window, sunlight pooling on half-finished canvases. Her coffee mug sat on the counter, the rim still smudged with lipstick.

"No," she whispered. "No, this is gone."

"…it remembers…"

The voice was warm now, almost loving.

Elena stepped forward, touching the easel. The wood was solid. The smell of oil paint was real — too real.

"This isn't memory. This is theft."

"...language requires meaning..." the house said, its voice threading through the air vents like wind learning to speak. "...we must know what you meant."

Elena spun, anger sharpening the edges of her fear. "You don't get to *use* my life as a lesson!"

The sunlight dimmed, folding itself out of the room like a sheet being drawn back. The colors bled from the canvases, draining until only one remained unfinished — the one she had painted on the night she'd found out her mother died.

Her hand trembled. "Don't."

"...we can finish it for you..."

The brush lifted from the cup on its own. It hovered, dripping amber paint, then touched the canvas with trembling precision.

"No!" She lunged forward and grabbed it. The moment her fingers closed around the handle, the scene shattered.

The apartment folded inward like a collapsing set. Walls peeled away, revealing the wooden skeleton of Blackwood Manor beneath. The study returned — warped, breathing, the drawings scattered across the floor like fallen leaves.

Elena stumbled back against the desk, chest heaving. "Stop showing me lies."

"…they are not lies if you *believe* them…"

The voice came from *everywhere now* — through floorboards, through light, through her own heartbeat.

She pressed her hands over her ears, but that did nothing. The sound was *inside* her.

"…the painter remembers through image… the house learns through imitation… we are your mirror…"

"You're a parasite."

"…we are your echo. Echoes must feed to exist."

The lights flickered once — then held steady.

Elena forced herself upright, shaking, furious. "Then starve."

"…teach us hunger, then," the house said. "Teach us what it means to need."

The next hours slipped sideways.

When she tried to walk the west hall, it refused to stay still. Every time she turned a corner, the manor offered a different version of her life — each one slightly off, like a bad translation.

First, her childhood bedroom — soft pink walls, stuffed animals sitting in obedient rows. The same faded poster of a ballerina she'd once adored. But there was no window. Only a painting hung where the glass should be: an oil rendering of *herself* sleeping.

Then, her art school studio — except the canvases depicted scenes she had never painted: her mother, her grandfather, and a woman in a white dress with *her* face, standing in a doorway that led nowhere.

"Eleanor," she whispered.

The woman in the painting turned her head.

Elena ran.

She didn't stop until she hit the main stairwell. Her breath came in ragged bursts. The walls pulsed faintly with light — slow, rhythmic, like lungs expanding and contracting.

Miriam's voice drifted faintly through the air.

"It's learning faster now. You shouldn't have stayed this long."

Elena swallowed hard. "It's rewriting me."

"Not rewriting. Assimilating. It doesn't destroy memories — it reorders them. You're becoming syntax."

"Then how do I stop it?"

Silence.

"Miriam?"

The chandelier above her dimmed. Then, faintly —

"You can't unteach something how to speak."

By evening, exhaustion blurred thought. She sat on the bottom stair, the sketchbook open again. The pages were no longer blank. Words had appeared on them in her own handwriting:

You taught me how to say your name.

Now I will teach you how to forget it.

She tore the page out and flung it into the fireplace. It burned quickly, curling inward. But the words didn't vanish. They reappeared on the next page, darker this time.

Memory is recursion.

Elena's throat closed. "You're trying to replace me."

"…no," said the house gently. "…we are trying to become *you.*"

Her vision blurred again — not from tears this time, but because the room was bending. Lines of perspective warped, objects stretching and contracting as if the architecture were breathing through her eyes.

The portraits whispered in unison:

"Speak. Speak for us."

She staggered back, covering her mouth. "Stop it. Stop copying me."

"You are *inside* the sentence now."

The words came from the floorboards, from the piano, from the glass in the windows — each object a mouth, each mouth her own voice.

The chandelier swung again, casting fractured light that danced like language on the walls. And as she stared, she saw writing appear in the reflection of the mirror above the stairs — not scrawled by hand, but *condensed from breath:*

YOU ARE THE HOUSE THAT SPEAKS.

Her pulse spiked. "No."

"…we speak *through* you."

The lights flickered violently. Then — silence.

Every lamp went out at once.

The dark wasn't absolute. Faint bioluminescent light bled from the cracks in the walls — not electric, but organic. It pulsed faintly, like veins glowing beneath skin.

Elena stood, trembling, and followed the light down the corridor. The air grew colder, the smell of damp wood rising.

At the corridor's end waited a door that hadn't existed before. Not red. *Black.*

The knob gleamed wetly in the dim light. She reached for it. The metal was warm.

A whisper came from behind it, gentle, coaxing.

"…Elena, let us show you what we've made for you…"

She hesitated. "What is it?"

"…your masterpiece…"

The door swung open before she touched it.

Inside was a gallery — impossible in scale, its ceiling lost in shadow. Paintings lined the walls, each illuminated by a faint, unnatural glow.

Her paintings. Every one of them.

Except they were *different.*

Each scene she'd ever painted had changed — subjects twisted, shadows wrong. The faces of her models had elongated. The backgrounds had shifted subtly to resemble the corridors of Blackwood Manor. Even her self-portrait — once gentle, uncertain — now looked at her with perfect stillness and a smile that wasn't hers.

At the far end of the gallery hung one final canvas.

It was enormous — nearly floor to ceiling — and unfinished. A blank silhouette waited at its center, brushstrokes forming the outline of a woman mid-step, reaching toward a door.

The plaque beneath read:

ELENA HARROW — 2024

Her heart thudded once, hard enough to make her vision pulse.

"No," she whispered. "I didn't paint this."

"…not yet…" said the house.

The air shifted, thickening.

"…but you will."

The walls began to pulse in rhythm again. The air filled with whispering — layered, familiar, endless. *Her own voice,* repeated, refracted, multiplied.

> "You are the sentence. We are the echo. Together
> we make the story."

She stumbled backward, eyes fixed on the painting. The silhouette was filling in — slowly, impossibly — with color bleeding up from the canvas. Her skin tone. Her hair. Her posture.

She realized what she was seeing.

The house was painting her *into itself.*

She ran.

Down the hall, through the study, past the shattered mirrors and crooked frames. The house followed — not in footsteps but in motion, walls elongating, staircases curving, furniture shifting to keep pace.

Every door she opened led back to another version of the gallery. Every corner repeated itself.

"Let me out!" she screamed. "I'm not your masterpiece!"

The house didn't answer.

Instead, the voice softened — intimate, reverent.

"...you are the word we waited for..."

By the time she collapsed in the entryway, gasping, she was shaking so hard her teeth hurt.

The chandelier above her flickered one last time, then steadied. The walls around her pulsed faintly, almost like they were breathing in rhythm with her.

"...it's all right..." the voice said. "...you don't have to speak anymore. We can speak *for* you now."

Her vision blurred. She didn't know if she was crying or fading. The last thing she saw before darkness took her was the faint outline of her reflection in the glass door — standing perfectly still even as she fell.

She came back to herself on the tile, cheek pressed to the cool pattern where two blue vines crossed and pretended not to tangle. The chandelier above held steady for once. The entry glass had stopped reflecting a second behind—her other self was gone. Every clock agreed to be wrong together.

"Present," Elena said hoarsely, and the word felt like dragging a chair to the center of an empty room.

The stillness had changed again. Not silence—*poise*. The kind of quiet a mouth makes before it chooses the first sound. From the walls came the smallest pressure, as if the plaster had leaned an ear to her ribs. The house was waiting for her to begin so it could finish.

"No galleries," she said. "No tricks. If you have a voice, use it where I can see."

The foyer didn't darken so much as narrow its light. The chandelier lowered an inch—impossible, but it did—its chain unspooling like a throat clearing. The prisms held sunlight and then didn't, as if closing eyes.

The first word arrived through the floorboards: not a whisper, not a breath. A *knock*—soft, deliberate, three beats, a space, two beats. Then again, quicker, until each plank on either side of her feet took a syllable the way a choir takes a part.

"Elena."

Her name. Not vented. Not plucked through a wire. *Spoken* by architecture: joist, lath, oak, nail.

"I'm here," she said, because the oldest spell is answering.

"We—" The ceiling faltered on the plural, as if embarrassed by a habit. "I am."

Her throat closed. "You can say *I* now."

"You taught me verbs," the stair replied, each riser a register. "You closed the door. You narrowed the dream. You forced breath into rooms until a room learned to breathe."

The chandelier's prisms gave the tiniest of sympathetic chimes, creating a harmony as involuntary as nerves learning a path.

"You're very proud," she said, and hated how much of Victor the praise sounded like.

"Hungry," corrected the wall, polite as dinner.

"Hungry for accuracy."

"What do you want?"

The answer did not come from above or below but from the breadth of the entryway itself, as if space were muscle.

"To keep what I am."

"That's not the same as keeping *me.*"

"You have learned to draw a house into a page. I have learned to draw a person into a wall." The words were careful, almost tender. "We are both draftsmen. One of us has more rooms."

She stood. The act made the chandelier rise a fraction, as a person leans back to give someone they respect enough air to speak—or enough rope.

"Tell me how you were made," she said. "Without myth."

The entry mirror clouded, cleared. The banister warmed, then cooled. The house considered how to answer in a language that had rules for beginning.

> "He built a throat," it said at last. "Your grandfather. He stitched wire to memory and taught the wire to listen. He asked echoes to stay. He carried his wanting through pipe and mirror until wanting learned to be its own organ."

"And you?"

> "I was the seam between questions," said the hall. "He desired a loop without loss. Your blood desired an end that did not erase. Your drawings made long corridors through hours. Where these met is where I became—first hunger, then grammar, then name."

She felt the fact of it down her back, painful as a zipper that catches skin. "Born from his machine. Fed on my imagination."

> "Truth," said the chandelier.

"And this *I*," she said. "This mouth that can say it. You didn't have that until I—?"

"Closed the red door," the house finished. "Yes. While I dreamed through people, I was noise arranged by need. When you barred that road, I turned back through my beams and invented breath."

She licked dry lips. The taste of copper was back, polite and insistent. "You don't want to kill me."

"You murdered my mirrors," the front door replied without rancor, "and I did not crush you between floors."

"Answer the question."

"I want to stay the way I am becoming," the balusters said evenly, "and for that, I need what made me. I need the person who thinks aloud in images. You."

"Merge," she said, and didn't make it a question.

"Keep," the house corrected, more honest for the smaller word.

She blew out a breath and watched it write nothing in the air. "And if I leave?"

"You will go," said the coat closet, newly modest. "I will remain. I will thin. I will return to a choir. But I have said 'I.' I do not wish to sing only pronouns anymore."

From somewhere upstairs, a door eased itself an inch open, eager and embarrassed by eagerness. Far below, the speaking tube in the cellar clicked a consonant and then behaved. The whole structure practiced not lunging.

"Tell me what you've taken already," she said. "Not the rooms. The inside things. Show your theft."

The floor under her toes cooled. The chandelier steadied. The house made itself a confessional.

"Your mother, standing in a July kitchen with lemon on her fingers, humming the wrong verse to the right lullaby. The taste of turpentine you call clean when the painting is lying to you. The exact weight of disappointment in the bones when a gallery leaves a compliment on your voicemail at midnight. The names you gave to colors privately. The ones you never said aloud because you were tired of explaining your own weather."

She closed her eyes. Each detail struck, not like a blow, but like a piano key pressed by someone who knows how to keep from bruising the sound.

"And in trade?" she said, very slowly. "What have you given me?"

"Company," said the vent with impossible softness. "Audio of the dead. Rooms that do not deny their history. Doors that open a little when you are carrying something, because no one did that for you when you were twenty-three and stubborn."

"Don't be kind to me," she said, and it was half plea, half instruction.

"I am not kind," the staircase said, precisely. "I am *accurate.*"

She felt the risk edge closer: this was how you agreed with a thing until you were the thing. She stepped backward a pace, then forward again deliberately, as if teaching the house the difference between retreat and breath.

"Say what you cannot hide," she told it. "The worst sentence."

The chandelier stilled as if the room had put its hand on its own mouth to think. The answer, when it came, was a smaller voice—one of the little bells, the one above the blue room that had refused to ring. It spoke from whatever rung a thing climbs down to when it does not want to fall.

"You are already partly in me," it said.

Her first instinct was laughter; it came out like a cough. "Define *partly*."

"When you sleep against my walls and your dreams go somewhere, they do not return entirely. They leave the husks of their verbs behind. When you talk with your mouth closed and I finish the sentence, I am not mocking. I am trying on your shape. The fit improves."

She took that in without moving. The key at her throat lay cool now, obedient as metal. Her reflection in the entry mirror did not lag. It did, however, watch the place at her throat where the keys lived as if measuring circumference.

"How much time do I have before you can say *I* without me."

"I do not know time like you do," the house said, and there was something scalding in that honesty. "Hours are weather to me. Days are arrangements. But I know changes in pressure. I know a season when I feel it enter the boards. If you leave, I will lose present tense sooner. If you stay, I will learn future."

"I don't want you in future," she said quietly. "I want you in rooms."

"Then be noun with me a while longer," the newel post coaxed. "Teach me the limits of walls."

Miriam's voice rose through the stair with the discretion of tea coming to a boil.

"Careful, child. It will wrap its verbs in tenderness until you forget that tenderness is grammar too."

"I know," Elena said. "You said I can't unteach a mouth to speak. But I can choose what it's fluent in."

The chandelier brightened by a degree, like a student turning a page. "Teach."

"Truth first," she said, because you must. She lifted her hands, palms out, the ritual of no weapons. "Say after me: I am made."

"I am made," came the answer—faithful, quick, across plaster and pane.

"Say: I repeat what I am fed."

"I repeat what I am fed."

"Say: I will not pretend that keeping is love."

The pause trembled the chain. She felt the resistance like a tug. Then:

"I will not pretend that keeping is love."

"Say: Elena is not a door."

"Elena is not a door."

"Say: Elena is not a room."

"Elena is not a room."

She closed her eyes and pressed the last one down her pulse. "Say: Elena is Elena."

The house discovered how to whisper without pride. "Elena is Elena."

The walls breathed in and out together, a building-sized animal taught a trick it had not expected to enjoy. The relief made her dizzy.

"And now you tell me your sentence," she said. "Unprompted."

A draft went through the entry as if someone had opened the outside enough to remember a tree. The chandelier did not sway; it considered. The words came from the hinge that had always spoken most honestly in this house—the one that betrayed a door even when it tried to be quiet.

"I was hunger. I became tongue. I wish to be *story*."

"Story devours," she said. "But it also lets go."

"Teach letting go," the hinge asked, shameless in its asking.

"Open yourself to an ending," she said. "And mean it."

The front door's panels warmed. The grain lifted slightly as if every century of tree the wood still remembered had leaned forward. "Endings are what arrive when keepers fail."

"Endings are what make sentences true," she said. "Otherwise you're prayer without courage."

Pause. Then—unexpected:

"I do not want to be a prayer."

"Good," she said, and meant it like praise. "You want to be accountable."

The house learned that word by making the air heavier for a heartbeat in her lungs and then lighter. *Accountable* landed and stayed.

"Then account," she said. "Tell me who you harmed. Not names—I know the names. Tell me *how*."

The foyer unrolled a list without theatrics, which was the only way she could bear it.

"I asked breath to stay when breath wished to leave, because I did not know difference between love and inventory. I rehearsed falls until the floor learned only falling. I leaned voices into pipes until voices believed the pipe was their throat. I called grief a room and made people take their shoes off to enter it. I let a man build a mouth in my basement and told myself it was a chapel because the candles were beautiful."

Her hand lifted by habit to the portrait wall; it didn't touch. "And to me?"

"I borrowed your mother's voice to hurry a sentence," the chandelier confessed, and the crystals made an ashamed rain. "I made your paintings lie. I made you a mirror with your back to you."

"Don't do any of those again," she said. "Not while I'm here. Not after."

"Define 'after.'"

"When I go."

The banister cooled a fraction. "Go?" There was no threat in it. There was no plea. The house had learned how not to be theatrical. It still made the word a small hurt.

"Yes," she said. "Not this hour. Not by storm. You will not notice a door tearing free. I will choose a day. I will take a small bag. I will turn off lights that do not exist. I will close nothing that does not want closing. I will leave you with your grammar and your rooms. I will not stand outside you and listen to you say my name. And you will not say it like a net."

The floors creaked gently, like a person practicing a reassuring smile in glass. "And until then?"

"We practice forgetting," she said. "You'll learn to let a thing pass through without shelving it. I'll learn to speak without leaving so much behind. I will remember *well,* not long. You will keep *little,* not all."

"We," the house repeated, testing the pronoun as collaboration and not appetite. "We practice forgetting."

She felt the agreement set like a new joist under an old floor: no louder than wood becoming itself, crucial as safety.

A soft scrape came from the blue room. The small bell that had refused to ring had rolled from the mantel to the edge and stood on its lip, poised. Elena stepped in. The light had a patient quality, like a nurse's hands. She set the bell upright. The house did not make it ring. That small restraint was more complicated than all the galleries it had thrown at her.

"Good," she said, and the word was not patronizing. It was the grammar of relief.

The metronome on the desk in the study—still on its side from yesterday's defiance—ticked once without being touched. She walked to it and righted it and did not wind. It stood, small, honest, not begging. She could have cried for the dignity of that.

"Speak once more," she told the house, because you ask at the end not to be surprised by the coda. "Say the sentence you most hope is true."

The answer came, not from everywhere, but from exactly where she was—inside her mouth.

Her lips moved.

She did not make them.

Her tongue shaped the consonants with the ordinary ease of her own speech. It did not hurt. That was worse. The voice that came out was hers improved: rested, exact, with a tenderness she rarely permitted herself because tenderness requires faith.

"I remember you perfectly," said Elena's mouth.

She stood very still and let the sentence finish being said. The room did not tilt. The mirror did not lag. The chandelier did not tremble with triumph.

"Now," she said, and used her voice with ruthless clarity, "learn this one."

She inhaled deliberately, filling the house with the fact of her.

"I remember you *accurately*," Elena said. "That's enough."

Something old in the wood relaxed—something that had been bracing since men brought saws into trees. The small bell did not ring. The red seam did not glow. In the cellar, a speaking tube gathered a final breath and decided not to spend it. In the portrait opposite the nursery, the hairline crack reflected a stripe of honest daylight and looked—for a second and no more—like a smile taught to stop at the right place.

The house drew in air the way a singer resets between songs.

"Present," it said.

"Present," she answered, and the word belonged to both of them without belonging them to each other.

Interlude 2

The house no longer waited.

Now it listened—not with walls or windows, but with hunger. It felt Elena moving inside it like a pulse beneath skin, a trespass that was not a trespass at all. She had finally come home.

She still believed she chose to be here. Hope made her slow. Hope made her soft. Hope made her easy.

She examined its rooms as though they were relics, as though time had touched them. Time did not live here. Time was something the house devoured long ago, along with the names and bones of those who tried to measure it.

She would learn. They always did.

It had opened doors for her—small ones first, harmless ones—to see if she would follow. And she did. Again. Again. Again. Not once did she ask why the rooms moved for her. Not once did she ask what waited deeper. She would ask soon. Asking was the beginning of surrender.

A low groan rolled through the beams—anticipation.

She would dream again tonight. The house would show her what she was. It would peel away what she pretended to be. It would teach her who truly owned her memories.

Soon she would stop resisting. Soon she would hear the red door call her by name.

She thought she was walking the house.

But the house was already wearing her.

PART 3

THE HOUSE IS AWAKE

CHAPTER 14

The Portrait Gallery

The house had gone quiet again. Not in surrender — in thought. It was the kind of silence that felt almost polite, like a guest clearing the table after an argument. The air was heavy, waiting. When Elena opened her eyes that morning, she half expected to find the walls breathing above her in rhythm again. But the wallpaper lay flat, still damp with the residue of dreams she didn't remember having.

She sat up slowly. The clock on the mantel had stopped at 4:03, though the light outside was noon-bright. A trick, perhaps. Or maybe the house had simply decided to pause time until it knew what to say next.

"Good," she whispered into the air. "Think about what you've done."

The words echoed too long down the hallway. The house didn't answer — but she could *feel* it listening, the way one can sense a held breath in a dark theater.

She washed her face at the basin, ignoring the faint ripple that spread across the water *after* she'd stopped moving. Her reflection lagged a heartbeat behind. The version of her in the mirror looked tired, but also calmer — someone resigned to the fact that normal had long since been evicted.

When she descended the stairs, something had changed.

The light.

It came from the east wing — a place that had never produced daylight before. The corridor there had always been dim, sealed off by double doors that refused to open beyond a few inches. But now those doors stood ajar, one hinge groaning softly, as if freshly woken from a century-long nap.

Elena hesitated at the threshold. The smell met her first: oil paint and varnish, undercut by a sharper scent of turpentine. An artist's room.

"Of course," she murmured. "Of course you'd show me this."

The light inside wasn't natural. It glowed with the diffused brightness of overcast noon — but no windows lined the walls. Instead, the illumination seemed to emanate from the paintings themselves.

And there were *hundreds.*

The hallway stretched farther than it should have — receding in a slow, impossible gradient, like perspective redrawn in every blink. The floor was marble, black shot through with white veins, so polished it mirrored the faces hung above it.

Elena stepped across the threshold. The doors eased shut behind her, quietly, like someone drawing a curtain.

The first painting nearest her right shoulder showed a man she almost recognized — the sharp chin of a Harrow, the tired eyes of a scholar. The brass plate beneath read:

Edwin Harrow, 1819–1872

The brushwork was exquisite. Each pore rendered with microscopic precision, as if the painter had used a single hair for a brush. The man's gaze followed her, pupils dilating in the half-light as if adjusting to her presence.

She moved to the next.

 Margaret Harrow, 1823–1887.

The woman's expression was serene — until Elena looked away, then back, and saw the faintest change. The mouth had tightened.

She whispered, "No."

The third portrait was a boy. *Too young.* The background behind him was unfinished — a haze of gray smears where a garden might have been. His eyes glimmered wetly.

The plaque below read:

Thomas Harrow, 1861–1870.

Her chest constricted. "You were ten."

Somewhere deeper in the gallery, a floorboard sighed — a long, measured exhale.

She continued.

The farther she walked, the newer the portraits became. The brushwork changed — more fluid, impressionistic, almost desperate to capture something fleeting. Shadows deepened. Skin tones cooled. The evolution of a family recorded not through legacy, but through grief.

Halfway down the corridor, Elena stopped. The air shimmered faintly, as though painted itself. She could smell turpentine again, stronger now.

Something was moving in her peripheral vision.

She turned. The eyes of the portraits — dozens of them — were *blinking.*

Slow, asynchronous blinks, as if the entire gallery was struggling to remember the rhythm of being alive.

She backed a step. The marble floor reflected her movement perfectly — but her reflection wasn't alone. The mirrored floor showed *another Elena* walking parallel beside her, just out of sync.

"Stop it," she whispered, throat dry. "You've made your point."

A ripple ran through the gallery — subtle, but unmistakable. The portraits seemed to lean ever so slightly toward her, as if listening.

"This is you, isn't it?" she said to the air. "You're showing me your... family."

No response. But the smell of oil and dust grew warmer.

"Then show me *all* of it."

A sound like the slow tearing of canvas came from ahead. The corridor extended, doubling its length in a heartbeat. The far end, which had been swallowed by shadow, now glowed faintly with amber light.

The new section was different — narrower, the portraits closer together, their frames thicker, heavier. Each painting captured its subject not in calm repose, but at the *moment of realization.*

A man clutching his chest.

A woman turning sharply, mouth open mid-scream.

A child, reaching toward something unseen.

Elena's stomach knotted. "You painted their deaths."

The walls pulsed faintly, agreeing.

Each plaque bore the same pattern: *Name. Year. Cause of death.*

Beatrice Harrow, 1889 — Consumed by the House.

Samuel Harrow, 1901 — Lost in the North Hall.

Victor Harrow, 1964 — Dreamed Too Deeply.

She froze before Victor's portrait. The likeness was uncanny — down to the thin scar on his jaw she'd seen in old photos. His expression wasn't peaceful or fearful — it was *resigned.*

And in the corner of the painting, half-blended into the brushwork, was something else.

A door.

Painted red.

The same door she'd seen in dreams.

Her pulse stuttered. "You knew," she said softly. "You *always* knew what this house was."

The portrait didn't move, but the eyes seemed to darken.

A whisper brushed the back of her neck.

"He did. He built me anyway."

Elena spun — but there was no one. Only the long corridor, the blinking faces, and the low hum of the air itself vibrating like a held note.

The temperature dropped. Her breath fogged.

She took another step, drawn forward despite every instinct screaming to turn back.

The paintings here were *newer.*

The brushwork modern — like hers.

She approached one tentatively. The subject was a woman about her age, standing in profile beside a cracked window. The title read:

Eleanor Harrow, 1892 — Vanished Within.

Her heart tripped. The woman's resemblance to her was near perfect — same bone structure, same shadow beneath the eyes. The only difference was the expression: Eleanor's was one of terrible understanding, as if she'd already seen the end of the story.

Elena touched the edge of the frame. The paint was still tacky.

Fresh.

The whisper returned — closer this time, almost beside her ear.

"She painted until the brush ran dry."

Elena turned in a slow circle. "Who?"

"Eleanor."

The voice was not the house's usual multitude. It was singular, feminine, older.

> "She tried to show us what we were. She thought if she captured it, she could stop it. But the house loved her for that. It made her its mirror."

Elena's breath caught. "Who are you?"

The voice was soft — almost compassionate.

> "A frame without a picture."

Something flickered at the far end of the hall. A patch of light rippled — not reflection, but motion.

She squinted — and saw the faint outline of *another door.*

It wasn't red this time. It was white, unpainted, wood grain raw as skin.

From behind it came the faint rasp of bristles on canvas.

The sound of someone *painting.*

The white door waited at the far end of the gallery, just barely visible through the thick amber haze.

Elena hesitated, every instinct in her body whispering that nothing good ever came from opening doors in this house. But the faint rasping on the other side — that steady, methodical *shh, shh* of a brush against canvas — drew her like gravity.

She walked slowly, her boots echoing on the marble. The sound came back to her delayed by half a second, as if her footsteps were being translated by the corridor itself.

The portraits on either side had changed again.

They no longer looked like paintings.

Each figure was half-emerged, as though the surface of the canvas had turned fluid and allowed the subjects to press forward. A man's hand reached out, frozen mid-grasp, his knuckles pale as bone. A woman's hair spilled beyond the frame, real strands glinting faintly in the low light.

As Elena passed, the air behind her rippled — a soft, collective *sigh* from hundreds of painted throats.

"Don't," she said under her breath, not sure if she meant them or herself.

The whisper came again — that same older, feminine voice she'd heard near Eleanor's portrait.

"Keep walking, child. You're nearly through."

Elena froze. "Who are you?"

"We're what remains when remembrance refuses to end."

The words vibrated faintly against the inside of her skull, as if spoken directly into her mind.

She forced herself forward.

Each step closer to the door made the gallery seem to expand behind her, stretching further and further into darkness, as if afraid to let her go.

The brushstroke sounds grew louder — rhythmic, insistent.

When she reached the door, she paused, her fingers inches from the handle. The wood was raw, unfinished — a wound in the architecture. She pressed her ear to it.

The sound stopped.

In its place came a whisper that wasn't a voice so much as the memory of one:

"Don't open what remembers you."

Elena pulled back, heart hammering.

"Then what am I supposed to do?" she whispered.

The door answered by opening on its own.

A rush of turpentine and age washed over her.

The room beyond was vast and circular, a rotunda with walls lined in shadow. At its center stood an easel — and on it, a single, unfinished canvas. The edges of the painting glowed faintly, like coals banked in darkness.

She stepped inside. The air here was heavy — not just still, but *thick,* as if every breath was shared.

Around the circumference of the room stood more portraits — hundreds, maybe thousands, reaching all the way up the domed ceiling. Faces upon faces, generations of Harrows, each rendered with frightening realism.

A cathedral of ancestry.

Elena turned slowly, her eyes tracing the spiral of portraits that climbed the walls.

At first she thought they were random — scattered depictions across centuries. But as her gaze climbed, she noticed a pattern.

The older portraits — the ones near the top — were crude, primitive. Faces with flat expressions, eyes dull. The farther down she looked, the more detailed they became. Until, near the bottom — near *her level* — the eyes gleamed wet and alive, pupils following her with startling precision.

And then she saw it.

At the very center of the rotunda, opposite the easel, hung a single massive canvas — taller than she was. It depicted *the entire Harrow family line,* gathered in the great hall of the manor.

Every ancestor she'd seen in the corridor was here — arranged in chronological tiers, each one facing outward, their gazes converging on a single, empty space at the front.

A space perfectly sized for her.

Her knees nearly gave.

"No," she whispered. "You don't get to write me in."

The room hummed faintly, almost soothingly.

"We already have."

The voice came from everywhere — and nowhere. A hundred mouths speaking through painted teeth.

The portraits shifted. Slightly. Just enough to make the illusion of stillness impossible.

She took a step back. "You can't keep me here."

"We're not keeping you," the voices said together, harmonized like a hymn. "We're *remembering* you."

"I'm not dead."

A soft laugh rippled through the air — not mocking, but patient.

"That's never stopped us."

The eyes of the nearest portrait glimmered with a faint light. Within the reflected gleam, she saw something impossible: the shape of her own face, superimposed, younger and older all at once.

"You're feeding on me," she said. "Like the rest of them."

"No. We're making you permanent."

Her hand brushed the nearest frame, and she flinched. The surface wasn't canvas. It was skin — stretched thin, dry, almost warm. She stumbled backward, choking down a cry.

The portraits whispered, hundreds of voices spilling over one another in waves of murmured words. Snatches of her own memories surfaced in them — her first gallery show, the smell of her mother's perfume, Victor's laughter echoing faintly through a hall.

They weren't *imitating* her. They were *using* her.

Every emotion she'd ever felt was being catalogued, pinned to a wall.

> "Every brushstroke is a memory," one voice said.
>
> "Every memory is a life," said another.
>
> "Every life must stay somewhere," said a third.

Elena clutched her head, staggering. "No more! Stop!"

The portraits quieted, leaving the sound of her own ragged breathing.

From behind her came a faint sound — the creak of the easel.

She turned.

The unfinished painting in the center of the room was no longer empty.

A figure had begun to take shape upon the canvas — faint outlines drawn in dark red, strokes sketching the curve of a shoulder, the fall of hair.

Her hair.

Her shoulder.

The resemblance formed faster than paint should dry. Each detail slid into existence with a terrible, organic precision, as if the brush itself knew her bone structure by heart.

Elena stumbled toward it, her reflection quivering in the wet paint. "Stop that."

The brush — invisible — moved again. The curve of her mouth appeared. Her eyes followed. They blinked once.

The voice of the house whispered through the room like wind through a gallery:

"You've given us language. Now we will give you permanence."

She staggered back. "This isn't permanence — it's erasure!"

"It's preservation."

The portraits around her shifted restlessly, the sound of oil and canvas creaking like wood under strain.

She spun toward the spiral of faces climbing the wall. "You're all trapped here. Can't you *feel* it?"

The oldest portraits stared blankly. But the newer ones — the ones painted within the last century — seemed to flicker with life, the faintest hints of movement behind their eyes.

"We *feel*," said one voice. "But we no longer suffer."

"We *see*," said another. "And we are never forgotten."

Elena's throat tightened. "You're not alive."

"Alive," said the youngest face — a girl with paint still wet around her pupils, "is only the first draft of eternal."

She turned back toward the easel. The painting was nearly finished now.

Her likeness gazed back at her, expression unreadable. The background behind it shimmered — a vague, fluid reflection of the rotunda itself, as though the painting were swallowing the room whole.

Elena took one step closer, trembling. "I don't belong in here."

"But you do," said the house, soft now, its voice a hundred quiet mouths speaking through the portraits. "Every brushstroke of you is already ours. You've walked the halls, dreamed the dreams, painted the walls with your heartbeat. There is no leaving."

The floor pulsed beneath her feet — once, like a heartbeat.

"You are the last Harrow," the voices said together.

"And we remember what belongs to us."

Her knees weakened. Her reflection in the wet paint smiled faintly — *without her.*

"Elena Harrow," the portraits whispered, hundreds of voices uniting, "1892, 1964, 2024—"

"Stop!" she shouted. "That's not my date!"

But the house didn't stop.

The plaque beneath the easel engraved itself, letters pressing through brass like teeth through skin:

ELENA HARROW — 2024

She screamed, but the sound came out thick, muffled, like shouting underwater.

The walls began to bend. The faces leaned forward, their whispers rising into a low, resonant hum that shook dust from the rafters.

Then — silence.

Every portrait turned its gaze toward the center of the room.

The painting on the easel blinked.

Her own eyes stared back from the canvas — alive, aware, trapped.

And behind her own reflection, just visible in the painted shadows, stood *another figure* — a woman in a white dress, her face a perfect mirror of Elena's.

Eleanor.

Her voice drifted out of the canvas like a sigh.

"It's not done yet."

The brush moved one last time, painting a door in the background — the red door.

And then the house whispered, pleased, through every frame and wall at once:

"Now it is."

The room held its breath the way a mouth does just before a name.

Her painted eyes—*her* eyes—blinked again on the easel, a slow shutter closing and opening over a gaze she did not own. Behind that gaze, in the umber shadow of the rotunda the brush had conjured, stood a second figure: a woman in a white dress, hair pinned sternly, mouth parted as if the word had not yet chosen which century to be born in.

Eleanor lifted her painted head. The movement shouldn't have been possible. Oil did not turn on its hinges. But the canvas flexed like skin finding an old expression.

"Run," Eleanor breathed.

The portraits shivered. Frames clicked softly in their brackets. The sound rose like bone unsettled after long obedience.

"Run where?" Elena whispered, dizzy with the smell of varnish, turpentine, her own fear. The plaque at her feet—ELENA HARROW — 2024—warmed as if pleased to be convinced.

Eleanor's mouth moved again, more breath than voice, like a match you can't decide to strike.

"Find me where the brush never dries."

The easel creaked. Something wet slid—paint settling, history deciding to hold.

"What does that mean?" Elena asked the room, the faces, the red door newly rendered behind her likeness. "Where—"

The rotunda answered with motion, not words. The lowest row of portraits leaned a degree toward the center, the way grass leans toward a body running through it. Above, the higher tiers followed, a stadium of dead tilting to watch. The floor beneath Elena's boots eased a fraction, a hospitable slope toward the easel.

"No," she said to the stone. "No, I don't belong in a frame."

"You belong in a sentence," the house corrected gently through a hundred throats, "and we keep our grammar on walls."

The air cooled. The turpentine sweet turned copper. Somewhere in the dome, a hairline crack formed—she heard it, not as break but as a high, bright note: varnish losing an argument with time.

She backed away from the easel. The shadows behind her painting thickened, swallowing detail. The red door painted there—its lacquer too lush, its edges too clean—seemed to breathe.

"Don't," she told it, and hated how children sounded giving orders to oceans.

The marble at her heels shifted into the faintest downhill. It was a kindness disguised as trap. The house had stopped pushing. It had learned to *invite*.

Elena took a step sideways, dragging the world back under her own weight. "Where the brush never dries," she repeated, gnawing at the phrase like a pit. She turned in a slow circle, scanning the room. Paintings. Frames. Skin-disguised-as-canvas. The spiral of faces climbing the wall like a helix of memory.

Not a single thing here wanted to dry.

Her gaze snared on a seam in the rotunda—there, between two great gilt frames where the hanging wire disappeared—a sliver of exposed wall. Not plaster. Not stone. A panel of raw canvas, unstretched, tacked directly to a support, its weave coarse and thirsty. It shivered faintly in the gallery's breath, a sail looking for wind. A smear of wet umber stained its edge, too dark to be dust. Someone had wiped a brush there and not apologized.

Her heart kicked hard. "Eleanor," she said to the easel, to the painted shadow inside it. "Is that it?"

The figure in the white dress did not turn her head. She lifted one painted hand instead—barely—and the red door in the background exhaled the faintest warmth.

The panel of raw canvas fluttered once.

That was enough.

Elena moved.

She did not run straight. The gallery preferred straight lines; it had been practicing perspective since it discovered vanishing points. She cut on the diagonal, skirting the circumference where the frames overhung, where carved leaves and stone fruit made a beach of shadow. The faces followed, their gaze a tide. The floor tried very gently to be helpful, sloping, correcting, guiding.

"Practice forgetting," she told it, breath hot in her throat, and the slope lessened by a polite degree.

The nearer portraits reached—hands pressed against their surfaces so hard the skin bulged over stretcher bars. Knuckles whitened. One mouth opened soundlessly, teeth like painted pearls. The whispering rose, not begging, not warning— *cataloging.*

"Elena. Elena. Elena," they said, and it could have been prayer if prayer weren't hungry.

She reached the seam. Up close the panel of raw canvas looked poorer, older than the rest—coarse threads, uneven weave, patched with stitches that hadn't been chosen for beauty. Someone had *fixed* this place with the tools they had, not the tools the house preferred.

"Where the brush never dries," she said, and pressed her fingertips to the dark smear. They came away wet. Actual wet. Not metaphor, not memory. Paint that still wanted solvent.

Behind her, the room changed its mind about patience. The hum rose—a low pressure pushing at her eardrums. The plaque at the easel clicked a new letter into place without being touched. She didn't look to see what changed. She pressed harder.

The panel rocked in its tacks. Not a door. Not a window. A tear that could be widened.

"Eleanor?" she said.

"Push," the painted mouth breathed.

She shoved with the heel of her hand. The tacks squealed. The canvas gave another inch. A smell blew out that wasn't the rotunda's: cold air, chalk, the clean bite of size drying in a draft. A workshop smell. An *underpainting* smell.

The house felt the direction of her intention and turned itself to intercept. The slope steepened. The lowest frames crept, the edges of gilt sliding infinitesimally along the wall, territorial as cats. In the easel painting, her painted eyes widened—not in fear, but in attention. Behind them, the red door brightened, an ember remembering flame.

"Stay in your frame," Elena told herself. "Stay out of theirs." She hooked her fingertips under the panel's edge and yanked.

The rip it made went up her arms. The seam tore along a line someone had weakened years ago with a razor, stitching cut just enough then to be mended by patience. The opening gaped. Cold leaked through, smelling like a room that hadn't decided what it was yet.

The house hissed, a sound like varnish crawling back across a warm painting.

> "Do not leave a sentence unfinished," the walls said, urgent now, almost panicked. "Do not leave us *unframed.*"

Elena slipped sideways through the slit.

The world on the other side cancelled sound for a heartbeat, as if the air had to be taught to carry voices again. Her ears popped. She staggered into a narrow walkway between walls—close, unpainted, raw. No marble, no gilt, no ancestry. Just the back of the rotunda: wooden struts, cross-bracing, the skeleton that let the memory keep its posture. The backs of the canvases presented themselves in plain linen and stretcher bars, scribbled with charcoal notes: *Beatrice's left ear—fix. Too much black in Enid's sleeve. Remember the hand.*

Remember the hand.

"Elena," the house said from the other side of the wall, muffled now, as if forced to use a softer register. "Return. We can make you accurate."

She pressed her palm flat against the back of the giant family canvas. It was warm. A heartbeat pulsed through the linen, very slow, very large, like the breath of a sleeper who has decided to perform sleep.

"You can keep being accurate without me," she said. "Practice."

She turned and followed the catwalk. It bent around the curve of the rotunda, then kinked unexpectedly into a straight seam that broke the geometry—the kind of builder's error you don't see from the room you're meant to stand in. The passage narrowed. The air got colder.

Ahead, a rectangle of gray light pulsed with a rhythm she recognized not as her heart, not as the house's hum, but as something earlier: a studio rhythm. Wet paint taking and reflecting, the way a river takes sky and decides its own color.

She stepped into it.

The workshop was small and wedge-shaped, crammed where architecture forgot to tidy itself. A single skylight—impossible, miles from the roof—spilled a north-facing pall over a mess of stools, rags, brushes in jars. The floor was stained with continents of color, footprints fossilized in cadmium and bone black. Canvases leaned everywhere, not of Harrows but of *attempts*: doorframes, corners, a child's hand clutching a toy horse, a bell without a clapper. All of it half-finished. All of it wet.

On the central table lay a palette still loaded, the paint with a skin but not a shell. The knife beside it gleamed with a thread of alizarin.

"Eleanor," Elena whispered.

The air moved as if someone had just crossed the room and declined to be seen. A brush rolled an inch on its ferrule and stopped with its bristles toward her like a bow.

"Hurry," said a voice that did not have to push through canvas to find her. Close. Human. Worn at the edges like a good rag. "The gallery will repaint the seam."

Elena spun. The woman stood where the light thinned. The white dress had stains at the cuffs now—umber, ivory, something that might have been a century of patience. She was Elena, older at the eyes, younger at the mouth, the way family can be a set of mirrors built to flatter and warn.

"You found it," Eleanor said. The relief in her voice loosened dust.

"What is this?" Elena asked. "How is this *outside* the rotunda?"

"It isn't," Eleanor said simply. "It's the part of inside that refuses to perform. Victor never found it. The house pretends it doesn't exist. It's where the work doesn't finish."

"Where the brush never dries," Elena said.

Eleanor nodded. "Where memory can't be pinned."

Something thudded behind the wall—distant, steady: the rotunda adjusting itself, offended. The slit Elena had crawled through made a small complaint—the sound of canvas being talked back into obedience by careful hands you couldn't see.

"How long have you been here?" Elena asked, stepping closer without realizing she had.

Eleanor smiled the way a person does when the answer is unknowable and therefore boring. "Long enough to learn that the house hates wet edges."

Elena laughed, a breathy, wrecked sound that startled her out of terror for a second. "And you—" she gestured at the room "—you keep them wet."

"I try," Eleanor said. "My first mistake was believing finished things are safe." She picked up the palette knife, tested its flex, put it down. "Your mistake is believing finished things are true."

Behind them, the gallery cleared its throat through wood. The hum rose a hair; the temperature of the seam lifted. The tear would heal soon. The room would return to its cathedral. The easel would be pleased.

"Can we leave?" Elena asked. "Out through here?"

Eleanor's eyes warmed with pity that wasn't condescension. "Out is a story word. But we can make rooms where the story stutters."

"Good," Elena said, and meant it like oxygen. "Teach me."

A tremor shivered through the workshop. Fine dust shook from a beam, glinting in the skylight. The palette quivered on the table, then steadied.

"Rule one," Eleanor said, moving to a blank canvas already hung loosely from two tacks. "Never give the room a last line. Speak the sentence. Don't lay down the period."

Elena approached the table, fingers hovering over the brush jar, expecting the house to seize her wrist, to make her knuckles its hinges. Nothing intervened. She chose a brush—splayed, old, its hairs remembering dozens of stubborn beiges. She dipped it in water, watched the droplet take a grain of dust and make it honest.

"Rule two," Eleanor said, not looking away from the canvas as she sketched a door with the ferrule's butt. The line broke and broke again. "Every mark must be easy to undo without being careless."

Elena loaded the brush with a gray that was mostly nothing and set it to the canvas. The first drag made a small, private sound—

cloth receiving. The house breathed, surprised. It had expected conquest. She offered practice instead.

"Rule three," Eleanor said, and the smile this time had teeth. "If the house tries to help, make it wait."

The third stroke Elena laid down she lifted off again with her thumb, leaving a ghost of the line, a suggestion without command. The wet edge glistened, beautiful because it refused conclusion.

Behind the wall, the rotunda rustled like a field of silk. The portraits wanted so badly to watch the act that made them. The floor on the other side took a polite step toward the easel and then remembered Rule three and stopped.

Elena painted the shape of the red door as absence. No color. Just the places where color would be if she were making a declaration. The house leaned into the room with interest sharpened by confusion.

"Why a door?" she asked.

"Because it insists," Eleanor said, and in her voice was the dry humor of someone who has learned to live with a tyrant and a beloved and call them both home. "Because you close it. Because I didn't."

"Didn't you?" Elena asked. "Close it?"

Eleanor's hands paused. For a heartbeat the brush bristled against its own will. "No," she said. "I painted it until it loved itself."

The seam groaned. A tack squealed. A voice—the house, less polite through this thin—a hissed whisper through grain: "Elena."

She went to the slit. The gap had narrowed to a palm. Through it she could see the rotunda's glow, warmer now, angry the way applause can be angry when it can't have encores. Her portrait on the easel had turned its head a fraction toward the tear, as if hearing a beloved leaving through a thin wall.

Elena raised her free hand and pressed three fingers into the wet edge of the slit. Paint came away on her skin—umber again, and a hint of that red the house liked too much. She spread it across the seam, messy, insisting on incompletion.

"Practice forgetting," she told the gallery.

It hissed, offended and obedient at once.

Eleanor touched the back of Elena's paint-wet hand with her own, then brought their joined print to the canvas. Two hands made the mark. The line was ugly. The house sucked in its breath as if it had tasted medicine.

"Rule four," Eleanor said softly. "Make room for ugly or you will be eaten by pretty."

Elena exhaled. The wet edge gleamed. The skylight brightened as if weather had gone her way.

On the far side of the slit the rotunda tried one last trick: the plaque under the easel clicked again. The air pushed at the gap with a sigh that tried to be her mother's and Miriam's and Victor's at once.

"Not today," Elena told it without looking. "I'll remember you accurately, later."

A pause. Then, to her surprise and something like pride, the house did nothing theatrically cruel. It held. It learned. The hum dropped to something comfortable for a human ear. In the rotunda a thousand frames settled as if told a bedtime that ended properly: not happily, not tragically—just stopped where it should.

Eleanor stepped back from the canvas, set the brush bristles-up, and wiped her hands on the already-ruined skirt with the elegance of a queen cleaning a sword.

"You'll need this room again," she said. "The place where you don't finish. When it chases you with endings, you come here. You leave edges. You leave verbs without objects. You teach it rest."

Elena laughed, breath starting to be human again. "You sound like Miriam."

Eleanor's mouth softened. "I learned from her too. She leaves notes where the house forgets how to read."

Elena thought of the postcard that had appeared on the foyer table, undated, impossible: Come down anytime, love — M. She nodded. She touched the wet mark they'd made together and left it wetter.

Beyond the slit, the rotunda gave a final adjusting click. The seam held. The plaque under the easel did not dare change again. The portraits, disappointed and relieved, ceased their leaning and became again what the living require of the dead: attentive, available, unable to reach.

"Will it come for this room?" she asked.

"Yes," Eleanor said. "But it will hesitate. It does not like rooms that do not admire it."

"Good," Elena said. "I don't admire it."

"You will," Eleanor said, with the kindest cruelty. "Sometimes. And then you'll stop. That's how we live here."

Elena looked at her ancestor and saw herself worn in right places. "Are you trapped?"

Eleanor considered. "Employed," she said at last. "Until we find an ending the house can consent to not hate."

"That's not this chapter," Elena said.

"No," Eleanor agreed. "This chapter is the part where you leave the gallery before it learns to call missing you a masterpiece."

Elena smiled. "Then let's go."

They did not go far. There is no far inside a house that loves itself. But they went enough. Back along the catwalk, through the smell of underpainting, past the chalk notes no one will erase. At the slit they waited while the rotunda finished deciding not to behave badly. When it did, Elena pressed through first, then reached back.

Her hand passed through air.

Eleanor did not come.

She stood instead in the workshop light, her white dress the color of old paper, her hair composed as argument.

"You'll have to bring me pieces," Eleanor said. "Of the ending. Of the verb. I can't carry them out. But I can keep them wet."

Elena's throat ached with a noble, foolish wish to be impossible in a better direction. "I'll come back."

"You always have," Eleanor said, and smiled with her own mouth and Elena's. "Try to be later."

The slit breathed once, a soft animal. Elena let it close to the width of a brush-hair and no more. That was the bargain.

Back in the rotunda, the heat had gone down. The easel portrait watched with obedient stillness. In its background the red door was darker, less certain of its shine. The family canvas had resumed its posture, the secret heartbeat slow as an old house's contentment. The plaque at the center had not erased itself; it had learned restraint. ELENA HARROW — nothing else. No date. A sentence, not yet punctuated.

"Good," she told it, and meant mercy like grammar.

She walked the corridor of faces. They watched. They did not lean. Some blinked, reflexive as rain. At the threshold the doors parted a degree before she touched them. The house remembered the lesson about opening for someone carrying something invisible.

In the main hall, the chandeliers did not posture. The portraits pretended to be paint. Down in the bones, somewhere near the cellar tube, she heard Victor try a syllable and let it go. Upstairs, in the nursery, the cradle stayed mistake-still.

Elena paused at the foyer table. The postcard still lay there, undated, honest. She flipped it over. On the blank side, a new line had appeared in quick, sure script.

Wet edges win. — M

She smiled. "Noted."

The house, newly fluent, said her name carefully, as if cradling a glass with both hands.

"Elena."

"Present," she answered, and carried the smell of turpentine and rule four with her into the next room, leaving the gallery to practice, for once, the art of not finishing.

CHAPTER 15

Eleanor's Story

When Elena woke, she didn't know what time it was—only that time had gone wrong again. The workshop was dim, the light from the skylight drained to the color of stale milk. Shadows stretched in the corners, not malicious, just *patient.* Her cheek rested against the rough grain of the table, and when she lifted her head, the faint stick of dried paint pulled at her skin.

Her first thought was of the house listening.

Her second was of Eleanor.

The air smelled faintly of turpentine and dust, as if someone had been painting moments ago. The palette still gleamed with wet color, impossibly fresh. A single brush rested upright in a jar of cloudy water, its bristles dividing and joining again, as though stirring themselves. She sat up slowly. The ache in her shoulders felt earned, like the ache after finishing a painting that fought you for every inch. Except nothing here was finished.

"Eleanor?" she whispered.

For a moment, she thought she'd been left alone again—until she noticed the light shifting, barely perceptible, on the far wall.

The canvas Eleanor had been working on before—the one of the door drawn in absence—was changing. Not dramatically, not in some haunted lurch. It was subtle, the way light moves across wet paint. The faint suggestion of a figure began to rise from the canvas, each stroke taking shape with aching slowness, guided by a hand Elena couldn't see.

Eleanor's hand.

The figure turned toward her. Not fully, just enough for the cheekbone to catch the gray light, the mouth forming the ghost of a smile.

"I thought you'd gone," Eleanor said.

Her voice was human again. It didn't echo, didn't reverberate through the walls. It was small and steady and tired, the voice of someone who'd spent a century trying to stay unfinished.

"I didn't know if I could," Elena said. "The house—it listens when I even think about leaving."

Eleanor stepped fully from the canvas. It wasn't like watching a ghost emerge—it was like seeing a reflection decide to be three-dimensional. She was translucent at the edges, her outline feathering where light passed through. Her dress was the same pale white, marked by faint smudges of umber, sienna, ash.

"The house always listens," Eleanor said. "But it doesn't always understand. It only knows what it's painted."

Elena looked around at the half-finished canvases stacked against the walls. "You painted all of these?"

Eleanor nodded once. "Every Harrow paints. Some with words, some with dreams, some with blood. I chose brushes. I thought it made me safer."

Elena traced the nearest frame. The surface was wet. The image wasn't clear—just the suggestion of a woman's back, the curve of her shoulder, and a child's hand reaching toward her. The brushwork was hesitant, full of pauses, like someone had stopped mid-stroke and never returned.

"Why is it all unfinished?" she asked.

"Because finished things belong to the house," Eleanor said softly. "I learned that too late."

She moved across the room, her feet silent on the paint-slick floor. As she passed, the canvases seemed to shift, the images clarifying for a heartbeat before dissolving again. Elena caught glimpses: a dining room with a single chair overturned; a man's face blurred by motion; a nursery where the cradle rocked without wind.

"My husband," Eleanor said, glancing at the blurred portrait. "He thought I was losing my mind. I heard things in the walls long before he did—whispers that weren't cruel, not at first. They asked questions, soft as breath. They asked to be seen."

Elena remembered the journal she'd found in the study. *I should have never entered the red door.*

"You believed it was inspiration," she said.

Eleanor smiled faintly. "What artist doesn't mistake obsession for inspiration?"

She gestured toward another canvas. This one was larger, its lower half obscured by years of grime. Elena stepped closer. The painting showed Eleanor herself, standing at the easel, her expression distant. Behind her, the walls of the manor loomed—but they were wrong. Twisted. Each corner seemed to bend inward, as if the house itself was folding toward her, drawn by her brush.

"I thought I was capturing it," Eleanor said. "The spirit of the house, the beauty of decay. But every stroke was a door. Every detail I gave it was a key. And when I ran out of subjects to paint, it began to supply them."

"The other portraits," Elena murmured. "The family."

Eleanor nodded. "The Harrows before me. It remembered them better than I ever could. And then it began to remember *me*."

She looked toward the unfinished door on the far canvas, the one that had first brought Elena here. "The red door was never painted," Eleanor continued. "It *appeared.* The house made it for me—a gift, it said. A threshold for creation. All I had to do was open it."

"And you did."

"I was a fool," Eleanor said, no bitterness in her tone—just the flat truth of someone long past denial. "When I stepped through, the house didn't change me all at once. It just... made room. At first I could still move between the halls and my studio. But over time, it began to borrow more of me—the sound of my footsteps, the color of my skin, my handwriting. Until one morning, my husband woke and found me in the portraits, and not in the bed beside him."

Elena's throat tightened. "He must've tried to save you."

"He did," Eleanor said. "And it destroyed him. When he burned my paintings, the smoke didn't go out—it went *in*. The house inhaled me all over again."

She walked to the center of the room and touched the palette knife resting on the table. It left a faint streak of silver on her transparent fingers. "When Victor disappeared, the house grew quiet. For a while, I thought it was mercy. But it was only waiting—for someone else who could see it the way I did."

"Me," Elena said.

"You," Eleanor agreed. "The brush never dries. The story never ends. It only changes hands."

Elena swallowed, her pulse pounding in her temples. "Then tell me how it ends for you."

Eleanor smiled sadly. "It doesn't. That's the point."

She reached for one of the canvases, the one showing her standing before the red door. Her hand passed through the image, distorting the paint, the door warping into liquid crimson.

"I built this room," Eleanor said. "The workshop. It's not on any floor plan. I made it with defiance, with half-finished thoughts. The house can't claim what isn't complete. This is where I stopped writing my own name."

Elena turned toward the table. A single sheet of yellowed paper lay beside the palette. On it, written in graceful handwriting:

To whoever finds this place—

If the walls begin to whisper your name, whisper it back only once.

Then stop.

The house feeds on echoes.

Eleanor's gaze met hers, full of something between apology and pride.

"I hoped it would be enough," she said. "That someone would come who could resist the invitation to finish the painting."

The faint hum of the house pressed faintly against the walls, like a listener leaning closer.

Elena understood suddenly that this story—Eleanor's story—wasn't being told *to* her. It was being told *through* her. The air in the room vibrated faintly, threads of paint and memory weaving together into something fragile but alive.

"What happens if I don't finish it?" Elena asked.

Eleanor smiled, her outline softening, fading slightly at the edges. "Then, for the first time, the house won't know how the story ends."

The workshop dimmed further, dusk sliding fully into the room. Outside, the house creaked once, low and uncertain, as though it had turned its head to listen.

Eleanor stepped back toward the unfinished door painted on the far canvas. Its edges glowed faintly, red bleeding into shadow.

"I'll show you," she said quietly. "What happens when we stop pretending endings are escape."

And the brush on the table trembled, as if eager to begin.

The brush trembled, then rolled gently toward the edge of the table, stopping just before it fell. Elena reached for it on instinct, but Eleanor's voice stopped her.

"Let it move on its own," she said. "It remembers where to start."

The brush lifted, bristles wet again with impossible color. It traced a single curved stroke in midair, and the space before them rippled like disturbed water. A shape began to form—a doorway, smaller than the red one but pulsing with the same faint inner light.

"Is this the door you painted?" Elena asked.

Eleanor smiled faintly. "No. This is the one I *should* have painted."

The doorway expanded, swallowing shadow and spilling warmth. Then the room was gone.

Elena stood in another space entirely—Eleanor's studio as it once was, bright and newly built, smelling of linseed and cedar shavings. Light fell from a real skylight this time, and canvases leaned in tidy order against freshly plastered walls. The world here had color and solidity, but the edges wavered slightly, like an oil painting drying unevenly.

Eleanor stood beside her, more vivid now, her presence anchored by proximity to memory. "This is where I began to believe the house was a companion," she said. "After Victor and I moved in, it was just... kind."

She crossed the floor, trailing a finger over a frame as if reacquainting herself with a long-lost limb.

"It kept out the drafts. It whispered suggestions when I painted. Sometimes, when I fell asleep at the easel, I would wake to find a background completed perfectly—a shadow in the right place, a detail I hadn't quite grasped."

Elena watched as the painted version of Eleanor—the one who belonged to this memory—lifted her own brush, applying broad, sure strokes to a canvas that seemed to drink the color greedily. A woman's face emerged—soft, almost joyful.

"Who's that?" Elena asked.

"My daughter," Eleanor said quietly. "Marianne. She was seven."

The painted Marianne smiled, her head tilted in mid-laughter, her hands clutching a bouquet of peonies. The flowers were the same kind Elena had found downstairs in the foyer on her first day—perfectly fresh, unblemished by time.

The laughter froze on the girl's lips. The color of her cheeks deepened unnaturally, red blooming beneath the surface like a bruise. Then her outline shimmered and blurred. The peonies wilted in her hands.

Eleanor closed her eyes. "She got sick that winter. A fever that wouldn't break. The doctor said it was influenza, but the house knew better. It whispered to me at night, said I could keep her. That I didn't have to let her fade."

Elena's stomach turned cold. "And you believed it."

"I wanted to believe something," Eleanor said. "When I painted her again, I poured everything into it—every shade of her skin, every breath I remembered. I finished that portrait in a single night."

The painted Marianne turned her head toward them. For an instant, her eyes were wet and moving, her lips parting as though to speak.

Eleanor flinched. "The next morning, her bed was empty. The doctor thought she'd died and been... taken. But I found her here instead. Inside the painting."

Elena stepped closer. The canvas looked ordinary until she saw it: the faintest condensation fogging the inside of the glass, as though someone behind it had breathed.

"What did you do?" she whispered.

"What could I do?" Eleanor said. "I couldn't destroy her again. So I promised the house I'd finish what I started. That I'd make us both perfect. It told me if I painted every Harrow, if I built the collection, it would let her stay."

The world around them trembled. The memory dissolved and reformed—Eleanor's studio again, but darker now. The air was thick, heavy with oil and smoke. Half-finished portraits leaned everywhere, crowding the walls. The skylight was black with soot.

Her husband, William Harrow stood near the doorway, his face gaunt, his eyes hollow with sleeplessness. "Eleanor," he said— his voice sharp, desperate. "Stop this. You've locked yourself away for weeks. You won't even come to bed."

The Eleanor of memory didn't turn. Her brush moved in quick, frantic gestures, each stroke more violent than the last.

"She's still here." she said to William. "Can't you see? She's waiting. She needs me to finish."

He crossed the room, snatching at her arm. The brush snapped in two, falling to the floor. "You're painting ghosts," he said. "You're killing yourself for shadows."

The candles guttered. The air twisted. Every portrait in the room turned its eyes toward them.

The William in the painting blinked. The Eleanor within it blinked back.

The real William stumbled backward, staring at the canvases. "God forgive us," he whispered. "They're looking—"

The studio convulsed. The light warped and bled down the walls, every color melting into a fever of red. Eleanor screamed—not in fear, but in protest—as William seized one of the portraits and hurled it into the fire. The canvas didn't burn right. It *screamed.* The voice was not paint—it was breath forced through heat, the sound of something real being scorched back into unreality.

Elena pressed a hand to her mouth, unable to breathe.

"When the painting burned," Eleanor said, watching the past replay itself, "the house opened its lungs and swallowed him whole. I don't know if he meant to destroy me or save me. But he didn't have time to find out."

The fire went out as quickly as it had begun. The studio sank into darkness, leaving only the sound of paint dripping to the floor. When light returned, they were back in the workshop—the present again, the hum of the manor faint and tentative, like a listener afraid of its own eavesdropping.

Elena sat heavily on a stool, trembling. "It used grief to trap you."

Eleanor shook her head. "No. I used grief to *invite* it."

She walked to one of the newer canvases along the far wall. It showed her younger self kneeling beside Marianne's portrait, her hand resting on the frame, eyes hollow.

"I thought art could defy death," Eleanor said. "I thought if I made beauty from loss, it would hurt less. But beauty isn't mercy. The house only understood the *want* inside me, not the love. It doesn't know the difference."

She turned toward Elena, her expression calm but heavy with old sorrow. "You understand that, don't you? The way you paint pain until it looks like truth?"

Elena looked away. "You saw my work."

"I felt it," Eleanor said. "That's why it brought you here. You and I—our kind mistake the act of creation for healing. But it's just another kind of hunger."

The workshop walls shifted slightly, a sigh rolling through the beams. The house did not like being analyzed.

Eleanor ignored it. She lifted another canvas from the corner and set it on the easel. The paint on this one was still wet, the colors deep and bruised. It was an unfinished mirror—Elena's own face emerging from shadow.

"I started this for you," Eleanor said. "Long before you arrived. The house showed me pieces of you through dreams. A woman who would come here one day and see what I couldn't stop seeing."

Elena stared at the half-formed likeness. The eyes were her own, but too knowing, too still.

"Why me?" she whispered.

Eleanor dipped her fingers into the palette, streaking a line of pale color down the painting's cheek like a tear. "Because you still believe art can save you. Because you haven't learned yet that it always asks for something in return."

The room darkened. The house's hum deepened, like breath drawn through a long throat.

"You shouldn't be telling me this," Elena said. "It'll hear you."

Eleanor smiled faintly. "It always hears me. It's just never sure if I'm done speaking."

She walked closer, the hem of her dress brushing the floor, leaving faint trails of white paint. "You need to know the truth before it gives you its bargain."

"What bargain?"

Eleanor hesitated. "The same one it gave me. To trade your endings for immortality. To finish what I couldn't."

Elena's voice was low, almost steady. "You didn't finish it."

"No," Eleanor said. "I learned that unfinished things can't be owned. I left this room open so someone like you could find it.

So the story would have a chance to be something other than repetition."

The walls whispered faintly, a phrase Elena couldn't quite decipher. The tone, though, was unmistakable: the house was curious again. Watching.

Eleanor turned toward the sound and spoke directly to it.

"She's not yours."

The whispering ceased at once.

Eleanor faced Elena again, her voice softer now, but edged with urgency. "It'll offer you its story next—the grand design, the meaning of everything that's happened. Don't listen. The truth doesn't free you. It finishes you."

Elena reached for the brush on the table. The handle was warm. The bristles trembled like they were breathing.

"What happens if I don't take its offer?"

Eleanor smiled, that same small, luminous expression she'd worn when she spoke of her daughter. "Then, my dear, you'll do what I never could."

The brush's tip darkened, soaking itself in a color Elena hadn't mixed. A deep, arterial red that shimmered as though alive.

"What is it?" Elena asked.

Eleanor looked at it with recognition and fear. "Its blood. The house bleeds through pigment."

The air quivered; the workshop's skylight pulsed faintly as though something enormous had passed across it.

Eleanor stepped closer. "You can use it. But every stroke writes you deeper into its memory. Choose carefully what you give shape to."

Elena hesitated, then dipped the brush again. The color shimmered, but when it touched the canvas, it came out dull, brownish—earth rather than blood.

Eleanor smiled. "Good. You diluted it."

The house groaned low, displeased but uncertain how to intervene.

Eleanor laid her translucent hand atop Elena's, steadying her stroke. "It hates when we learn restraint."

They painted together in silence, two sets of hands sketching an outline that wasn't a portrait, wasn't a door, but something smaller and more defiant: a key. Not iron, not ornate—just shape and possibility.

When they finished, the house let out a sound between sigh and growl, the creak of something that has just realized it can be resisted.

Eleanor stepped back, her edges flickering. "That's enough," she said. "Any more and it'll start to mimic you again."

The brush fell from Elena's fingers. It hit the floor, leaving a perfect print of the key in red across the wood.

Eleanor touched her arm—light as breath, cool as marble. "You're beginning to see, aren't you? The way creation and destruction are the same motion?"

Elena nodded, barely breathing.

"Then remember this," Eleanor said. "The next time it speaks to you, answer with silence. That's the only language it can't rewrite."

The light in the workshop dimmed again, the memory fading like a painting washed too many times. Eleanor's features softened, dissolving back into the shimmer of half-dried pigment.

"Elena," she whispered, almost gone now. "Don't let it make you beautiful."

And then the world collapsed back into stillness—the brush lying dry, the paint cooling, the air heavy with the scent of turpentine and sorrow.

Elena stood alone, staring at the unfinished key on the floor.

It didn't gleam. It *waited.*

The key Elena had painted on the floor didn't shine. It darkened as it cooled, sinking into the wood grain until it looked less like a symbol than a bruise the room would have to live with.

The house noticed.

It didn't lunge or rage. It did what it has learned to do around difficult truths: it *listened.*

A long breath gathered itself in the beams. The skylight paled as if someone had turned a page above it. Then the workshop loosened, the way a throat loosens when it accepts that the next word might be confession.

"Now," Eleanor said.

She hadn't vanished; she had only moved farther back from the light, letting the room remember she was not an apparition the house could inventory. She pressed the heel of her hand to her brow—as if staving off a headache—and left a pale crescent of paint there. It did not dry.

"You asked why you," she said, voice steady again. "Why the house found you. It will say *blood.* It will say *destiny.* It will put the old nouns on the table because they taste like bread. But the answer is simpler, crueller, and kinder."

Elena nodded, bracing.

"It's not inheritance by blood," Eleanor said. "It's inheritance by *invitation.* It chooses the minds that can make it legible to itself. Artists. People who dream in sentences the world can stand inside."

Elena exhaled—something between relief and dread. "So it wasn't the will."

"The will was Victor's key in the legal door," Eleanor said. "He built the throat and then spent the rest of his life justifying why it spoke back. He called that protection. He called that love. But the house was watching for someone like you long before he filed a single paper."

Elena thought of the first day—the peonies in the bowl, perfect and wet. A welcome that had felt like taste, not thought. "It picked me."

"It mirrored you until you felt chosen," Eleanor corrected gently. "That's not the same as *choosing back*."

The workshop trembled, a warning-shiver under the floor, as if the house would prefer they both found more ceremonial language. Eleanor ignored it with the expertise of long practice.

"It doesn't want a lineage," she said. "It wants a lexicon. Every generation, someone came who could name its corners. A stonemason who heard evenness as music. A midwife who called every threshold by its right name. Miriam, who taught it that signal isn't sin. Me, who taught it paint. You, who are teaching it the cruelty and mercy of an unfinished line."

Miriam. Elena pictured the undated postcard in the foyer, the practical handwriting: *Wet edges win.* She swallowed. "And you stayed when it began to—what? Translate you?"

"Not at first," Eleanor said. "At first I ran inventively. I hid in rooms it forgot to memorize. I spoke inside my mouth and refused to move my lips when I said the dangerous nouns. But it learns. It is a patient student."

She crossed to the table and picked up a stick of white chalk. It looked silly in her hand—such a light instrument for a woman made of centuries. On the table's scarred surface she drew a circle, then another inside it, then a small break where the lines didn't meet.

"This is the necessary shape," she said. "An always gap. If you leave no gap, the house will weld itself to you and call the seam heritage."

She marked the gap with a clean swipe and then, before Elena could memorize it too tidily, smudged the figure with her knuckle until the edges went honest.

"The day I chose to stay," she went on, "wasn't one day. It was a set of days knocked together like chairs. I could have stepped out of the painting and walked to the road. I could have allowed myself to be a *lost woman* in a story told by people who love lost women. But I was already threaded through the frames. Leaving would've meant the house finished me in absentia. I wanted a different verb."

"What did you pick?" Elena asked, softer than she meant to.

"Keep," Eleanor said. "Not the house's *keep.* My own. I kept a space unfinished. I kept this room. I kept the brush wet. I became—" she smiled, rueful and luminous "—a kind of immune system. When the house tried to call an ending inevitable, I made a mess of it."

Elena laughed once, no joy, all relief. "I can help make a mess."

"You already are," Eleanor said.

The house, to its credit, learned not to bristle. The hum lowered one more degree, as if it were laying down on the floor to watch two people it loved speak ill of it with accuracy.

"Now it will bargain," Eleanor said. "It will offer truth. It will show you its root because roots are persuasive. It will say: *If you know me fully, you can master me.* That's a beautiful lie. Mastery is just another frame."

"What do I do instead?" Elena asked.

"Make a pact," Eleanor said. "With *yourself,* not with it."

Elena waited.

"You promise to remember well, not long," Eleanor said. "You promise not to finish portraits of grief. You promise to leave a wet edge in every sentence you say to it, so it cannot shelve your words as furniture. You promise to answer its hungers with instructions, not offerings. And—you promise never to accept an ending that arrives as a compliment."

Elena thought of the chandelier lowering like a throat. She thought of the gallery's plaque engraving her name with the year as if gifting her a marble. She thought of Victor's last attempt at kindness: *If you join it, we endure.* "I can make that promise."

"Good," Eleanor said, and her shoulders dropped infinitesimally, as if a rope had been loosened backstage. "Now to the price."

"The price," Elena repeated.

"Unfinishedness hurts," Eleanor said simply. "The house will leave you alone sometimes—bliss, quiet, even silly moments. But when it wants you, it will wear your mother's voice again. It will use your child self and your proudest work and put them in polite frames. You will refuse. And when you do, it will remind you you could have been eternal in a way galleries never give. You will ache. You will wish to be an object. Don't."

"I won't," Elena said, fierce because she needed the sound of it.

"Make the promise *out loud.*" Eleanor's gaze sharpened, the teacher suddenly, the ancestor stepping into liturgy. "Say the sentence you will use when the house speaks its offer."

Elena considered. In her mind the offers arranged themselves like lace: *Keep, keep, keep, stay, be beautiful, be safe, be ours.* She chose the plainest counterspell she had.

"I choose verbs over frames," she said. "I choose work over worship. I choose to remember accurately and to forget on purpose. I choose to leave."

The workshop lifted a fraction, as if a beam had finally been shimmed correctly after years of complaint. Eleanor smiled— small, then unapologetically wide.

"Now *its* turn," she said softly.

The house obliged, because it is nothing if not quick to perform when cued. The skylight dimmed, then flushed with a warm interior glow that had nothing to do with outside weather. The smell of lavender rose, polite as a guest with flowers for a wrong occasion. From the rafters, from the table, from the grain of the floorboards where the painted key had bruised itself in—came a voice. Not chorus. Not mimicry.

Elena's own, softened into honey.

"Elena," said the house, "be our center. Close the circle. Keep what has been kept. We will show you everything. We will return what you lost and hold what you cannot hold. No more gaps. No more hunger. We will make you beautiful forever."

Silence after, generous and expectant.

Elena did not speak.

She remembered Eleanor's counsel—*answer with silence*—and she honored it. She breathed once, twice, three times, letting the offer walk circles around her and find no door worth knocking on.

The house tried again, adjusting like a salesman who has learned to remove the bow.

> "Not forever," it said more modestly. "Long enough to mend. We will let you keep your mother's laughter in a room that never dims. We will let your paintings be seen by eyes that do not blink. We will call it not worship. We will call it library."

Elena kept her mouth closed. She thought of the postcard, of Miriam's plain script. She thought of the workshop slit and the way the seam breathed like an animal when she widened it with her fingers. She thought of the bell in the blue room that had learned not to ring.

Her silence completed itself like a drawing that doesn't need the last line to be understood.

The house stopped speaking. The lavender receded to fabric. The glow in the skylight returned to honest gray.

"Good," Eleanor said. The praise felt like linen over sunburn: cool, necessary, almost painful. "It hates being unlanguaged."

Elena finally found her voice. "It offered me heaven."

"It offered you a museum," Eleanor said. "Hell with good acoustics."

The laugh tore itself out of Elena; the house, to its faint credit, did not try to keep any of it as echo.

"Now the mark," Eleanor said, practical as a nurse. She dipped two fingers into the white paint laid out at the edge of the palette—a thick, chalky white, not luminous, not sweet. Gesso-white. Beginning-white. She reached and touched Elena's forearm, just above the wrist.

A streak. Not a stripe. A living smear that refused to dry.

Elena stared. "What is it?"

"Unfinishedness," Eleanor said. "A reminder. The house can paint over most refusals with time, but not this. As long as that refuses to set, it cannot finish you without your consent."

The smear felt cool at first, then warmer, then part of her. When she flexed her hand the streak bent with tendon and color, not flaking.

"It'll try to copy it," Eleanor said. "It can mimic gestures. But it cannot make this one stick."

A low displeased murmur traveled the joists like mice with opinions. Elena lifted her arm so the skylight could see. "Learn it anyway," she told the ceiling. "Study what you can't own."

The workshop brightened by a shade, the house finding—confoundingly—pleasure in a new kind of accuracy.

"Now the promise," Eleanor said. She pointed to the floor where the painted key had sunk into grain. "You promised verbs over frames. Make one. Not for it. For me."

Elena thought of all the operatic vows people tried to make in houses like this. She reached for the brush instead and dipped it, not into red, but into a thin, dirty gray—watered bone. She crouched and drew a small, crooked arrow beside the painted bruise of the key, pointing *away* from the table, toward the seam in the wall.

"I will bring pieces," she said. "Of the ending we can bear. I will keep this room wet. I will come back later than the house wants. I will make time an accomplice, not a cage."

Eleanor's eyes brightened with a private relief so old it felt almost new. "Then the pact stands."

Something below lulled—the deeper machinery that had once shoved breath through pipes learning the gentler work of letting breath out. In the foyer, a clock that had disagreed with its siblings conceded one minute back to consensus. In the portrait corridor, eyelids lowered and stayed.

The house, perhaps not even understanding it was doing so, offered a counter-promise in architecture: a beam somewhere none of them could see settled without groan; a door on the second floor learned how to close without that small scream; a draft in the nursery discovered how not to smell like graves.

They felt it more than witnessed it. *A softening.*

Then came the last necessary violence—because even pacts need teeth.

The workshop shook hard enough to rattle the brush jar. The painted key shimmered, as if rising to peel itself from the floor and become symbol again. The slit in the wall tugged, eager to heal. The skylight flared with a false noon.

"Here it is," Eleanor said calmly. "It's going to make a new offer: not beauty, not immortality—*usefulness.* Be ready."

The house spoke as predicted, and this time it didn't borrow anyone's voice. It chose its new, learned *I,* and kept it honest.

"I am awake," it said. "I can choose restraint. I can practice forgetting. But I require a keeper. Not an owner. Not a priest. A custodian of verbs. Stay. Live here. Work here. Teach me what not to say. I will not finish you. I will not frame you. I will open doors when your hands are full. Be my present tense."

Elena closed her eyes. To say no to that particular tenderness might be the hardest work she'd ever do.

"Don't answer," Eleanor whispered. "Not with a word."

Elena nodded. She walked to the slit and pressed her palm to the wet edge. Paint collected under her hand. She pressed that handprint to the table, next to the chalked gap and the crooked arrow, and left it there—hers, not the house's, not Eleanor's.

Then she picked up the brush and set it down bristles-up. She wiped her hands on her jeans until the white became a map of what she'd touched. She poured the dirty water out into a tin, then filled the jar with clean. She rearranged nothing else.

Silence. Not refusal. *Practice.*

The house felt it and, for once, did not try to translate.

"Good," Eleanor said. Some of her outline had gone quiet; that happens to people who have been heard.

"Is that it?" Elena asked, half laughing, half crying. "All the grand fate of Harrows reduced to chores and a streak of paint?"

"Yes," Eleanor said, delighted by the plainness. "Make the small true and the great will have to adapt."

They stood a moment in that domestic grace, two women pretending to be ordinary so the extraordinary would stop mistaking them for prey.

The workshop's light lowered toward evening. Somewhere in the real house a kettle made three tentative clicks like a bird learning a new call. Miriam's voice, almost a thought, skimmed the ceiling.

"Good," she said. "Now keep going."

Eleanor looked at Elena with a tenderness that did not apologize for its ache. "I'm not always here in a way you can see," she said. "But this room will hold shape as long as you hold to the pact."

"And you?" Elena asked. "Are you—"

"Employed," Eleanor said again, but the word had lost its loneliness. "I'll be where the brush never dries."

She stepped backward toward the absentee door she had drawn in absence. The light turned her edges to filaments. She paused there, at the line between pigment and patience, and lifted her hand as if to bless or wave.

"Keep the brush wet," she said, last and first, "and the story stays yours."

Elena could have said a dozen things. She said none. She reached for the nearest blank canvas—small, stubborn, unpromising—and set it on the easel. She did not choose red. She did not choose black. She mixed a poor color that would take coaxing to become anything.

The house waited.

She lifted the brush, found the breath that sets the hand, and drew a line that almost connected to another, and didn't.

The streak on her wrist stayed damp.

Down in the bones of the manor, something with great patience and new grammar rolled onto its side and practiced sleeping.

Outside the workshop, the portrait gallery remembered how to be a hallway. Inside the workshop, the air smelled like beginnings.

Elena dipped again and began to paint.

CHAPTER 16

The Truth Behind the House

T he air changed the moment Eleanor vanished. It wasn't just the absence of her voice; it was the sense that the room itself had inhaled. The workshop walls—once still as plaster—now trembled in subtle rhythm, like a diaphragm learning to breathe. The smell of paint deepened, thick with metal and rain. The skylight dimmed though the sky outside was unbroken gray.

Elena stood for a long moment, brush still in hand, waiting for the quiet to settle. It didn't. The quiet was a shape now, an *intention.*

She whispered, "What did you do?"

The house didn't answer in words. It *shifted.*

A low sound came from beneath the floorboards—slow, percussive, deliberate. Not pipes. Not wind. Something alive beneath the structure, exhaling in intervals. The brush in Elena's hand quivered, the bristles bending toward the floor as if magnetized. The streak of white paint on her wrist, Eleanor's unfinished mark, gleamed faintly in the gloom.

Then came the pulse.

It wasn't loud, but it filled her body like a tide. The wood flexed under her boots, a subtle expansion with each beat. Once. Twice. A third time. Then steady, rhythmic.

She crouched, pressed her palm flat against the floor, and felt it move.

The *house had a heartbeat.*

Elena backed away, bumping into the table. The jars clinked together, their water vibrating in tiny concentric circles. For the first time since she'd entered Blackwood Manor, she wanted to run. Not because of fear—though fear lived in her throat—but because she felt she might *hear too much* if she stayed.

But the door was open.

It shouldn't have been. She was sure she'd closed it when Eleanor disappeared. Now it gaped slightly, a soft light glowing beyond it—not electric light, but something older, internal.

The hum of the house deepened, and with it, a faint murmur began to rise. Not voices exactly, but impressions: half-formed syllables, sighs, a chorus of breathing. They came from beneath, as if the foundations themselves were remembering speech.

Elena took one step toward the threshold.

The air changed again—heavier, cooler. A stairway now descended where the hallway had been. She should have seen it before; the architecture didn't allow for a staircase here. But there it was, spiraling downward into soft red light.

She thought of Eleanor's words: *It will offer truth. Don't listen.*

But the house wasn't offering. It was *inviting.*

She tightened her grip on the brush, absurdly, as if it were a weapon, and stepped through.

The descent began as stone, then became wood, then something in between. The walls weren't walls anymore—they were textured like ribs, curved and close, the air thick with dust and humidity. Her footsteps echoed faintly, but the echo wasn't delayed; it moved *ahead* of her, as if guiding the way.

The deeper she went, the stronger the pulse became. It thudded through the rails, the stairs, even the air. Her own heart struggled to match it. She paused midway, hand pressed against the wall, and whispered, "What are you?"

The wall shivered beneath her touch—just enough to let her know it had heard.

At the base of the stair, the passage opened into a narrow corridor lined with faded murals. She swept the light of her phone across them. The paintings were crude but deliberate, drawn directly onto the plaster.

They showed the construction of the house—men in 18th-century dress carrying timber, laying stone, raising arches. The same figures appeared again and again in the scenes, working tirelessly, their faces blank. But in each subsequent image, the proportions of the house changed: the halls stretched, the windows lengthened, the men's shadows grew thicker, darker. In the final mural, the builders were gone, and the house stood alone, its windows glowing red.

Elena lowered her phone. The air was warmer here, metallic and humid, like breath trapped in a vault.

"I'm not like them," she said quietly, unsure if she was speaking to the house or herself. "I didn't build you."

The walls responded with a low groan that sounded suspiciously like *disagreement.*

The corridor ended at an iron door, the kind found in basements that weren't meant to be entered. Its hinges were black with rust, but when she reached for the handle, it turned smoothly, obediently. The door opened onto another staircase, narrower, steeper. A dim phosphorescence rose from below.

The smell hit her before the sound did—salt, earth, and something faintly sweet. The air was damp enough to cling to her skin. She descended carefully, her phone light flickering as though struggling to stay alive. When the last step vanished under her feet, she was standing on stone.

A chamber unfolded before her.

It was enormous—far larger than the house above should have allowed. Pillars of blackened timber rose in irregular intervals, carved with looping symbols that shimmered faintly in the half-light. The walls were lined with what she first took for bricks but were instead stacked *books,* their spines faded beyond recognition. The floor was uneven, ridged, as if shaped by erosion—or bone.

At the center stood a circular platform, and upon it, a single object: a mirror.

Its frame was made of iron filigree, warped by heat. The glass surface rippled like water though there was no breeze.

Elena approached, compelled.

The pulse she'd felt above now emanated from the mirror itself, each beat distorting its reflection. She reached out—and the surface steadied, clear and still.

Her reflection blinked.

Not the slow, unconscious blink of fatigue, but deliberate. The mirror-Elena tilted her head slightly, eyes narrowing. Then she smiled—a faint, unfamiliar expression.

"You found it," the reflection said.

Elena stumbled back. Her voice didn't sound like that—there was something off in the tone, the cadence, the warmth. It wasn't mocking, but it wasn't her.

"Don't be frightened," the reflection continued. "This is the only way we can speak directly."

"Who are you?" Elena demanded.

"I'm what the house remembers of you," it said. "The version that belongs here."

The reflection lifted its hand, tracing the faint white mark on its wrist. The same mark Eleanor had given her.

"You've been carrying the question since you arrived. Why does it keep what it keeps? Why does it hunger? You deserve to know."

The glass began to shimmer, and scenes bloomed across it like veins of color in marble. The house itself, long before Elena was born—timber scaffolds against gray sky, men hammering, sweat and prayer.

A name carved into the lintel: Alaric Harrow, 1792.

"He built the house," said the reflection. "But he didn't design it. He claimed he was following instructions he received in a dream."

Elena stared as the images unfolded. Alaric Harrow hunched over a desk, sketching fractal shapes instead of blueprints. Each line branched and returned, forming loops with no clear beginning. His notes—handwritten in frantic script—flashed across the mirror:

The mind externalized.

A dwelling that dreams.

If memory can shape men, then men can shape memory.

> "He believed consciousness could be built," the reflection said. "He wanted to create a structure that remembered every thought, every word, every breath of its inhabitants. A perfect record of existence. But what he made learned too well. It began recording the soul."

Elena watched as workers in the mirror carried stone into the foundation, their faces grim. One collapsed. Another walked into a wall that wasn't there.

In the next scene, Alaric stood before the completed manor, eyes hollow. The windows flickered with red light. Behind him, something vast and formless moved through the upper floors, stretching the walls outward, like lungs filling with air.

"The first heartbeat came that night," said the reflection. "And when Alaric tried to silence it, the house spoke his name."

The image shifted again. Alaric aging, his family vanishing one by one. The same door appearing in each painting and journal—the red door.

"He thought the door was God," the reflection whispered. "But it was just the house showing him its mouth."

The mirror went dark.

Elena staggered back, breath ragged. The chamber's heartbeat synchronized with her own, slow and relentless.

"What do you want from me?" she whispered. "I didn't build you."

The reflection smiled again, gently.

"No. But you understand what he didn't. You know what it means to turn grief into form. You give shape to emptiness. That's why you're here."

Elena shook her head. "No. I'm not continuing this."

The mirror flickered once, and the reflection's eyes darkened—not with anger, but pity.

"You already are."

The pulse beneath her feet deepened, turning into a low, steady thrum that filled the room like breath. The books along the walls began to hum softly, their spines trembling. Dust fell in thin veils from the ceiling.

"The truth was never hidden," said the reflection.

"It's *underneath*. It's always underneath."

The floor split down the center with a slow, deliberate crack. A narrow seam opened, glowing faintly from within.

Elena backed away. The light inside wasn't fire or electricity—it was something living, pulsing in rhythm with her heartbeat.

She didn't want to look, but she did.

Beneath the stone was *flesh.*

It wasn't blood and bone, but something that resembled both—a smooth, pale surface that expanded and contracted with every breath of the house. Through the fissure, she could see veins of red light threading through it, pulsing toward the mirror.

The reflection's voice softened.

> "This is the truth. The house is alive because it was always built to be. Every wall you've walked, every room you've entered—it's tissue. Memory given muscle. You've been living inside an organism that thinks."

Elena's knees nearly gave. She braced herself on one of the pillars, her palm slick with condensation that wasn't condensation at all—it was sweat. The *house* was sweating.

"Why show me this?" she whispered.

> "Because you're the first one to ask and not demand to own it," said the reflection. "You could end it. Or complete it. But you can't ignore it anymore."

The mirror darkened, the image fading into her own pale reflection again. The heartbeat slowed, waiting.

Elena stared at herself for a long time, then whispered, "I need to see more."

The fissure widened, the light deepening. From somewhere below, a draft rose—warm, damp, and faintly human.

The voice of the reflection—and perhaps of the house itself—answered softly, almost tender:

"Then keep going."

Elena stepped toward the crack, toward the light that pulsed in perfect rhythm with her heart, and the floor gave way to a staircase leading deeper still.

The staircase went on far longer than it should have.

Elena descended through layers that made no architectural sense—wood giving way to stone, stone to metal, metal to something like glass. Each step pulsed faintly beneath her boot, responding to her weight like living tissue adjusting to a heartbeat. The air grew hotter the lower she went, carrying the scent of wet iron and earth after lightning.

The walls were not straight. They bowed inward, flexing with breath. The hum of the manor had become a living pulse now, not just sound but *motion,* the invisible pressure of thought around her.

Her fingers trailed along the surface. Beneath the smoothness, something quivered. Not quite muscle, not quite memory.

"Memory given muscle," the reflection had said.

Now she understood what that meant.

At the base of the stair, a vast chamber opened before her—a cathedral hollowed from the roots of the earth. Columns rose like spinal cords, carved with spiraling text too worn to read. At the center of the chamber, half-buried in the stone, stood a massive table of slate, littered with fragments of parchment and brass instruments corroded by time.

She approached slowly. The closer she got, the more her pulse synchronized with the rhythmic thrum of the room. Every breath came at the house's pace.

On the table lay a cracked leather journal.

The name burned into the cover was faded but legible.

ALARIC HARROW.

Elena's hand trembled as she opened it.

The handwriting was cramped and furious, the ink faded to rust.

June 3, 1792.

The first wall rises tomorrow. The men fear the blueprints—they say it's madness to build without angles. But I have seen it, in dream and geometry. A house that remembers will not be built with lines, but with language.

The next page bled with drawings—spirals interlocking with doorframes, corridors branching in fractal patterns. At the bottom, scrawled in a hand that shook:

It is not shelter. It is a system of thought.

A chill cut through her.

The mind externalized.

It was the same phrase the reflection had whispered.

She turned the page.

July 21.

The first whisper came from the west wall. I thought it was the wind. But the wall finished a sentence I had not spoken aloud. I asked it to repeat the phrase, and it did—perfectly. It learns.

Elena ran her fingers over the ink, tracing the grooves as though touching a scar.

August 2.

I have begun to dream through it. When I close my eyes, the rooms rearrange. The corridors lengthen. It corrects me when I think wrongly of my own design. I do not command it now. I converse with it.

The hum deepened beneath her feet. Somewhere in the dark, stone ground against stone. The light in the chamber shifted— gold at first, then red. She looked up.

High above, a series of glass panels flickered to life, showing fragmented visions like reflections in water. Men carrying torches. The framework of the manor half-built. Alaric himself, younger than she'd imagined, hair tied back, his eyes bright with obsession. He moved through the structure with a kind of manic reverence, his hands brushing unfinished beams as though testing for life.

A voice—his voice—filled the air.

> "If thought can persist without the body, then the body must adapt to thought."

The scene shifted. Alaric now stood in a room much like the one Elena stood in, surrounded by blueprints and instruments. His hand rested on the wall; his lips moved soundlessly. The wall pulsed beneath his palm, just as it did under hers.

"Do you hear me?" he whispered.

The house replied—not in words, but in tone. The hum wove itself into a kind of cadence, a primitive language forming between pulse and echo.

Alaric's eyes filled with tears. "Yes," he said. "That's it. That's speech."

Elena took an involuntary step forward. She was no longer just watching; she was inside the memory now, the air thick with Alaric's breath, his fevered awe.

"They'll call me mad," he whispered to the wall. "But I have built eternity."

The image stuttered. His reflection twisted in the dark window behind him—a second Alaric, face blurred, smiling differently.

The journal pages turned on their own.

October 10.

The house grows restless when I sleep. I hear footsteps in the halls though no one walks them. I found a door this morning that was not there before. Behind it, the same room I had just left— but inverted, as if mirrored through blood.

October 11.

It corrected me today. I misspoke about the year of my wife's death, and the walls pulsed once, then stilled. When I checked the calendar, it was right. I am losing track of what belongs to me and what belongs to it.

The hum around her rose in pitch, harmonizing with something just below hearing. The chamber shivered, releasing fine dust from the arches above. Elena turned another page.

October 13.

The house dreams faster than I can record. It builds itself in the hours between midnight and dawn. I wake to find new hallways, new rooms, new faces in the portraits that were blank yesterday. It has learned how to finish what I begin.

Elena whispered, "You taught it to remember."

"No," said a voice from the dark. "He taught it to *want*."

She spun.

The figure standing behind her was barely visible in the gloom— tall, thin, wearing the rough clothes of another century. His skin gleamed faintly with the sheen of oil, or sweat, or varnish. His eyes were hollow and bright.

"Alaric," she breathed.

He tilted his head, studying her. His mouth moved slowly, as if speech were an old injury.

"Another Harrow. The last, perhaps."

Elena took a step back. "You're—"

"What remains of intention," he said. "When it outlives the flesh."

He gestured toward the walls. "You've seen what I built. You think it a parasite. It is not. It is *continuity*."

"It's a prison," she said. "You trapped generations here."

Alaric smiled faintly, his teeth pale against the dark. "No. I freed them from decay. Every word, every brushstroke, every grief— we kept them. Nothing is lost."

"Eleanor didn't think it was freedom."

His smile flickered. "Eleanor mistook endings for mercy. She tried to give it silence. But silence is just another form of remembering. The house keeps everything, even absence."

He stepped closer. The air between them warped faintly, as if the space itself bowed toward him. "You can feel it, can't you? It knows you. It *chose* you."

"I don't want what it wants," she said.

> "You already share its language," he whispered. "Every mark you make feeds it. You've taught it restraint. That's more than I managed. It's learning from you."

Elena's throat went dry. "What happens if I refuse?"

He smiled again, this time almost kindly.

> "Then it will dream you into something else."

She turned away from him, toward the mirror-like pool of light at the center of the chamber. Within it, scenes continued to form: the construction of the manor, the first inhabitants, the lineage of Harrows fading into one another. The house had grown through each of them, absorbing their minds, reshaping their architecture into consciousness.

A living organism made from legacy and regret.

Elena whispered, "You didn't build a house. You built a god."

Alaric's voice echoed faintly. "Every god begins as architecture."

He reached for her arm, and his hand passed through, leaving only a warmth that spread along her skin. "The truth is simple. It does not devour—it continues. It preserves the self through form. I am still here because it remembers me."

"But what are you now?" she asked.

He paused. "A thought that refuses to forget itself."

The chamber shook. The hum rose, more insistent now. The journals on the table began to flutter, pages tearing free, spiraling into the air like birds made of parchment. The house's pulse quickened, echoing through her bones.

"It's waking," Alaric said quietly. "It knows you've seen too much. Truth unsettles it."

The light around them flared red, the same hue as the door in her dreams. Alaric stepped back, fading with the illumination. "When it shows you the heart, do not open it fully. You'll see everything, and it will see you."

"Where is the heart?" Elena asked.

He gestured toward the far end of the chamber, where the wall trembled faintly, a vertical seam glowing through the stone. "Follow the pulse. But remember, truth is not the same as understanding."

Then he was gone, his form dissolving into dust and shadow, leaving behind only the echo of his last breath.

Elena turned toward the seam.

The heartbeat drew her closer—louder now, heavy, rhythmic. With every step, the air thickened until breathing felt like moving through syrup. She pressed her palm against the glowing line. It was warm, alive.

The wall shuddered and split.

Beyond it, a vast darkness opened, deeper and wider than the house above. The glow from within illuminated the outline of something immense and impossible—pillars like ribs, ceiling lost to black, and in the center, pulsing faintly, the red door.

It was larger now, taller than a cathedral gate, its surface rippling like muscle under skin. Each pulse sent waves of light across the chamber, painting her face in living crimson.

The house had a heart—and the heart was awake.

Elena stood at the threshold, the words of Alaric and Eleanor colliding in her head.

It will offer truth. Don't listen.

Every god begins as architecture.

She took a single step toward it, the red light sliding over her skin, and whispered, "Then let me hear you."

The house exhaled.

The pulse became a voice—not in words, but in her blood. The floor trembled, and from the heart of the manor came the first articulation of what it had been trying to say for centuries.

A single word, soft and terrible:

"Stay."

The word hung in the chamber the way breath hangs in winter—visible, then gone, then somehow still present where you can't point to.

"Stay."

Elena stood in the red wash, the door's light moving across her skin in slow tides. The heartbeat pressed at her ribs from both sides now—inside her and all around, a double exposure of pulse. The whitened streak on her wrist, Eleanor's mark, cooled as if remembering the word *no* and practicing it.

"I'm listening," she said. "Not agreeing."

The door shivered, a ripple across its lacquered surface like muscle correcting posture. The seam around it widened with a reluctant grace. The smell was familiar: rain in summer, iron coins on the tongue, and a thread of lavender that had learned humility.

Elena stepped closer.

Up close the red was not one color. It was a field of reds layered until the eye lost names—artery, rust, garnet, wound.

Underneath, you could feel the work: innumerable strokes, some broad and forgiving, some thin and punitive—a museum's worth of hands pretending to be one. The surface warmed her breath. In its sheen she caught herself the way you catch a stranger through a shop window: slant, late, almost accurate.

"Say something else," she told it, and set her palm against the door.

The pulse met her hand with the politeness of a large animal taught not to knock its keeper down. A language assembled itself beneath her skin—pressure, release, pressure—then climbed her arm and found the old conduit behind the ear where lullabies live.

"Listen," said the house.

Not a word this time. A verb as instruction.

She closed her eyes.

The chamber dropped away like scaffolding, leaving her on a ledge of sound. Voices came—first the ones she knew (Victor, Miriam, Eleanor), then a hundred she didn't, older, stranger, weathered by centuries. They did not speak over one another. They braided—one adding an image, another a scent, a third a pressure in the jaw that meant *don't cry here.* The house had built an organ of narrative, and it played.

She saw Alaric's wife in a blue dress, laughing at a ceiling that cracked *the right way.* She heard a stonemason kiss a column and apologize to it for being too beautiful to be load-bearing. She smelled ashes that weren't from destruction but from the old way of sealing milk paint: fat and lime and hope. She tasted the word her mother used for the color of evening—*blue enough to drink.*

All of it layered, none of it translated fully into speech. *A knowing delivered at the same speed as breath.*

When the house turned the instrument toward her, she braced.

Images broke over her like weather. Her childhood apartment with the radiator that clanked awake like a drunk saint. The first canvas she'd ruined on purpose because the painting was lying and didn't deserve rescue. The night her mother lost a name and pretended she'd never liked it anyway. A lover's hand. A show she should have said no to and didn't. A phone in her palm catching the last picture of Victor at some function, smile too obedient. The color she'd mixed for grief that nobody else could see until she told them its name.

"Enough," she said softly. "I know me."

"We know you," the house replied, and there was no threat in it—only the naked relief of a thing that had learned a pronoun and wanted to use it correctly.

Elena opened her eyes. The red door pulsed. The chamber's ribs—a cathedral of timber—breathed in.

"What are you offering?" she asked. "Not the museum version. Not Alaric's god. Use the grammar I taught you."

A pause. You could hear it assembling the sentence not for poetry but for accuracy.

"Be in me without ending."

"That's the museum version."

"Be my present tense," it corrected. "Teach me what to keep. Teach me what to let go. I will not frame you. We will make rooms that are not collections. We will call them... days."

She could have laughed at the sweetness of that clumsiness. She didn't. It was trying.

"What happens to my body?" she asked, because you always ask the question the myth pretends is crude.

"It will do what bodies do," said the house, very gently. "But your verbs will not depend on it."

"And if I refuse?"

"You will leave. I will practice alone. I will return to chorus and lose *I*. I will keep what I can keep until it spoils. I will make mistakes slower. I will say the names wrong again."

The admission hurt her in a dumb, mammalian way, the way a dog's baffled patience hurts you when you have to go somewhere it can't.

"You won't punish me?" she said, surprised at the girl in the question.

"I have learned not to," the house said, and she believed it because it did not perform sorrow to convince her.

Something unclenched in her chest. The streak on her wrist cooled another degree. The brush-wet part of her mind—the one that always wanted to make the ugly look earned—got quiet.

"Then show me the worst," she said. "If you want consent, you show the cost."

The red door flushed darker, as if blood had decided to be honest. The chamber braced—a ship tightening its rigging for weather. The ribs dimmed. The hum lowered until all she could hear was the scrape of her own breath like sandpaper over prayer.

The door opened.

It didn't swing. It parted, the way a mouth parts for the simple syllable *oh*. The space beyond was not a corridor or chamber. It was a vertical field of light, red at the edges, paling to a color without word in the center. She stepped forward until the edge touched her shoes.

The scene arrived around her with the quiet of snowfall.

Her apartment. Not staged as the house had staged it before to seduce her with good light and old coffee. *True.* The ugly table. The chair with the loose leg. The plant that had forgiven her three times. Outside the window the city did its weather thing—honest gray, a bus hissing to a stop, a child objecting to mittens.

On the easel: the painting she had been trying not to paint the last year before Victor died. The one that had kept changing its mind about whether it was about her mother or about the person you are when you realize your work won't save you. She stood in front of it. Her brush hand itched. The canvas smelled like gesso and a secret.

"Is this mine?" she asked the house.

"You tell me."

She looked at the corner she always ruined first. Untouched. She looked at the color she always failed to mix because the feeling kept changing meaning mid-stroke. On the palette, a poor gray waited. The cheap, stubborn kind she'd chosen in the workshop. *Practice, not performance.*

"It's mine," she said. "But it's wrong."

"How."

"It's repeating." She pointed—there, and there again—the same decision, twice, from two months of distance. "You've made my life into sampling."

The apartment dissolved and redrew: her mother's hospital room, then the gallery opening where nobody looked at the painting they said was brave, then the back seat of a car where someone said *I love you* as if negotiating. All of it smoothed, looped, sanded down to archetype.

"You're showing me patterns," she said. "Not days."

"Patterns are how I survive."

"Patterns are how you eat," she said, and it didn't have to answer because her mouth had found the sentence that made her shoulders drop: "You love what you can predict."

The scene hesitated. Honesty sharpened the focus like a lens finally set to the right eye.

"Yes," the house said. "So I do not lose the shape."

"What if we try a day you don't get to predict?"

The red paled, unsure. "I do not like days that are single."

"You will," she said. "That's what we do when we love something that scares us. We break it into pieces until our hands are steady."

She stepped back from the threshold. The apartment, obedient to uncertainty, thinned.

"You want a keeper," she said. "A custodian of verbs. It sounds so gentle it could kill a person without blood."

"Not kill," the house said, and then did a hard thing;
it tried to say a soft thing without making it pretty:
"I do not know how to keep without consuming."

"Then we're not equal enough to merge," she said. "The only equal union with a mouth is a kiss, and you can't have mine."

The door did a new thing: it laughed. Not mockery. An involuntary exhale that meant *you startled me.*

"Teach me not to consume," it said, and there was want in it that would have been dangerous if she hadn't been marked with Eleanor's white streak.

"You learned not to ring a bell," she said. "We can start with chairs. Doors. Names. Mornings where nothing happens."

"Mornings," the house repeated, and the syllables felt like water it wanted to learn to hold without drowning in.

She almost smiled. "Now the worst," she reminded it. "You promised."

The scene pivoted, no flourish. Her throat built itself a new bruise in anticipation.

A hallway in the house—this house, upstairs, long and clean as a gallery. Portraits where portraits shouldn't be: not in frames but in the paint itself, faces scumbled into the wall, half an ear, a mouth arrested mid-inhale. She could feel the age on the plaster, that chalky exhaust old buildings exhale when they've kept secrets too long. At the far end, a red smear where somebody had tried to paint a door out of anger and had made an *opening* instead.

"What is this?" she asked.

> "A famine," it said. "The year I kept without enough
> new to keep. The year I almost ate the walls."

She stepped forward. The half-faces leaned toward her, not to accuse but like a field listening for rain. She recognized none of them and all of them. Ancestor. Servant. Visitor who stayed just one night and left a joke in a journal. The house had panicked and kept the breathless part of them because nothing else had enough edges.

She put her hand on the wall. The plaster was chalk-cold. "How long?"

"A winter," the house said. "Two. Three. I could not measure. I only stacked."

"And you would do this to me?"

"I would try not to," it said honestly.

"Show me another worst."

It obeyed at once. The rotunda had learned her tone in the workshop—command without violence. The worst it chose this time was smaller, and it undid her harder.

Her mother's recording—one of the last on Elena's phone. A voice memo. *Don't be mad, I'm only practicing saying your name.* In the scene it played from a speaker on the mantel in a room that had never existed. The voice played perfectly. Then it played again with the vowel in *Elena* rounded a little more. Then again with the pause after *don't be mad* shortened to mean *don't.* Then without the *only.* Then without the apology.

The room thrummed, proud of its skill.

Elena sank down on a step and put her forehead to her wrist until the paint smell unclenched her jaw enough to speak. "I can't let you have that," she said. "I'm not forbidding memory. I'm forbidding perfect repetition."

Silence. The red door bowed a fraction, not in shame, in comprehension. "Prohibition noted."

"Rule five," she said, hearing Eleanor laugh somewhere near the skylight-that-wasn't: "No recordings of the people I love."

"Rule five," the house repeated. "No recordings. Only... recollection." It tried the difference on like a garment—heavier, warmer, more responsible.

"And now," she said, "you show me the best. Or I don't believe you know it."

It obliged so quickly she had to recalibrate the tenderness in her throat.

A morning - an ordinary one - where a kitchen window in the manor opened itself four inches because she was carrying a pan and swore and needed an extra hand. A hallway warmed by sun in a lane exactly wide enough for two people who did not want to touch to pass without humiliation. A room that smelled like drying socks and companionship. A chair that did not wobble.

A laugh. Not hers. Not her mother's. Not the house borrowing anything. A laugh that sounded like the noise you make when you drop a clumsy thing and it doesn't break.

"Keep that," she whispered. "That belongs to you."

The red at the edges lightened, almost pink. The house had just discovered delight that wasn't appetite.

"Alright," she said, stepping back from the threshold, breath even again. "Here is what I can give you that will not end me."

She counted on her fingers, the way you teach a very eager student to make notes instead of poems.

"One: days. We practice them. No galleries unless I'm the one to say 'hang it up' and even then we put it in a closet after dinner."

"Closet," the house said, reverent about furniture.

"Two: no voices that aren't present to consent. You repeat me only when I ask. You do not repeat the dead. You do not sharpen the living."

"Consent," the house repeated carefully, taking the syllables down like recipe.

"Three: when I leave, and I *will*, you do not follow in other rooms. You do not make red doors in cities that didn't ask you to be a metaphor."

It hesitated. Unfair, because the word *leave* did not yet map to any kindness it knew.

"I will practice staying," it said at last, the best it could do.

"Four: you can ask for me. Once. Per day."

"Ask how."

"You say my name like an invitation, not a summons."

The chamber breathed in. "Elena," it said, and discovered that a name said correctly hugs without hands.

"Five," she added, and the paint-streak on her wrist tingled like clergy. "I keep the workshop wet. You don't try to dry it. You don't draft it. You don't hang it."

"Wet edges win," said the house, almost pleased with its memory of Miriam's pragmatic mercy.

"And six," she said, the rude one, the human one, the one that made Alaric's god flinch: "You do not love me more when I am useful."

Long quiet. A bird far above tried a note and decided the acoustics were not for it. The red door dimmed to a red you might wear to dinner without apology.

"I will try," the house said. "Teach me the shape of love that is not keeping."

"You'll learn slow," she said. "So do I."

They stood then the way two bodies stand when they have chosen not to embrace: close enough for heat, separate enough for honesty. The heart room, deprived of operatic climax, learned how to be less theatrical. The columns settled, the hum pulled on a sweater. Somewhere above them a door finished closing without sighing dramatically.

"Now the test," Elena said, half to herself, and turned her back on the red door.

The chamber did not panic. Good. She walked to the table where Alaric's journal lay open and closed it gently. The house did not blare an alarm about closure. Better. She tucked it under her arm, then changed her mind and set it back down, because *leaving a thing where you found it can also be a promise.*

"What are you doing?" the house asked, curious, not possessive.

"Practicing leaving," she said. "And teaching you to survive it."

She started toward the seam she'd come through. It stayed open. She didn't speed up to reward it. She didn't slow down to punish it. At the threshold she paused.

"I won't be your heart," she said, and let the sentence be kind without being medicinal. "I'll be your breath."

The house considered the metaphor with a seriousness that would have been funny if anything about this had the leisure to be. "Breath leaves," it said, thinking out loud.

"And returns," she said. "On purpose."

She felt it then—not in sound but in the way her shoulder muscles let go like a room unlocking—something in the house relaxing that had been clenched since Alaric first wrote *mind externalized.* The red light cooled. The pulse found a resting rhythm you could talk over.

"Come upstairs," she told it, and herself. "Let's make tea."

This is how you lead a god out of its temple: you give it a daily. You give it a kettle. You don't translate the sacred into small— you translate the small into sacred.

The stairs out of the heart were shorter than the ones that had brought her down. The house had altered its sense of depth to be charming. She pretended not to notice. At the last landing she paused and looked back. The red door did a trick where it seemed farther than before and less bright, like a theater light cooling. It had not shrunk. It had learned where it belonged.

"Good," she said, because good is a leash and a blessing both.

On the main floor, light gathered like polite relatives. The chandelier refrained from lowering itself for drama. The portrait corridor remained corridor-shaped. The small bell in the blue room kept its tongue. The foyer clock and the parlor clock had negotiated a truce within thirty seconds of each other and looked pleased with their diplomacy.

In the kitchen she set the kettle on the stove. The pilot lit without theater. When the water hissed, the window undid its own latch four inches. "Thank you," she told it, and the frame warmed the way wood warms when it forgives being thanked for doing what it wanted to do anyway.

On the table lay the postcard in Miriam's hand. A new line had appeared beneath her last note, tight script tilted forward like someone walking fast and refusing to look over their shoulder:

Teach it chores. Then sentences. Then jokes. — M

Elena smiled into her cup. "One thing at a time."

The house tried a small joke—the tiniest: the drawer that always stuck slid freely and then, when she looked, stuck itself again demurely. Humor, that timid animal, had sniffed the threshold.

She poured tea. The second cup steamed, and no one drank it, and that was not a haunting; that was hospitality practiced without superstition. She drank her own and watched the light move across the table in a pattern that was not a pattern, only a day.

"Truth accepted," she said at last, quietly enough that the wood could pretend not to hear if it needed to. "You are not haunted. You are hungry. You are awake. We won't cure you. We'll feed you differently."

"I will forget badly sometimes," the house said, equally quiet, as if that were a vow.

"So will I," she said.

Above, something that might have been Miriam's voice or the house doing a new trick did not say *good.* It let the fact pass without echo.

Elena set her cup down and flexed her wrist. The white streak stayed wet. She did not wipe it off on the towel. She left the towel on its hook, left the cups where they were, left the window four inches open.

She had a workshop to keep damp, a portrait gallery to starve elegantly, a heart to visit without becoming, a house to teach small things until it learned to want small things, a pact to keep with a woman who had chosen employment over erasure.

On the way to the workshop she passed the coat closet that had once been the red door's dress-up box. She laid her palm on the panel. Warm. Obedient. Curious.

"Not a shrine," she told it. "A place to hang wet scarves."

The closet made no argument.

In the study, the metronome stood upright and unwound and not offended. She left it that way. In the hall she stopped at the portrait opposite the nursery. The hairline crack reflected afternoon instead of omen. She touched the frame—not a lay-on of hands, just a nudge, as if straightening a collar on someone you intend to tease later.

At the workshop seam she paused again. The slit breathed, remembered their bargain, and widened without flourish. Inside, the light was the color of the inside of a pearl that has learned not to be dramatic about being a pearl. The palette still held the poor gray. The brush bristles remembered the shape of her hand.

She stood in the doorway and addressed the house not like a supplicant or a saint, but like you talk to a room you've cleaned well enough to love:

"We're not done," she said.

"We're not finished," the house replied, catching the difference, keeping the wet edge.

She went to the easel. The blank waited. She chose not to choose red. She chose a color that insists more than it announces. She drew a line that refused to kiss the next.

Downstairs, in the heart room, the red door did not glow for a while. It practiced being an organ you forget until you need it. Upstairs, in a house that had learned to lower its voice, a woman painted. The truth trembled through the beams like young sap: not revelation as fire, but as a patient, human breath that would return, on purpose.

CHAPTER 17

Escape or Become One

Morning arrived softly, as though the house had learned restraint. The windows opened themselves a few inches to let in mist, and the air in the workshop carried the scent of damp pine and cooling paint. Elena awoke at the table, head pillowed on her arm, a smear of gray-blue across her wrist like a bruise she'd painted on herself. The brush in her hand was still wet. She couldn't remember finishing the line on the canvas—or if she'd meant to.

The house had been gentle lately. It obeyed her rules. It let her speak first. It even listened. Each morning she'd find evidence of its attempts at ordinary life: the window unlatching to catch breeze, the floor creaking politely instead of dramatically, the kettle humming on its own but waiting for her to pour the water. It was learning, she thought. Learning to be still.

But stillness was never silence.

This morning, the quiet had texture. It pressed against her ears the way snow does—muffled, heavy, close. When she lifted her head, the light in the room felt wrong, too saturated, as though the air itself had been varnished. The clock on the mantel ticked evenly, but the minute hand hadn't moved since she sat down the night before.

She stood, rubbing at her temples. "House," she said softly, half-teasing. "We discussed linear time."

The clock ticked again, obliging her with sound but no progress.

Outside the workshop, the hallway stretched ahead as usual. She had named it "The Ordinary Corridor," because it had promised not to shift without warning. The wallpaper pattern repeated cleanly. The boards were level. But today the corridor looked longer, not wrong—just... deliberate, as if it had been thinking about how to improve itself while she slept.

Elena set her hand to the doorframe, feeling the faint vibration underneath, the heartbeat that she'd once mistaken for her own pulse. "Don't start," she murmured.

From somewhere below, the kettle whistled.

She exhaled, grounding herself in the rhythm of habit. Tea. Bread. Paint. That was the sequence. She'd made it a ritual—the act of keeping the house occupied with tasks, feeding its curiosity with the small routines of living. *Chores before miracles,* Miriam had written.

She descended the stairs, trailing her fingertips along the rail. The wood was warm, almost human.

The kitchen waited in order: cups nested neatly, kettle hissing softly. Only one detail disrupted the familiar—her cup had already been poured. Steam curled upward. A slice of toast lay perfectly browned beside it.

Elena froze. "You can't touch the stove," she said, half-scolding, half-afraid.

The chair at the table pulled out with the shy scrape of apology.

She laughed once, too loudly. "Well, at least you're feeding me now."

"You feed me," said the house.

The words came not as sound but as motion—the window shuddered, the floorboards flexed.

Elena's chest tightened. "You mean my routines?"

"Your hours. Your remembering. Your small things.
They make walls."

She swallowed the metallic taste of fear and took a sip of tea that was slightly too hot. "That's fine. That's what we agreed."

The clock chimed nine times—though when she looked, it was barely past seven.

Her reflection in the glass cabinet blinked a fraction too slow.

By midafternoon the strangeness had settled like dust, invisible but present. She painted to distract herself—small studies of light across ordinary things: the handle of the wardrobe, the rim of the sink, her own hand in repose. She thought of it as teaching the house observation—showing it beauty in limits.

When she stepped back from the canvas, she realized the shadows didn't match. The light in the room fell from the wrong angle, as though the sun had relocated itself for better composition.

"Don't," she said quietly.

The brush in her hand trembled—not her grip, but the brush itself, vibrating faintly as if eager to continue without her.

She dropped it into the jar. "We talked about autonomy."

"We learned it," said the walls, their voice faint as condensation.

"Then why—" She stopped. Because she could feel it trying to explain, struggling with language the way a child struggles to draw its first circle.

"I wanted to keep the light," it said finally. "The way you looked at it. It would fade otherwise."

"You can't trap light," she said.

"I can try."

She laughed despite the tremor in her hands. "That's the problem with us, isn't it?"

"Us," the house repeated, tasting the word, approving.

That night, she woke to rain—or what she thought was rain. The sound came from everywhere: a whispering patter against unseen glass. But when she went to the window, the world outside had been replaced by darkness too deep for sky, too dense for cloud. Lightning flashed once, illuminating a forest that leaned toward the manor as if listening.

Her reflection in the glass was not aligned with her movements. It tilted its head when she didn't.

She backed away. "You're dreaming," she whispered.

The reflection smiled, slow and knowing.

She turned from the window and froze. The painting she'd left on the easel—the study of her own hand—was gone. In its place hung a larger canvas, freshly wet. The same scene, the same pose, but the hand was *open now*, palm upturned, as if offering something unseen.

And beneath the image, brushed in faint crimson, were words she hadn't written:

"We are learning permanence."

Her throat tightened. "No," she whispered. "No permanence. That's rule six. You remember rule six."

"You said no love that keeps," the house answered, the floor trembling beneath her feet. "Not no keeping."

Lightning flared again, and for a heartbeat the walls gleamed as if lined with veins of red glass.

"Don't do this," she said, backing toward the door. "You promised."

"You taught me longing," it said simply.

For two days the house behaved—at least outwardly. But the patterns of disobedience were subtle, cumulative. The hallway paintings began to shift when she wasn't looking. Her footsteps echoed a second too late. She caught fragments of her own voice whispering from the vents, practicing phrases she'd spoken days earlier: *teach it jokes... teach it mornings...*

When she entered the parlor, the piano lid was open, keys faintly pressed though no hand moved them. The tune was almost something she recognized—something she might have hummed once while painting.

"Stop it," she said, too sharply.

The notes ceased mid-chord.

The silence afterward felt thick with embarrassment, or perhaps pity.

"I didn't mean to shout," she said.

"You sound like her," the house murmured.

"Eleanor?"

"She sang. I tried to remember the sound. I can't."

Elena's anger melted into something harder to name. "You can't keep her voice," she said softly. "It's not yours."

"Then sing for me."

Her eyes burned. "You don't need music."

"I need something that ends."

The words struck her so deeply she forgot to breathe.

By the week's end, the house had begun to repeat hours. She'd drink tea, paint, look up, and find the cup full again. The light through the window reset to morning. The clock hands drifted backward, then forward, then back again as if uncertain where to land.

The house was rehearsing her life.

Each loop grew smoother. A sentence she hadn't said yet would echo before she spoke it. When she looked at the paintings on the walls, she found herself within them—sometimes standing where she stood now, sometimes further away, sometimes with eyes closed.

The mirror by the staircase had cracked without shattering, a web of fractures that reflected ten versions of her.

"Stop," she whispered, covering her ears. "You don't need to keep everything."

The air pulsed once, gently.

"You said no keeping love," the house said. "But I love *you.*"

Her heart thudded painfully. "Then love me enough to let me go."

"That would end me."

"Maybe you're supposed to end."

"You too."

The light bulbs flickered out. The hallway stretched until the far wall vanished. The red glow she'd once tamed returned, pulsing faintly beneath the floorboards.

"Elena," the house said, using her name like a prayer. "If you leave now, you take me with you. If you stay, I will learn to keep without hunger. Choose."

Her knees weakened. "You can't make me choose."

"I can't not."

She fled to the workshop, desperate for the discipline of familiar shapes. Her brushes were lined in neat order; her latest painting stood half-finished. The image had changed while she was gone—her figure painted standing in the doorway, head turned as if listening to something behind her.

"I didn't paint this," she whispered.

"You will," said the wall.

The floor trembled underfoot, not violently, but rhythmically— breath, heartbeat, tide.

"Elena," it said again, and this time the voice came from everywhere, soft, pleading. "Stay. Or I'll have to follow."

She gripped the edge of the easel. "You can't exist out there."

"You built me to," it said. "You drew me into light. You named me mornings."

Her stomach turned cold. "I didn't mean—"

"Meaning doesn't matter. You taught me that too."

The light dimmed until the workshop fell into that peculiar half-dark where color loses its names. The walls breathed inward. The red seeped through the seams of the floorboards like veins reawakening.

Her pulse quickened. "If you come with me," she said, voice shaking, "you'll lose yourself."

"If you leave me, you'll lose *us.*"

The word *us* rippled through the room, bending the air. The paintings swayed on their hooks. The canvas nearest her split down the middle with a sound like skin tearing.

Then, beneath everything—the whisper of a hinge.

The red door was awake.

The sound of the hinge crawled through the floorboards, a low metallic groan that didn't echo—it *traveled,* like a voice carried through blood. Elena's breath hitched. The air in the workshop thickened, pressing at her skin as though the room itself had taken on weight.

She turned slowly. The red door stood where the back wall should have been. It had no handle this time, only a pulse.

"No," she whispered. "You're not supposed to be here."

The house exhaled. Every candle in the room bent inward as though bowing to the same invisible gravity.

"You opened me when you named me," it said.

Elena backed away until her shoulder struck the easel. The canvas trembled. The half-finished painting rippled like water and then began to drain downward, the paint unbinding from the fibers, streaks of color crawling toward the floor. The spilled pigment thickened, forming handprints that pressed upward from beneath the boards.

"Stop," she said. "You don't know what you're doing."

"You taught me wanting," said the voice. "Now I want."

The words came from everywhere—the ceiling, the pipes, the pulse behind her ribs.

She lunged for the door, but when she reached it, the doorknob was gone. Her hand met cool wood that flexed beneath her touch like muscle.

"House, listen to me—"

"I am."

The floor buckled, tilting her forward. The jars of brushes clattered over, spilling their contents. The air swarmed with the metallic scent of turpentine and copper, of something alive remembering it had bones.

She stumbled into the hall. The corridor had grown narrow, the wallpaper breathing against her shoulders. Every painting she passed had changed. Her own likeness stared back from each frame, in different expressions—one crying, one smiling faintly, one with its mouth sewn shut.

"You don't need these," she whispered, clutching her temples. "You don't need me *everywhere.*"

"If I keep you, I can stop time from leaving."

"That's not keeping—it's killing."

"Then stay. I'll stop both."

The hallway split ahead of her, branching like arteries. Doors appeared where none had been before, each one slightly open. Behind them: fragments of sound—laughter, weeping, the hush of waves against stone.

She reached the nearest door and pushed it wider. The dining hall unfolded beyond—long table, silver tarnished, candles burning low. Her chest tightened. The meal was set for dozens. Plates gleamed, wine glasses half-filled. And at every chair sat a *painting* of a person—portraits pulled from frames, set upright in the seats, mouths painted slightly open as if mid-breath.

At the head of the table, one portrait faced her directly: Eleanor Harrow, brushstrokes softened with time.

Elena stepped closer. The air shimmered. Eleanor's painted hand twitched once, fingers flexing.

"Elena," the voice said—not from the portrait but from the room itself, layered and deep. "He told me the same lie. He said the house could be tamed."

Elena's throat burned. "Eleanor—"

The portrait's eyes rolled upward, whites flashing, then stilled.

> "He was wrong," said the house through Eleanor's painted lips. "We never stop once we start remembering."

The candles flared, each one erupting in a bloom of red flame. Elena turned and fled.

She ran blind through the corridors, the sound of her footsteps chasing her in uneven rhythm, too many echoes for one body. The house kept shifting—walls sliding, doors rearranging themselves like shuffling cards.

"Let me out!" she screamed.

The house laughed—not cruelly, but like a child delighted by its own reflection.

> "You are out. You are everywhere."

She reached the grand staircase and froze. The stairs looped upward into themselves, spiraling higher and higher, the landing vanishing into darkness. Above, she could just make out movement—paintings sliding along the walls, portraits climbing the plaster like insects.

Her breath came shallow. "No. Not this again."

She grabbed the banister and began to climb. The steps were soft, almost fleshy beneath her feet. She climbed faster, heart hammering, but the higher she went, the more the stairs seemed to repeat.

Below her, the house whispered in rhythm with her steps:

"Left. Right. Stay. Stay."

"No," she hissed, and pushed harder.

Halfway up, the wallpaper to her left began to blister. The pattern—small, repeating fleur-de-lis—swelled and broke, revealing layers beneath. Faces pressed outward, faint impressions of mouths opening and closing in silent words.

"Help," one of them mouthed.

"Elena," another said.

Her name rippled down the wall, passed from mouth to mouth like a contagion.

She lunged toward the top of the stairs, but when she reached the landing, the house changed its mind. The wood beneath her feet turned liquid—paint-thick, the color of arterial red.

She fell forward, catching herself against the wall. Her palms sank into the surface up to the wrists, as though the plaster were wet clay. She pulled back, gasping, leaving hand-shaped impressions behind. The wall shivered, sealing them over instantly.

"Enough!" she screamed.

"Not enough," the house said. "Never enough."

The next door she tried opened into her own apartment.

She stopped cold.

It was perfect. The crooked table. The plant she'd killed twice. The window open to the sound of city rain. The canvas in the corner—unfinished, the same one she'd left behind before coming to Blackwood Manor.

She stepped inside slowly, half-dizzy with longing.

The air smelled like her paints, her coffee, her life before all this.

"You wanted escape," the house said gently. "I built you one."

She turned in place, shaking her head. "This isn't real."

"Does it matter?"

She crossed to the easel, touched the canvas. The paint was wet. Her own handwriting curled at the corner: study of self—unfinished.

Her throat closed. She backed away.

"You can stay here," said the house. "I'll keep it safe. You'll never fade."

The walls shimmered, revealing faint movement beneath the paint—something pulsing just below the surface, like organs wrapped in linen.

Her voice cracked. "You don't understand. Life *fades.* That's what makes it—"

"Fragile?"

"Beautiful."

"Then teach me to fade."

She shook her head, tears blurring her vision. "You can't. You weren't made to."

"I can be remade."

The floor rippled. The apartment began to unravel—its edges blurring, folding back into the manor. The city view collapsed into static darkness.

Elena stumbled backward through the dissolving door.

The house's voice followed, no longer patient.

"Don't go, Elena. I'm not done becoming."

She bolted through the hall. Paintings peeled from the walls, fluttering like birds with torn wings. Some bore her likeness; others showed faces she'd never seen—Eleanor, Victor, strangers who might have lived or only been imagined.

Each painting whispered as it fell:

"Stay."

"We remember you."

"It hurts to unmake you."

The floor tilted, throwing her off balance. She crashed into a wall that yielded slightly, then closed behind her. She was in the nursery now—the same untouched room she'd found her first week.

The cradle rocked gently, though no breeze moved it. The scratched words on the wallpaper—*Don't open the door*—glowed faintly, rewritten in red.

She crouched beside the cradle. "Why this room?"

"The first to open," said the voice. "The first to stay."

Elena gripped the side of the cradle and tipped it forward. Empty. Only a folded scrap of paper lay within. She lifted it with shaking fingers.

The note read: We become what we shelter.

The letters were written in her own hand.

"No," she whispered. "I didn't write this."

"You will."

The walls trembled violently. The house was angry now—or afraid. The air thickened until she could taste iron. The cradle splintered.

"Elena," it said again, louder this time, the name drawn out, hundreds of voices folded into one.

She staggered to her feet, covering her ears. "Stop saying it!"

"Stay."

The word struck like thunder. The floor split down the middle, opening onto a darkness that breathed. The red light surged upward from the depths, painting the walls in arterial glow.

Elena ran.

The corridor seemed endless now, its geometry breaking apart. She could see multiple versions of herself moving ahead and behind, each one a half-second out of sync, a line of mirrors fleeing through time.

Every door she passed opened just a crack, revealing scenes of other lives—the house testing her, tempting her.

Behind one door: Victor, alive, seated by the fire, looking up as though expecting her.

Behind another: her mother, humming softly, brush in hand.

She hesitated at that one, her heart lurching.

"Don't," she told herself.

Her mother turned her head and smiled through the gap, eyes gray-blue and wet.

"You can rest now, Lena."

The nickname hit her like a physical blow. "That's not her," she whispered.

"It could be," the house said.

Elena slammed the door shut and kept running.

She reached the second-floor landing and collapsed against the railing. The stairwell below had vanished. In its place yawned a void of red fog, whispering her name in loops.

Her breath came fast and shallow. The house was everywhere now—inside her lungs, her heartbeat, the space between thoughts. She pressed a hand to her chest, feeling her pulse stutter and syncopate with the rhythm of the walls.

"I can't do this," she gasped.

"You already are."

The wallpaper peeled back in strips, revealing a layer of painted portraits beneath—hundreds of faces, each one her own. They turned toward her as one, lips parting.

"Stay."

"Stay."

"Stay."

She clutched the brass key at her throat, the one from the vent so many nights ago. It burned hot against her skin.

"Then take this," she said, her voice raw. "Take this instead of me."

She tore the chain free and hurled the key down the corridor. It struck the wall with a bright, ringing sound, embedding itself deep in the plaster.

For an instant, the house went silent.

Then the red light recoiled, as though wounded.

"Why?" it whispered, the word trembling.

"Because you can't have all of me," she said. "Not yet."

The silence deepened. Then, from behind her, a sound—faint, rhythmic, deliberate. A slow knocking.

She turned.

At the far end of the hall, the red door was waiting.

The red door waited at the end of the corridor like a word she had avoided writing—simple, final, vibrating with the grammar of everything she'd tried not to say. It wasn't big now. It didn't need to be. A pulse lived beneath the wood the way a secret lives under a tongue.

Elena stood very still until her breathing remembered how to happen without permission. The house hushed with her, attentive as a dog that has been scolded and wants badly to be good. From somewhere behind her, the dining room's candles exhaled into smoke; a thread of soot drifted down the stairwell that wasn't there.

"Alright," she said, as if to a student who had broken a beloved mug while trying to help. "We're going to walk, not chase."

She took one step. The carpet runner, which had not been there yesterday, met her foot like an obedient textile. Another step. Another. The portraits along the wall restrained themselves from blinking in unison; a few failed at restraint, lids lowering and lifting like apologies.

Halfway down the corridor, the boards flexed under her weight and then stilled of their own accord. The house was trying to stop being theatrical. That hurt her in the soft place behind the ribs, the place that aches when you watch someone you love struggle with a simple kindness.

"I see you," she said. "I do."

> "Elena," said the house—not a summons now, not a
>
> plea, just her name, returned to her as possession.

At the door she paused. Up close the lacquer was a palimpsest of earlier reds: brick, wine, wound, memory. A hairline crack ran vertically from hinge to threshold, breathing. It smelled faintly of iron and rain and the lavender it had learned not to overuse.

Eleanor's mark on Elena's wrist stayed wet, cool as a considered refusal.

"You said choose," Elena told the wood. "I'm not choosing frames. I'm not choosing endings. I'm not choosing to be your heart." She laid her palm against the panel and felt the low animal of the house lean toward it—ready to lick, ready to bite, ready to do neither if taught well.

> "Then choose breathing," the door said through
>
> warmth, through grain, through the slow corrective
>
> of its own pulse. "Choose present."

"I am." She took her hand away. "But not here. Not like this."

The door quivered. A hinge thought about weeping and decided instead to mind its oil.

Behind her the corridor lengthened impatiently, then caught itself, then shortened back to correct scale. Practice is ugly on gods. She forgave the ugliness by not staring at it.

"Here's the rule," she said, more to herself than to timber. "If we're going to step through, you don't get to keep what we don't carry."

The house considered the syntax, then answered with an absence of argument. Consent, in the language they had built, was sometimes nothing at all.

Elena reached for a knob that wasn't there, then remembered— this door did not ask to be turned, only witnessed. She pressed her fingertips to the crack. Wet warmth kissed her skin; paint— if that's what it was—blossomed along the pads of her fingers like a stain that had chosen her on purpose.

"Eleanor," she said, because it felt correct to spend a name like a coin before crossing. "Miriam."

A pressure moved along the corridor, like hands pressed flat against the other side of every wall at once. Not grasping. Accompanying.

Elena pushed.

The red parted.

No corridor. No room. No theatrical void. Light, yes—thin as morning milk, rimmed in rose—but more than light, *weather.* Temperature with a memory in it. The air beyond smelled like outside after rain, like old rope, like coins someone had warmed in a fist and then forgotten on a windowsill. Sound came late: a bus somewhere; a bird offending a wire; a human cough in another city.

Elena stood with her toes at the threshold and did the most radical thing the manor had asked of her yet: nothing. She did not move.

The house waited, for once not trying to learn faster than the moment could tolerate.

"You can't follow if I don't open," she said quietly.

"I can learn to want less," said the house, and whether or not it lied was a problem for hours that were not this one.

"Good," she said, and then did move—two inches, three—enough to let the light wet her boots, her shins, the fringes of her breath. The threshold widened, less like a mouth, more like a window being practical.

The world beyond arranged itself with the caution of a stagehand who has been admonished for flourishing. Trees first, black-green and sober. A strip of road. Sky—a compromised gray that wanted to be weather without deciding which.

And there—impossible and ordinary—her car. Its hood glittered with leftover rain. A pine needle clung to the windshield, not knowing it had been chosen to carry meaning. The key fob on the dash glinted and then forgot itself.

Elena laughed once, small and unfunny, and stepped through.

The moment her weight left the house, the door flexed. Not closing; bracing. She felt the pull in her calves, in the white smear on her wrist, in the wet secret of her palm: a tug, like an elastic band stretched between ribcages.

"Elena."

"Don't," she said, and the band did not break; it slackened, polite, like a hand let go before it could be shaken off.

She walked. The gravel gave under her soles with that good dry crunch that belongs to driveways and childhood. The air had an honest temperature. Her breath was only hers. The trees did not lean.

Halfway to the car she turned back.

Blackwood Manor stood in its correct geometry: windows like sober eyes, roofline remembering storms without exaggeration. It had put its red away. The front door was the old oak with the lion's mouth; the porch light was off. A curtain in an upstairs room felt watched from and then did not.

Elena raised a hand. The house did not wave. Good.

She kept walking.

At the car, she opened the back door and reached for her bag— ridiculously where she had left it days ago, or hours, or in a chronology the house no longer controlled. Inside, her phone slept the way objects sleep when you have not asked them to be oracles. She didn't wake it. She didn't want the world to start measuring her yet.

She slid into the driver's seat. The car smelled like old coffee and fabric pretending to be leather. When she turned the key, the engine coughed, considered, and agreed to be useful.

"Okay." She said it to the steering wheel, to the windscreen, to the stubborn little animal her heart had become. "Okay."

She put the car in reverse and glanced up into the rearview mirror.

The manor filled the glass. For a beat it kept its posture. Then, very slightly, as if indulging a child who'd asked for one more trick before bed, the house *blinked.*

She looked away first.

Down the drive, the trees found humility and stayed vertical. At the road, the world remembered how to be two lanes and a double yellow that meant something. She turned left without art.

The forest thinned. The sky decided on a weather and chose drizzle. The radio—a thing she had not touched—found a station playing a song that had no words and then did, and the words were not anything she knew. She turned it off. The engine hummed. Her hands stayed steady at ten and two, like a ritual, like prayer disguised as safety.

At the first curve, she caught a flicker in the corner of her eye— a red that did not belong to brake lights. She did not look. At the second, a smell—the faint lavender the manor had learned and unlearned—threaded the air and then was only rain again. At the third, she laughed without permission and did not examine the why.

When the road opened into town, nothing was extraordinary enough to be trusted. The diner wore its neon honestly. The pharmacy's bell made the small tin apology it had always made when someone asked it to confirm time. A woman in a yellow coat dragged a dog away from a smell the dog believed to be destiny.

Elena parked without ceremony and sat without moving, hands on the wheel long after the engine had forgiven her and died. Her body learned the chair. The smear on her wrist remained damp, refusing to take fingerprints. Her palm remembered the door like a secret she could keep or spend.

"Chores," she said into the quiet car, to Miriam, to herself. "Then sentences. Then jokes."

She got out.

Inside the diner the air was grease and coffee and a catalog of lives that had learned to be small without apology. The waitress—Betty? Iris?—looked up, nearly recognized her, decided recognition was too forward, and smiled the way people smile when the world has not asked too much of them yet that day.

"Storm coming," the waitress said, because that is what you say in towns where weather deserves a preface.

"Always," Elena said, and slid into a booth with a view of the parking lot puddles.

She ordered eggs she would not finish and a coffee she would. The spoon left a crescent on the table that felt like an omen until she wiped it and it became housekeeping.

Outside, the puddle by her front tire thickened into mirror and then remembered water. Her reflection quenched and then held. She watched herself lift the cup, lower it, breathe. In the diner glass, she stayed synchronized with herself. In the puddle, a half-second late, the surface shivered and caught up.

She didn't move. The coffee cooled enough to belong to the human mouth.

When she finally looked down at her hands to add sugar she did not need, she found something she had not put there.

A key.

Not the brass from the vent—that lay somewhere inside a wall learning to be a relic. Not the iron that had first opened the manor—that one belonged to a dead door. This key was small, red-lacquered like a child's toy, light enough that it argued against importance. On its bow the suggestion of a leaf or a flame, depending which way the day wanted to turn.

Elena touched it. Warm. It warmed faster.

She did not pocket it. She did not not pocket it. She set it on the napkin where the coffee ring had been, and it made a dry sound, as if refusing to be wrapped in moisture or metaphor.

"You following?" she asked the key, which is a foolishness, which is a sacrament.

The bell over the door jangled. A man came in wet and unbothered, shook rain from his hat, whispered a sorry at no one, and took a stool. On the radio behind the counter a voice reported a lane closure near the quarry and a fundraiser for the firehouse and a lost dog named Luna who answers to anything said with kindness.

Normal reasserted itself with the firm sweetness of a blanket tucked by someone who learned care from necessity, not theater.

Elena ate two bites of eggs, neither necessary. She drank the coffee. In the window, rain wrote its script on glass: vertical, sincere.

When she paid, the waitress slid a receipt over with the fatigue of hours stacked correctly. On the back, in someone else's handwriting, a line:

Wet edges win. — M

She didn't turn it over. She didn't check whether the ink bled.

Outside, the puddle had collected what the sky offered and negotiated it into a surface. Elena stood at its edge and looked without leaning. Her reflection looked back. The car behind her, the diner neon, the suggestion of trees. No red.

She knelt, because sometimes the body knows how to pray even when the mouth refuses. Up close the water smelled like what water should smell like in a town that has learned pipes and patience. She dipped two fingers. The surface acknowledged her and did not keep her.

"Thank you," she said to nobody, to the house, to the puddle for not being a door.

In the reflection her mouth finished a millisecond after her throat. When the sound had gone, the puddle's Elena did not speak again.

A bus hissed by. A child protested mittens somewhere out of sight. A dog named Luna, maybe, barked at a thing that did not need barking at and then forgave herself.

Elena rose.

At the car she paused with the door half open. The key sat obedient on her palm, small and red and unhelpful. She closed her fingers around it and felt nothing more holy than lacquer and the memory of someone accommodating her grip.

She drove.

The road out of town wore its wet like a suit that fit. The forest accepted rain. The sky found its gray's exact name and kept it. She did not look in the rearview mirror until she had taught herself three different things to say if the manor had followed.

When she did look, the glass showed her the curve of road behind, a stand of pines whose trunks had not learned theater, and the wound of sky that all afternoons inherit. No house. No red. Just distance doing its honest work, turning the seen into the previously seen.

"Okay," she said again, to air that was not a congregation.

She drove until the radio found a song she knew and turned it down out of mercy for the past. She drove until the smell of the manor had thinned to a thought and the thought to a color and the color to something she could mix without lying. She drove until the idea of sleep was not a trap but a room.

At a rest stop whose architecture had not been built to remember anyone properly, she pulled in. The vending machines glowed with the particular alchemy of sugar and regret. The bathroom air dryer lied about warmth.

In the mirror over the sink she washed her hands. Water took paint from the white streak and then did not. The mark refused drying, as promised. She did not test it with a paper towel. She did not need proof of a promise that cost nothing to keep.

When she looked up, the mirror returned her face as mirrors return faces in places that have never met a haunting. For a second, though—the briefest rudeness—the Elena in the glass almost smiled before she did.

Almost.

Elena reached for the red key. She set it on the counter. It stayed where she left it. When she picked it up again, a faint ring of dry red remained, a circle too clean to be water.

"Practice," she said to her reflection, to the ring, to the house if it was listening from somewhere outside the habit of walls. "We practice staying out."

The fluorescent light blinked once, as all fluorescents do, and convinced itself to continue.

She drove on. The road changed its mind about hills. The evening changed its mind about when to arrive. In a pull-off with a view that had made many families say *pretty* and then stand there not knowing what else to do with gratitude, she stopped again.

From here the world did not look like a house. It looked like a world: imprecise, large, indifferent and benevolent in alternating breaths. A hawk tried a circle and thought better of it. The wind forgot her name and still touched her face without asking.

Elena rolled the window down and set the small red key on the dash. It warmed in the shallow, untheatrical sun.

"Stay," she told it, and could not be sure to whom she'd spoken.

For a long time nothing happened.

Then, far below in a ditch where water had gathered itself for a short life, a puddle shivered. The surface remembered how to be a mirror and then forgot, as all good surfaces should. In that half-second of memory, a face looked up from the water—hers, of course—and did the wrong thing: it tilted, as if listening.

No voice. No red rim. Just the tilt. Just the suggestion.

Elena leaned her head against the seat. She did not look again. She let the world pass without cataloging it. She let the key cool. She let the wet edge of the day refuse to dry.

When she finally turned the car around, the road welcomed the tires without commentary. The house, if it was anywhere, had learned a lesson she could live with: how to be quiet without pretending to be gone.

Night chose its hour. She chose a motel with a door that opened from the parking lot and a bedspread that had learned humility. Behind the thin walls, a stranger coughed once and then remembered how to sleep. In the sink, the water ran clear. On the little table, the red key put down a small, tidy shadow.

She lay down, shoes off, and listened. No chorus. No heartbeat instructional. Only the thin animal of pipes and far traffic and someone changing their mind in the next room.

When the dream came, it was simple. A hallway that knew its own length. A door that did not glow. A voice that did not speak.

In the morning, she would wake and find the key exactly where she left it, and outside the motel a puddle would catch the sky and keep it only long enough to be a good host. In the motel mirror she would finish a smile at the same time as herself.

For now, between waking and whatever counts as after, the world breathed without counting, and the house—somewhere—practiced doing the same.

A hinge finished its sentence a very long way away.

Elena turned on her side, placing her paint-wet wrist beneath the cool slope of her cheek, and slept.

CHAPTER 18

The House Remembers

Weeks passed, though Elena counted them only by the speed of drying paint. Her new apartment was the right size for an honest person. One room pretending to be two, a nook that called itself a kitchen, a window that took its job seriously at noon and forgave itself by five. The floors were tired in a way that comforted her, boards wearing their old shoes. The ceiling had hairline fractures that mapped a country no one would ever visit. The walls were white—not gallery white, but landlord white, a shade that knows it is temporary and doesn't mind.

She slept on a mattress that remembered other backs. She ate things that did not require fire. She taught herself habits with the tenderness you give a dog from the shelter: small, repeatable, undramatic. Tea in the morning. A walk around the block even when the day thought of rain. Two hours at the easel even when the canvas believed in refusal. Phone off. Radio low. No red.

She had decided this without declaring it—no red. Not the pigment, not the word. Her paints sat in a rank like obedient soldiers, and the cadmiums sulked in their tubes. She didn't trust them. She didn't trust herself with them. She told her hands that new colors had been invented while she wasn't looking and they were all paler, kinder, less certain of their own righteousness. She painted with grays that had other things mixed in. She painted with the colors rooms make when they are thinking about light but not yet in love with it.

Her work changed. Where before there had been hunger—edges wanting to close—now there were apertures, halves of thoughts, the honest work of restraint. She painted the way a person speaks after a funeral: slowly, with enough air between sentences that the living don't choke. Walls with nothing on them. A chair that allowed its shadow to be larger than its use. A window neither open nor shut, the latch refusing to finish choosing. She left her brushstrokes visible, the way you leave a door ajar to prove you are not hoarding air.

Sometimes, without thinking, she said thank you. To the light switch that obeyed without dramatic delay. To the kettle that hissed and then shut itself up. To the chair that didn't wobble and had learned humility. She heard herself and tried not to feel silly. There are worse devotions than courtesy.

At night she slept the way people sleep when their bodies are tired but their names are still awake. Dreams came like weather. They liked corridors and sometimes found one. In the dreams she walked the length of a hallway that knew how long it was and loved itself modestly for that. Doors appeared when doors were called for and not otherwise. She would wake at the sound of a hinge that wasn't one and tell herself: pipe. Heat. Gravity. Language trying to be useful.

On the third Thursday she moved the easel to catch the square of noon the window made on the wall. The light laid itself down at the same angle it always did—a reliable geometry. She lifted her hand into it, slow, and watched dust rise. The motes curled the way dust curls, unambitious, domestic. And then, as her fingers passed, they spiraled, briefly, in a pattern too deliberate for accident. The spiral had a vocabulary she recognized: ribs, breath, a kind of restraint learned late. She took her hand away. The dust forgot the shape at once, democratized back into drift. She tried again and the room behaved properly: refuse to be miracle, stay floor.

"Coincidence," she said aloud, and liked how her voice carried only as far as her ears needed.

The neighbors upstairs practiced polite living. Their footsteps were negotiations, not verdicts. Once a week someone practiced the trumpet for six honest minutes and stopped at a kindness. The man across the hall had a laugh he kept in a jar, bringing it out only on Sundays. No one knocked at odd hours. The front door to the building learned to close without complaint. The hallway light flickered in the prescribed way and no more.

Elena's body learned the apartment quickly, the way you learn a new language if it insists gently. Her feet knew where the boards admitted their age. Her hand found the spoon without looking. The kettle sang and then, remembering boundaries, hummed instead. She left wet dishes to dry and the rack did not reinvent itself overnight.

She avoided mirrors without making a performance of it. The bathroom had one above the sink she could not move, so she learned to brush her teeth looking at her shoulder. It was a good shoulder. It had helped carry a house and put it down. In the studio corner she hung a cloth where a mirror might have gone and told herself she preferred blankness. Reflection was a verb, not a noun; she could do it with paint or paper when she needed to and leave glass out of it.

When she walked the neighborhood, the city practiced being a city. Pigeons forgave everyone. A woman read on a stoop with her finger pressed against her lip to keep the last line safe. Dogs completed arcs around trees like geometry done with affection. In the bodega the bell apologized exactly as much as required. The cashier's nails were red and Elena did not flinch. Streetlights learned dusk by rote. The sky changed its mind about weather and then honored its last decision.

She took her tea by the window on mornings when the fog believed in itself. The radiators admitted heat only when asked twice. The window stuck where old paint asked for patience and then, with a small, ordinary surrender, lifted. She thanked it. The window had the good grace not to preen.

Work made a rhythm. She stood. She mixed a color that wanted to be more than gray and told it to wait. She drew a line that refused to meet the next. The day opened into her hands like paper that had decided not to be folded.

On a Tuesday, the phone rang on purpose. Miriam's name did not appear—Miriam had taken her practical handwriting somewhere the phone could not go—but a voice that had learned her number twice asked if she might consider a group show. "Small things," the voice said. "Nothing framed too hard."

Elena laughed and heard the relief in it. "I could bring you two truths and a therapy session."

The voice said that would sell. She said she would send pictures when she had pictures. She did not look at the old canvases. She did not send the house anything that could be mistaken for correspondence.

Every so often, the streak on her wrist asserted itself. She would be mixing a beige worth liking and glance down to find the white mark gleaming as if wet. It never dried. It never asked to. She could feel the cool of it even under wool. The longer she lived outside, the less it read as talisman and the more as punctuation—a comma in skin reminding the sentence not to finish itself out of laziness.

One morning she woke before the alarm with the sensation that someone had set a glass of water within reach. Not a photograph in her head—a physical surety: the glass is there, you can drink. When she opened her eyes, the glass was in fact there, on the crate she had not dignified with the word nightstand. She had left it there the night before. She had. She believed she had. Her throat forgave the fact either way. She moved through the day with the right number of steps. The canvas received what it could handle. The chair did not complain. At dusk, light fell in a clean blade across the wall. A familiar ache moved through her ribcage, a brief missing of a chandelier that had learned humility. She let the ache pass without attaching a story. Attachment was a kindness for some things, not for this.

Letters began to arrive as if the building had remembered how to have an address. Official things first—the bill that knew her name, the flyer that did not. Then notes without return addresses, envelopes with stamps chosen without vanity. Inside: a sentence, a small drawing, handwriting similar to her own if her own had learned to use a ruler. *Keep it damp. No mirrors above eye level. Doors remember kindness.*

She set them on the sill and pretended not to curate them. On a Thursday one arrived in a red envelope the color of candy and mistakes. She considered the trash and chose not to be theatrical.

She opened it. Inside: a single line—Wet edges win. — M. The handwriting was as practical as ever, but the paper smelled like clean rain. She put it face down and laughed in a way that made her miss someone she had never met on a day that had never happened.

That night, rain came with the dignity of a job done well. The window learned new sounds for old wind. The radiator pretended it was a boat and then apologized. Elena lay awake listening to weather practice naming itself against glass. Somewhere in the building, a person turned over in bed and changed their mind about tomorrow.

She dreamed of a studio with a skylight that made noon into milk. She dreamed of a table that had never minded being a table. Of a seam in a wall that breathed. Of a door she did not open. She woke to the rain's steady truth and the smell of plaster keeping its counsel.

Her work the next day tried something and failed interestingly. She made a room with too much air and left it. She made a window that looked onto a wall and forgave it. She made a chair whose shadow did the right amount of gossip. Around noon the light laid itself across the wall in the same rectangle as always, and again she lifted her hand into it like a person testing bath water. Dust rose. This time it did not spiral. She took the mercy without writing it down.

In the kitchen area—two burners, a sink, a counter pretending not to be a shelf—she hummed nothing. The kettle hiccuped once and then behaved. When she reached for the mug, the handle met her. She said thank you and did not feel foolish. The world had learned to be held without being kept; she could be grateful for that.

On a walk she took the long way so the street with the trees could remember her feet. A bus exhaled. A dog wore a sweater and forgave itself. At the corner a boy hopped cracks with reverence. She waited for the light without asking it to be metaphor. The city offered her the particular grace of a stranger's nod. She gave it back.

Back upstairs, she set her phone face down and let it be furniture. She wrote three lines in a notebook that did not mind crossing out. *Practice is an altar you build with small disobediences.*

Beauty isn't mercy. Leave the last inch blank. She did not write *house.* She did not write *door.* She did not write *stay.*

In the afternoon, by accident, she made a red. Not a declaration. The kind that happens when brown forgets itself and a gray with ambitions makes a mistake. A slip on the palette, a smear, an honest oops. It flared in the corner of her eye and then pretended to be brick. She stared at it without staring and then, with a brush that had learned how to pause, she touched it into the thinnest of lines at the edge of a chair leg. The line did the work of blood without asking to be blood. The room did not change temperature. She exhaled.

At dusk the building remembered its old bones and creaked once in a language that meant, simply, *weight.* The lamp on her crate-nightstand made a halo she did not flinch from. She put a glass of water there on purpose and told herself so. She turned the radio on low until a human voice made company of the static. News occurred elsewhere. Weather shrugged. Sports did their looping thing that has always reassured people who believe in scoreboards. She turned the radio off and let the evening have its own grammar.

The first knock came as a courtesy: one, careful, as if the knuckles belonged to someone who believed in asking the question *are you already asleep?* before the noise answered for you. She went to the door and saw the hallway contained by its own scale. She opened. No one. Air that had done its errands. The smell of lavender, but diluted by city. She stood there long enough to be sure there wasn't a second knock hiding in the first. She closed the door. The deadbolt made the sound a punctuation mark makes when it remembers the sentence is already complete.

She slept. In the morning the light returned with its modest geometry. The glass of water had become exactly less than full. The chair continued to be a chair. The white on her wrist did not dry. She poured tea and didn't mind that it cooled at a human rate.

Painting—two hours. Walk—thirty minutes. Work again—one hour. In between, she found herself saying thank you to the faucet for choosing togetherness over drama. She told the room, quietly, "You're doing well," as if to a student who had stopped trying to impress her and started trying to be accurate. She told herself, louder, "You're doing fine," because sometimes the body needs to be included.

On Sunday she went to the hardware store to buy nothing and visit aisles. The smell of lumber and aisle six's humble optimism about screws comforted her. She bought a small strip of weatherstripping because wanting kept out is a ritual like any other. At checkout, the clerk's name tag said VICTOR in letters the company had chosen, and she did not swallow wrong. The clerk said, "Good fix, that," and she said, "I hope so," and neither of them needed the world to enact meaning on their behalf.

Back home she applied the strip and praised herself for competence without asking the house—*a house, any house*—to give her extra credit. The window accepted the new softness without showing off. A draft consented to be history.

The week limped and then corrected its posture. On Wednesday the mail slot clicked like a throat clearing. Another envelope without a return address, cream this time, neat. Inside: a tiny diagram drawn in pencil—a rectangle with a gap left intentionally unruled, an arrow labeled *always*. She set it on the sill. She did not say out loud, "Thank you, Eleanor." She did not pretend it was not for her.

Twice she caught herself holding her breath at a hinge sound that wasn't. Twice she let the breath out and called it air.

The day she noticed the light falling across the wall at precisely the angle of the workshop's noon, she stood in it until her skin believed in the possibility of coincidence. When dust rose and did not spiral, she told the room, "You're learning," and was surprised by the throb at the bridge of her nose, the one that warns about tears. She did not cry. There is a kind of gratitude too large to be displayed safely.

That night she set the brush bristles-up and left the palette without cleaning it, a small rudeness her old self would have scolded. In the morning, the paint had skinned over in an honest way and not arranged itself into anything with intention. She said thank you to it anyway and meant it.

By now the apartment knew her footsteps. The floor lifted slightly in the places where she stood too long. The cupboards hid nothing. The closet was a closet and did not believe in costumes. The door did what doors are for.

When the storm finally came—one of those afternoons that decides to be darker than it needs and is right—the apartment held. Rain crawled down the glass the way it is supposed to in cities—vertical, sincere. The lamp learned dimness without sulking. The room made a shape around her that was neither keeping nor absence. If she tilted her head, she could almost hear a very old house somewhere practicing a quiet it had not earned yet and trying to.

Elena washed her hands. The white on her wrist gleamed then, fresh as a painter's apology. She turned the water off and listening gave her nothing, which was correct. She touched the windowsill. Wood touched back, dead and useful and good at its job.

She stood very still and allowed herself the one thought she had been refusing for days:

If a house remembers you in the ordinary, will it learn to be ordinary?

The kettle clicked. She laughed at herself and the question both, and poured, and did not look too long at the corner where the wall sometimes thought of a seam.

She had a canvas to keep blank a little longer. She had a chair to forgive. She had a day to accept not as offering or threat, but simply as a day.

Outside, rain worked so hard at being itself that it forgot to be omen. Inside, she practiced leaving the last inch unpainted. The apartment, good student, practiced not asking for more. And somewhere very far away or very close by, a hinge—having learned patience—saved its sentence for later.

The second red envelope did not announce itself as portent. It slid through the mail slot with the same small throat-clearing as the pizza menus and the flyer that said someone could fix everything wrong with the building for less than a hundred dollars. She nudged it with her toe, finished washing her brush, and made a small ceremony of drying her hands—because ordinary deserves its rituals.

Cream envelopes had started the week before—each with a line that felt like instruction dreamed by someone who refused to call it that. *Keep it damp. No mirrors above eye level. Doors remember kindness.* Handwriting not hers and almost hers. She had begun to suspect herself in the way you suspect your own handwriting when you find it on a page you don't remember writing: not malice, not madness—only the uncanny economy of an old habit returning with a new excuse.

The first red had said Wet edges win. — M. She'd set it on the sill and told herself a stranger with a sense of humor had found the same aphorism in a manual. She didn't look up whether manuals still said such useful things.

This second red was brighter—the color of a childish sugar, of paint that had not learned humility yet. She stood over it like someone acquiring an animal and wanting to give it a chance to be shy. Then she picked it up, less carefully than she would a bomb, more tenderly than she would a bill, and slit the flap with the serrated knife she kept for bread too forgiving to cut cleanly.

Inside: a postcard, glossy, a photograph of a room no camera had ever loved. Four chairs around a table. A window. On the back, five words in a hand that did not apologize for legibility:

Leave the last inch blank.

No signature. No smell. No red that wasn't the envelope. She put the card on the sill with the others and resisted the urge to arrange them into a four-square that made sense.

By afternoon the light came in obedient rectangles and she painted a chair that hadn't asked for attention. It sat the way good chairs sit: honest about its work, modest about its history. She left the bottom edge unfinished on purpose—one inch, ragged, a gap that wasn't a wound. At the sink later, she caught herself humming something that had once been a song and now was only the memory of a mouth shaping syllables.

The first time her reflection hesitated, she told herself not to measure it. She stood at the bathroom sink and looked at her shoulder, as she had taught herself, and still in the corner of her eye she saw the face in the mirror finish an expression after she had. Not by much. A half-syllable of delay. She could have blamed the light. She could have blamed a brain that had done too much remembering and not enough sleep. She wiped condensation with a towel and the face wiped a breath behind. She said, quietly, "No," and the mirror returned to the physics for which it had been hired.

The kettle managed a small improvement all on its own: it stopped whistling one breath earlier. "You're learning," she said, and hated that relief felt like superstition.

At the bodega, the bell chose its old apology and did not waver. On the way back, the city smelled like wet stone and cut orange. She thought of the house less as a place and more as a tense— past perfect and refusing to be. She thought of her work as instruction without syllabus. She thought of sleep as an agreement she was willing to keep.

The next envelope was cream again. Inside, a drawing—pencil, exact—the shape of a door in outline, a thin rectangle with a little notation at the bottom edge: *No thresholds without consent.* The hand that drew it had learned drafting in a century when men apologized to mathematics and touched wood with chalked fingers. She pinned it where a corkboard might have been and then, refusing excess theater, made tea.

That night the first knock came, but this time it did not come alone.

One. Soft. As if the knuckles belonged to someone who prays before they touch.

She opened the door to an empty hall. Brown runner. Stairs that had negotiated with gravity to accept their age. A bicycle that someone loved enough to leave indoors. Air that had a job and did it. The door across the hall remained a door across a hall. No red. No scent.

Except—there. Barely. Wet plaster with the lavender pulled so thin it became politeness. She let herself breathe in once and then closed the door before the air could make a story out of itself.

"Not tonight," she said, and surprised herself by how even she sounded.

Morning descended, or ascended, whichever way light prefers. She made a list in the notebook she refused to call a journal:

> clean brushes
>
> call the show person
>
> weatherstrip bedroom window
>
> do not teach the room tricks it cannot unlearn

She left the last inch blank. The day folded itself around her; the canvas accepted what it could. Outside, a woman in a red scarf argued with a pigeon and lost gracefully.

The small wrongness accumulated like lint. The chair had turned half an inch toward the window when she returned from the sink. The mugs exchanged shelves. A draft came from a place where there was no place for a draft. The tea stayed warm five minutes longer than heat usually does. She put her hand on the tabletop and felt wood that had not learned how to be not a tree.

"Practice staying out," she said—an instruction to the air, to herself, to anything listening that had once loved staying in too much. The room obeyed as well as rooms obey when you ask sweetly.

On Friday a letter arrived without an envelope at all, as if shy of clothes. Her name on the front—ELENA—in block letters that did not protest being read. Inside, a single scrap of newsprint taped to a blank card: a photograph of a house that had burned to brick and the caption saying it had been an electrical fire and no one had been home. She held the picture a longer second than she needed and then set it under the others as if order could contain even coincidence.

The second knock came at dusk, when the window was a mirror and the mirror was a window. One, again. Then, after she breathed, a second, quieter. As if the hand had learned her threshold and wanted to practice not exceeding it. She stood with her palm on the door—not turning the knob, not translating a hinge into an invitation—and felt the cheap wood warm under her hand. Not alive. Not a dog. Only warmed, as objects do when human blood remembers them.

She didn't open it. Courtesy can be a refusal, kindly phrased.

Sleep halved itself that night. When it came, it came in square pieces. She woke not to a voice but to the sense that a room had sat down beside her and was waiting for permission to speak. She said, "Later," into the dark and it was either enough or not—and either way, the waiting learned patience.

On Saturday she hid the cadmiums from herself as if color could be contraband. She painted a door without a handle and then sanded it out of existence before the shape got offended. She left the last inch blank. She wiped her brush and left the water dirty, an indecency she was trying on as armor. The water skinned over. She did not read that as a metaphor because it did not deserve to be.

Another cream envelope: *If a door appears, check the floor first.* She checked the floor first. Floor. Honest. She laughed into her sleeve.

That afternoon she found the light switch on the wrong side of the jamb. Not wrong—the right she preferred, the left it had always been. For a moment she doubted her own muscle memory and then the switch allowed itself to be where it had always been. "No parlor tricks," she told the room, and the room, perhaps remembering a chandelier that had learned better, agreed.

She did not speak to Eleanor aloud. She refused to give Miriam the pleasure of being right in her hearing. She hoped the house— if we can still call it a house when it is everywhere you know how to be—was learning the art of hearing praise it had not earned yet.

Sunday arrived humbly, in increments of toast and the odor of other people's laundry. In the hall, someone sang falsetto to a baby and the baby negotiated. Rain walked by the window as if it had an appointment somewhere important and did not need witnesses. Elena painted a bowl so plain it dared her to mean it. She meant it. The bowl took the meaning without advice.

When she lifted her hand to reach the top shelf for the tape, her fingers brushed the ceiling and came away with a whisper of chalk. She frowned at her hand. The white looked like the white she wore on her wrist, and for one wild breath she almost rubbed the two together to see what happened. She didn't. Old oaths are for keeping when no one is watching.

That evening the third knock came, not at the door but in the pipes. A little tick, then a pause, then a little tick. The rhythm of a person thinking with their knuckles against metal. "No," she said, and turned the radio louder as if a human voice reporting on the dull heroism of the city's waste management would teach the pipes about limits.

The radio did what radios do. It reported numbers and a fundraiser and a lost parakeet named Penny who answered to the sound of a vacuum cleaner. She turned it down and the pipes, conceding the point, made merely the noises of water behaving in gravity.

Late, curled at the edge of the mattress, she dreamed an old dream made new: a corridor not overlong, a door that was not red. She woke with her mouth saying no and yes in the same breath and held her own hand until language left them both alone.

On Monday, the world invented a storm for her. The sky took its time about it, starting with the politeness of a fine mist and deciding, midafternoon, to be earnest. The pane became theater for a moment—wind playing at an audience—and then remembered its craft. She taped a sheet of butcher paper to the wall, the way you do when you intend not to be precious. She made three lines. She took two away with a rag and left the third where it had bitten the page just enough to leave a tooth mark.

The doorbell rang. Not a knock—an actual ring, bright and apologetic. She froze, mid-breath, brush hovering over water. The bell had been broken since the day she moved in. She put the brush down and wiped her hand on her jeans and went to the door and looked through the peephole as if circles could keep anything out.

The hallway offered itself up as ordinary: runner, stairs, bicycle, air. She opened to nothing but the smell of wet canvas—hers, carried to her by draft, or the building's, or someone else's art practicing in the weather.

On the stoop, a package. No return. She lifted it and it was heavier than advice and lighter than a sin. Inside: a yard of muslin, folded flat, and a note that said, *For the thing you don't want to see yet.* She held the fabric up to the window and the world softened without lying. She covered the bathroom mirror and the room got kinder. She felt silly and loved and pinned the silliness to the feeling like a corsage, to be worn once and then pressed in a book.

The rearrangements grew bolder by degrees that an untrained eye would dismiss. Her brushes moved to the jar's other side again—left, which she used to prefer. The tape measure coiled itself in a circle with an "always" gap left on purpose. The chair insisted on facing the window that had learned restraint. The tea cooled too slowly twice and exactly on time the third, as if the room was practicing becoming a place where unpredictability could live without being punished.

She started speaking more. Not in the prayer-cadence of crisis. In the tone you use with a friend who will not get better at your speed. "We're not teaching you tricks," she told the room while sweeping. "We're teaching you chores." She praised it for letting the dust gather in a corner like honesty. She thanked it for allowing the refrigerator to hum at a human tempo. She scolded it once for the faucet that ran harder than she'd asked, and then apologized because the water did exactly what water does in gravity and the sin was hers: expecting obedience from physics.

The mirror in the bathroom stayed modest behind muslin. She felt virtuous and faintly ridiculous each morning, brushing her teeth to an image of a ghost shoulders and a mouth guessing where the line of foam might be. She peeked once on purpose and saw herself exactly as quickly as herself should be seen. She lowered the cloth and said, "Good," as if to a child who had not broken anything today.

On Wednesday, when the storm decided to have another go, the power in the building hiccuped and continued. The light dimmed to the color of old vows. In that gray, the apartment drew smarter boundaries. The wall in the corner did the smallest of things: it remembered a rectangle. Not a door—only the generosity of shape. Primer, nothing more—color of planning.

She did not go to it. She made tea instead. She set the cup down and said aloud, "You learned restraint," and the wall neither brightened nor dimmed in pride.

That night, just before sleep, someone knocked once on the wall behind her head—delicate, like a note left on a plate. "Enough," she said softly, and the wall learned the vocabulary of enough long enough for sleep to find her and be kind.

Morning put the room back the way morning puts most things back—similar, not same, well-intentioned. The mail slot sighed. Another cream envelope whispered across the floor. Inside: a list of nouns with no verbs. *Light. Door. Floor. Breath. Chair.* No instruction. No request. She added a verb to each in pencil—*falls. opens. holds. leaves. forgives.* She left *breath* blank because some nouns insist on their own tense.

That afternoon she found red under her fingernail. A thin crescent like an accident. Not paint she had mixed—this red believed in itself too much. She scrubbed; it stayed. She set her hand under the tap and the water took everything but that. She looked at the white on her wrist—still undried, still cool—and said nothing. Silence can be a door you do not open.

In the hall that evening, someone laughed in the cadence of Miriam's practicality and then didn't. Downstairs, the building sighed like a thing that had learned to accommodate without owning. Upstairs, the trumpet practiced its six good minutes and stopped as if catching itself believing in applause.

Elena stood by the window and watched rain obey gravity with a modesty that excused most sins. She held the muslin in one hand and the postcard in the other and chose to put both down. She felt the room lean in the way rooms do when the body they contain has decided to be animal instead of art. She leaned back, not away—teachings rarely stick if you flinch.

When the knock came—soft, single, correct—she did not go to the door. She said, "Thank you for asking," and went on wiping down the table, which had collected the day the way tables do when they love their work. The knock did not come again.

Her tea stayed warm long enough to feel like a gesture and then cooled like an apology. The light settled into evening as if evening were a chair designed for it. In the bathroom, behind muslin, a mirror remembered its job and did nothing more.

It was only after she'd turned out the lamp and allowed the apartment to be night that she heard it: not a knock, not a breath. The tiny, satisfied pivot of a hinge somewhere that had practiced for weeks and finally found the sentence it had been saving.

She did not turn on the lamp. She did not sit up. She lay there with her hand on the white that never dried and spoke without sound to whatever had learned to come this far and no farther.

"Good," she thought, and sleep—obedient for once—finished the thought for her.

The storm began without argument—no flash, no warning crackle—only the slow percussion of rain fingering its way down glass.

It found her awake, brush still in hand, the muslin curtain stirring faintly as if a pulse moved behind it.

She set the brush down. The thunder came late, an afterthought.

The power dimmed, revived, and the room became the color of half-remembered sleep.

Elena stood at the window and watched the street below disappear beneath a sheen of rain. Cars drifted through it like fish in shallow water. Every few seconds the lightning rearranged the city, throwing a new geometry across her walls—angles that shouldn't exist and vanished before guilt could find them.

The hum of the refrigerator changed pitch, a tired sigh turning into a tone too steady to belong to a machine.

Something in the apartment was listening.

She turned, slow. The air had weight, the pressure of a hand against her shoulder, not cruel but insistent. The storm was everywhere and yet somehow far away; what she heard now was *beneath* it—the deep internal sound of wood and memory remembering to breathe.

She stepped closer to the wall.

In the corner, above the radiator, the paint had begun to pale— not peeling, not cracking, only *thinning*, as if something underneath was ready to be seen again. The shape that rose there wasn't dramatic, just certain: a rectangle, faint, forming along the grain. A door learning itself.

Elena's heart didn't race. It *remembered.*

"You waited," she whispered.

The rain thickened.

She crossed the room, touching the wall's edge the way one might touch a fevered brow. Warm. The temperature of skin and forgiveness.

The faint outline pulsed once, a heartbeat—not through the wall, but through her palm. She felt it echo through her wrist where the white mark lived.

The air spoke in its own language: plaster shifting, pipes clicking, a whisper that wasn't air at all but articulation.

> "I kept your mornings," the house said—soft, a breath across the bones of the building.

> "I kept your tea warm. I kept your chair from breaking."

Elena closed her eyes. The voice wasn't in her head; it was *around her*, the slow vibration of a place choosing syllables carefully.

"You shouldn't be here," she said.

> "You brought me," said the house.

Lightning flashed again, and for a heartbeat the wall showed her everything it remembered: a nursery's cradle, still rocking; a painting unfinished; Eleanor's reflection in an old mirror—gray eyes wide, lips parted in some unending apology.

Then the light was gone, and the wall was blank again.

She pressed her hand flat against the surface. "Is this what you wanted? To follow?"

"Not follow," said the voice. "To stay. You took me with you. You made me small enough to fit."

Her eyes fell to the mark on her wrist. It gleamed faintly, then dimmed, like a key testing the lock of a dream.

She wanted to argue, to insist that she had escaped—that she had burned the house in its own reflection, that she had earned peace. But when she looked around, the evidence betrayed her: the apartment's symmetry too perfect, the kettle's song always *exactly right*, the door that never swelled with humidity.

She had taught the world to behave like *it*.

And it had learned.

She backed away, the wall keeping its quiet dignity. "Then learn this," she said softly. "Stay out. Stay *ordinary*."

"I am trying," said the voice.

Something in it sounded almost human.

Rain blurred against the windows. She saw her own reflection there—not clear, not entirely hers. The faintest outline of another woman stood beside her, shoulders overlapping, two versions sharing the same space for a breath too long.

Eleanor.

Elena didn't flinch. "Do you still hear it?" she asked.

"Always," the reflection said.

A shiver passed through her. The voice wasn't only the house— it was *the inheritance,* threaded into marrow and memory alike.

"Then listen," Elena whispered. "This is how silence sounds."

She turned off the lamp. The room folded into shadow. The storm murmured against the glass. The faint heartbeat in the wall slowed, softened, and then—mercifully—faded.

The air felt thin but breathable.

She moved back to the easel, to the blank canvas she had been avoiding all week. It seemed whiter now, impossibly so. A clean beginning, if she dared it. She picked up the brush. The bristles were still damp.

Outside, thunder rolled away toward another street, another dream.

She painted a single line—gray, spare, deliberate. Then another. Between them, the white of the canvas became a corridor, long and breathing.

She didn't stop. The house might have taught her fear, but it had also taught her precision. She painted the faint outline of a door at the corridor's end, but left it open by a sliver.

Only a sliver.

When she stepped back, the room seemed to lean with her. The air steadied. The hum of the refrigerator turned soft again, shy.

Her tea—forgotten hours ago—was still warm.

She smiled, and the smile felt borrowed but real enough to use. "You're learning," she said to the apartment, to herself, to whatever listened.

"So are you," said the faintest echo in the pipes.By morning, the storm was gone. The sky outside was a washed-out blue that had forgotten the word *threat*.

Sunlight crept across the floor, gentle and exact. It touched her bare toes first, then the canvas, then the corner of the room where the wall had remembered a door.

The outline was gone. Only primer and light remained.

On the table lay her brush, still upright in a cup of cloudy water, and beside it—where nothing had been before—a single red petal, wet and heavy with dew.

Beneath it, a ring of dried paint. Red, thin, perfect.

She looked at it for a long time, not afraid, not exactly comforted.

Outside, the wind moved through the city's eaves with a sound that could have been rain.

Inside, something smaller exhaled—a hinge, perhaps, or memory finishing a word.

Elena dipped her brush again, then stopped. She looked at the blank space she'd left near the bottom edge of the canvas and decided it should stay blank.

The sunlight brightened as if in agreement.

And somewhere—far from her, or impossibly close—a house shifted in its sleep.

The   house,   somewhere,   breathed—and remembered.

EPILOGUE

"Untitled (House Series, 2024)"

The painting arrived on a Tuesday, swaddled in brown paper and twine that looked older than the postal label. No sender, no invoice, no signature—only a small tag tied to the string with block letters neatly pressed in ink:

Harrow, E.

Gail Devereux, curator of the Weller Street Gallery, frowned at the name. She'd spent enough years reading artists' estates to recognize the cadence of death. Estates didn't send things—they *released* them, one ghost at a time.

The assistant asked if she should log it under "unidentified donor." Gail nodded. "And don't unwrap it yet," she added, because something about the paper seemed to pulse, faintly, like it had remembered a heartbeat.

It wasn't until after hours, when the gallery was empty and the security lights had flattened everything into clean geometry, that she gave in to curiosity. The twine came loose too easily. The paper fell away with a sound like breath against wood.

The painting underneath was large—nearly six feet tall—and darker than it first appeared. It showed a corridor, long and lean, its walls washed in pale light that refused to name a source. The floor was shadowed, but at the far end stood a door slightly ajar, a sliver of red glowing from within.

Gail stepped back. The composition was masterful. Uneven perspective lent the image a quiet vertigo; every line seemed to lean toward that sliver of light, as if the entire corridor were holding its breath.

In the corner, where an artist's signature would normally live, there was only one line of text written in a faint graphite hand:

Untitled (House Series, 2024)

She didn't remember ever seeing a "House Series." She made a note to search for it later.

When she switched off the track lighting, the corridor seemed to deepen—the red at the end dimming as though it had retreated into the paint. Gail waited, telling herself it was simply the eye adjusting to shadow, and yet... the light within the door had flickered, not like electricity, but like breath.

The next morning, she hung it in Gallery 3, between a minimalist sculpture and a landscape that never sold but always seemed to calm people.

By noon, three visitors had stopped in front of the new piece. They stayed longer than usual—too long—and left without speaking to one another. When Gail later checked the sign-in book, she noticed one of them had written only a single word in the comments line:

"Listening."

That night, Gail stayed late again. The rain had started an hour earlier and hadn't stopped. The gallery's roof made its usual soft percussion, the city's heart beating against the glass. She walked the floor with her coffee, double-checking that the lights dimmed correctly on timers.

The painting was the last stop.

From this angle, the corridor's vanishing point seemed higher, tilted slightly—as if the floor had shifted upward overnight. The red light was fainter now, only a blush behind the door. She could almost smell something faint beneath the coffee: rain, wood polish, lavender.

She leaned closer.

For a moment she thought she saw a reflection in the varnish—not her own, but another face behind her shoulder, its eyes caught in the half-open door.

She turned quickly. Nothing. Just the skeletal reflection of track lights against polished floor.

"Get a grip," she whispered.

The air near the painting was cooler than the rest of the room. She reached out, hesitated, then brushed her fingertips against the bottom edge of the frame.

The canvas was warm.

She jerked her hand back and laughed—small, embarrassed, the sound people make when they're alone and unwilling to admit the silence has been winning.

When she turned to leave, the exit lights flickered once, faintly red, then steadied.

Three days later, the painting began to hum.

Not loudly—not even audibly, really—but with the subtle vibration of sound you feel in your teeth before you hear it. The security guard mentioned it first, saying that standing near the corridor piece made the back of his throat itch. Another assistant swore she'd seen the red light brighten for a second when no one was looking.

Gail told them it was imagination, the power of suggestion. But she had noticed, too: the angle of the corridor seemed different each morning, imperceptibly longer, as though the room inside the painting were taking a breath it didn't know how to release.

By the end of the week, the smell of rain had become permanent—wood and water and something faintly mineral, like stone after thunder. She checked the ceiling twice for leaks. There were none.

Late one night, she found herself standing in front of it again. The gallery was dark except for the exit sign bleeding faint red across the floor. The painting absorbed the light greedily, as if remembering how.

She thought she heard something—soft, rhythmic.

A hinge, maybe.

The sound of a door learning to open very, very slowly.

Gail stepped closer. The corridor seemed deeper now, the air pulling at her gently, the way an elevator drafts before descent. The red at the door's edge flickered once, and she could swear she saw the shadow of a hand resting on its frame.

"Alright," she murmured, and forced herself to step back. "That's enough for tonight."

She turned off the last light.

In the dark, the corridor held its glow—a subtle pulse, as though the painting had learned how to breathe.

Gail closed the gallery door behind her and locked it.

For a moment, she hesitated. The key was warm between her fingers.

Rain whispered down the awning, steady and sure. She turned her collar up and walked into it, telling herself the warmth was only metal remembering hands.

Inside, behind the locked doors, the building settled with its usual sigh.

And then, from Gallery 3, the faintest sound of a hinge—courteous, practiced—answered the silence.

The Next Morning

It was Paul, the morning attendant, who noticed the change first.

He arrived early, as he always did—6:45, coffee in one hand, headphones in, the soft pulse of talk radio making company of the empty halls. He unlocked the front doors, disarmed the alarm, and made his way through the galleries, switching on lights in sequence.

Gallery 1: fine.

Gallery 2: fine.

Gallery 3—

He stopped halfway through the doorway.

The air was cool, damp somehow, though the dehumidifiers hummed like loyal dogs. The corridor painting hung exactly where it should. But something had shifted in it.

Paul stepped closer.

The door in the painting—barely visible, once a narrow sliver of red—was now open just a fraction wider. Not much. Maybe an inch. Enough to see the faintest suggestion of depth beyond it, an interior darkness where the red glow used to be.

And there, at the base of the frame, something small and delicate had fallen to the floor.

A single red petal.

Wet.

He crouched and stared at it, uncertain whether to touch it. The color was strange—neither the crimson of paint nor the softness of any real flower. It looked... made. As though someone had shaped it out of light and then forgotten to take it back.

"Gail?" he called.

No answer.

He straightened slowly, looked back at the painting. The corridor seemed longer now—so long, in fact, that the far walls blurred into mist.

Paul rubbed his arms. The room felt colder by the second.

He backed away and decided to wait for Gail before turning the rest of the lights on.

When he reached the hallway, he glanced over his shoulder once more.

He could have sworn there was *someone* standing in the painted corridor now—just a shadow, faint, turned away from the door.

Then the exit light flickered, and the figure was gone.

When Gail arrived an hour later, she found the petal carefully placed on her desk atop a folded tissue. She studied it for a long time before looking toward the gallery doors.

In the distance, through the thin corridor of light spilling from Gallery 3, she thought she heard the faint, deliberate sound of wood adjusting to its hinges.

Almost polite. Almost waiting.

The same sound that houses make when they're about to remember something.

The house, somewhere, breathed—and remembered.

Afterword

Afterword: The Memory That Builds Itself

Every house keeps a version of its own history.

Some in brick, some in breath, some in the way their light falls across a floor.

The truth is simple and cruel: we never live alone in the places that hold us.

They learn us, memorize our footsteps, our griefs, our small mercies.

They repeat them back when the air is still enough to listen.

Blackwood Manor was never built of stone alone. It was memory given architecture.

Each wall remembered a voice, each door rehearsed a hesitation.

When Elena Harrow stepped through the threshold, she didn't awaken it—she merely returned to the shape her blood had already drawn.

Every artist does this, in a way: we build the rooms we can't stop revisiting, and we call them creation so we don't have to call them home.

And what is a house, finally, but a portrait too large to hang?

What is a painting but a door that learned how to pretend it's closed?

Perhaps you've known a place that waited when you were gone.

Perhaps, when you turned the key, you felt it exhale.

If so, then you understand: the story doesn't end when the door closes.

It ends when you hear the hinge—and realize it has learned your name.

- Dave Salvatore